Shaman's Blood

BY

ANNE C. PETTY

JournalStone

San Francisco

JournalStone books may be ordered through booksellers or by contacting:

JournalStone
199 State Street
San Mateo, CA 94401
www.journalstone.com

The views expressed in this work are solely those of the authors and do not necessarily reflect the views of the publisher, and the publisher hereby disclaims any responsibility for them.

ISBN: 978-1-936564-20-0   (sc)
ISBN: 978-1-936564-21-7   (dj)
ISBN: 978-1-936564-22-4   (ebook)

Library of Congress Control Number: 2011932591

Printed in the United States of America

JournalStone rev. date: August, 2011

Cover Design: Denise Daniel
Cover Art: PhilipRenne
Author Photo: Mona Lisa Abbott

Edited by: Elizabeth Reuter

Acknowledgements

First off, many thanks to the staff of JournalStone for bringing this book to life. Ned's story has been waiting to be told, and I'm grateful that it's finally going to happen. Thanks as well to the fans of *Thin Line Between*, who kept asking me what happened to Alice and Margaret.

Thanks also to supportive readers who have helped me hone this manuscript over the years – Bill, Lynn, April, Lissa, Kate, and probably others I don't remember.

A few words about my source material: To find out what the Australian Aboriginal Dreaming is all about, you can dip into any number of books on Aboriginal mythology and culture, but I recommend beginning with the works of James G. Cowan, Percy Trezise, Bruce Chatwin, and K. Langloh Parker, among many others. Online, you can sample the resources of the Australian Government Department of the Environment & Heritage at www.deh.gov.au, as well as the numerous Australian Aboriginal cultural heritage centers represented on the Internet, or Aboriginal publishers such as Magabala Books.

See other JournalStone Published books!

Ghosts of Coronado Bay

The Gargoyle Prophecies, Part I, The Savior Rises

The Traiteur's Ring

Imperial Hostage

That Which Should Not Be

Duncan's Diary, Birth of a Serial Killer

Prelude

July 1953

Flames roared through the pines, crisping their tops and scorching the night sky. Orange sparks swirled in a mad dance, carried high and far on the breeze.

Running flat out, Ned crashed through brambles and underbrush. Saw palmettos tore at his bare feet and ankles. He splashed headlong through a bog of red-leaved snotbonnets, their mucous undersides sliming his shins. Reaching higher ground, Ned searched in the dark for the narrow surveyor's trail he knew to be somewhere ahead. Tall for his sixteen years and starvation thin in threadbare overalls a size too large, the boy looked like a demented scarecrow.

The fire behind him filled the swamp with smoke, its ravenous red mouth popping and hissing as it ate the roof of his mother's house and low-hanging branches from patriarch oaks. The homesteader's cabin had been roughly built of heart pine nearly a century ago, and its resin-soaked timbers fed the furious blaze.

Ned bit his lip. He couldn't let himself grieve over what he'd done—that would come later. Flight was all that consumed his mind now as he tore through the underbrush. . Stumbling onto the trail, lungs sucking air, he felt rather than saw the cool reptile body that whipped over his foot and off into the underbrush. Cold fear stopped his breath for a beat as he felt the fleeting sting above his instep. The snake had tagged him.

Panic drove him now, and soon he was staggering and gasping for air, his tongue thickening against his palate. A metallic tang invaded the back of his mouth. Shit! Ned knew the signs—he was a dead man. Venom boiled along the network of arteries, pushed by his pounding heart from his swelling foot up his leg and into his trunk. The trail tilted and Ned fell heavily into a titi thicket, its elongated spires of tiny white flowers bobbing back and forth over his head.

The boy lay on his side, gasping in ragged heaves, his leg a lava tube of red pain. The surrounding slash pines and hardwoods dimmed to a blur, but the scurryings and scratchings of tiny creatures in the sand near his face seemed louder than his labored breathing. A distant crash and whump told him the house had collapsed, but he could barely lift his head to look. "Shit," he breathed, "shit." He understood … she'd sent the snake as punishment. Which he deserved and more.

Somewhere back beyond the oak grove his old life was burning away, but the fact of the snakebite reversed all his future plans. Struggling to his feet, Ned tried to limp forward, but his bitten foot refused to respond. Would his mother be amused now at his predicament? She had been a snake handler, a hex woman who made potions for a price or an exchange of goods when the customer had no cash. They often ate the offerings left on their doorstep—tomatoes, squash, pole beans, eggs, even an occasional live chicken. Sometimes clothing would be left as well, mostly for Ned. He was especially fond of the striped overalls someone from the county's volunteer fire department had donated. His mother didn't mind; she had no money to spend on clothes for him anyway.

From an early age he'd helped her in obedience and shivering terror as she trapped and milked copperheads, cottonmouth moccasins, and their most venomous cousin, the Eastern Diamondback rattler. He'd seen what that witch's brew of poison blended with nightshade and other vile filth could do. And now, he understood for the first time how it felt inside the body, working its way through the tributaries of veins and capillaries, wreaking its destruction.

Steadying himself against the rough bark of a loblolly pine, Ned tried to examine his foot. The bite site was turning mottled purple, and the swelling of hot, stretched skin that engulfed his ankle was headed up his shin. Ned dropped to his knees and retched heavily, his stomach turning inside out as the toxins invaded his gut. How long, he wondered, did it take to die from a rattler bite? If it had been a moccasin, he might have some small cause for hope; he knew their bite, bad though it was, rarely proved fatal and could be survived without treatment. He spat out bitter saliva, pretty sure which of the Florida pit vipers had scored the hit. Ned would've cursed his luck, but a gagging cough was all he could manage. The ground rose up and punched him in the face as his cheek hit the sand.

"Here, Neddy, hold onto this fella while I get the glass," his mother had said, thrusting a prime rattler at him nearly as long as he was tall. "Just grab it behind the head and hold tight." His ten-year-old mind had shut down at the thought, and he'd blindly reached out for the infuriated serpent with a hand marked by tiny white dots from dry bites where no poison had been injected. Snakes hoarded their venom, she'd said, saving it for prey catching, and half the time the bites were warnings not meant to kill. "Hold still now." He could hear her voice clearly as he lay in the sand. He'd done as he was told and held the snake in a death grip, staring into its beady eyes—he was her good, obedient son.

Most of the snakes she freed into the woods once they were milked out, keeping only the fat ones to eat. He could still see her lopping off their heads and splitting them down the belly with a sharp filleting knife. The image brought a darker memory.

She'd held him smothered in her great fleshy arms and whispered, "Your father's dead, Neddy. His own doing, just so you know. Do you want to see?" Her voice had crept around his ear, comforting and chilling. "Do you?" He didn't, but couldn't avoid looking. The blood was bright and dark at the same time, crimson red and muddy brown. It oozed from the spot where the filleting knife had torn open the man's stomach. Five-year-old Ned had stared, barely comprehending.

Ned heaved and retched again. His leg was on fire. Sweat slicked his face, and a crust of sand formed where his mouth met the ground. Rolling onto his back, he lay helpless in a bed of wiregrass.

"My love," his mother had said, stroking the soft dark hair that framed his father's perfect face. "So pretty..." Her voice had trailed off, as she'd pushed the curtain of hair away from his unfocused eyes. It was true. His father was deemed beautiful by all who met him, and although Ned's coloring, which mirrored his mother's sandy hair and hazel eyes, didn't resemble his father much, he had inherited the man's prominent brow, sharply defined nose, and heart-shaped mouth. His father was much younger than his mother, or, as Ned's childish mind had thought of it, his mother just seemed a lot older than everybody else. They didn't fit as a pair, but at the time of his father's death, he was only vaguely aware of the mismatch. The few children he knew had mothers roughly his father's age, and women who looked like his mother were either called Auntie or Granny.

"Nnngh," Ned grunted, sitting up. Sparks flashed behind his eyes and he was falling again, clawing on his belly with his dead leg stretched out behind him. Frogs chorused from unseen ponds, and a symphony of nighttime noises he'd listened to as long as he'd been alive sang around him. Then, unexpectedly, he was aware of the Other.

"Bassard ... f-finally comin' to get me?" he wheezed, his chest constricting and his tongue going numb. He was breathing in shallow gasps now. "Hope I poison ya!" Ned spat into the dirt, trying to remove the horrible taste pooling in his mouth at the base of his swollen tongue.

The dark presence that had stalked him ever since he could remember came out of the tangle of blackberry brambles lining the path. His mother had wanted to harness it, to use its dark magic, but she didn't have the mojo. It hovered over him now, a darker blotch in the center of his tunneling field of vision.

"What do you fear?" Its soft rasping voice whispered in his head, like wind in the reeds at the edge of the marsh.

The shadow began to coalesce, twisting itself into an enormous fat-bodied snake with a flat wedge-shaped head and rounded snout. The thick, heavy coils were reddish-brown with darker jagged crossbands and a sharp backbone ridge that tapered down to a thin, nervous tail tip. Its bright eyes fixed on him from beneath prominent brow scales. An Australian death adder. Ned recognized it instantly from the many images of serpents his mother had painted and taped to the cabin walls. His mind recoiled; it was the very snake-shape that repelled him the worst. Ned scrambled away from it in horror.

"You're not an ordinary boy." His mother had held his chin in her hand, her eyes probing, looking for whatever it was that made him different. "You can *see*, can't you?" *Yes, Mama, I'll draw you the magic, so please, love me* ... Six-year-old Neddy wept with pencil and paper in hand as the terrifying images of a place and a time that were not his own flowed and splashed through his mind like river rapids.

"You're my gift, my precious Neddy," his mother had crooned, smothering him against her chest, her sweat and the scent of her hair filling his nostrils. He saw it now, that cascading gray-streaked waterfall of hair that reached past her waist. She wore it straight and loose, parted in the center, even on the hottest, most humid of days, when her sweat strung it into long snakes down her back. It was her sigil, her woman's power, and Ned would never be rid of its image and weight in his mind. "Draw me the visions, Neddy," she would coax him.

He knew the particulars of the death adder: lightning fast strikes from a mouth that held the longest fangs of its serpent family. Its venom attacked the nervous system and voluntary muscles, causing massive swelling and tissue destruction. Screaming in his mind, Ned reached out and pushed the fanged mouth away from his face. Whether real or a poison-induced hallucination, he little knew nor cared; he fought it with every sinew, thrashing into a stand of sweet pepperbush and black ti-ti.

"No, Mamma, please, I don't wanna ... no!" His mother held his arm stretched out over her knees. "Please don't," seven-year-old Ned had begged, choking his tears back. She'd stroked his forearm, her fingers brushing the many tiny scars that covered it like a gauntlet, looking for an unblemished spot. His other arm was similarly marked.

"Hush," she'd whispered, "it's just a drop, just a little drip I need. It won't hurt." She pressed the tip of the filleting knife against the soft skin and a bright bead of red appeared. "Nhuh huh huh." Ned gasped for air as his mother held his arm over a small ceramic bowl and guided several ruby drops into a pool of yellow venom. "There, now." She kissed his forehead and pressed a wad of toilet paper over the nick, then walked away with the bowl.

Neddy had wiped his tears on the cotton undershirt donated by a soldier who'd come for a good luck charm to take back to his carrier in the South China Sea. It was supposed to ensure his safe return after the war. "I hate you," Neddy snuffled, watching his mother's back as she bent over her work. A shiver had passed through him as he'd sensed the Other and felt its hungry need. It wanted to lick his arm.

"Get the fuck away from me!" Ned's poisoned vision was a red blur, but he could make out the flattened snout of the death adder too close to his face. Bucking under its weight, he held the monster at arm's length with all his failing strength, but it was within inches of winning. Then, with a jerk that sent him sprawling, the adder whipped out of his grasp. Above him, two snakes now writhed, grappling each other with sinuous, muscular necks. They pushed backward and forward against each other, their upper bodies twisted into a tight rope of rasping snakeflesh.

The new snake was longer and more slender than the adder, with glossy olive scales and a small, elegant head. Its body emitted a faint golden sheen as it fought with its heavier, clumsier opponent. With a sharp ripple of its whiplike tail, the taipan pressed the adder to the ground, forcing its head into a fire ant mound.

"You bin know better," she hissed at the adder. Ned shook his head, trying to stay conscious. He recognized her, that other voice that sometimes lived in his head, the one that held the dark presence at bay. "Neddy-boy got a job to do—can't be dyin' yet," the Taipan Ancestor scolded as the death adder beat the sand with its tail, its head covered in ants. It gave one loud honking hiss at its captor and disappeared in a curl of gray smoke.

"Well. You bin want looking after, don't you?" The liquid reddish-brown eyes of a slender, golden-skinned woman looked down at Ned, her soft brown hair streaming outward from her head in a halo of spirals. She took both his hands in her long thin fingers, and he felt a stinging, burning heat flow from her into his poisoned body. Blinking, he watched in shock as the taipan bit into his hand and held him firmly. Ned spasmed, his body absorbing the counter-venom as it scoured the battleground of his ravaged body.

"Neddy," the golden Aboriginal woman continued, pressing his hands against the cool silky skin of her small breasts, "you bin left that little boy behind. You a big man now. That mob up in Sky Home, they bin watching you. They bin tell me, go down there, tell him to fix that dingo-clan taboo, make things up right."

"Wha...?" Ned was beyond coherent speech

"You got to put back the *tjuringa*."

The what? Ned wanted to complain that he didn't know what the fuck she was talking about, but his tongue wouldn't function. He was dying and too weak to move. The taipan released him, stretched to her full height—nine feet of swaying olive-golden serpentine beauty—and then was gone. Ned gasped as a cramp knotted his guts. He let out a shuddering breath and, finally, lay still.

Smoke from the burning blew up from the marsh and over the piney flatlands, catching the nighttime attention of owls and raccoons, shy deer, and a nervous gray fox that lashed the underbrush with its black-tipped tail. A flash of lightning lit the sky, and a few tentative raindrops soaked into the sand, but Ned was beyond caring about such things. He slept the sleep of the dead.

Chapter 1

July 4—Present Day

"Alice! Wake up."

Alice Waterston struggled to the surface of a dream. She'd been standing on an escarpment of weathered limestone and darker boulders, looking down into a narrow gorge with outcroppings of palms and eucalyptus. Far below, the hiss and boom of restless water pounded ancient rocks as an incoming tide brought the open sea into a bottleneck between sheer cliffs. Across the gorge she saw a galaxy of stars. Someone grabbed her shoulder from behind and pushed, she was falling …

"Holy shi…oh. Nik." She jerked, then rolled toward him, sleep-fogged and relieved.

"The phone's ringing."

Alice sat upright, and then bolted out of bed. In the dark kitchen, she cracked her little toe against a chair leg as she grabbed for the receiver. *Motherfuck!* "—ello?" Her voice was a frog's croak. She cleared her throat, curling her foot in pain. "Hello? Yes, this is Alice Waterston."

She listened in silence to the ward nurse calling from Gull Harbor, informing her in carefully measured tones that her mother Suzanne had just passed away. Standing naked in the predawn darkness, Alice noted the time on the microwave—two forty-five in the morning. It was Monday, July 4. Independence Day. Suzanne's liberation. The obituary was already writing itself in her mind as she listened.

Nik came into the living room, pulling on his jogging shorts and turning on the light. Alice blinked at him and mouthed, "She's gone." Nik nodded, tossing her his well-worn Mycological Society T-shirt. Alice put the phone down for a second and shrugged into it—the shirt engulfed her, the hem reaching halfway down her thighs.

The nurse was saying something about a quiet, peaceful passing. Alice bit her lip. "Right, it's for the best. We're all glad she didn't linger," she said, her thoughts spiking ahead to funeral plans and back to images of Suzanne and Margaret playing together on the beach. "Thank you so much for calling. Florida Shores Funeral Home, that's right. They should already have her instructions on file. Yes, her brother, Harold Blacksburg, will take care of the arrangements. You should call him to pick up her things from the hospital—oh, he did already? Was he with her when she...? Well, thank you again for everything. Yes, goodbye."

Alice hung up and stood quietly, ignoring her throbbing toe, letting the news sink in. It was what she'd been expecting, even hoping for, and yet now that it was true, she felt strange.

Margaret slipped into the living room, rubbing her eyes.

"Mom? What's going on?"

Alice reached out and pulled her daughter close.

"Grandma Suzanne's passed on."

"Oh." Margaret's face was a mask, but Alice knew the loss was severe. Suzanne doted on her only granddaughter, and Margaret had adored her in kind. Alice felt the girl's chest rising and falling. When at last Margaret pulled away, there was a damp spot on Nik's shirt, just over the mushroom logo.

"What'll happen to Carlisle?" Margaret raised her head, damp strands of hair stuck to her face.

"Hal's keeping him." Suzanne's Afghan hound had been her companion for the past eleven years, but Alice supposed he could keep Hal company just as well. "Carlisle's an elegant dog, pedigreed with papers and all, but they never showed him. Poor Carlisle. Hal says he's pretty sad. Looking for Suzanne."

"I want him if Uncle Hal doesn't." Margaret wiped her cheeks.

Alice watched her pad back to her room, face shielded by her tangled mass of red curls. The bedroom door shut softly.

"Will she be all right, then?" Nik touched her hand.

Alice nodded. "It'll be hard, they were tight. But yeah, she'll deal with it. You know how she is."

"*Ja,*" said Nik. "And you?"

"Me? I'll miss her, I guess. I can't say I loved her. Shit, let's be honest, I didn't even like her. But ... there's a hole." Alice shrugged. "I don't know how to explain it."

"Do we need to do anything tonight?"

"No, Hal's in control, as usual."

"Then come back to bed, try to sleep. You haven't done much of that while she's been ill."

"I know." *Ahhhh.* Alice leaned against Nik as he massaged the base of her neck with his big hands. Nik was tall and lean as a lodge pole, like his Viking ancestors. His flax-colored hair fell loose over his bare shoulders. Alice yawned and thought about the week just past.

She'd spent the last six days in Suzanne's hospital room, keeping vigil. The doctors told her the stroke was massive and that her mother might not wake up again and, in fact, might remain unresponsive for however long it took her to die. Your basic vegetative state, she'd told Nik on the phone. She'd called Shelton, her boss at the Hardison Museum, and asked for a short leave of absence to help Hal with doctors and lawyers, and to sit beside the hospital bed waiting for some sign of consciousness beyond the steady hiss of the respirator.

That sign had come the second night, when Alice sat staring at Suzanne's thin, remote face, thinking about nothing in particular. Her mind had been wandering, mulling over mundane stuff like getting Margaret enrolled in the university's summer Science Camp for gifted middle-school kids and taking Dawg to the vet for his annual rabies shot. Then she'd seen a single tear pool at the corner of Suzanne's closed left eye and slide down the sunken cheek into her ear. From that point on until yesterday when Alice had driven the hundred miles back to her own safe haven, her house in the pines near Citrus Park where the museum was located, she'd talked to Suzanne. Saying things she'd wanted to say for years and trying to take back other things, hurtful things, that she'd actually said. But that single tear was all she got for her effort.

Now, settled comfortably back in bed with Nik, all that seemed so pointless. It was over; Suzanne was gone and couldn't care less how Alice felt about her or what kind of parent she'd been. Alice pressed her back against Nik and tried to sleep, but she couldn't stop thinking.

With Suzanne gone, she was now officially an orphan. Which meant she was no longer anchored to a family, had no parent to impress with the way she'd turned out. But had Suzanne ever praised her or openly demonstrated love that she could remember? She couldn't think of a single instance, but other memories fought their way to the surface.

"Mama, can I come in?" five-year-old Alice asked, peeking around the doorframe. Her mother sat at her bedroom window, watching a summer squall blow sheets of rain through the palms lining the driveway. It had taken her a full minute to respond. Alice knew because she'd counted to sixty-three before Suzanne turned around.

Alice's memory rendered the scene in CGI detail. She'd approached her mother, holding her breath. "Papa says," she'd whispered, "that he's going to the market and wants to know if you want anything." Suzanne had stared at her as if she'd spoken a foreign language.

Tiny-boned and fine-featured, Suzanne Blacksburg-Waterston sat still as a porcelain doll on the cushioned window seat, her flame-red hair unbrushed and her white satin dressing gown untied. "Come here," she'd said, and stretched out a thin hand toward Alice. Alice had gone to her, hoping for but not really expecting some sign of affection. Suzanne had taken Alice's face in her hands and looked her in the eyes with such unblinking fascination that Alice had begun to tremble.

"You have his eyes," she stated to no one. "They're not natural. Yellow, with blue rings around the pupil. Who has eyes like that?"

"Papa says they're hazel," Alice responded, shaking. Her mother's fingers reached up into Alice's thick hair, pulling her head back. "His hair," she said, "That thick sandy …" Then she'd erupted, scratching Alice's cheek and hitting at her in a blind fury. "Get out! OUT!" Alice had fled down the stairs at a pounding run, ending up in Hal's study where she'd recounted between sobs what had happened.

Squirming against Nik, Alice endured the memory to its end. Hal had washed her face, put an antiseptic on the scratches, and taken her out for ice cream. She'd stayed away from her mother's room after that.

Nik rolled over and fitted himself to the curve of her body, his free arm holding her lightly, reassuring but not binding. His lips brushed her shoulder, and she smiled in the dark. She should marry this man before he got away, the eight-year difference in their ages notwithstanding. The age gap seemed irrelevant to them now, but when he eventually reached his forties, she would be fifty. It was something to think about.

Listening to Nik's even breathing, she began to doze.

"But why? Why would she call me something like that?" Nine-year-old Alice's face was flushed, her voice hoarse from yelling. Hal had picked her up from school just in time to derail the shouting match between Alice and a schoolmate. On the way home, she'd poured out her fury and embarrassment, her voice rising until all she could do was squeak.

"She asked me if I was adopted. She said my mother and father are really brother and sister, and if I'm not adopted then I'm a sin against nature 'cause they would have to commit incest to have me."

Hal had looked at her with an unreadable expression. In her enraged state of mind, his silence had been worse than any answer. Furious, Alice had plunged ahead. "I looked it up. Incest means that a brother and a sister—"

"I know what it means." Hal shut off the car. They were sitting in the curve of the long driveway, halfway to the house. "Let's go for a walk. I need to explain some things to you." The tone of his voice, normally so reassuring, was constricted, and Alice remembered how much that had frightened her.

They'd walked a block down to the Miami River seawall and sat on a park bench, watching joggers and skaters pursuing their quest for physical perfection. Alice had cried until she had no tears left, and Hal had waited patiently until she'd finally asked, "Is it true?"

"Only half. Yes, Suzanne is my sister, but I am not your father."

Alice sat stunned. "Then who is?"

"A man you've never met, nor ever will." He'd then told her of the death of Ned Waterston during his honeymoon expedition to Australia with his bride, twenty-four-year-old Suzie Blacksburg. Hal explained how, a few months after their departure, Suzanne had called home, barely in control of herself, with the news that she was stranded, alone and terrified, somewhere in Queensland and that something unspeakable had happened to her new husband. Beyond that, she was not very coherent.

Hal had gotten on a plane and gone to fetch her. He explained how Suzanne, just visibly pregnant, had suffered a mental breakdown upon arriving home and how, when her baby was born, she seemed afraid to hold it or look at it, as if it might have some deformity. She was diagnosed as clinically depressed and spent time in and out of various private hospitals.

Hal confessed with a catch in his throat that when Suzanne's mental state did not improve as Alice entered childhood, he took it upon himself to become father as well as uncle, ignoring the fact that some day he would have to come clean. He'd apologized repeatedly that she'd had to learn about it from someone who didn't understand the facts. Poor Hal, he'd been so truly miserable, she'd been afraid he would cry, too. As it was, the incident brought them closer, and she could not have loved him more if he'd been her real father, whose face Suzanne apparently saw whenever she looked at Alice. Why that was so horrible, her mother would never explain. Not even on her damned deathbed.

Over the years, and once Alice had made her own life with a suitable husband and child, Suzanne had managed to reinvent herself. Still living with her brother, she'd become a fairly competent business woman. Something in real estate, Alice remembered. When Hal reached retirement age, they'd bought an upscale beach house on the Florida Gulf coast to be closer to Suzanne's granddaughter. Alice frowned, remembering. After her divorce, Suzanne and Hal had tried to convince her that moving in with them would be safer, but she'd told them nothing doing. She loved her house in the woods with its second floor deck that faced into a sea beech, pine, and oak. Margaret had agreed with her—they weren't leaving. Adjusting to life as a twosome had its rough patches, but they were making it work. And then, unexpectedly, there was Nik.

Alice sighed and pressed herself against him. He'd been in the States a number of years, pursing a degree in Mycology, paying his way as a part-time illustrator at the museum, where she'd met him. They began seeing each other not long after her divorce. The fit was good, intellectually and other ways, and most importantly, Margaret liked him. He was her anchor now, with his wholesome Swedish family of parents and siblings overseas who cared for each other no matter what else was going on in their lives. She wondered what it would be like to live in a family like that.

Suzanne had wanted to know all about Nik when Alice finally confessed, a few years ago, they were an item. It was ironic, thinking about it now, how Suzanne had kept Alice at arm's length for so long and then performed a one-eighty once she became a grandmother—wanting to know every little thing that might have the slightest impact on Margaret's welfare. Alice smiled against the pillow. Over the past week Suzanne had gotten an earful as she lay trapped on her deathbed, listening without reprieve to Alice's memoir of love and pain and loss.

"Did you care the least little bit about me? What did you hate seeing when you looked at me?" Alice had demanded of the comatose figure. "Hey, are you listening?"

As usual, Suzanne refused to be interrogated, and Alice was left to fill in the gaps with her own imagination. In life, and now in death, it was the only relationship mother and daughter had ever known.

Chapter 2

July 1953

"Hey boy, you alive?"

Ned cracked an eyelid. Daylight lanced his skull, and he clamped the lid shut. He tried to speak, but there was no feeling in his tongue. He willed it to form words.

"Unnggh."

"Shit, he *is* alive! Gimmie a hand here. We'll lay him in the truck."

"Dead weight," another voice grunted.

"Just a skinny kid. Here, hoist up his legs ... holy fuck, lookit that."

"Snakebite. See them double fang marks?"

"Cottonmouth?"

"Nawsuh, rattlesnake. This fella's lucky to be alive."

"Wouldn't wanna be alive in that shape."

Ned felt his body lift off the ground. The motion was nauseating, but then he felt a sublime sensation of floating. He sprouted wings and soared high above the pine scrub and palmettos. Far below, he saw a battered gray pickup truck with two dark-skinned men wrestling something into the truck bed. Then his wings evaporated, and he was plummeting toward the tiny figures, landing hard with a loud metallic clunk.

"Hey, watch his head there."

Merciful darkness descended.

* * *

When the light returned, it was muted. Ned opened his eyes and blinked a few times. He was in somebody's bedroom. Sun-faded lace curtains shielded the single window, and late afternoon light heated a patch on the bare plank floor beside the bed. Against the wall directly opposite the bed, a chest of drawers in dark wood dominated the room, its top covered by nearly a dozen framed photos. A few were in color, most were black and white, and some seemed quite old. He sniffed. The room had a clean, scrubbed smell.

He tried to sit up and wished he hadn't. Pain stabbed through his head and his left leg, and he fell back, cursing. His envenomed foot was propped up on a stack of pillows, looking evil and misshapen. It was sticking out of the leg of a pair of faded pajamas, something he'd never worn in his life. *Whose*? he wondered.

Lifting his hands to rub his eyes, Ned realized with a shock that something else was not right—the tiny scars dotting both forearms were gone, replaced by a pattern of faint overlapping crescents. Ned stared in disbelief. *What the fuck*? He ran his hands over the skin and its surface was smooth, with no ridges at all. He wet his finger and vigorously massaged a patch of the design, but it wouldn't rub off. On top of that, the skin of his hands and arms, and probably the rest of him if he could have looked, had turned olive complexioned instead of pasty white and freckled like his mother. Ned was stunned. What had happened to him?

"You've been through one nasty ordeal, young fella." A small black man stood in the doorway, dressed in a crisp white shirt and dark trousers. "But Doc Avery says you'll survive. The worst is over. We put you in my father's pajamas, hope you don't mind. They seemed a pretty good fit."

Ned didn't remember any doctor, and he had for sure never seen this person before. He stared at the man, who could have been anywhere from thirty to fifty years old for all Ned could tell.

"Where...?" he croaked. His vocal cords felt like they hadn't been used in years.

"I'm sorry," the man said, coming into the bedroom. "I shouldn't have surprised you like that. My name is Cecil Rider, pastor of Saint Christopher's African Methodist Episcopal Church. It was two of our church members who found you and brought you here. If the Lord hadn't brought you to us, you likely would have died out there in the woods."

Woods! Ned saw in a flash the burning house, his crashing escape through the underbrush, the snakebite … He shut his eyes and convulsed.

"Easy, now, have a drink of water." The Reverend Cecil Rider picked up a glass from a nightstand near the bed and held it to Ned's mouth as he helped the boy sit up.

"Thanks, mister," Ned said, swallowing the water in a single long gulp.

"More?"

"Naw, it's just … my mouth is so dry." He ran his tongue over cracked lips. "How long I been layin' here?"

Cecil settled himself onto the faded gunnysack cushion of a cane rocker, crossing one leg over the other and folding his small brown hands over his knee. "Three days. It was day before yesterday when Thaddeus and his son pulled up in the yard with you in the back of their truck. Said they found you on a dirt road inside the National Forest, soaked to the skin from that big rainstorm that passed over. You were out of your head, but alive, so I sent them to fetch the Doc, and he came yesterday. Dressed your foot up and said he didn't think he'd need to amputate—"

"What?" Ned sat up straighter. "Nobody's cutting my foot off!"

"Easy, that's what I'm telling you. The swelling's gone down a lot, so looks like you'll survive. The Lord's doing, like I said."

"I don't know about that, but yeah, I'm still here."

The man nodded and smiled. "You want to tell me your name and how can we contact your ma and pa? They must be worried sick, wondering what's gone with you."

"I'm just Ned. No parents. My dad died when I was five … hunting accident." He sat still for a moment, wondering how to explain what had happened to his mother. It occurred to him that he shouldn't give his full name, in case the police might accuse him of murdering his mother by burning her up, which was exactly what he had done.

"I … lightning hit the house. It burned up in a flash. I tried to get my mother out, but couldn't do it. So, I'm an orphan." He closed his eyes and chewed on that notion for a moment. An orphan. That meant he was now free and had no family at all and could do whatever he wanted, for the first time in his life.

Cecil rose from the rocker, a look of anguish on his smooth features. "You lost your mamma in a house fire?"

Ned looked up at him. "Yeah, I did."

He touched the boy gently on the shoulder. "That's a terrible thing, but I'm sure the Lord spared you for a reason. You should be grateful to be alive and ask Him to help you through this terrible time. Maybe there was some reason He brought you to me." He folded his hands in a prayerful gesture. "You're sure there's nobody we can contact? No aunts, no uncles?"

Ned shook his head. "There was just my mother and me. No relatives."

Cecil sat down on the edge of the bed. "Do you still go to school?"

Ned's defenses went up. "Naw, I quit goin' to school when I turned thirteen," he lied. "Mamma needed me at home. It was hard, but we had some charity help." He shut up. The fact that he'd never been to school wasn't anything this old colored guy needed to know.

Cecil sat there and just looked at him. Ned fidgeted under the gaze of those soft brown eyes that were kind enough, but a little cagy, like the eyes of a vole he'd once kept in a homemade cage. Ned didn't think this was some dumb old darkie you could fool in a heartbeat. He'd better be more careful.

The Reverend Rider got up. "Well, don't you worry yourself, son. You can stay here a bit. This was my grandmother's room. She's been dead quite a few years, but I don't s'pose she'd mind you using it," he said softly. "You lie back. I'll check on you when it's suppertime."

Ned slumped back on the pillows, sweating, his mind churning. He'd expected to die, but now he'd been rescued. He'd never interacted much with black people, and the few who'd come to his mother for her services had been either shaking in their worn-out boots while the witch mixed her potions or dangerous as the snakes that fueled the brew. In any case, he knew he couldn't stay.

* * *

"So, what're we gonna do with that white boy? He can't stay here without it causing trouble." Estell looked at her husband in the fading light. They were sitting on the front steps of the small frame house the congregation of St. Christopher's had built for Cecil's father and his extended family back in 1925 when Cecil was in middle school. Now, half-a-dozen years after the second world war, Cecil's father had passed on, leaving the church and the house to his son, who lived in it with just his wife. They were hoping for children, had been hoping for nearly a decade, but so far the field had proved infertile.

Cecil took her hand. "Why? He's homeless and from what he says, motherless and fatherless. You want to just turn him out?"

"Find some whites who'll take him in. Ask up at the Methodist Church, they'll find somebody. Or maybe a schoolteacher knows him. I just don't want any trouble."

Cecil sat with bowed head. "It doesn't feel right, after he was sent to us half-dead."

"*Brought* to us, if I remember rightly. Don't act like a darn fool. We can't adopt him, and how do you know he's really an orphan? He could be a runaway, just as easy. It'll be Hell to pay, us keepin' him." She was frowning, keeping her voice down. "You know I'm right."

Cecil continued to stare at the tops of his shoes. He sighed deeply. "I'll ask around. At least let's feed him a good supper. He seems like a nice boy."

Estell looked her husband in the eyes. "Don't you go getting attached to him, you hear me? I know you—take in every stray dog that wanders into the yard. This ain't your stray dog. He belongs to somebody else, and we can't keep him."

"All right, I agree. Satisfied?"

"Yes." She pecked him on the cheek and stood up, fanning herself with a magazine. "Now I'll go start dinner. This summer sure is a scorcher."

Cecil sat, chin in hand, wondering why he felt so unsettled. She was right, of course. Although some brave souls had recently tried protesting the segregation of the races in schools and public places, it wasn't a crusade he wanted to jump into. Last year he'd read in the paper about that little girl Linda Brown in Topeka, Kansas, whose case had been taken to court by the NAACP. But Kansas was a long way from Magnolia, Florida. A childless black couple taking in a homeless white teenager ... it wouldn't be tolerated. The Klan didn't seem all that visible in this quiet rural community, but he didn't want to test that assumption.

Cecil sighed again and stood up. At forty, he was well respected in the colored community and on friendly terms with some open-minded whites as well, but he was not like his father. Antoine Rider, the late pastor of St. Christopher's, had been courageous in life and a source of strength to his flock and family even after his death. Cecil missed him still. He wished his father was here now, to give guidance. He'd looked long and hard into the eyes of that skinny child lodged in his grandmother's room, and he wasn't at all happy with what he saw. The boy was lying, of course, concealing his real situation. But there was something else ... something in his eyes and sharp-boned face that gave Cecil a start every time the boy looked at him. It was unsettling, like feeling anxiety or dread over something you couldn't name.

He'd also taken a good look at those ritual markings on the boy's arms. What kind of voodoo was that? Again, the sense of unease tightened his stomach.

The Reverend Cecil Rider said a silent grace as the aroma of ham and turnips seared in butter and onions reached his nose. Be thankful for what life gives you: he'd always preached that to his flock. But he wondered, as he opened the screen door, what life had just dropped in his path.

Chapter 3

July, Tuesday — Present Day

"Well, that sucks," Alice said aloud. She highlighted a paragraph on her computer screen and hit DELETE. The introduction she was supposed to be writing for an expensive picture book the Hardison Museum was publishing wasn't flowing. It wasn't even trickling. The book was a follow-up to last year's highly successful *Land of Legends* Australian Aboriginal art exhibit. The photos were beautiful, the book design top notch, but Alice couldn't get focused.

Opening her well-worn *Guidebook to Australia*, a tome larger and heavier than the Greater Miami phone book that she remembered from the years she'd grown up there, she turned to the sacred sites chapter and read:

> Sacred sites are vital to Aboriginal culture.
> Aboriginals claim that Ancestor spirits still linger in
> such spots, and to enter them without permission or the
> proper initiations and rituals can be highly dangerous.
> These so-called "dangerous places" are not listed on any
> tourist map; in fact, Aboriginal guides will refuse to pass
> near them or even divulge their existence to outsiders.

Alice frowned. She wanted to explain how the Wandjina rock paintings and artifacts appearing in the *Land of Legends* exhibit had been blessed by clan leaders and sanctioned by the Aboriginal community. Nothing in the show had come from any so-called "dangerous place," disturbing accidents around the exhibit notwithstanding, including the fact that she'd had a mental meltdown once the show opened. In her heart of hearts she knew what she'd seen, and felt. The electrical discharge in the Wandjina spirits' touch during a thunderstorm, she still remembered that. The oversized wild dog that attacked her in the yard of her house in the woods … that'd felt damned real. But what came after … Alice felt the sweaty palms of a panic attack gearing up. She'd taken a leave of absence, gone to a shrink and gotten convinced it had all been in her head, and then tried very hard to get on with her life. But Margaret knew, and so did Nik. They just weren't saying. The three of them were living as if last year hadn't happened. On some level it was working.

She did the deep, calming breath technique the shrink had taught her, and her heartbeat slid back to a normal rhythm. Alice sagged in her chair, feeling tired and stupid. Suzanne's impending funeral was draining away her concentration and making her irritable. She reached for the phone.

"Doris, what's the deadline on this intro copy for the *Legends* book?" Alice rarely had occasion to call Doris Manley, the museum's Education Director, but everyone had agreed Alice should write the introductory chapter for this special collector's edition book. The exhibit had been her baby, her first big show as Arts Curator.

"Alice, is that you? I was sorry to hear about your mother. There's no hurry, we don't need the introduction yet."

"No, I can do it. I'm flying down to Miami for the funeral, but I'll be here all this week before that. My uncle Hal's taking care of the arrangements, so I don't have much to do. Just show up for the ritual, I guess."

Alice winced; she hadn't meant to sound that flip. It was just that she felt removed from the entire death and mourning process. She was dealing with the fact intellectually, but her emotions weren't connected to it.

"Don't push yourself," Doris was saying. "Anytime this week is fine."

"Right. I'll get on it, then. Thanks."

In the lunch room down the hall she found Hannah, her research assistant, leaning against the counter, watching the corporate coffee pot ooze a vile black liquid into a glass decanter that could use a good scrubbing.

"Alice!" Hannah came around the lunch table, her arms extended. "I'm really sorry."

Alice returned the hug with minimal response. "I'm fine. We're all glad she didn't linger. My uncle Hal's in control of the situation, so..." She shrugged. She was beginning to feel a little guilty that she couldn't pretend even a small display of bereavement.

"Well, that's good. We've missed you. Nik stopped by and brought us up to date. He's looking good," she added.

Alice finally smiled. A vision of tall, skinny Nik with his blonde ponytail and wire-rimmed glasses, rummaging through the museum's library stacks on his first assignment as technical illustrator, invaded Alice's mind. She'd been newly divorced and initially not interested, but the attraction had taken hold anyway.

"Have you met Milton?" Hannah was saying.

"Who's Milton?"

"I told you. Part-time artist hired for the *Legends* book. Knows his Florida history, but he's just a little too full of himself for my taste. Says he's a local history expert. I think he's a camp activities coach, too, or something like that."

A gong went off in Alice's head. "What camp?"

"Apalachee? It's that one Margaret went to, I think."

Alice was suddenly very interested. "Where's he located?"

Hannah poured the dark sludge from the pot into a Styrofoam cup. "Downstairs in the Conservation lab. They promised to find him some space up here, but I don't know who's got room. All the double offices are full."

"What's he look like?"

"Big burly guy, built like a fullback. His illustration skills aren't that bad, but Nik he ain't."

"How old, would you say?"

"Um, thirtyish?"

Alice turned to leave. "I think I'll go search him out. If he's working on *my* book, we need to get acquainted."

Alice took the elevator down to the basement where the Conservation lab took up most of the real estate. She went down the hallway, poorly lit and drab as a fallout shelter, and pushed at the heavy double doors to the lab. At a new desk pushed against the wall behind the receptionist area a large man in a yellow golf shirt and khaki pants leafed through the print pieces from the *Land of Legends* promotional campaign.

"Hi," she said, approaching him.

Startled, he turned, dumping flyers onto the floor.

"Alice Waterston," she said, extending her hand. "I was the curator for that exhibit."

"Oh, cool! I've been wanting to meet you!" He pumped her hand up and down. She looked him over. Curly brown hair shaved close on the sides of his head and up his neck, with the top a little longer. Bit of a belly hanging over his belt, sweat rings around his armpits, rundown deck shoes, and white cotton socks bunched around his ankles. He grinned at her, his head tilted sideways. A big old sloppy dog, that's what he was. If he'd licked her hand and sprouted floppy ears and a tail, she wouldn't have been half-shocked.

"Milton Crouch, glad to meetcha. I'm just part-time for this job," he gestured toward the flyers, "but who knows, it might turn into something if they like me."

"Hannah mentioned something about Camp Apalachee?" She phrased it as a question, giving him the lead.

"Oh, yeah, activities director, just a summer job. The pay's not that good, so if I went fulltime here, I'd give it up. Not that I don't like it—the kids are great—but I gotta pay the bills, you know."

Alice nodded, keeping her distance. "My daughter's been a camper there for the past couple of years."

"Hey, that's cool! What's her name?"

"Margaret."

Milton scratched at his wooly thatch. "I'm pretty good with names, but I can't remember a Margaret Waterston."

"Sorry, it's Margaret Sullivan. Her father and I are divorced."

"Ohhhkay! *That* Margaret. Skinny little red-haired girl. Hey, she's your kid?" He leaned forward, the too-small secretary's swivel chair creaking under his weight.

Alice backed away. "That's her."

Milton let out a guffaw that would have dislodged bats if they'd had any. "That's a ballsy kid you got there!"

Alice blinked. "I'm sorry if she caused any problems for you—"

"No, no, no. She and a couple of guys from the boys' cabins made a little midnight raid on that abandoned church property just past the camp fence last year. We didn't catch 'em in the act, but it was the buzz of the camp for days. Nobody got hurt or anything, so we just let it slide. Scared the bejeezus out of them enough that nobody tried that trick again."

"I should hope not." Alice was frowning. "I was just wondering … She told me the camp's wakeup bell came from the belfry of that same church." She was fishing, despite her resolve to let the memory of what she'd encountered there fade into oblivion.

"It sure did, and that's mainly thanks to me. That old geezer who was the pastor, Cecil Something-or-other, wasn't going to let us have it at first."

"Really?" Alice moved a bit closer.

"Oh hell yeah. Listen, anything you want to know about that old landmark—well, it's torn down now, of course—I'm your man."

"Is that so?" She sat down on the edge of the receptionist's desk. "You know what, I've often wondered about that old church," she said, throwing out the line and wondering what it would hook. "What finally happened to it? I was on vacation in Norway last February, and after I got back, I drove past the spot and saw it had been dismantled."

Milton gave her a toothy grin. "The bell tower got hit by lightning and set on fire. The main roof was tin, but the tower was wood shingled and burned pretty good. County's volunteer fire department is only a mile and a half down the road, so they put it out pretty quick. But the belfry fell on top of the roof and took a wall with it. Last time pays for all." He grinned and leaned toward her, a conspirator. "The place was a lightning rod. Been hit a couple of times that I know of, maybe even more."

Now it was Alice who leaned forward. "Really."

"Hell yeah, the place has a history of bad luck … snake bites, you know?"

"What makes you say that?" Alice's mouth was dry.

Milton scooted his chair a little closer and held up a huge paw. "First," he said, ticking off his pudgy fingers, "all kinds of things happened to the construction crew hired to tear the place down. One guy steps on a rusty nail and gets tetanus. Another one gets bit by a coral snake. Standing in all those deep weeds around the foundation, they figured it must have crawled into his boot and started chewing on his ankle—he didn't even realize it was there until he'd gotten a good dose. Darn near killed him."

Alice hoped she wasn't gawking too openly, but she was riveted by his rambling tale as it filled in holes in her personal history of the First Church of the Heavenly Powers, a name the primitive one-room building had not borne since its founding in the late 1800s. Her own part in its history, played out over three terror-filled months near the end of last year, haunted her nightmares still.

"Then you got that first preacher," Milton continued, "a gold-plated weirdo by all accounts, who *also* gets hit by lightning and fried right there, right in the belfry. After that, there's no record of what happened to the church until nineteen seventeen, when it was used as a meeting hall for young black men being recruited into the World War I armed forces."

Alice's brain was on fast forward. "What year did the first preacher die? The one you said was hit by lightning?"

"Well, you can look up his obit, February of nineteen-hundred. Cause of death wasn't listed, but there's anecdotal evidence from a separate newspaper story and a coroner's report, if you're interested."

"*You're* obviously interested in the guy," Alice said, watching him. "How come?"

Milton shrugged. "I'm a history buff, in case you hadn't noticed. I do research for the Massalina County Historical Society, and some for the camp, too. Like when we asked if the bell was for sale. I mean, the building had been abandoned for years, what with the congregation moving up the road to a new brick church. They sure didn't have any use for it. That preacher guy—"

"Cecil Rider," said Alice.

"Yeah, him. He didn't want to sell anything from the church, but that bell is pretty valuable. I offered them a hundred for it, but it's worth more. I saw the maker's mark on it: McShane Bell Foundry, Baltimore. That one in the church tower was bronze, seventeen-inch diameter, about a hundred pounds, made in the eighteen-hundreds. I've started a camp fund to have it restored. Say, how do you know old pastor Rider?"

"I'm a bit of a history buff myself. Job requirement."

"Oh, yeah, I forgot that. You got a degree in history or archeology or something like that, right? I read your bio when I got hired."

Alice stood up. "Nice to meet you, Milton. I'm glad we'll be working together."

"Hey, you betcha!" He waved as she slipped out the door.

Alice rode the elevator back up to the third floor lost in thought. Her mind was circling around the periphery of forbidden territory, events she'd promised herself she wouldn't get sucked into again. She'd moved on, and yet, there it all was again, right in her face. She went to her office, sank down into the wing chair by the door, and stared into space.

She had to drive past the camp and the old church grounds on her way home, but the church and its blighted past were gone now, so who the hell cared anyway, besides Milton and maybe Cecil Rider. Alice remembered him, hunched over in the January wind, watching her drive away with a church artifact he'd begged her to burn. She silently wished, for the millionth time now, that she had taken his advice.

Chapter 4

July 1953

"Who's that guy in the uniform?" Ned was pointing to the oldest photo on the dresser.

Cecil picked it up. "My father. He was in the Army Supply Service corps, World War One. He got an honorable discharge when the war was over. When war broke out again after Pearl Harbor, he wanted to reenlist, but by then he was too old, so he did a lot of volunteer work for the war effort, ministering to those who came home alive. I was very proud of him. He died in nineteen forty-five … too early to see the war come to an end."

"That's tough," said Ned, not wholly comprehending. War had been a distant drumbeat in the background of his childhood, but he neither knew nor cared much about it.

Ned shifted his healing leg and leaned back against the pillows. Roughly a week had passed since the bite, and he could now put weight on his left foot and hobble around a little. The preacher and his wife took good care of him, feeding him and dressing him in clean clothes. That doctor came by once more, pronounced him "one lucky sonofabitch," and went away. He was the most comfortable he'd ever been in his life, and hoped they wouldn't turn him out too soon. He knew he couldn't stay indefinitely, but he didn't want to think about what he would do once he was completely well. He had no money and no knowledge of how to get along in the world outside the forest swamps and titi thickets where he'd been born.

The cabin of his birth had not originated with his parents. His mother said she'd found the old "cracker" cabin before her marriage, during excursions into the woods. Few people knew where it was, and his mother had kept him there most of his life, except for a few trips into a nearby town for supplies.

"I heard some stuff about the war, but don't understand much about who started it or why." Instantly, he regretted letting that slip, because it revealed he hadn't been in school. He would have been consumed with war news like everyone else if he'd been a student.

His mother and father had not kept him very well informed of how life went on outside their homestead among the blackgums and magnolias. They occasionally interacted with farming families in the area, but he was too antisocial to make any friends among the children. When questioned about schooling, he simply said he was needed at home, which was the same excuse all the farm kids used. No truant officer ever came looking for him. His parents—mostly his mother—taught him to read and how to add and subtract numbers, but his skills lay elsewhere. He twitched as painful memories crowded his head.

"This one here," said Cecil, indicating a black and white photo of a very old woman seated on some porch steps with three much younger men, "was taken in nineteen-thirty-four during the Great Depression, which I guess you wouldn't know anything about. People living on farms at least had a little bit to eat, but nobody had any money." Cecil shook his head. "That was the last year all of us were together."

"How come?" asked Ned, squinting at the picture.

Cecil lifted the photo off the dresser and handed it to Ned. Pointing, he said, "This is me, just twenty-one. In those days I was working day labor in the turpentine camps, chipping pine trees for the resin. I hadn't received the call to the ministry yet, as you can see."

Ned looked from the small, well-groomed pastor in his white shirt and black trousers to the skinny smiling youth in the photo, his dark face shiny with sweat. He slouched against the steps in rumpled work shirt and loose-fitting patched pants rolled up to the knees. His feet looked huge in lace-up men's boots with the soles peeling off. Ned felt a momentary pang of kinship with the grubby, tattered boy in his ill-fitting clothes. He imagined that the only real difference between them was the color of their skin and the smile. Ned had rarely, if ever, felt a smile that broad cross his face.

"This, of course, is my father, pastor of St. Christopher's A.M.E. church." Ned could see the resemblance. The father's expression was stern and his black suit and white shirt buttoned to the neck with no tie seemed severe, but he looked like someone you could trust.

"And this is my grandmother. I called her Granny Yoo, although her actual name was Yula. My father, Antoine, was her son. Sadly, she died the year this picture was taken."

"Yeah?" Ned was now genuinely interested. He decided he liked the Reverend Cecil Rider, although he couldn't say as much for the reverend's wife, who he could tell wanted to shuffle him out the door as soon as possible. Ned knew sneakiness when he saw it; he was more than adept at it himself.

"Heart attack," Cecil was saying, "which I guess is not too surprising. She was nearly blind, in her seventies. It took a toll on her … her older son running off with a woman she didn't approve of. They had some terrible arguments over it, but he was under that woman's spell and there was no turning his head. Some people said she put a hex on my grandmother, but that's just foolishness. That's him," said Cecil, pointing to the other man sitting beside Yula Rider. "We never heard another word from him when those two took off. To this day, nobody knows what happened to him."

Ned looked, and his heart stopped. He stared hard at the young man's face, with its liquid dark eyes and bow-shaped mouth. He looked back up at the reverend, not even bothering to disguise his expression of confusion.

"I guess I should explain," said Cecil. "He wasn't blood kin; he was adopted into the family as a baby when my father was about eight or nine, I think. He wasn't colored, but he wasn't a white boy either. But my grandmother loved him as much as she did my father, who treated him like a brother."

Ned's hands were shaking as he held the photograph. "W-what was his name?"

"My grandmother named him Lazarus, but everybody called him Lacy because he was so pretty. Black hair and light coffee-colored skin, he was kind of mulatto looking. He liked to tell people that he was from New Orleans, but that was just a fib, of course. He wore his hair long, too, braided in a pigtail like a Chinaman. He was working for Mr. Clarence Bradley at the funeral home just before he took off, which was a good job to have because work was so scarce back then. But that witchy-woman stole him away."

Ned had ceased to listen because the blood was pounding in his ears. There could be no doubt. The face was younger and less careworn, but it was him. The man in the picture was his own father.

Ned put the photograph down carefully and grasped the side of the bed to steady his trembling body. He thought he might faint dead away. Shadows thrown into the corners of the bedroom turned fluid. A voice whispered in his head.

"Ned, is something wrong?" Cecil took the photo and placed it back on the dresser. "You don't look so good."

"I ... just felt sick for a minute. It ain't nothin'." His mind was reeling. He'd accidentally stumbled through a door into his father's past, which neither of his parents had ever explained to him. His guts were churning, and the skin along his arms began to sting.

Cecil headed for the door. "I'm sorry, I've been talking your ear off, and what you really need is sleep. I'll just turn the light off."

"No! I mean, wait, please." Ned leaned forward. "I'm not sleepy. Could you ... talk a little longer?" He tried to keep his voice level. "About that picture. Did all of you live together?"

"Oh yes, in this very house. When my father left the Army and returned to preaching, the congregation built this house for him and his family, which included me, Granny Yoo, and Lacy. My mother died birthing me into this world—she was only sixteen—so our family was just the four of us."

"I was just wondering," Ned hesitated, not sure how to get what he wanted to know without giving anything in return. "Um, how you all got along together ..."

"I think I know what you mean," said Cecil. "An old woman, two young men, and a little boy living together in the same house. Yet it made perfect sense to us. My grandmother ruled the household, and this was her room, as I've told you. The biggest bedroom down the hall was the one I shared with my father, and Lacy had his own small room. Poor boy, he had brain seizures that were sometimes pretty bad. He kept to himself a lot of the time."

Ned licked his lips and tried to swallow. He was definitely feeling toxic. "What's a seizure?" This was sneaky, because Ned knew very well what Lacy's fits were like and what he'd claimed to have seen when they were coming on. To five-year-old Ned, it was more frightening than milking serpents of their venom.

"Well now, I don't think you want to hear about all that." Cecil got up and reached for the light switch. "Maybe you'll feel better in the morning."

"That w-witchy woman, what was she like? I mean, I'm just curious."

"Well sir, she wasn't somebody you wanted to cross, that's certain. Sure had her heart set on Lacy. She was a lot older than him, and that was partly what got off with my grandmother. She didn't think it was right, with his condition and all. Broke her heart when he left. Well. Good night, son." Cecil turned off the light and softly shut the door behind him.

Ned lay on his back, listening to Cecil's footsteps retreating toward the kitchen. He was trembling and couldn't get his thoughts lined up straight. Something scraped against the baseboards near the dresser, but when he sat up and looked, there were only shadows.

Cecil had met his mother, interacted with her, maybe knew more about her than Ned did. But Ned knew the rest of Lacy's story and savored the thrill of knowing something others did not—it was a form of power, and it felt good.

He wondered about those fits. His mother had said his father was a gifted seer whose brain was wired funny; it was the price he paid for being the vessel of power. She'd been sure, she'd also told him, that her husband's seed had carried the gift into his son. But the problem was that Ned didn't want to be a great shaman or whatever she called it. He just wanted to get away.

Ned sat up and stared at the photo again. Could he be mistaken? His father had never called himself Rider. Ned had been taught that his last name was Waterston. Had that been his mother's name, instead? Ned felt as if his head might explode.

He lay awake a long time, watching the shadows. He could barely hear the two voices that lived in his head—they seemed very far away and he hoped they would stay that way. His forearms itched like crazy, but he forced himself not to scratch. Closing his eyes, he tried to sleep.

Just as he was dozing, a scraping noise along the baseboards brought him wide awake. He sat up and stared around the darkened room. Ned rubbed his eyes, and abruptly something bumped underneath the bed.

"Shit!" he yelped and pulled his knees up to his chest. The room seemed to tilt and slide, and the floor appeared to be *rippling*, the bare boards no longer wood but the scaled hide of a vast living beast. Spots danced before Ned's eyes as he gripped the side of the bed. His hands went numb, and he fell over the side onto the undulating surface. It was icy cold and froze Ned's heart on the moment of impact. He gasped a quick breath, and all went black.

* * *

Morning sun bathed Yula Rider's bedroom as Ned opened his eyes. He sat up slowly, looking around at the old woman's room, sedate and undisturbed. Head in hands, Ned decided he'd had one of the worst nightmares of his life. He slowly swung his legs over the side of the bed and waited. Nothing bumped the bed or grabbed him by the ankles, so he stood up. Whatever he thought he'd seen in the room last night, there was no sign of it now. His stomach rumbled, and he concentrated on getting dressed in his newly washed overalls, ignoring the massive headache that threatened to turn his stomach sour.

As Ned hobbled down the hallway and into the kitchen for breakfast, the phone rang. Estell went to answer it, leaving Cecil to dish out cheese grits, bacon, cornbread, and scrambled eggs onto Ned's plate. When she returned, she seemed more relaxed than she had been since Ned arrived. He watched her with suspicion.

"It's been decided," she said, smiling. "Cecil, will you go take the phone, please?"

"Who is it?"

"That man from the Methodist church that you talked to."

Ned kept silent, watching them both.

Cecil got up, and his eyes slid over Ned in a quick glance.

Estell sat down in her usual place at the end of the table nearest the stove. "Eat up, honey. We don't want you to go hungry."

That was the nicest she'd been to him. Ned tensed, wondering what was going on. He wolfed his eggs and bacon and kept an eye on the hallway where Cecil had disappeared. Whatever they were plotting, he wouldn't meekly go along with it if he didn't like it. He could hear the minister's soft voice, but couldn't make out any words. At last, Cecil returned and sat down at the table.

"Well, Ned, I think we've found a good family who can take you in. Mr. Campbell and his wife are fine church-going people, couldn't ask for better."

"He's a deputy sheriff," added Estell, "and his wife teaches Sunday school."

Ned stopped chewing. There was no chance in Hell he was going to go live with an officer of the law.

"His brother's a forest ranger, and he said if you can tell them how to find your cabin, they can go retrieve your mother's remains so she can have a decent burial."

Ned put his fork down. "When're they coming to get me?"

"This afternoon," said Estell, "so you need to go get a bath, and we'll find you some pants and a shirt to wear. I don't know what to do about shoes, though."

"They're planning to buy him new clothes, so don't fret over that," said Cecil. "Well, Ned, how does all of this sound?"

"Fine." He could feel the panic rising. "I think I'll go get in the tub now." He got up, clutching the table for support.

Cecil rose and followed him down the hall. "I'll go look through my father's closet and see if I can find something decent for you to wear to meet the Campbells."

Ned went into the bathroom and turned on the water. He stared at the floor, thinking, trying to calm his beating heart. Then he went to the small, high window that faced the back yard of the property. Standing on the closed toilet lid, he pushed out the screen, scrambled up onto the sill, and then eased himself out. Dropping to the ground, he landed with a painful jolt, but bit back a yelp.

By the time Cecil knocked on the door of the bathroom to check on him, he'd caught a ride with a farmer hauling bags of manure and was miles down the road, heading west.

Chapter 5

July 9, Tuesday — Present Day

Alice got out of her car and stretched.

"I'm not looking forward to this," she said. Standing barefoot in the gravel drive in front of her mother's house, she held her hair up off the back of her neck as a stiff breeze whipped her gauze skirt around her legs. Shielding her eyes, she squinted beyond the house at the windswept dunes fronting the Gulf of Mexico. At one o'clock in the afternoon, heat waves shimmered over the sand. The beach was dotted with people, even in the baking heat.

"I wish we'd brought Dawg," said Margaret from the back seat.

Nik unfolded his legs from the passenger side and got out, pushing the seat down for Margaret to crawl out. "Me too."

"Don't you two start. I'm not in the mood. Dawg smells and he's not getting in my car."

She hadn't been sleeping well and had come close to dozing off at the wheel during the two-hour drive from Citrus Park to Gull Harbor. She caught the look that passed between Margaret and Nik.

"Sorry," she said. "I'm stressed. It'll pass."

Alice stood looking at her mother's Lincoln, still parked in the drive. She hoped Hal would be able to sell it because she certainly didn't want it.

She could hear Carlisle inside the house, barking like a demon. Hal opened the door, and Suzanne's Afghan hound galloped down the porch steps with wide, wagging sweeps of his feathered tail. Hal opened his arms toward Alice and folded them around her.

"I'm glad you've come. There are so many things I need to do ... you'll be a huge help."

Alice pressed her face against his chest, hugging him tightly. "It's funny," she said, her voice muffled. "I don't miss her, not in the normal sense, but I feel ... unmoored. I don't like it."

Hal gave her a squeeze and turned toward Margaret and Nik. "Thank you both for coming. This probably isn't how you'd like to be spending your Saturday afternoon."

Nik stepped forward and offered his hand. "It's good to see you again, sir," he said.

Hal nodded, one arm still around Alice's shoulders. "It's been a difficult week, forgive me if I'm not very attentive. I was a better host when Alice brought you here for Christmas."

Carlisle galloped around them, heading for Margaret. She squatted down and grabbed his neck as he landed on top of her.

Hal managed a small laugh. "Poor Carlisle, he's been quite unhappy. Maybe he'll be better when we move."

"Ah, so you've decided to sell Dunescape?" Alice linked arms with her uncle as they headed inside. "I wondered if you might think about moving."

It was mercifully cool inside. "God, this feels good," Alice said, fanning her neck. "I don't know how those idiots on the beach can stand it."

"I like it hot," Margaret said, taking Carlisle into her lap on the couch. "It doesn't bother me like it does you." The old dog lumbered his thin body up and over her knees with a whuffing noise. "Poor old woof," she said, hugging him. "Misses his person." Margaret wiped at her eyes. "Me, too."

Nik scratched the dog behind the ears and settled himself into an armchair beside the couch. "How old is he, then?"

"Nearly twelve," said Hal. "Suzanne got him when he was a puppy. He's pedigreed, you know ... papers and all. He was her companion."

Alice watched them, allowing herself a small pang of guilt for not feeling weepy. Well, Margaret could do the proper mourning for both of them. The one she was most concerned for was Hal, who had been Suzanne's shadow for most of their lives. Hal never married—she'd wondered for a while if he was gay—but he appeared to be perfectly happy living platonically with his widowed sister. It had seemed the perfect arrangement for them both, but now it was over.

Hal went to the kitchen and returned with a pitcher of lemonade and four glasses on a tray.

"I'm thinking of moving back to Miami," he said, "if I can get a decent price for the house. I still have friends and business associates there that I wouldn't mind seeing again. And Suzanne will be there."

Alice winced. He meant, of course, that her mother's ashes would be entombed in the Blacksburg family mausoleum. "So, is everything set for the funeral?"

Hal nodded, pulling a pack of Luckies from his shirt pocket and lighting up. Alice did a double take. He'd never smoked in the house before, because Suzanne didn't and never had. But now she supposed he could smoke wherever he damn well wanted to.

"I've booked our flights," said Hal. "You'll be leaving fairly early Monday morning, returning on Tuesday. I hope Nik won't mind being left behind."

Nik shook his head. "Not a problem."

Alice sat down on the floor and leaned against his leg. "Nik's a hermit. He'll enjoy having the house to himself."

"And somebody has to take care of Dawg," Margaret said, holding Carlisle against her chest with both arms. His tail thumped the couch cushions.

Alice turned to Hal. "I assume you're keeping Carlisle?"

"Oh yes, we're a pair now. Two old bachelors with nothing more important to do than fetch the morning paper and fall asleep in front of the television. We'll be all right together."

Alice poured herself a glass of lemonade and sipped it slowly. This was probably the last, or maybe next to last, time she would be sitting here in this house. Hal was decisive when it came to business, and she knew that once he'd found the right buyer, he'd close the deal and be moved out in the time it took to sign the papers and do the handshake. He'd bought Dunescape with Suzanne on a whim some years ago and, Alice was sure, would move out of it just as quickly.

She thought of Nik, so perfectly content with his own company. After a year of living together, she still sometimes wondered what went on in his head. She had seen him sit still for long stretches of time without moving, just thinking. Margaret had once poked him from behind to see if he was breathing, and they had all laughed.

"You're awfully quiet," Hal said.

"Huh? Sorry, I kind of zoned out." Alice yawned and swallowed another gulp of lemonade. It wouldn't take much for her to fall asleep on the spot.

"Can I take Carlisle for a walk down the beach? We won't go far." Margaret heaved the dog off her lap and headed for the back door.

"Don't go any further than the boat house," Alice called. She checked her watch. One thirty-five. She'd give them half an hour, then send Nik to fetch them.

She refilled her glass and got up. "Well, no sense putting it off."

Hal leaned forward in his chair, elbows on his knees. "If you could bag up all her clothes and such, that would help. Keep anything you want, the rest I'll take to Goodwill. Her expensive jewelry goes to you and Margaret, listed by item in her will. She's made a rather nice endowment for Margaret's education."

"Well, that doesn't surprise me," Alice said, walking back to her mother's bedroom. "Nik, would you go after Margaret and the dog if they're not back by two o'clock?'

He nodded and gave her the slightest wink. "*Ja, min kärlek.*"

That seemed to bring Hal out of his funk. He said to Nik, "How'd you like to sample a little Wild Turkey I keep for special occasions? No reason to save it."

Nik shrugged. "No reason at all."

They went to the kitchen, where Alice heard glasses and ice clinking, then the back door slammed as they went out onto the patio. Alone, she turned to the task at hand.

She went to Suzanne's bedroom and looked around. The room was neat, bed made, no clothes piled on the floor or spilling out of drawers.

Alice sat down on the edge of the bed, feeling morose. No wonder Hal didn't want to do this job. It was disheartening. She thought about all the things a person accumulated and kept because they held meaning, defined who the person was. And once that person was gone, the objects had no purpose, no value. Alice felt smothered—it made her want to go home and throw away every useless object taking up space on dressers, shelves, tables, and the floors of closets. It was all so pointless. She stared at the floor.

Suddenly, her stomach lurched. The polished hardwood floor appeared to be fading; through it, she could see a field of stars. *No, no, no.* Alice panicked, breathing sharp, shallow breaths as if her lungs had forgotten how to function properly. Her mind reeled as images of Namarrkun, the Wandjina spirits, the Dreamland Ancestors played a slideshow on her retinas–she was losing it again. The room receded around the edges as her vision tunneled. She looked down at the dark well opening up under her feet and tumbled headlong into the void. A moment of freezing cold, and all went black.

Alice came to sprawled on rough ground, gasping and slightly nauseous as her brain groped to find equilibrium.

Chilled air brushed her ankles and lifted her hair, circling in a raw, bone-shaking dance. Within moments her entire body was shaking uncontrollably in her summer tank top and thin gauze skirt.

"H-holy sh-shit," she whispered, and then caught her breath. Not far off, a group of young Aboriginal women stood watching her. Their long silver hair swirled around their waists and knees in the frigid air, and their naked bodies glistened with a coating of ice. Long icicles sparkled from their earlobes and fingertips. Several wore tall tasseled headdresses, and others were adorned with bangles of crystal and armbands tufted with sprays of ice needles. They laughed and whispered among themselves in voices like the surface of frozen water cracking or icicles falling from tree limbs. Frost was in their breath. Alice's hands and feet began to go numb as she listened to their voices, rising and falling like a cicada's chant, although there was no hint of summer in their frozen song.

Alice tried to stand, but the marrow in her bones was freezing, her breathing slowing to long, shuddering gasps of frost-laden air. She was turning to stone and for a fleeting moment understood what glacier-entombed mammoths must have sensed as they slowly went to sleep.

The frost-maidens were approaching. Where they stepped, the ground became a glistening sheet of ice. Her brain had slowed to a crawl, but she listened to their tinkling, crackling song with an unbearable desire to join them. The song was ancient and primal, creation business of the Ancestors, yet she heard words that were familiar and held meaning. *Kungkarangkalpa.* The syllables danced in her mind and rolled like pebbles over a watercourse of ancient language and memory. One of the women bent down toward her, reaching out with silvery elongated fingers.

Alice's face lost all feeling as the woman touched her forehead, then her cheek, with long fingernails of ice. Blinding cold flashed up her sinuses and into her brain as the ice maiden's thumb and index finger pinched the septum of Alice's nose, making a tiny hole. Blinded by cold and pain, she barely noticed the small dingo bone sliding through her nose as the woman's shining hair whipped around her face. But the instant the bone was in place, it became a sounding board through which Alice's entire body began to resonate with the sirens' song—it was filling her up like the rising tide in the gorge below. She sank below the surface of consciousness, immersed in the trance woven by the seven sisters.

The Aboriginal maidens surrounded her, touching her hair and shoulders, intoning their song of creation. They sang their name, *Kungkarangkalpa*, the Dreamtime Seven Sisters whose beauty touched the land from high cliffside to water's edge at creation's dawn. Alice felt drunk on their song. She wondered in a loopy sort of way where her essence had skittered off to, but at the same time something about the place felt familiar. And then it all came back, only in much better detail than she'd given the shrink.

She'd been writing a book, a fictional history of the abandoned turn-of-the-century rural church she'd passed so many times on her drive into town. During her research, she'd found a folder of crumbling documents that belonged to the church's founder, a mysterious foreigner named Cadjer Harrow. Alice had believed–and perhaps some small part of her still did–that her discovery of the documents had triggered something. Her psychiatrist called it a psychotic episode brought on by the stress of curating an international exhibit and a much too vivid imagination. Alice's neighbor Raine told her she'd had a paranormal experience, maybe even manifesting a thought form of the appalling Rev. Harrow.

In the event that put her breakdown into overdrive, she thought she remembered cowering in the abandoned First Church of the Heavenly Powers, as it had been named, confronting the physical specter of Harrow, just as she'd described him in her manuscript. Black, flat-brimmed hat, mud-stained riding boots, black coat, dark skin like tanned animal hide, soulless eyes. Had the historical Cadjer Harrow looked like that? She had no idea, but this was the image that embedded itself in her mind's eye when she began to write about him. He'd materialized with a great black beast with red eyes that was more mutant dire-wolf than dog. She'd also sensed a dangerous tension between it and the man, as if they could not agree which of them was the master.

Though the specter wore a man's body and a preacher's suit, and was corporeal enough to inflict pain, he'd claimed to be from the other side. Exiled there, he'd said, by Namarrkun, a terrifying Dreamtime Ancestor humans called the Lightening Man. In the wake of Namarrkun's arrival to fetch him back, Alice had been swept with them into the frozen void, where she'd hung, for an hour or an eon, listening to the hum of the stars. When she'd struggled back to consciousness, the black shaman Harrow was gone, and the wreckage around her house and yard had been attributed to a monster thunderstorm that had swept across the county. But she knew. Namarrkun who commanded the rain and thunder and the Wandjina who followed him on the storm had scrambled her molecules.

Months of mood-calming drugs and private sessions with the psychiatrist recommended by her sister-in-law had helped her get a grip enough to return to work, and in the end she'd accepted the explanation that none of it had been real. Nik had taken her to Norway with him for a mycological convention, and life returned to normal, whatever that was. If she were honest, Alice didn't think she'd ever feel normal again.

Margaret had been her unwavering ally through the whole fiasco because, as Margaret had confessed to Alice, she'd known without doubt the wild dog big as a pony that hid in their woods was the same shape-shifter who met and taunted her in her nightmares. In fact, Margaret had been talking to it since early childhood; she just hadn't told anyone. Sometimes it appeared to her as a scruffy dingo, sometimes a blood red lizard, and sometimes just a dirty smear of shadow that Margaret could barely see. She further revealed that it came and went from her closet, mostly before she was fully awake. Raine had suggested they both read up on psychic phenomena and had loaned them some books.

Alice agreed that knowledge was power and, as a result of what she'd read, burned her book manuscript with the hope it would incinerate the tie that bound Harrow to her waking world. That was the point at which Namarrkun had arrived, trailing chaos and destruction.

To carry on day to day in the months that followed, Alice and Margaret had taken their cue from Nik, the nonbeliever, and tried to pretend there was a physical or mental explanation for everything they'd gone through.

But now Alice opened her mouth and felt the chanting resonance of the Kungkarangkalpa. The dingo bone amplified vibrations through her mind and body, shaking the foundations of that pulsing collection of atoms known in another dimension as Alice Waterston. Her identity was slipping away again, dissolving in the swirling, circling song of the Pleiades Ancestors. She was panicking in slow motion, powerless to do anything except intone the long notes into the seamless dark.

Turning slowly, atom by atom, she faced a wall of stone. In it, a man's frozen body glistened, arms wrapped around a darker splotch on the rock. The creation song thundered in her ears, as she stared, uncomprehending. He seemed familiar. Was he someone she should know? She reached out to touch him.

A hand suddenly gripped her shoulder, too hard it seemed–her frozen body cracked into a mosaic of splintered ice. She was disintegrating.

"Alice!"

Strong hands were shaking her to pieces. Her eyelids fluttered, thawing.

"Mom! Wake up!"

Alice shuddered and opened her eyes. She was lying on the floor of her mother's bedroom, with one canine and three human faces hovering above her. She rolled over, coughing.

Nik knelt beside her, his hands supporting her shoulders. Carlisle licked her neck. Hal's face was creased into a frown of worry. "Alice, what happened to you?"

She sat up, disoriented. "I have no idea. I was sitting on the edge of the bed and then sort of blacked out."

"We found you lying on the floor," said Margaret.

Nik helped her to her feet and kept his arm around her. "We couldn't tell if you were passed out or just asleep."

"Yeah, you were breathing really loud." Margaret was staring at Alice with that look that signaled alarm—the pupils of her ginger eyes had gone wide.

"Excuse me," Alice said and lurched for the bathroom. Shutting the door, she looked at her face in the mirror from all angles. Her nose was perfectly normal, no perforation. *What the fuck?* Alice felt sick to her stomach. She'd had a shock like this once before—she'd written about an injury Harrow supposedly inflicted on one of his followers and immediately experienced the sensation herself. It'd shocked her senseless, yet she could find no visible evidence of it on her body at the time. She'd rationalized it as a product of her overactive imagination, but here it was, happening again.

She sat down on the toilet lid and leaned her head against the sink, trying to get her atoms collected. Although she sat in the bathroom of twenty-first century reality, that other world clung to her like a gray fog. She got up and promptly threw up in the toilet bowl.

"Mom, are you okay?" Margaret was pounding on the bathroom door. "Can I come in?"

Alice flushed the toilet and opened the door just enough to pull Margaret inside.

"I need to talk to you," Alice said, taking a glass from the medicine cabinet and rinsing her mouth out. She took a washcloth off the shelf and bathed her face. Finally, she turned to Margaret.

"It's happening again," she said, holding onto the edge of the sink.

"Uh oh." Margaret's eyes were deep black.

"I think I went out of body … like before." Alice was shaking and found it hard to get the words out. She wrapped her arms around her chest, clutching her sides and wondering if she would ever be warm again.

"You looked like you were passed out," Margaret said, wary.

"The last thing I remember clearly was sitting on the edge of Grandma Suzanne's bed and staring at the floor. Then the bottom dropped out." Alice kept shivering.

Margaret closed the toilet lid and sat down. "Let me know if you need this again."

Alice wet her face again with the washcloth.

"Are you gonna be okay now?" Margaret's voice sounded tight, controlled, but not scared.

Alice relaxed a tiny bit. Thank the gods for Margaret—Raine had called her an old soul in a child's body. Alice didn't know about that, but she did know that Margaret was the closest thing to a best friend and confidant she had. At times they felt more like siblings than parent and child.

Alice looked at Margaret. "In this dream state or whatever it was, somebody poked a hole in my nose and put a bone through it, and it resonated so loud it started pushing my body apart. I felt that whole experience with every nerve, but do you see any marks?"

Margaret shook her head.

"Right, neither do I." Alice ran her hands through her hair. "Do me a favor, will you, and don't tell Nik or Uncle Hal."

"Alice? What's going on?" Hal's muffled voice from the bedroom was urgent.

She looked at herself in the mirror again, smoothed her hair, and opened the bathroom door. "I'm all right now. Must have been something I ate. I'm over it now. Can I have another glass of lemonade?"

Hal looked her over, doubt in his eyes. "Certainly." He went to the living room and left the three of them standing together.

Nik put his arm around her shoulders, and she leaned against him. "Are you ill?"

"Hell if I know."

"What does that mean?"

She bit her lip. "It means, let's just get this business over with and go home."

Following Hal out to the living room, she added, "I really wouldn't mind if I never came back here again."

Chapter 6

August 1956

Ned stood at the edge of the clearing. Sundown. Dry heat scorched the parking area in front of the windswept tent. Brown dust devils whipped dirt toward beat-up vans and trucks, an old Packard station wagon missing its hubcaps, and a few nicer cars jammed in front of Brother Micah's Southern Tent Revival.

"Gloryhalleluiahamenbrother praiseJesuspraiseJesus … praise*Jesus!*" Voices of the faithful peaking, falling, then building again toward climax. And over the top a strident nasal voice Ned assumed must be Brother Micah. Or maybe a lieutenant, if Brother Micah already had his hand in the box. He understood how this worked. He'd heard it all before, a lifetime ago.

Ned shivered in the heat, rubbing his arms through his long-sleeved shirt. Tall and rail-thin, he hitched up his pants and cast a look over his shoulder into the trees. Nothing he could see, but his arms and chest stung like he'd taken a nap on an ant bed. The demon stalked the fringes of his perception, sometimes serpentine, sometimes just a shadowy smear. He didn't figure anybody else could see it, but he wouldn't bet money on that. He saw it plenty good enough, mostly in his fitful dreams but occasionally in broad daylight.

Which was why he was here in hot, dusty Texas instead of dark and sultry Louisiana where he'd been the past year. How long had it taken him to get here, coming full circle to witness that spectacle of belief and terror from childhood that he hated most in the world? For Ned, counted time had crawled by with little attachment to dates, but he reckoned he'd been on his own for close to three years. Not such a bad accomplishment, when he stopped to think about it.

After his desperate escape from mosquito-bitten Florida, he'd hooked up with migrant workers heading to Chilton County, Georgia to pick peaches, strawberries, and sweet Vidalia onions. He'd fit in okay with the crew, who took him for an odd Tex-Mex mix with his olive-golden skin and tawny hair that threatened to bush out all over his head unless he kept it razored close to his skull. The only thing that mattered to them was that he didn't look one hundred percent Anglo, which meant he could get in line at soup kitchens and climb into pickup trucks heading out to the onion fields without too much of a wayward glance. He would come back to the migrant camps in the evening, covered in gray-brown dust from bending over the onion beds in ninety-degree heat, his long-sleeved sweat-soaked shirt clinging to his body like another skin. Conditions were primitive, some said inhumane, but it was nothing different from what he'd grown up with– no plumbing or electricity, just the oppressive heat and drone of insects in summer or brief but sharp bouts of cold in winter.

Following the migrants on their seasonal odyssey, he'd drifted from Georgia to Alabama to the Carolinas and back without much ambition, just going where the vegetable farms and orchards were hiring and where his thumbed rides took him. Sometimes he stayed a while in those places, depending on whether there was a job he could do without drawing too much attention to himself. He was mostly homeless.

In 1954, he'd joined a crew working the strawberry harvest on a farm not far from Atlanta. It was early April and the dogwoods were clouds of white on slender gray-brown branches. Consuela and her brother Manolo, friends he'd worked with all season long, had persuaded him to go with them in Mano's battered pickup over to Atlanta for the Dogwood Festival. It was an arts and crafts shindig held each spring in Piedmont Park. Consuela wanted to hear the live music and Mano just wanted a change of scenery. Ned could sell his drawings, they'd argued, when he'd balked at the idea of big crowds and curious people. But he'd gone with them in the end, and that day—especially that night—became etched in Ned's brain forever.

It was true what Mano'd said—people were willing to pay Ned good money for his little drawings of peach blossoms and wooded hillsides. But more lucrative than these were the quick-sketch likenesses he could draw of children, pets, families, boys trying to impress girlfriends, and sharp guys decked out in fancy suits and fedoras with pencil-slim gals latched onto their arms.

By the time the Contreras siblings were ready to call it a day, Ned had enough money to buy some serious whisky. Mano had done the actual buying, of course, Ned being underage. Back in their tiny shack in the migrant camp, squeezed among others just like it, they'd quickly drained one bottle of Johnny Walker and started on another. By the time the whisky slammed into his cerebellum big time, Ned knew he'd made a cold, hard mistake, the kind there was no backing away from, because he felt it coming at him full tilt. He fell to the rough plank floor of the shack and buried his head between his knees.

"Hah!" the creature hissed in his ear. "Gotcher attention now, Neddy-boy." Even through clinched eyelids he could see the red eyes inches from his face, smell its fetid, blood-soaked breath up his nostrils.

"Eh, Ned, whatsa matter?" Consuela was smiling a big alcohol-blurred grin. "You're not gonna be sick on the floor, are ya?"

"Cut him some slack, he's just a kid. Probly never been fallin' down drunk before. Right, *amigo*?" Mano touched his shoulder all friendly like, but Ned slapped it away.

His head came up. "Don't...don't—" he croaked, scrambling away on his knees, away from ...what?

"Shit, it's just me," Mano said, sort of smiling, sort of not.

"I...I can't tell." Ned knew the creature could mimic human voices perfectly, all the better to lure them into whatever black hole passed for its lair. What it did with them after that, he didn't want to imagine.

The shack was awash in shadow, the single oil lamp on a low table throwing everything into sharp-angled relief. A hand reached and grabbed his shirt front. Ned went into overdrive, punching and thrashing as if the very devil had hold of him.

Manolo switched from cool drunk *amigo* to pissed-off Mexican in a single breath. "What the shit, man? You cruisin' for a bruisin', *hombre*." He punched back.

A moving shadow leaped along the wall, and Ned lunged away from it. The table jostled, the lamp toppled over. Oil spread. Caught fire. Other flames flared in his memory. Ned was screaming, or maybe that was Consuela…he couldn't tell.

He'd hopped a boxcar headed south by the time the embers were cold.

* * *

After that, Ned kept moving. Day-to-day subsistence was a challenge, but he relished his independence, hard as it was. At age nineteen, he felt he could take pretty good care of himself, minus the shapeshifter that dogged his trail. He'd sworn off alcohol completely after that terrible night in the migrant camp. Clearly it brought his defenses down, and he had no desire to hear that rasping voice with its hissing tongue so close to his ear again. Although he was dimly aware of its malice, the creature had retreated for the most part, as if it kept vigil from a distant hilltop. The scale marks on his skin had begun to fade, and Ned rested more easily.

What had led him to knock on the door of the tiny office behind Delphine's Soul Food in New Orleans in search of a job he couldn't say. Delphine Savoie, expert cook and voudou priestess, had put him to work washing dishes in her tiny café in the French Quarter, and it was she who'd shoved him onto the path that led eventually to Brother Micah. Which meant his dishwashing employment lasted just a few weeks. He'd felt sorry about that, having to leave the eatery before he'd even learned the names of the regulars who came for dirty rice and ham hocks topped with okra and tomatoes and a side of corn fritters laced with chipotle peppers. But when she'd spotted those faint scale-like designs below his rolled-up sleeves, the jig was up. She'd hauled him through her office, asked him what the markings were, and then in a full-on panic dragged him out the back door and pushed him into the alley, wild-eyed. Actually, the dragging and pushing had happened after she'd held him by the arms for several jagged heartbeats and gotten a second-sight glimpse of his hidden companion.

"It's like a caged dog … it paces away and then comes back to lunge against the fence again," he'd told her. That was when she'd decided to have a closer look.

Between clenched teeth, she revealed what he'd already suspected. "Those marks are the sign of a barrier, put there for protection against some great wickedness."

That was the one piece of useful information Ned gleaned from her terror. She couldn't tell him anything about who'd put them there, but she could see the fluid malevolence held in check by their presence. It made sense. Sometimes the scale-like images faded to the point where only Ned knew they were there. When that happened, he couldn't feel his nemesis, either.

Delphine claimed to be a rival of the famed Marie Laveau, whose backyard rituals caused many a New Orleans resident in the 1950's to sprinkle salt over their doorsteps. According to the hand-lettered sign tacked beside the Soul Food office door, Mistress Savoie knew about protection, how to cast it and how to break it, but what she'd seen in Ned, or just behind him to be more precise, was apparently more than she felt prepared to confront.

"That's old serpent majik," she told him, "but somethin' else, too." Her voice had dropped to a whisper that Ned strained to hear, and she'd made a protective hand signal in the air in front of his nose.

"Go find yourself a Pentecostal snake-handler. I don't want nothin' to do with this." He could smell her sweat, patchouli laced with something musky, making dark circles on her cotton blouse under her ample arms. And then he'd found himself curbside, watching the street lamps come on in the tepid Louisiana night and wondering what the hell to do. True to form, he'd hitched a ride out of town within the hour, heading west. It was a pattern that felt disturbingly familiar.

*   *   *

In the fading sunlight, Ned heard what he'd been waiting for.

"Eloi shandai, shandai, harakushka, eloi …" The tongues of angels, according to St. Paul.

The high nasal voice set the tone, and others in the congregation took up the chant.

"Jesuslord … shandai … release Your Holy Spirit, lord … harakaharaka shandai …"

Ned started walking toward the tent. Voices murmured, someone wept. A woman screamed, a baby began to cry and was shushed. Nasal Voice upped the ante and built the crowd into a frenzy.

"Behold! The power of the Holy Ghost! Fill us up, fill up these sinners—witness the power of His protection!"

Ned knew without a doubt what was going on by now. He pushed the tent flap aside and stepped into the sweltering confines of Brother Micah's Southern Tent Revival. The stench of raw sweat and mildewed canvas filled his nose and mind. How many years ago had he been in one of these tents? The gloom was lit by a couple of hurricane lanterns hung from the tent struts, their sharp white light revealing maybe a hundred folding chairs set in rows bisected by one long aisle. A low wooden stage took up the space in front of the chairs. Onstage, Ned saw what he'd expected to see: several middle-aged men, thin to skinny, dressed in the kind of nondescript plaid shirts and shapeless pants you'd find in charity clothing centers. But the one who worked the crowd wore a cowboy-styled shirt and bolo tie. Ned pegged him for Brother Micah. A high table dominated center stage, and on it sat a couple of wooden boxes, each about two feet square with their lids closed. Except for one.

The oldest man dipped his hand in the opened box and hauled out a timber rattler. He held it high over his balding head, its buzzing tailtip brushing his eyebrows. More shrieks from the crowd and loud yelps of "Praise Jesus!" The serpent began to thrash its tail, and the man danced around with it a bit, then reached into the box again, extracting another rattler. Ned felt a wash of old fear.

"Behold! The power of the HOLY SPIRIT!" shouted the man in the bolo. Ned stood transfixed at the back of the crowd, drinking in the scene, the moaning, praying, weeping, shouting, and singing voices wrapping him up in the group trance. A gaunt, gray-haired woman who'd been standing at the back of the stage stepped forward and opened a second box. Ned felt sweat running down his ribs and mingling with the sour smell of the tent, not so much from the spectacle in front of him as from the unbearable stinging across his chest and the barest suggestion of a rasping voice inside his head. Or maybe it was the agitated buzzing of the captive serpents—he couldn't tell.

The woman flipped her long braid over her shoulder and reached into the second box, pulling out an even longer, fatter snake. A western diamondback, by its markings. More shrieks from the crowd. Ned felt lightheaded. He wasn't sure why Mistress Savoie had thought this was what he needed to do to get his answers, but some enlightenment had better happen soon or he would be out the tent flap and running flat out toward the dirt road behind the trees. And then he froze. There was a boy, a little younger than Ned had been when his mother had dragged him to handlings like this. The kid stood motionless at the edge of the stage. Ned didn't need a close up of the tight mouth and pallid cheeks to know paralyzing terror when he saw it. The woman turned to the boy and thrust the diamondback toward him. "Take it!" he heard clearly over the cries of the faithful and the fearful. The boy took a step forward and reached out, grabbed the reptile clumsily from the woman, and then promptly dropped it.

The enraged rattler hit the tent floor with a resounding *thwap* and snake-warped its way down the aisle, amid shrieks of panic and tumbling chairs as men, women, and children fought to get out of its path, which was aimed directly toward Ned.

Without blinking, Ned reached out as he'd done on many other such nights long ago and grabbed the serpent firmly behind the head, hauling it up. Its body whipped the air for frenzied seconds and then wrapped around his arm up to the elbow. It felt dry and heavy against the meat of his forearm, hanging on for all it was worth.

"Don't be scared, son," said his mother. He felt her at his back, close to his shoulder. "She's milked dry." Ned turned fast, swinging the arm with the snake in a wide arc, scattering screaming worshippers in its wake. She wasn't there to see, but he'd felt her. He looked back toward the stage and saw Mr. Bolo hurrying toward him. Ned shifted his attention to the snake.

She glared at him with vertical-slitted pupils, the striped ridges over her eyes giving her a cat-like expression. Her gaping mouth showed recurved fangs, fully extended. Ned's grip was firm behind the wide triangular head, holding her as tightly as she held him. The snake was channeling all its aggression and panic into its madly buzzing rattles. Below the black and white stripes of her tail he counted nine, with a broken tenth. He knew you couldn't precisely date a snake's age from the number of rattles, but from her girth and length, she had the feel of a reptile that'd been around for awhile.

Ned held her face up at eye level and touched the ridge over her eyes, ran his finger over the snout, and lightly traced the curve of one perfect fang and then the other. The snake shivered all along the length of his arm, squeezing him in a death grip. Someone near him screamed and he barely heard Brother Micah's high-pitched voice saying something about aiming for the open box at his elbow. Ned shut them out and focused entirely on the red-brown eyes of the serpent. She held his gaze, and then, unexpectedly, her pupils widened and it seemed to Ned that her head changed shape, becoming rounder, smoother, smaller, with wide-set eyes and no brow ridge. Her stripes faded to a smooth brownish olive-green with diagonal rows of darker scales forming an all-too-familiar chevron pattern down her body. Ned choked and nearly let go. Somebody had him by the shoulder. He blinked hard, coming out of the vision.

"That's some fancy handlin' you done there, son. Here now, I'm gonna peel 'im offa you and you can just ease 'im back in the box quicklike." Brother Micah held the empty snake box just under his hand. Ned nodded and watched, still as stone, as the older man wrestled the coils loose. Ned aimed the snake's head down into box and let go. It fell heavily into the container without offering to bite. He let his breath out.

Brother Micah handed the box to one of his subordinates and turned back to Ned. "What's your name, son? You from around here?"

Ned shook his head, avoiding the question of his name. He rubbed his arm, getting blood flowing properly now that the snake tourniquet had been removed. To his relief, the ant-sting illusion was gone, too.

"You know, I could use a cold-nerved fella like you. You handled that snake like a pro. In fact, I'm thinking mebbe the Lord sent you here, to help us keep doing His work."

Ned was suddenly painfully, aware that everyone was staring at him. "No, I don't think so," he managed. "I was just…" He frowned, unable to articulate exactly what he was just doing there. He'd found them more or less by instinct and a few lucky questions back in the last town.

Ned stumbled out of the tent, his mind a blur. He tried to orient himself toward the road, and then realized someone had fallen in step with him. A young guy, nearly as tall as himself, loped along beside him. White t-shirt with the sleeves rolled up over his biceps, well-worn jeans, scuffed cowboy boots, dark blonde hair swept back from his face in a pomaded wave, unlit cigarette clamped between his lips—the essence of cool. He vaguely reminded Ned of that popular young actor whose name escaped him. The one who'd taken himself out in a blaze of race car glory last year. It had been all over the news.

"Need a ride somewhere?" The stranger's voice was friendly, with a hint of amusement.

"Yeah, I do. Much obliged."

"This way, then." He steered Ned toward the edge of the clearing where the Packard rested near a stand of blackjack oaks and sumacs. Ned climbed into the passenger seat and sank against its cracked leather. His rescuer slid into the driver's seat.

"Name's Earl Wayne Marshall II. You?"

"Ned…Waterston." Ned chewed his lip. It'd been a while since he'd actually used his own name. Nearly three years now since his mother's death, and nobody'd come looking for him. He guessed it was all right.

"Nice to meetcha," Wayne said, digging his keys out of his jeans. "Been to my dad's funeral in Macon. I was heading back to Frisco by way of Ft. Worth and took a wrong turn. Saw the tent revival back there and was gonna ask somebody for directions, but the show was more interesting. Especially your part."

"That wasn't intentional," Ned said. "It just happened."

"Well, you sure looked like you knew what you were doing. I thought, now there's a cat's got some brass ones."

Ned sighed. He wished he'd never listened to Delphine and her idiotic suggestion. The less anyone knew about him, the better he liked it.

Wayne reached under the seat, scrabbled around for a minute, and then produced a bottle of bourbon about two-thirds empty.

"You look like you could use a drink."

Ned eyed the bottle, remembering. "No, sorry, I don't touch alcohol."

"Don't worry, I'm over twenty-one, by a day or two. Hundred percent legal," he laughed, uncorking the bottle and taking a quick pull. "Sure?" He held out the bottle.

"No, I can't."

Wayne shrugged. "Suit yourself, though most cats I know would never turn down a taste of boss Kentucky gold."

Wayne cranked the wagon and put it in gear, backing away from the crowd of people gathered in front of the revival tent. The great metal beast lumbered across the parking area, bumped over a shallow gulley in the gathering dark, and found its way out onto the dirt road that eventually aimed toward Ft. Worth.

Wayne pulled a flattened pack of Luckies from his sleeve roll and tapped one out. "Smoke?" he asked, offering the pack. Ned shook his head. "Well, you're just a barrel of laughs, aren't you?"

"Sorry," Ned muttered. He watched the line of trees roll by in the Packard's headlights.

After a few minutes of silence, Wayne asked, "So, how come you were hanging there watching all those snakes get abused? Since you weren't looking for a job or anything."

"A voudou priestess sent me," Ned answered. No point in lying, since he couldn't think of a good cover story anyway.

Wayne nodded. "I can dig it." He steered the wagon with his knee against the wheel and lit up, inhaled deeply, and blew smoke out the window. "Did you get what you came for?"

Ned chewed his lip. "I don't think so...I don't know."

"Where you headed, then?"

"West, I guess."

"You running from the law or something? I mean, you just have that jumpy look."

Ned turned and stared at his new companion. He didn't seem like the kind of guy who'd rat on you, but you never knew.

Wayne stared back. "Hey, don't have a cow, it's okay. You got secrets, we all got secrets. It's a long ways to San Francisco, and I wouldn't mind having you hang with me. Keep me from falling asleep at the wheel. Can you drive?"

Ned shook his head.

"Well, hell, Ned," Wayne laughed, "what *are* ya good for?"

"I can draw," he answered.

"Artist, huh?" Wayne laughed again, "You might find San Fran is just your kinda town."

Chapter 7

March 1965

"Want a toke?"

"Yeah, man." Ned lifted his head and reached out as the joint came around to him. Barely inhaling, he passed it on. He held the smoke in a few seconds, and then slowly let it out in a long exhaling sigh. Phosphenes glowed in his peripheral vision. "That's some serious shit," he said.

"Homegrown. Mostly buds," said the young woman to whom he'd passed the thin hand-rolled joint. "Doesn't take much."

"Religious experience," said the long-haired man in whose lap she was draped. He took a final drag and stubbed out the lighted end. "Roach jar?"

Ned felt around under the cushions of a sagging couch and produced a mayonnaise jar partially filled with the butts of joints past. He tossed it to the man, who caught it clumsily against the NO NUKES logo on his T-shirt.

His other companions, a black man about Ned's age dressed in military surplus clothing, a tousle-headed boy who might have been in his teens, and an older woman voluminous in a kaftan printed with a disturbing pattern of dark red paisley, laughed appreciatively. Ned barely knew these last two, but didn't think they were related. They were pals of

Tripper, the man with the hair, who was also the source of the premium weed.

Cannabis smoke and incense hung in the air of the small upstairs room. Ned sighed and lay flat on the bare wood floor with his hands locked behind his head. The familiar pot-disconnect fuzziness began to steal over his body and brain. He'd only just rolled out of bed when Tripper and his entourage had descended on him with the grass, so it didn't take him long to drift away.

"—and my brother said it took him over a month to get out of jail," the black guy was saying. "Selma, Alabama, man. It was a fucking scene like you can't imagine."

"At least he's not in Nam," said the woman in paisley. "My son is."

"Bummer," said the teenage boy.

"Now, *that* is a serious governmental crock of shit," observed Tripper. "They draft me, man, I'm over the border in two seconds!"

In Ned's mind, soldiers with machine guns morphed into oriental faces being clubbed by blue-uniformed police with Dobermans on leashes, then faded to images of the ocean pounding against rocks on the shore. He lay for a long time, thinking about a lot of things and about nothing. Definitely first-class weed.

It had come as a pleasant surprise to find that he could get a little high from smoking pot without rattling the cage of his personal demon. Unlike alcohol, ganja seemed to dull their connection rather than enhance it. The creature hadn't bothered him in a long time anyway, so he rarely thought about it these days.

"Later, man." Tripper, once known as Wayne, was leaving with his old lady. The other three were nowhere to be seen. Ned hadn't noticed them make an exit, but that fact worried him for less time than it took to heave to his feet and pad down the hallway to the communal bathroom.

A high-ceilinged, oak-paneled room containing a claw-footed bathtub of nineteen-twenties vintage, the bathroom belonged to the third-floor denizens of the house on Fulton Street, mostly unemployed musicians and artists like himself. The couple who lived in the larger suite of rooms on the ground floor actually held regular jobs and made sure the rent was paid. He knew their first names, but that was all.

Ned relieved himself, thinking about food. He had a serious case of the munchies, but no money. It was sad. He zipped up his faded brown cords and tucked in his equally faded work shirt. Ned regarded his rumpled image in the mirror on the back of the door—a tall lean young man with hair like a bird's nest. It was just long enough to brush the tops of his shoulders and thick as a lion's mane. About the same color, too. Ned ran his fingers through the tangles. It had taken Tripper several years to grow the unkempt blond ponytail that reached halfway down his back. Ned wasn't about to let his hair get that long.

Yawning, he wandered back into the room he marginally called his own. Because he only occasionally donated rent money, he couldn't really claim the room all to himself; anybody who moved into the house and at least pulled their share of kitchen duty or other chores could stay, as long as there was a vacant mattress or couch to sleep on.

He'd found the third-floor room with its westward-facing window much to his liking because it was good for painting or drawing in the afternoon when San Francisco was bathed in soft natural light. He'd parked his few belongings under the room's single rollaway bed and pushed it against the westward wall. Over the head of the bed he'd taped his two best watercolors, alien landscapes with broken scarps and scudding cloud formations in brilliant reds and deep magentas. Friends told him he should be doing science fiction book covers or black-light posters. They also wanted to know what he'd been on when he'd done them and where they could get some.

The couch on the opposite wall was variously occupied by the teenaged boy, Tripper, and other heads who knew him—mostly dealers or an occasional runaway. They came and went; the bedroom door was never locked. In fact, it didn't even have a lock. Ned really didn't care as long as nobody messed with his paints or brushes. They were his livelihood.

He flopped down on the bed and felt under it for his shoes. In his twenties, he considered himself mobile and self-sufficient. He traveled light, needing only a battered backpack to carry his meager wardrobe and artist's supplies. He'd been in San Fran for nearly nine years, living first in the North Beach area, not a stone's throw from the City Lights Bookstore where at age twenty he'd heard the beat poet Allen Ginsberg read from his crazed new poem "Howl," that had got Ginsberg and the bookstore owner arrested for indecency.

Ned had not understood most of the poem when he'd heard it, but the rhythm of its language and the intensity of its imagery made him immediately shoplift a copy and commit whole passages to memory.

Ned had found it a tough go with his limited reading skills, but he continually pushed himself and was improving daily. When someone had loaned him Burroughs' *Naked Lunch*, it had put new words into his vocabulary and scoured his soul. Like many in the literate circles he aspired to belong to, he agreed that Aldous Huxley had probably written the ultimate handbook on the truth of existence. Ned could still quote the line from William Blake that had spawned the work: "If the doors of perception were cleansed, everything would appear to man as it is, infinite." He also still believed that to be true.

But as the beat poets grew in notoriety and rent around their artists' enclave escalated, Ned had been forced to look for cheaper digs. He'd scoped out other neighborhoods, ending up in Haight-Ashbury in 1962, the same year Timothy Leary founded some research group whose name Ned couldn't remember to promote LSD research. A lot of people around Ned were experimenting with the stuff, but he'd yet to give it a try. His grasp on reality was loosey-goosey just on weed, so he didn't feel a great need to open his personal doors of perception all that wide. He feared what might come through.

It was Sandy, the female half of the couple who rented the ramshackle Victorian on Fulton Street, who'd invited him home one November night after Joan Baez had sung to thousands of students on the Berkeley campus in support of the Free Speech Movement. After all the speeches and dancing were done and the university Board of Regents had screwed them over yet again, Sandy had commandeered him and some other freaks as company for the long drive home. She'd stoned him, fucked him, introduced him to her husband, and invited him to stay. Together, they'd smoked hashish, drunk a gallon of Ripple, and played and replayed "Masters of War" from Bob Dylan's *Freewheelin'* LP until the people in the next room had banged on the wall. Ned smiled. That had been one fine night.

Now, five months later, he was no longer servicing Sandy, but she remained his friend, as did her husband. But Sandy was heavily into the SDS and some fledgling civil rights group called SNCC, which they referred to as Snick, and Ned, basically apolitical, had not measured up to Sandy's recruitment standards. When he admitted he'd only been on campus for the free concert and not the cause of free speech, their relationship had cooled. Ned didn't mind; there were plenty of other chicks more than willing to get chummy with him beneath their Indian-print bedspreads.

He found his battered desert boots and extracted the socks he'd stuffed in them. He'd walked miles in those boots and although most of the suede had eroded from them long ago, he cherished them like extensions of his body. He resolved to get them resoled as soon as he had enough money. Toward that end, Ned finished dressing, gathered his art materials, and headed downstairs.

Ned took off at a brisk walk downhill, his backpack over one shoulder and two folded campstools under his arm. Reaching the intersection of Ashbury and Haight, it didn't take him long to hitch a ride out to his old stomping grounds around Telegraph Hill. By noon, he'd set up shop on a stretch of Fisherman's Wharf thick with tourists and aspiring bohemians. Within an hour, he'd made a couple of quick-sketch portraits and nearly forty dollars. Ned stretched and took in the blue horizon reaching out beyond the Bay Bridge. At this moment in time, life was damned near perfect.

"Neddy. How's it going, man?" Tripper slid onto the stool beside him.

Ned grinned. "Working the crowd, same as you."

"You wound me, friend. I never offer anything to anyone that they don't need. It's Zen archery, man—I put myself in the right place and the target appears." Tripper pulled off his T-shirt and sat bare-chested in the afternoon sun, letting his hair fall loose down his back. "Ain't life great?"

Ned nodded. "Where's your old lady?"

"She had something to do that didn't involve me. No sweat."

Tripper's fidelity seemed questionable, but then maybe his girlfriend's was, too. At first, Ned had been a little annoyed at Tripper's interruption, but now it occurred to him that he couldn't ask for a better advertisement of the San Fran hedonistic lifestyle, and sure enough, a trio of nubile maidens from out of town was snapping their picture and approaching them. He looked at Tripper.

"Good job, man."

"Do I get a commission?"

"Like hell. Hello, there." Ned smiled up at the nearest girl. "Want your portrait done?"

She smiled back. "How much?"

"Just ten dollars for a charcoal sketch. Or twenty, depending on how detailed a likeness you want, and if you want it in color."

"Are you a famous artist?" She looked at him sideways.

Tripper laughed. "Our Neddy is quite famous, among some circles. As an artist, he is untouchable."

"Well, okay, then. Just a sketch." She looked at Tripper with the same questioning expression. The other two girls hung behind her, their eager faces taking in the total experience of being in San Francisco and talking to *real* hippies.

Ned removed Tripper from the second campstool and seated the girl so that the direct sun was out of her eyes and her face was at a three-quarter angle to him. With a charcoal pencil, he began to sketch quick, deft lines that within ten minutes resembled the subject remarkably well.

"What's your name?" he asked.

"Linda."

With a flourish, he wrote *For Linda, welcome to SF, March 25, 1965 — N.W.* underneath the portrait and handed it to her. The others crowded around to see.

"Far out. That's amazing," said the one whose ample thighs were barely contained by her new bell-bottom jeans.

Linda was blushing. "You made me better looking than I really am."

"Let me see," said Tripper. Kneeling down beside her, he draped his bare arm around her shoulders, drawing her close. "Perfect likeness." He gave her a squeeze. She beamed at him, her shyness evaporating as quickly as fog on the bay. Ned grinned. Old Trip was a master; with a little luck, they might score some entertainment for the rest of the day.

"Where are you girls from?" said Tripper, settling on the ground and pulling Linda into his lap.

"Arizona," said the one in tight jeans.

"Flagstaff," said her companion, a slip of a girl with a high giggly voice. Ned had serious doubts about the legality of that one, but her green eyes were quite beautiful. He offered her a sip from his thermos.

"What's in it?" She adjusted her peasant blouse over her slim shoulders and reached for the thermos.

"Just water," he said, charmed.

"Okay." She took a drink, and watched him from under long lashes.

Ned retrieved the thermos and kept hold of her hand. "You have a great profile. Want me to paint you?"

"Uh uh." She shook her head. "No money. I spent it all already." The girls laughed as a unit. "I love your tattoos," she said, pointing at his arm. The scale pattern had been fading over the years and was barely visible now. Occasionally someone noticed it enough to comment, but they had to look up close in just the right light to see it. Ned didn't mind—it was cool.

"Where are you staying tonight, and do you want company," said Tripper, his arms around Linda.

Ned admired his approach. No use dallying with them unless it was going somewhere.

Tripper wriggled back into his T-shirt. "Want to get turned on?"

The girls exchanged quick glances. "Um, yeah, why not?" said Linda.

The others agreed, nodding and shuffling their feet, as if they'd been hoping for such an offer but had been too embarrassed to ask. Ned knew this body language all too well; he saw it repeatedly as more seekers of hippie heaven flowed into the city each summer.

Ned began packing up his paints. "Where to?"

"We have a hotel room near Union Square," said Linda. She named an older hotel near the Powell Street cable car line.

"Cool." Ned folded the stools and handed one to Green Eyes, as he'd named her in his mind. "Hope you girls don't mind walking."

They assured him they didn't.

"I'm Ned, and this is Tripper." The girls laughed on cue.

"Gloria," said the one in the tight jeans.

"Mary Catherine," said Green Eyes.

They moved as a gang down the Embarcadero, laughing and flirting and barking back at the sea lions, heading generally toward Union Square.

They rode the elevator in a cozy wad up to the room and immediately ordered out for pizza and sodas. Ned knew that if they waited 'til after the bong had gone around a few times and the screaming munchies had settled in, it would be next to impossible to order coherently over the phone. They settled onto the two double beds, just talking and getting comfortable with each other, waiting for the food to arrive.

When it came, Tripper paid for the pizza and locked the door. He put the unopened box on the dresser and pulled the curtains closed over the narrow window that looked down on the busy street below.

"Oh cool, a water pipe," said Gloria, watching Tripper assemble and fill the bong. He puffed on it dramatically, producing the familiar gurgling sound that was music to Ned's ears. He lay back on the pillows beside Mary Catherine and waited for his turn.

Linda choked and had to be comforted, and, to her credit, gamely tried again. She was red in the face from coughing, but Ned could see by her pupils that she'd gotten a big enough hit. She passed the pipe to him, and he handed it to Green Eyes.

"You go first," he said. If she needed help, he wanted to be clear-headed. To his surprise, she took in a lungful and held it like a pro. Ned quickly reassessed her possible age and experience level, and considered the possibilities.

By the time they'd smoked it all, Tripper had established himself on one of the beds with Linda, which was fine with Ned, as long as Gloria and Mary Catherine didn't object to a threesome. He stripped off his clothes quickly, unselfconscious and comfortable in his own skin. The girls were less forthcoming, but he'd been there before and did what he needed to do to put them at ease. By the time the sun went down and the room was mostly dark, he had made love to them both and taught Green Eyes how to perform a proper blow job.

He was lying flaked out on his back when his stomach growled in a hideous, long, gurgling complaint. Gloria shrieked with laughter.

"Open that pizza, man," said Tripper, emerging from under the sheets.

Ned got up obediently and plunked the opened box down on the bed so they could all reach it. Like starving hyenas, they devoured the deluxe extra-large pie with double cheese and olives within a matter of minutes.

"God, plain old tomatoes and cheese never tasted so good," said Tripper. He burped loudly, sending the girls into a fit of the giggles.

Finally, silence settled around them.

"Have you guys read *The Psychedelic Experience* yet?" Mary Catherine asked.

Tripper nodded. "Religious experience."

"Not me," said Linda, looking at Tripper with the kind of adoration that Ned recognized; it meant he'd become her Guru of gurus.

"Me neither," said Gloria.

"Ned? What about you?" Mary Catherine was licking pizza grease from his fingers in a damned good imitation of what he'd showed her how to do with another part of his body.

"No, I haven't read it yet. Been meaning to, though."

"You gotta read it," she said. "I would love to trip with you, Ned."

"Your wish is my command," said Tripper. He rolled out of bed and searched around for his pants. From an inside pocket, he produced a small brown envelope, folded twice. He opened it and emptied three tiny squares of white paper, each with a pink circle in the center, onto his palm.

"This, ladies and gentleman, is Owsley's finest: pure Sandoz LSD-25 in that little dot, undiluted and unadulterated. Not cut with uppers or rat poison or anything vile. This is the very best blotter acid money can buy."

"Wow," breathed Mary Catherine with reverence.

Ned's brain balked, realizing where this was heading. He was not averse to others tripping their brains out, and had, in fact, sat around mildly stoned on grass while friends were finding worlds within worlds in the carpet threads. But he hadn't really intended to do it himself—too risky. The current situation, however, wasn't lending itself very well to refusal.

"That is so far out, how did you get it?" Mary Catherine was still staring, bug-eyed, at Tripper's outstretched hand.

He smiled and put the blotters side by side on the nightstand between the beds. "Like Neddy here, I am an artist. Only difference is I don't paint with water colors." He took a pocketknife from his pants and carefully sliced two of the blotters in half. "Half a hit for each of you, and a full hit for me, because I've done it before and know what to expect."

He gave them each a slice of paper like a priest dispensing holy wafers. Then he picked up one of the sodas. "Just fold it up and swallow, like this." He put the blotter in his mouth, tilted the soda can back, and swallowed the paper down with a couple of gulps. Then he handed the can to Ned.

Ned hesitated, feeling bile in the pit of his stomach. But Mary Catherine slid her slender fingers up the inside of his thigh and gave him that look that no dude could refuse.

"Don't you want to know how it feels to do it on acid, Ned?" Her green eyes were pools of desire.

There was nothing for it. Ned took the tiny piece of paper, put it on his tongue, and chased it down with the sharp tang of Dr. Pepper.

"Me next!" Mary Catherine took the can and downed her dose.

Linda and Gloria followed suit, and then they sat still, looking at one another, waiting.

"How long before it takes effect?" Linda asked. She settled into the crook of Tripper's arm, looking up at him.

"Depends," he said. "Five or ten minutes, maybe longer, maybe shorter. If we hadn't eaten anything it would probably come on faster."

"W-what does it feel like?" asked Gloria, licking her lips.

Tripper shrugged. "Hard to say. It's different for each person. I usually start to feel like I'm floating, like being in a plane when it hits an air pocket."

"Cool!" said Linda and wedged herself tighter under his arm. Ned could see she was putting a brave face on, but he suspected she was scared.

Gloria was sitting perfectly still, saying nothing.

Ned was monitoring his own bodily functions, counting his pulse, running his tongue over his lips, keeping his breath even. He didn't feel much different from the way he felt after a few tokes, so he relaxed a bit, letting his breath out. It was then he realized with a jerk that he'd been staring unblinking at the veins on the back of his hand, thinking of snakes. Sweat trickled down his body. He decided with a rising panic that it wasn't so much what your body felt like that was the true power of LSD—it was where your mind went.

"Neddy, make love to me." Green Eyes was pushing him down and climbing on top of him. He flowed into her body effortlessly, absorbing her molecules one by one into his own gravitational field. He was burning hot and freezing at the same time. Somewhere far away someone was crying, in long slow sobs that could only come from the deepest black hole of despair. It sounded like Gloria. But the instant he thought that, he couldn't remember who she was. He wasn't even sure who he was, but that was compounded by the confusion of merging with another creature whose eyes burned above him like emeralds. He could no longer feel his body, but was aware that his essence was flowing out of him like a tidal wave, building as it raced unhindered over the open sea. The entity above him moaned, but that fact held no meaning that his brain could decipher. He was an energy wave, roaring over the ocean of the mind.

Somewhere, someone was weeping. Ned sat up, listening. Mary Catherine lay beside him, breathing heavily, eyes closed. He couldn't tell if she was asleep or just following her own eyelid movies; it pleased him that he could remember her name. In the bed next to him he could make out figures under a sheet and a long strand of blondish hair. They did not seem to be the source of the sobs. He tried to course the sound, but it was slippery, changing location just as he thought he'd nailed it down. Then he spotted her.

Gloria was curled into a tight ball in an armchair by the window. Wrapped in one of the bedspreads, she sobbed into its folds as if her heart would break. Ned got up unsteadily and went to her.

"Are you …?" He couldn't think of what he'd intended to say.

Gloria shrank from him, shaking her head. "Don't touch me," she whispered, her face red and swollen. "I don't know where I am. Where is this place?" She was trembling.

"You're … here." It was all he could think to say. "Don't worry." Why he added that, he couldn't imagine. His mouth tasted funny and seemed to be over-salivating. He swallowed, sensing an odd metallic taste, but couldn't figure out why it seemed familiar. Feeling dazed and disconnected from his body, Ned went in search of the bathroom. He found it with difficulty and clumsily flipped the light switch.

An explosion of light seared his retinas. Slowly he let out his breath and tried to relax. He made himself remember that he'd dropped acid with a friend and three strangers, that they were all accounted for, and that he was here, in the flesh, in a hotel bathroom staring at his reflection in the mirror over the sink.

The face that stared back at him was his own, yet not. The eyes were wrong. Then he realized with a shock that the pupils were vertical slits in a yellow field. Drool pooled in his open mouth and spilled over his chin. The face was morphing before his eyes, turning serpentine and filling the glass until it shattered with an ear-splitting crash. Then he was writhing on the floor under the full weight of the reptile as it wrapped its coils around him, squeezing his breath and life out.

Ned tried to scream but no sound came out. He fought harder, thrashing to free himself from the death adder's grip. In his head he heard its rasping voice.

"At last!"

Ned struggled and bashed his head against the floor, trying to dislodge the serpent's hold. Its enormous fangs slashed at his face as he rolled to the side. They struck his neck with such force that his carotid artery was severed and his hot life's blood poured out, salty sweet, over his face and chest.

"Damned human!" it hissed and spat poison in his ear. "My kind should never be coupled to a human! We eat them for sport!"

Fangs slashed at him again. Ned crashed against the side of the bathtub, his mind screaming. "Wh-what are you?" he managed through clenched teeth.

"What am I, the human wants to know." The adder's eyes turned blood red, its fangs yellow-white. "Quinkan. QUINKAN!" The voice scraped Ned's brains raw. "SAY IT!"

"Q-Qu-Quinkan," Ned choked, every muscle in his body convulsing.

"The serpent's not my preferred form," it hissed, "but I know it's a shape you loathe."

"W-what do ..." Ned beyond articulating.

"What do I want? Your father was next to useless. But *you*, you can find where your bastard grandfather hid the *tjuringa* and put it back where it belongs. Then you and I can part company." Venom dripped from its fangs onto Ned's cheek.

And then Ned found his voice. He screamed and screamed, raking his throat raw, emptying his crushed lungs of air. And still he screamed, as if by that one ragged sound he could remain attached to the shred of humanity that was Ned Waterston. If he stopped, he knew beyond doubt, that he would be lost for all time.

Chapter 8

July 10, Sunday—Present Day

Screams ripped the air, explosions boomed one after another. Panicked voices yelled over the din.

"They're attacking the pilot trainees' barracks!"

"What news of Lieutenant Zechs? Is he safe?"

More booming and screeching sirens. Shouts disappeared in the crash of masonry collapsing under steel girders. It was a cacophony of destruction.

"Nik, could you turn the TV down?" Alice buried her face in the pillows.

"*Ja*, sure. Sorry."

Alice got up and shuffled down the hall. So much for sleeping in on the weekend. Nik and Margaret were ensconced on opposite ends of the long sofa bisecting the single large room that served as living and dining area. The southward facing wall was mostly taken up by sliding glass doors that opened out onto a wooden deck. Saturday morning anime flamed and exploded across the television screen.

Seeing her, Nik pronounced with a grave face, "It appears we have been busted."

Margaret kicked at him and grinned wickedly. "Turn it up."

He shook his head. "Experiencing the full power of Chang Wu Fei's Shenlong Gundam is not worth the price of your mother's wrath."

"You're so weird," said Margaret, grinning. "That's why you're cool."

"*Tack*, I think." He found the remote and lowered the volume, cutting his eyes toward Alice.

She headed for the kitchen alcove, rubbing her eyes. "Who am I to interfere with your Gundam addiction? I'm up now. Do what you want."

She yawned hugely for their benefit and nuked a cup of water, tossing in an instant coffee-singles bag and swirling it around.

Nik leaned over the back of the couch, watching her. "Want to go run, then? Before the heat sets in?"

Alice stood at the kitchen counter, sipping her coffee. It was slightly bitter and about as nasty as the corporate stuff. She sucked it down. "Sure."

Nik turned to Margaret. "You?"

"Uh-uh. You guys go on." She dug the phone out from under the couch cushions and punched some numbers. "Is Judy there?"

Alice put her cup down in the sink. "Don't go anywhere till we get back."

Margaret scowled darkly and took the phone to her bedroom, shutting the door.

Alice got dressed and stepped out onto the deck, Reeboks in hand. Nik followed, stopping just long enough to grab a piece of toast left on the breakfast table. Dawg met them at the head of the stairs and danced around, wagging and salivating.

Alice sat down on the top step to tie her shoes. "You know, she's developing a really smart mouth, without even saying anything."

Nik pulled his hair back into a tight ponytail. "I can't imagine where she gets that."

"Half the time you're her accomplice." She stood up and stretched. "But it's okay. I'd much rather have you two get along than not."

"Dawg—fetch!" Nik tossed the piece of toast into the sandy yard below, sending Dawg thumping down the stairs. A rescued shelter mutt, Dawg appeared to be equal parts Labrador, German Shepherd, Collie, Pointer, and who knew what else. His personality, however, was all Lab.

"You know, I had my doubts about Dawg when you moved in. Now I can't imagine life without him." She clumped down the steps behind Nik's back. *Or you*, she thought.

They walked briskly out to the dirt road that ran for a straight mile past the wooded property, and then turning north, they headed toward the intersection with Magnolia Parkway, the main road into the county seat of Magnolia. Dawg caught up with them and galloped ahead, his black-and-tan tail wagging in wide circles.

They walked in silence for half a mile, just pacing each other. Alice lifted her hair off her neck and reveled in the early morning breeze. Later on, toward noon, the heat would become humid and stifling. Then all you could do was hole up somewhere with air conditioning.

On both sides of the road, butterflies swarmed over thickets of leggy Spanish needles crowned in star-shaped white flowers with yellow centers. To most people, they were just weeds, but Alice considered them an attractive fill plant and butterfly magnet, which was why she tolerated them in her garden. But she knew that by fall she would be cursing them within an inch of their lives as their spiny seed pods stuck to socks and skin.

It was Nik who finally broke the silence. "Have you looked through the briefcase yet?"

"No, I haven't."

"Why not?"

Alice watched her feet. "I just haven't felt like it yet."

Nik rubbed the bridge of his nose. "I would have thought that would be the first thing you would want to do. Did your uncle tell you what's in it?"

"Sort of. He said it was mostly letters from Suzanne that he'd saved when she went to Australia and now felt should be mine. I don't know what else. I can't believe he's been keeping them for so long and never said a word."

"He must be very good at keeping secrets."

"Mm. Better than I ever guessed."

They walked past the cut-off road to Judy's house and continued on down to the divided paved road that was Magnolia Parkway. At this time of year, it was a beautiful sight, with a long line of crepe myrtles running all the way to the town, about five miles westward. Clusters of pink, white, lavender, and dark red blooms bent their necks in the breeze as bees clung to their flowers.

Alice and Nik stood at the intersection, admiring the view. A car whizzed by, and Nik grabbed Dawg's collar to keep him off the highway.

"Ready to jog back?" she asked.

"In a moment." Nik stepped into the shallow roadside ditch to examine a small *amanita* poking up through the leaf litter. Alice waited, used to his mycological diversions. He was always on the lookout for something he could photograph for the field guide that was his doctoral dissertation-in-progress.

"Not worth collecting," he said, coming back to the road. Alice fell in step beside him and soon they were running at an easy pace. Dawg galloped on ahead, aiming for home.

Alice frowned, annoyed that she was feeling a little winded. She'd let herself get out of shape over the summer, eating too much ice cream and not burning it off. Nik could run and carry on a conversation with little or no effort, but she was having trouble keeping up. Finally she slowed to a walk.

"What's the matter?" Nik stopped and waited for her to catch up.

"Stitch in my side." She was feeling the tiniest bit wheezy and wished she'd stuck an inhaler in her pocket before they'd left the house.

"We'll walk the rest of the way, then. Don't breathe in shallow gulps like that. A stitch is caused when you don't get enough oxygen."

Alice nodded. He was always right about shit like that.

They turned down the driveway and stepped into the shade. There was a noticeable difference in temperature between the baking road and the cooler winding track under the trees. Alice's hair stuck uncomfortably to her face and neck.

Her thoughts returned to the briefcase. After she'd helped Hal clean out her mother's closet, when he'd gone upstairs to his study and brought down the case. "Go through it when you have the time," he'd said, and that was all. No explanation beyond what she'd told Nik. She hoped it might tell her something about her father, and especially why her mother had returned from that faraway place so damaged.

She hurried across the yard and up the steps to the deck, Nik right behind her.

"What's the hurry?"

"I think it's time," she said over her shoulder.

Inside, she went to the small extra bedroom that served as a home office and workspace for Nik, with floor-to-ceiling bookshelves and a computer desk squeezed in beside a day bed. Margaret was sitting at the computer, completely engrossed in web surfing, and jumped when Alice came in.

"What?" she said, looking up.

Alice saw the flash of a webpage disappear as Margaret minimized the screen. Normally, she might have quizzed her about her internet surfing habits, but not just now. The briefcase contents were more important.

"I want to go through the stuff from your Grandma that Hal gave me." She took the small brown case down from a shelf and sat on the floor, shoving books and a basket of laundry out of the way.

Nik stood in the doorway, his expression uncertain.

"You might as well come in," she said. "No secrets. We'll just all three see what's here."

Nik nodded and stepped across Alice to the day bed, where he moved notebooks and papers out of the way and sat down.

Alice turned her attention to the briefcase and undid the latch. As Hal had told her, it contained bundles of letters and postcards. They were bound with disintegrating rubber bands that broke apart when she picked up a packet. The letters on top bore Australian postmarks: Sydney, of course, and towns in Queensland such as Brisbane and Cairns. But she sucked in her breath at the sight of the small dark green pamphlet among the letters. It was a passport. Which meant a photo.

Putting the letters aside, she opened it to the first page and read: IN CASE OF DEATH OR ACCIDENT NOTIFY THE NEAREST AMERICAN DIPLOMATIC OR CONSULAR OFFICE and *Harold Blacksburg, Miami, Florida.* Alice swallowed. She turned the page, and there they were, Ned and Suzanne, sitting together in an obvious studio passport, shot in color. The date stamped beside their photo was November 20, 1969. Alice stared, speechless, at the man who had been a phantom all her life but now appeared in the flesh beside a young-looking Suzie Blacksburg. The date on the passport would make her twenty-four. The man beside her seemed not much older—anywhere from twenty-five to thirty-five, Alice guessed.

"Can I see?" Margaret reached down for the booklet. Alice gave it to her without a word. She was blinking, trying to clear her vision.

"Wow, he's hot! Is that your dad?" She handed the passport over to Nik, who looked at the photo, then at Alice, then at the photo again.

"I can see the likeness," he said, smiling. He gave it back to her.

It was true. His hair was a shade darker, but tawny like hers, and about the same length. His nose was sharper and his cheekbones higher, but the mouth was the same. His eyes were the same yellowish-bluish-hazel. Suzanne sat in front of him, leaning against his chest, and both were turned slightly to their right, looking into the camera with open, smiling faces. Suzanne's hair was flame-red and long enough to trail down her chest and out of the picture. She wore a string of "love" beads in several loops around her neck. Ned Waterston, whose signature appeared on the opposite page, wore a black T-shirt and a silver hoop in one ear.

Alice couldn't stop staring. Here they were, setting out on a great adventure together. What could possibly have happened to them so far away on the other side of the globe? She closed the passport and lifted out the remaining bundles. There were three, labeled in the broad strokes of Hal's pen, from different chunks of Suzanne's young womanhood: college, her post-graduation tour abroad, and Ned. A few unbundled Christmas cards and some folded sheets of paper lay at the bottom of the case.

Alice unwound the disintegrating rubber band, peeling off a piece that was stuck to the paper. The envelopes were in chronological order, with the most recent on the bottom. How like Hal, she thought. Nothing in his life was helter-skelter, not even his collection of letters from his sister. The fact that he had saved such a collection for so many years was vaguely unsettling to Alice; was this something siblings typically did?

"Looks like she sent him a bunch of postcards when they first landed in Sydney," Alice said, fanning out half a dozen cards with colorful images of Sydney Harbour, the controversial opera house under construction, the Sydney Harbour Bridge, Bondi Beach, the Great Barrier Reef, and Ayers Rock, now called Uluru. She turned them over—they were all dated within a few weeks of each other, from late November to early December of 1969.

"This one says, 'Hi, we made it here safely. Sydney is beautiful, it's springtime! More later. Hugs to all, Suzanne.' They're all like that, just touristy-type messages." She handed the cards to Margaret.

Margaret stared at the image of Ayers Rock at twilight, then turned it over. "What's she mean by 'Please don't be angry at us'? What did she do?"

"Huh? Let me see." Alice took the card back. "I don't know. Hal never said anything about being mad at her when she and Ned went overseas."

"Maybe they eloped," said Nik.

"Yeah, I bet they did! Hey, this is getting good." Margaret swiveled the computer chair around to face Alice. "What else is in there?" She poked the briefcase with her toe.

Alice put the letters down and took out the remaining papers. There were Christmas cards mailed from France and Italy, postmarked 1967. "She must have spent the holidays in Europe after college," Alice said, reading the inscriptions inside the cards. She was shocked to see that they included greetings to Hal in both French and Italian, respectively. This was something she'd never known, that Suzanne had learned enough of two foreign languages to compose brief notes in them. A picture of Suzanne was emerging that had nothing to do with the distant yet controlling individual she had grown up with. This Suzanne was exuberant, accomplished, vibrant—worlds away from the emotionally constricted woman Alice had yearned to embrace as a child, then rejected with dislike as an adult. Such a waste of a life. What could have happened?

Alice opened the two folded pages and caught her breath. They were watercolors.

"Awesome!" Margaret reached for them.

Alice's chest constricted, sweat dampening her neck. Hard as she might wish, there was no denying the fact that she recognized that surreal landscape—she'd stood there in her dreams. She felt lightheaded.

"I like his style," Nik said. He was holding up one of the paintings to get better light on it. "Too bad it's creased. You could have these framed."

Alice wiped her face with her shirttail. "I don't think so," she managed. "Are they signed?"

Nik nodded and handed her the paintings. "Down in the right-hand corner. See?"

N.W, 1964 the inscription read, in a small crimped hand.

"Mom, are you crying?"

Alice wiped at her face. "He … always felt imaginary to me, like I was spontaneously conceived or something. And now, here he is and there they are, together." Alice sniffed. "It's just a little overwhelming."

"I've never seen you cry," said Margaret. She looked embarrassed, but Alice didn't care. The discovery that she and her father had seen the same dreamscape was a revelation she had not expected. And then something else dawned on her—was this a landmark somewhere in Australia?

Nik sat down on the floor beside her. "You all right?"

Alice nodded. "Let's see what else is here." She smoothed the two watercolors out flat and put the postcards on top of them. Then she turned to the letters. There were only three, two in regular envelopes and the third a folded blue aerogramme. She opened the first one and read aloud.

"'Dear Brother. Just want to say we're fine. Went to see the historic convict buildings near Sydney but Ned was spooked and didn't want to stay. He's very sensitive to surroundings and places, says he can feel who's lived there. I have no idea what he means, but it's part of why I love him. I know you hate to hear that, but it's true. If you got to know him better, I'm sure you would come to like him. I want the two men I love most in this world to become friends. When we return, which we think will be after Christmas, I hope you will think better of us both. Please hug Mama and Daddy for me. Love, Suzie.'"

"Where were they when she wrote that?" asked Nik.

Alice looked at the letterhead. "Townsville, Queensland. Pretty fancy hotel stationary."

"Bet it was the honeymoon suite!" said Margaret.

Alice opened the second letter. "This one's from Cairns." Alice tried to locate Cairns on her mental map of Australia; it was somewhere on the eastern coast, up near the Daintree rainforest that had a lot of rock art sites.

Nik sat up straight. "Cairns is where the International Mycological Congress will be held next year."

"They have mushrooms in Australia?" Margaret seemed genuinely surprised.

"Of course. It's not all desert. They have *Panaeolopsis nirimbii* and *Amanita muscaria*, lichens, giant boletes, truffles. We ought to consider attending."

Alice gave him a wry face. "And what am I supposed to do while you're chasing down Outback fungi?"

"I'm sure they have a spouse program with sightseeing and other—"

"You guys aren't going without me! And she's not a spouse, anyway."

Alice looked at Margaret, startled.

Nik cut his eyes to Alice and then looked away. "What I mean is, anybody who comes as a guest of a conference attendee can take advantage of being there."

An uneasy silence settled over the room. Alice was thinking hard about things she and Nik had not talked about in the open.

"Can we table that discussion for now? But you're right," she said, looking at Margaret's pinched face, "if we make any more trips overseas, we'll all go." She picked up the letter from Cairns. Unlike the previous one, it was several pages long. She scanned through them, seeing nothing worth reading out loud until she hit the last page.

"Listen to this, she mentions the watercolors.

'Ned has been showing his pictures around, trying to find anybody who might recognize the location. He says he needs to find these places. I don't know about that, but it does seem like fate because we met this Aboriginal man on the beach at Nielson Park in Sydney who told him those places were in Queensland, and then Neddy met some people at the Foundation of Aboriginal Affairs who said the same thing, so here we are in Cairns. It's hot and humid, but no worse than Miami, and since we are both Florida natives, we are not suffering too much.'

Alice looked up. "My father was born in Florida? I never knew that."

"It looks like your uncle is extremely good at keeping family secrets," Nik said.

"But why would he not tell me something like that? I don't get it."

"Call him up and ask him. Now that your mother is gone, he's not obligated to protect her anymore, for whatever reasons he may have been doing so."

Alice looked back at the letter and chewed her lip. "Maybe I will."

She scanned the rest of the letter, but there wasn't much else of interest, just more apologetic language about Suzanne's marriage to Ned.

It was pretty clear they had eloped, or at least married against the family's wishes. The more facts she uncovered about her father, the more questions surfaced. She looked at the passport photo again. What sort of man was he? Was he educated, did he love animals and children, could he be trusted? If Hal knew, he'd never let on. It was time to call him on that.

She folded the letter and put it back in the case. That left the blue aerogramme. Alice noted the postmark—Cooktown, Queensland, December 20, 1969—and unfolded the flaps. The message it contained was brief and hastily scrawled. It was a plea for money.

"It looks like they've maxed out Suzanne's credit card and are short on funds. She wants Hal to wire them some money. They're getting ready to make some kind of trek and have hired a vehicle and a guide, and bought provisions, but it's taken most of their cash." Alice read another paragraph to herself, then put down the aerogramme and stared at Margaret. "They're headed into the bush, in search of Quinkan cave paintings."

Alice didn't even bother to explain; her brain was derailed. She'd suddenly realized that what her late-lamented parents were doing in Australia wasn't a honeymoon, or even a fun adventure. Ned was on the trail of something. With a sour feeling in her gut, Alice guessed what must have happened to Ned in Australia. He'd found his quarry, or it had found him. Which suddenly explained a whole lot about Suzanne and her crazed state of mind when she'd come back to the States as a widow instead of a bride.

It also meant something equally chilling. That desolate landscape of canyons and caves, high bluffs and raging winds was the place of her waking nightmares—the Outback of the Dreamtime.

Alice gathered all the papers together and shut them up in the briefcase. She wiped sweaty palms on her shirt.

"Excuse me," she said, getting up. "I need to make a phone call."

Chapter 9

April 1965

"What was it like?" The teenage boy sat on the couch, watching as Ned got dressed.

"What was what like?"

"Tripper said you freaked out on an acid trip. I wondered what it was like."

Ned put his only good long-sleeved shirt down on the bed and turned toward the boy. "Tripper doesn't know shit. What else did he tell you?"

The boy shrugged. "Just that he was scared the fuzz was gonna come bust the door down, you were yelling so loud. He said you scared the shit out of everybody."

He turned his back on the boy. "Tripper has a big mouth."

"Where you going? I've never seen you dressed up like that."

Ned buttoned his shirt, leaving the top two buttons undone. He straightened his cuffs. "You're fucking nosey, you know that?"

"Just wondering, is all." The boy felt around between the couch cushions and produced a joint. He retrieved matches from his jeans and lit up, toking with practiced ease. He held the joint out to Ned.

"Pass. Maybe later, when I get back."

"Ain't gonna last that long," said the boy. "You got a date or something?"

Ned brushed his hair, pulling out tangles. "None of your business."

The boy inhaled with a loud sucking hiss and spoke holding his breath. "Is she a fox?"

Ned stopped brushing and looked at the boy. "How old are you?"

"Seventeen."

"Bullshit. How old?"

The boy shrugged. "Thirteen. But I'll be fourteen in a couple of weeks. And I got laid already. So, like, is your date a fox?"

"There's no date." Ned checked his pants pockets for his wallet and other essentials and headed toward the door.

"Oh. I get it." The boy started to smile. "You're hustling. Have a good time."

Ned shut the door behind him a little harder than necessary.

* * *

Nighttime in the Castro district could be a surreal experience, even without pharmaceutical enhancements. However, Ned wished he'd taken at least one toke from the kid. He was jittery, and a little grass would have been welcome right about now. He piloted his body down Market Street, feeling disconnected. He hadn't felt right since last week when he'd dropped the blotter with Tripper and those girls. It had taken cold water in the face and a bath towel shoved in his mouth to shut off the screaming, but that had brought him back to his senses and the worst was past within a few minutes. Shaken, he'd sat on the floor of the bathroom staring at his forearms, as the scale pattern pulsed dark green-gold against his lighter olive skin. Mary Catherine had slid down onto the floor behind him, leaning against his back with her arms around his waist. The warmth of her body had been an unspeakable comfort.

Fortunately, his shouts had also jarred Gloria loose from her crying jag to the point that she could recognize her buddy Linda, and Tripper had snuggled both girls into bed with him, talking them through the experience like the old pro that he was.

"Neddy," Green Eyes had whispered.

"Shh. Just sit." With glacial slowness, the vibrations along his veins began to let up, and the objects in the room became more solid, their outlines more stable. Once the amoeboid acid pattern that pulsed over his field of vision began to fade, he started to feel closer to normal. Mary

Catherine sighed and curled up in his lap, her eyes closed. Soon, her regular breathing told him she was asleep. Ned had held her slight body close to his chest with a king-sized hotel bath towel wrapped around them both and wondered if he would ever sleep again.

After that night, his forearms continued to prickle in a way he hadn't felt in years, not since he'd confronted the serpents at Brother Micha's tent revival. In fact, since the acid trip, his shadow nemesis had returned with a vengeance. A piece of Ned's mind was very frightened, realizing he'd opened forbidden doors again. He lay in his bed in the house on Fulton, telling friends he'd caught a virus and to leave him alone. But his mind chewed and chewed over what to do. By the end of the week, he could see only one solution. He had to go home. All the way back to the ashes of his mother's house where he'd been born and where the Quinkan, as it called itself, had killed his father and possessed his mother. Would it eventually kill him as well? Ned was scared down to his bones, but he was also resolute.

*   *   *

Stopping at the intersection of Market and Castro, Ned surveyed the crowd. He needed a place that was expensive, but casual enough that he could get in dressed as he was in plain white shirt and khaki pants. He knew of several possibilities, one close by and the others another block away. Ned had concluded, sitting on the cold bathroom floor with Mary Catherine, that he had to get home, which was going to take much more money than he could make selling sketches. In this town, there were really only two ways of making that kind of quick cash, and both of them involved selling. Since he didn't have a stash of drugs he could unload, that left the other option. If it didn't work out, Ned was grimly prepared to hitchhike his way across the country; he'd done it before, but needed to get home quicker.

Resolved, he jaywalked across the street and pushed open the glass and brass doors of a well-known piano bar. A hostess approached him, menu in hand, but Ned shook his head.

"I'm just going to the bar."

She smiled and nodded. "Enjoy your stay, sir."

Ned sat down at the bar and looked over the crowd. The place was expensive yet laid back, a casual-but-upscale kind of place he'd been in only once before. He looked over the drink menu and saw that he had just enough cash in his pocket for one order.

"Ginger ale on the rocks," he said, looking past the bartender at the array of tables and booths reflected in the expanse of mirror behind the man. The place was moderately filled, mostly with couples, but there were enough singles scattered around to get his hopes up.

He drained his drink, and sat fingering the empty glass. He didn't have to wait long.

"Can I get that refilled for you?"

Ned looked the guy over. Not too old, conservative clothes, understated jewelry, new shoes. Bland Midwestern face. He could have been anything from a college professor to an advertising executive, or a successful dealer.

"All right."

The man picked up Ned's glass and handed it to the bartender. "Give him a refill of whatever he's drinking." He sat down beside Ned. "Name's Grant. Yours?"

"Ned."

"Do you come here much? I haven't seen you before."

"Now and then," said Ned, watching as the man took a money clip from his inside jacket pocket and peeled off a twenty from a sizeable wad. The edge of a Rolex peeked out from under his shirt cuff. He paid for the drink and put the money back in his jacket. Ned decided drug dealer was a definite possibility. He needed to be careful.

"What about you?" asked Ned. "You come here much?"

"Whenever I'm in town."

"You're not local, then?"

Grant shook his head. "I do business around the country, but this is my favorite town. I always try to arrange it so that my west coast connection is in San Francisco."

The bartender returned with a full glass, and Grant took it from him. He held it, looking at Ned with frank appraisal.

"And you?"

"I've lived here for about nine years; I guess that makes me sort of local." He reached for the glass, his fingers barely grazing Grant's hand.

"You here by yourself?" Grant asked.

"Yes."

"Want some company?" Then Grant laughed. "Well, of course you do. Why else would you be sitting here talking to me. Am I right?"

Ned allowed himself a grin. "You're good. Pegged me right away."

"So, Ned ... let's cut to the chase. How much do you want?"

"I'll do whatever you want for a thousand dollars," said Ned without blinking.

Grant's barking laugh ricocheted off the leather and brass surfaces of the bar. Heads turned, then looked away.

"Nobody's butt is worth that much! I'll pay you four hundred."

Ned hesitated. It wasn't nearly as much as he needed to get him across the country in a hurry, but he also wanted to get this over with.

Grant was leaning toward him. "Why do you need so much? Debts to pay?"

Ned swallowed. "Family emergency. I need to get home."

"And where is that?"

"Florida."

Grant leaned back on the stool. "I tell you what, Ned from Florida. You show me the best time I've ever had, and you might get more than four hundred out of me."

"Done." Ned stood up. "Where do you want to go?"

"I imagine my hotel suite is more comfortable than whatever loft you live in. Am I right again?"

Ned smiled with his teeth. "Lead away."

Riding in the cab to Grant's hotel, Ned was relieved that the man made no overture to touch him or in any way indicate that they were more than two business colleagues out for a drink. The cabbie dropped them off in front of a restored turn-of-the-century luxury hotel near the Financial District. It wasn't until Grant had unlocked the door to his suite and dropped his suit jacket on a velvet side chair that he made any reference at all to their business in hand.

"You're a pretty boy, Ned. Are you part Mexican, or what?" He took two beers from a small icebox and handed one to Ned. Then he sat down on a chaise beside the wide window looking out over the lights of the city. "Make yourself at home. I'm not in a hurry ... unless you are."

"I'm not," Ned lied, barely sipping his beer. He sat down in an overstuffed chair opposite the man from out of town.

"I like you, Ned," Grant said, taking a long swallow from the bottle sweating around his fingers. "I don't really have any basis for that, since we barely know each other. But I promise you this—you do me right, and I'll take good care of you."

"Ready whenever you are, but I'd like to see the money, if you don't mind."

Grant laughed. "Before I even find out if you're worth all that cash or not? You're pretty demanding." He sat still, looking at Ned. "I like that."

He got up and went to retrieve his jacket, pulling out the money clip. He tossed it onto the glass table between them. "It's all yours if I like what you're selling."

Ned reached out for the clip and unfolded the wad of bills. He stopped counting when the quick tally in his head went past six hundred. "I think it's enough."

Grant turned out the lights in the sitting room and walked to the bedroom. Ned followed.

"So, Ned, do you like to give or receive?"

"Doesn't matter."

Grant unzipped his expensive trousers and let them fall to the carpet. "You *do* know what to do, right?"

"Yeah," said Ned, biting his lip. "I know."

Chapter 10

July 11, 2009—Present Day

"There he is," said Margaret, waving.

Hal came toward them across the baggage claim lobby, impeccable in a well-tailored black suit, oblivious to the midsummer Miami heat.

"I hope you haven't been waiting long," he said, a bit breathless. "Airport traffic is worse than I remembered."

"No problem, we just got here." Alice hugged him; he kissed her cheek and gave Margaret a quick scrunch around the shoulders.

"I've booked rooms for all of us at the Sheraton on the beach, so it's a bit of a drive." He helped them find their suitcases and carried them out to a waiting taxi.

Settled into the back seat with Margaret, Alice watched the cityscape roll by, white and tan and shaded glass set against the impossible blue that was the sky on a clear day over the Miami coastline. She hadn't been home in years and couldn't resist pointing out familiar landmarks to Margaret as they cruised along the Dolphin Expressway. Passing over the MacArthur Causeway to Miami Beach, they were soon rolling past Art Deco hotels resplendent and uniquely tacky in their restored facades of pastel aqua and shell pink.

"As I told you on the phone last night, South Beach is where your mother and father met each other," said Hal over his shoulder from the front seat. "I believe he was working as a waiter in one of the hotel bars, or something like that."

Alice and Margaret craned their necks, taking in the row of hotels along Ocean Drive. To their right lapped the blue-green waters of the Atlantic Ocean.

"Ned Waterston held several different jobs in the year we came to know him," Hal continued. "Being a waiter was only one of them. Suzanne told us he painted portraits as a street artist. I can't confirm that, although his artistic talents were genuine. I have a pencil sketch he did of Suzanne that is quite good." Hal's voice was level, yet Alice now knew about the strife over Suzanne's sudden and all-encompassing passion for this mystery man.

Questions and misgivings swirled in Alice's mind as they got checked into their hotel room and dressed for the funeral service. Throughout the brief private ceremony in the chapel of the moss-covered Episcopal Church long supported by the Blacksburg family, all Alice could think of was her shifting assessment of Ned Waterston. At the interment, attended by a handful of ageing family friends and Hal's business associates, an urn containing Suzanne's ashes was installed in an alcove of the Blacksburg mausoleum beside both her parents. Alice realized Hal was telling her something.

"—here next to her. I'm showing you this just so there's no confusion when my time comes, which I hope will not be soon." He said this last with an off-center smile, as if half of his mouth could not decide whether it was an appropriate reaction.

"What? Oh, right. In the slot beside her." Alice nodded, hoping her face didn't mirror what she was thinking. Where was the line between sibling affection and unhealthy obsession, and how long had it been since Hal crossed over? The thoughts she was trying not to think made her skin crawl. Was her family completely screwed up on both sides? It seemed lately that the people most important to her were not at all what they seemed.

* * *

That evening, the three of them sat poolside, watching the lights of cruise ships on the horizon. The night sky lit up far out over the water where a distant storm silhouetted the clouds. A stiff breeze was kicking up the surf, silvery dark in the gloom, in stark contrast to the rippling, lagoon-style swimming pool with its golden artificial lighting.

"I'll drive you to the airport in the morning," Hal said, "so don't worry about calling a cab."

Alice watched the light show behind the growing thunderheads and then finally turned to Hal. "So, I guess now's the time."

Hal glanced at Margaret.

"No secrets," said Alice. "Ned was Margaret's grandfather. She has as much right to know about him as I do."

Silence again, and then Hal began. "The family, myself especially, considered him completely unfit for Suzanne. She was bright, educated, had been abroad. That trip to Europe was our gift for graduating from college with high marks. She had ambitions to become an interpreter or teach internationally. Ned Waterston ruined all that."

"What did he do," asked Margaret, "get her pregnant or something?"

Alice glared. "No! They were already married when I came along."

Hal nodded. "That's true. In fact, you were probably conceived in Australia. We were concerned to learn about the marriage because no one in the family trusted him. Somehow he'd convinced Suzie to move in with him, but we'd hoped it wouldn't last long. Obviously, those hopes were futile."

"Where was Ned from?" Alice tried to keep her expression neutral.

"That I don't know."

"But you do," she pressed. "In one of those letters you gave me she said he was from Florida, like her."

"Well, then, you know as much as I do on that score. I had a background check done on him, just as a precaution. Not only was there no record, the man did not even have a birth certificate."

Alice was stunned. "But you have to have something, don't you, to get a driver's license or a passport?"

Hal shrugged. "Apparently he found a way. I'm just telling you what I know."

Alice chewed this over. "But there must have been something worthwhile about him, don't you think? I don't know what Suzanne was like before she met him, but I just can't imagine her falling for somebody who was an outright con artist." There. She'd said what Hal was implying, but it didn't make her feel any better.

Margaret was watching them closely, and Alice wondered how all this was going down. Almost fourteen, Margaret was savvy in many ways, smart, bratty, with Alice's stubbornness. There was another inheritance, more disturbing and ephemeral, but the dim trail leading back to its origin was slowly coming to light with the discovery of Ned's artwork. Margaret experienced what their neighbor Raine referred to as "prescient" moments, which was to say images of future events or details of places she had never been washed across her waking mind. These episodes were often accompanied by headaches or a loud ringing in the ears that persisted for up to an hour. Sitting in the safety and comfort of the Sheraton cabana, Alice faced the knowledge that both she and Margaret were carriers of something dark, something lethal, that came from Ned.

Plus, there was the shadow-shifter that had defined Margaret's childhood nightmares. She'd seen the Quinkan rock art images in Alice's *Land of Legends* exhibit at the museum and looked it up on the Internet where Queensland rock art websites were a dime a dozen. Margaret claimed to have encountered it, physically manifested in the real world, much as Alice had seen it in that terror-filled afternoon in the old church.

"Anyway, it's all water under the bridge," Hal was saying, draining his drink. "This tired old man needs his sleep, so I'll see you in the morning." He bent over and pecked Alice on the cheek. She smiled back at him, but not as openly as she once would have done, and that hurt. They watched him climb the cabana steps back to the hotel lobby.

Margaret shifted in her chair. "Mom, what do you think?"

"Let's go for a walk."

Margaret pulled off her shoes, and together they headed down the boardwalk and past the hotel's low retaining wall to the sand. The half moon was rising, barely dusting the lapping waves with its pale light. As far as they could see in either direction, the beach was a gray-white ribbon. Barefoot, they walked side by side just at the margin of the surf where the sand was damp, but not mushy.

"What I think," Alice said, "is that my father was a complicated person. And I think Uncle Hal has … issues that made him not like Ned."

"I think he liked his sister a little too much and felt kicked to the curb when she fell for your dad."

Alice nearly choked. Once again, she had misjudged Margaret's grasp of the adult subtext going on around her.

"For the record, I don't believe there was anything going on between Uncle Hal and your grandmother. I think he may have been overly devoted to her, especially because of whatever happened in Australia, but I'm sure their life together was platonic."

"Know what else I think? I bet my art talent came from him … Ned … my grandfather."

"I'll agree on that much," Alice said. They linked arms and walked in comfortable silence, the rising sea breeze at their backs.

Without warning, Margaret dropped to her knees in the sand, doubling over as if in pain.

Alice was beside her in an instant. "What?"

"Migraine coming on," Margaret said between clenched teeth. "I think I'm gonna be sick. Have you got my pills?"

Alice shook her head. "They're on the bathroom sink in our hotel room. C'mon, let's go back. Can you get up?" Gently, she pulled Margaret to her feet.

"It's not that far. Can you make it?"

Margaret nodded, saying nothing, but holding on as if the whipping wind might blow her mother out of her arms.

* * *

With Margaret safely settled into bed after a dose of phenobarb, Alice locked the sliding glass door to the small terrace overlooking the cabana, and then stretched out on a deeply cushioned sofa, intending to read for awhile. She propped the fantasy novel she'd picked up in the airport on her knees and read a couple of pages without much comprehension. Alice turned another page and yawned. The cushions were so soft. Nestling down into a comfortable position, she began to doze.

Her body was shivering. She'd probably set the air conditioning too high, which meant she'd have to get up out of her warm nest and reset it. Forcing her eyes open, she sat up and gaped at a sky streaked with indigo, purple, and gray-blue storm scud flying eastward over the edge of a ragged scarp. Monumental blocks of weathered red and gray sandstone littered the horizon as far as she could see. A chill wind blew up her back.

The landscape was barren, with a few windblown bloodwood trees stretching out at improbable horizontal angles. Dark red resin oozed from their trunks and glistened as an occasional shaft of sunlight lanced through the cloudbank. A gang of black cockatoos, crests raised, fought for purchase among the branches, their strident calls ripping the air. They hopped from branch to branch, quarreling, and then suddenly the entire mob lifted into the air and flew screeching over Alice's head, disappearing down into the gorge behind her. She sat, speechless and terrified.

A single small bird sailed down the wind and lit on a branch nearest the ground. Glossy black with a white breast and white patches over its eyes, it wagged its tail at her in nervous twitching jerks, spreading its white eyebrow feathers in an insistent display.

Alice got unsteadily to her feet. She was still in the clothes she'd worn to dinner, but they were torn and soiled, as if she'd trekked miles through the Outback. The willy-wagtail cocked its head at her and chattered its distinctive call.

Alice framed the thought in her mind and then said it aloud: "This is a nightmare. I'm going to wake up now." In response, a blast of chilled air tore at her thin blouse and skirt. In its wake, a different sound intruded: something was being dragged, scraping over the rocks behind her. Alice turned and gagged.

A pencil-thin figure with no neck and no discernable features in its knob-shaped head was pulling an inert human form toward a flat rock not far away. The creature was as tall as the leaning bloodwood, and its shoulders were rounded as it bent to hoist its prey up onto the boulder. Its sticklike limbs were the same color as the tree resin and glistened, slippery wet, in the failing light. Darker drops of red came from an area of its head where a mouth might have been, and then Alice saw that it had been feeding on the body flung across the rock.

In dream paralysis, Alice could only watch as it bent down, arms and legs akimbo, and tore at the throat of the body, which she now saw was a human child. Mingled with the dark crimson of its blood was a lighter red. Hair, matted and tangled. The creature flipped the body over onto its back and Alice screamed with her entire soul. The face of the child belonged to Margaret.

Alice fell to her knees, heart pounding out of her chest, and felt soft carpet under her hands. Looking around the darkened room, she realized she had rolled off the sofa.

"What the hell ...?"

Staggering up, Alice went to Margaret's bed. Her daughter slept deeply under the Sheraton's blue satin coverlet. The world she knew was back, but that other place clung to her; she couldn't see it, but she could feel its tendrils brushing her face and arms.

Trembling, Alice went to the bathroom and washed her face and hands. In the bright lights over the sink, nothing seemed amiss. Her clothes were just a bit rumpled. But her face in the mirror wore a look she'd seen before—controlled terror.

Lightning split the clouds as she came out of the bathroom. The storm they'd seen on the horizon was blowing in. With sudden fury, rain lashed across the hotel with enough force to send long rivulets pouring down the glass door and pooling around the sill. Thunder boomed in hollow thuds that rolled out over the ocean. Alice watched and shivered.

Dread settled into a tight knot in her stomach. She'd had no trouble of any kind for nearly a year, but now she was reliving that terrifying rain-soaked afternoon where she'd been cornered in the abandoned church whose bell Cecil Rider had been reluctant to sell stupid Milton Crouch. The demon Harrow had come out of the shadows near the belfry staircase, a darker shadow in his black parson's coat and hat, his mud-spattered riding boots echoing across the plank floor. At his heels trotted the soot-black dingo, tall as a Great Dane. It glared at her with one flickering red eye; the other was blind.

Trembling, she remembered how the dingo had morphed into a salamander the size of a Komodo dragon. Even now she could see its mottled skin pulsing dark muddy red as it flicked a forked tongue over rows of needle-sharp teeth. Muscles along Alice's back spasmed as rain fell across the hotel pool in torrents.

And she remembered what the hellspawn preacher had breathed into her ear as he'd held her fast with fists of ice. "The shifter and I are bound to you." Alice shuddered. She couldn't get the guttural, strangely accented voice out of her head.

Watching cabana patio chairs tumbling in the storm's onslaught, Alice allowed herself to remember the worst Harrow had said. It had been about Margaret.

"Perhaps she'll do what your father and you apparently cannot."

Memory brought back in fine detail how those black eyes, soulless in his weathered brown face, had frozen her, filling her with a deep-space cold that stopped her brain and heart.

"One day, we'll conclude this business," he'd said and vanished in a spiral of dust motes where sunlight from a high window hit the staircase. Since then, she'd talked herself into believing the encounter had been delusional, brought on by the high stress of mounting her first museum show and fueled by the menacing content of the exhibit, the Lightning Man himself being the central image on a floor-to-ceiling mural. *Namarrkun.* The name rumbled through her mind.

Margaret coughed in her sleep and turned over. Watching her, Alice racked her brains for an explanation she could accept. Ned had been painting the ancient Outback landscapes Alice saw in her visions. How was that possible? Thunder crashed outside.

"Mom?"

"I'm here."

"Why are you still up? What are you looking at?"

"Just watching the rain. A bad dream woke me up, that's all."

"I was dreaming, too. What was yours about?"

Alice went to Margaret's bed and without undressing and slipped under the comforter. She related the dream in a general way, including a few details like the black cockatoos chased away by the small black bird with the white breast, but omitting the final scene. She wasn't putting that image into words.

"Weird," was Margaret's only comment. "I had a chase dream. I kept hiding and running away and hiding again. It scared me awake. Can I have a glass of water?"

"Sure, I'll get it." Alice went to the bathroom and filled a glass. Margaret drank it all, and then settled back under the covers. "I'm okay now. 'Night, Mom."

Alice kissed her forehead and turned off the light.

Getting into her own bed she lay awake, staring at the shadows of the darkened room. She was tired, but no longer sleepy. In fact, she intended to stay awake the rest of the night.

With dread, she began doing something she'd promised herself she would never do, which was to go back over those unbearable few months where beings from the Dreamtime had somehow come into her waking world and threatened her life and that of her child. And only then did she remember something very important.

In last year's research on the old plank church, among the clippings and other documents in a dust-covered folder in the county library's Florida Collection, she'd discovered a notebook belonging to Harrow, the church's founder. Showing it to the church's current pastor, Cecil Rider, had nearly given him a heart attack. He'd implored her to burn it.

In spite of that, she'd kept Harrow's notebook, assessing it to be a valuable artifact of the county's history. Only now did she remember the hieroglyphic-like images sketched on the back pages. She had no doubt now what they were: Dreamtime sorcery symbols like those painted on the rock caves of Queensland. She'd stored the book away somewhere, and in the fog of her breakdown and subsequent months of recovery, it had slipped out of her memory. But now, she knew the very first thing she had to do when they got home was to take it someplace far away from the house and burn it to a fine ash.

Settling back into the pillows, Alice watched the rain beating in torrents against the glass. It was well into the gray dawn before her chin sank onto her chest and the world slipped away.

Chapter 11

April 1965

"Thanks, man. I appreciate it."

"You sure this is the place?" Rain beat against the windshield in counterpoint to the wipers' steady thump-thump. Set off from the county road by a waist-high hedge, the house was barely visible. Just beyond it, a post and chicken-wire fence defined the front yard.

"Yeah, this is it." Ned opened the truck door and stepped down into a puddle deep enough to soak his resoled boots over the insteps.

"Awright, then. You be careful on a night like this." The driver pulled the door shut and drove away, the taillights of his pickup disappearing in the downpour. That was a stroke of luck, catching a ride from the airport in Citrus Park as soon as his thumb was out, and the irony of arriving here the same way he had departed so many years ago was not lost on Ned.

Shouldering his backpack, he opened the fence gate and ran for the house. A single light gleamed through lace curtains from a side window, which gave him hope the occupants were at home and that someone was still up this late at night.

He was soaked to the skin as he sprinted up onto the porch and knocked at the screen door. Thunder boomed overhead, and he knocked harder. Shaking his head like a dog, Ned sprayed water in all directions.

Thoroughly miserable, he hoped like hell the old man would recognize him.

More moments of waiting, and then he heard slow footsteps coming down the dim hallway. A shadowy figure appeared in the doorway.

"Who's there?"

"It's Ned, sir." He slung the backpack off his shoulder and set it down. Wiping rainwater out of his face, he presented his most engaging smile.

"Who did you say?" Cecil Rider turned on the porch light, the naked yellow bug-light casting a bronze sheen over Ned's face and arms.

"Ned, Mr. Rider. You took me in twelve years ago, remember? I was a kid half dead from a rattler bite."

The screen door opened wide. "Good Lord! Ned!" Cecil offered his slim brown hand, and then changed his mind, giving Ned a quick half-hug instead. Patting him on his rain-soaked back, Cecil stepped aside so Ned could enter.

"Come on in, son, you're soaking wet. Estell and Pearl, that's our daughter, have gone to bed already, but I can get you a glass of tea. Ned! What a surprise!" The reverend was shaking his head as if unable to believe the evidence of his own eyes.

Ned followed him inside and down the familiar hallway to the kitchen, where the light was on and the remains of a midnight snack sat on the same masonite-topped table where Ned had eaten his last Massalina County meal a dozen years ago.

Cecil motioned Ned to his regular spot at the table, and then sat down in his own chair. He stared at Ned with such open amazement that Ned self-consciously looked away. He hoped his bedraggled appearance hadn't put the old man off too much.

"Forgive me, I just couldn't help staring. You look so much like someone else. I thought for a minute you might be a ghost from the past."

Ned smiled. "You don't believe in ghosts, do you, Reverend Rider?"

"The only ghost I believe in is the Holy Ghost, but you sure enough gave me a start when I saw your face through the screen." He was still staring, his head cocked to the left, as if that would bring Ned's features into sharper focus and explain everything.

Ned put his elbows on the table and leaned forward. "The thing is, I have to know something very important, and you're the only person who can tell me." No sense wasting his time or the old man's with useless small talk.

Now it was Cecil Rider who smiled. "And you waited twelve whole years to ask me this thing that's so important you had to come out here in a thunderstorm in the middle of the night? It must be mighty important, this thing of yours." Then his voice took on a hurt tone. "We had everything set up for you. Why'd you run away?"

Ned shrugged. "Reasons." He leaned toward Cecil, his skin stinging as if he'd stuck his arms in a fire ant bed up to his elbows. "You say I remind you of somebody. Take a good look. Do you know who I am?"

"Just Ned?" Then suddenly Cecil leaped up and scrambled away from the table, knocking over his chair. He backed up against the kitchen sink, horror in his eyes. Lightning popped nearby, filling the room with a bright flash. More thunder boomed and subsided.

Ned stood up. "What's the matter?"

"Keep away!"

Ned froze, barely breathing.

"Your face. For a minute I thought …"

"What did you see?"

The old man was shaking so violently he could barely speak. "When you leaned toward me, I thought … your eyes turned reddish, then yellow, with slits like a reptile. But that's not possible."

Ned said softly, "I'm sure it was just a trick of the light."

Two figures in bathrobes appeared in the shadowy doorway.

"Cecil, what on earth was that noise—" Estell stopped in mid-sentence. Ned had no trouble recognizing a slightly older and larger version of the woman who'd facilitated his sudden departure from the Rider household.

"Mama, who's that?" A young girl of around seven or eight peeked at Ned from behind her mother's ample hips. Ned smiled at her. Unafraid, she returned the smile and then some.

Recovering himself, Cecil set the chair upright and skittered around Ned to stand beside his family.

"See, Estell? Ned's come back. We're just talking. He's got some business or other, but he won't be staying long." All three of them looked at Ned.

"No, I won't stay. But I left something here, way back then, and I came to see if I could retrieve it."

"What's that?" Estell asked, her jaw set. Ned could tell her temper had not improved with age.

"A photo."

"What photo? Of who?" Estell left no doubt as to who was in charge here.

"My father."

Ned counted a full ten seconds before anyone responded.

"I cleaned up that room after you took off and there wasn't no photo laying around anywhere." Estell's jaw jutted even further.

Ned sighed and sat back down at the table. "No, that's not what I meant. You might want to have a seat, too, and hear me out."

Estell and Cecil looked at each other in silence and then discussed the situation in heated whispers. Finally Estell took Pearl by the hand and led her away. "Just one night. No more."

Cecil Rider waited until a door closed loudly down the hall, and then he turned to Ned.

"You shouldn't sit there in wet clothes. Don't you want to change first? Then we can talk. We'll put you up in my grandmother's room again."

Ned shook his head. "I've come a long way to find out about him, and I don't want to wait any longer."

"All right." The reverend came back into the kitchen, keeping his distance from Ned.

"Sit down. I won't hurt you."

Cecil mopped his brow with a white handkerchief and said, "I been living out in the country all my life and, Jesus forgive me, I damn sure know snake eyes when I see them." He dabbed at the back of his neck.

Ned's forearms burned, but the rest of his skin had gone icy. He was pretty sure what Cecil had glimpsed. He'd seen it himself. Did that mean he'd become wholly possessed by the thing? And where was that other presence, the one who'd fought off the death adder that night he'd burned his ancestral home to the ground? Would she come to his defense if the Quinkan finally decided to kill him?

Ned swallowed. "What do you see now?"

"Just Ned." Cecil eased back into his chair. He took his glasses out of his shirt pocket, rubbed them on his sleeve, and put them on.

"You know how it is, once you get past fifty your eyesight starts to go." His voice was steady, but his face still broadcast his fright.

"Sure," Ned said. He started to smile, but held it back. "Reverend Rider, I'm not here to cause you or your family any trouble, but I need to know everything you can tell me about that boy your grandmother adopted, Lazarus, or Lacy. My father."

"What makes you think it's him? I showed you that picture when you first came to us and you didn't say a thing."

"Sorry about that. It's true I recognized him right off. And so did you, just now, when you let me in. You want more proof? Let me describe my mother to you. A big woman, probably weighed over two hundred pounds. Hazel eyes, pale freckled skin, straw-colored hair with gray streaks that she wore parted in the middle and down to her butt. Silver and turquoise rings on most of her fingers. She made charms out of snake venom for a living. Her name was Teresa. You knew her, didn't you?"

Without speaking, Cecil Rider nodded. Then he said, "I always felt you were sent to us for a reason." He folded his hands in his lap. "What do you want to know?"

"Everything you know about them, especially Lacy. You said he was adopted. Where did he come from? That's what I most want to know."

"And that, sadly, is the one thing I can't tell you. I never knew who his parents were. My own father only told me Granny Yu took him in as a newborn when his parents were killed in a hurricane. Their house was demolished. Trees fell on it, and no one survived but that tiny baby. My father was about eight when that happened."

"But, there has to be some way to trace it, a public record of some sort."

"All I know is that Lacy was born in nineteen-hundred and that we always celebrated his birthday on September eighth, so I guess that's the day he was born. He lived with us 'til he was just past thirty, and that's when he ran away with Teresa Waterston, or as Granny Yu said, she stole him off us. He had fits, which I think I told you, and Granny was always scared he would hurt himself by accident. For years we wondered whatever happened to him."

"Your fears came true," said Ned. He sat still for a moment, remembering. "He had a seizure and fell on a filleting knife."

"Horrible! I'd hoped for better things for him. Was he a good father to you?"

Ned nodded. "We had some things in common. We both enjoyed a healthy fear of my mother."

"A hateful woman," Cecil said, and then looked down, studying his hands. "I shouldn't say that. No soul is without merit in God's eyes, so who knows what part she played in His great design."

"You grew up with Lacy in this house ... I'd like to know what you remember." Ned tried out his most polite tone of voice.

"Well, understand that he was a teenager when I was born, so what I know about his childhood I only heard from others. I remember him as very sweet-tempered, but he always seemed ... not complete. You could be talking to him and realize he'd gone blank and hadn't heard a word. Or he would just cry out for no reason, or hide in his room with the door locked. Cheerful and fearful at the same time. I never understood why he was so spooky. Granny Yula just told us to hush up and leave him be. My father knew, I think, but he never told me. He's been dead since nineteen forty-five, so you can't ask him, either."

Ned slumped in his chair, bone weary. "What I wouldn't give to be able to talk to one of them. Maybe you'd let me look through Lacy's old room, in case there's some clue left behind."

"That's not possible. When Estell became pregnant, we cleaned out that back room and turned it into a nursery. It's been Pearl's room ever since."

"Then I'm at a dead end."

Cecil's smile of sympathy appeared genuine. "I'm truly sorry." He got up and touched Ned's shoulder. "Get out of those damp clothes and go to bed. In the morning we can rummage through my father's papers and see if there's anything that might help."

He stopped in the doorway. "I'm glad you came back, Ned. Just finding out who you are and knowing what happened to Lacy fills in a gap for me, too. You're no real kin to me, but in a way you are. You're a fine-looking young man, and I hope you do well in life. God bless you."

* * *

Ned put his pack on the floor of Yula Rider's bedroom and shut the door. He removed the expensive diver's watch Grant had insisted on giving him, and laid it on the nightstand; although its crystal was water-spotted, he assumed its waterproof case had protected it from the downpour. He then stripped off his sodden clothes and pulled a second pair of jeans and a T-shirt out of his pack. After getting dressed and draping his wet clothes over a chair, he flopped down across the bed and let his muscles go slack. God, he was tired. For two cents, he could drop off to sleep right now, but there was something he wanted to do before he could go to bed.

He got up again and went to the dresser. There was the group photo he'd carried around in his mind for a dozen years. He looked long and hard before pulling himself away. Once again, there could be no doubt that Lacy Rider was his father. Ned stood barefoot, staring at the floor, thinking. Then he pulled out the top drawer of the dresser.

It contained female things like slips, bras, stockings, panties, nightgowns, and an ancient rose-petal sachet bag. He poked around, feeling under them, but found nothing of interest. He pulled open the second drawer. More of the same. Pushing it shut, he opened the third drawer. This one was filled with moth-chewed knitted scarves and sweaters, and at least a dozen carefully folded pairs of men's white socks. Again, nothing out of the ordinary. Ned was beginning to feel a little guilty, snooping like this among an old black lady's personal things and possibly those of her long-dead son. Maybe he was wrong in thinking there might be stuff belonging to Lacy still stowed away in the house.

He pulled out the bottom drawer, and a shiver passed over his skin. Pay dirt! Ned sat down on the floor and pulled the drawer all the way out. Instead of clothing, it was filled with a row of neatly stacked bank envelopes that stretched side-by-side from one end of the drawer to the other, more old photos, and most promising, a small metal strongbox. Ned pulled out one of the envelopes, which had been slit open across the top, and saw that it held a deposit receipt. The date on it was from 1940. A quick thumb through the others revealed a span of time roughly covering five years, ending in 1945, shortly before the Second World War was brought to an end. They were all just deposit and withdrawal receipts from a bank in Magnolia, so he turned his attention to the photos.

Most of the pictures were black and white snapshots, wartime photos of black soldiers, some with injuries. A yellowed envelope held over a dozen photos documenting the construction of a large brick and stone church, plus a few showing a newly built wood-frame house he recognized as the one he was in now, although the hedge and surrounding fence were missing. In several of these shots he saw the matriarch of the family, Yula Rider, surrounded by her menfolk: her son Antoine the preacher, a young boy of about twelve that Ned guessed must be Cecil, and a comely young man with long black hair tied in a braid that he knew was his own father. He was tempted to pocket one of those photos, but decided against it. Instead, he put them all back in the drawer and took out the strongbox. As soon as he touched it, a distant murmuring crept into his head, voices arguing, water rushing.

Holding the box up, he saw that it had a hasp but no accompanying padlock. It was pretty old, judging by its scuffed and discolored surface, and surprisingly heavy for its small size. It occurred to him that it might be lined with lead, for fireproofing. Lifting the lid, Ned saw two things. On top, a large wad of money, which did not surprise him much. That was typically what people hid in strongboxes. Under the bills was a small notebook.

He put the box down and picked up the notebook. He judged it to be a little larger than a five-by-seven photograph, with flexible leather covers cracked with age. He flipped through the yellowed pages, noting that a lot of it was unused. Ned turned it over in his hands, trying to guess whose book it was or why it was in the strongbox with a small fortune in hundred-dollar bills. It was then that Ned realized his fingers were growing numb. Clumsily, he turned pages until he reached the back, and what he saw nearly caused him to drop the book. Serpents! The images were crudely drawn in coiled and undulating lines, but he knew that's what they were because he'd created similar icons when he was drawing the "magic" for his mother. Some had stripes along their bodies and others were outlined in dots. One formed a sweeping arch over the smaller images.

He couldn't imagine godly and harmless old Cecil Rider scribbling those symbols, but he sure as hell wanted to know who had done them. As he stared at the page, he began to hear a high whistling sound, faint yet unmistakable, scratching at his eardrums. With a shock, Ned saw one of the images ripple over the page, as if it lay underwater and a pebble or a raindrop had disturbed the surface above it. Blinking, he looked again. The other images closest to it had begun to slide across the page toward it, slowly but inexorably being sucked into its vortex.

Mesmerized, Ned reached out with trembling fingers and touched the undulating serpent shape.

The instant he did so, a thin line of light pulsed in front of his face like the frayed end of a fishing line. He fell back, dropping the book. Still the filament of light floated and pulsed in the air in front of him, almost winking out and then glowing brightly again for a few seconds. The room around him dimmed, but Ned scrambled to his feet away from the tiny rope of light that spiraled and dipped as the shadows closed in. The frayed end of the line seemed to be tasting the air, like a serpent's tongue, seeking the heat of its prey.

"Shit!" Ned backed out of its way and fell over his pack on the floor. The swaying filament of light became still, and Ned saw with terror that tiny globes were traveling down the line, glistening like drops of resin, red as blood. The floor heaved like a leviathan breaching, and as Ned fell across the phantom rope, all the lights winked out.

* * *

Ned found himself on his hands and knees, face down in cold water. It was too dark to make out his surroundings, but not far off the thread of light pulsed ruddy bronze. It stretched in a quivering horizontal line as far away as Ned's eyes could make out.

Staggering to his feet, Ned slogged toward it through knee-high water. Without thinking, he reached out and took hold of the shining cord; it had substance in his fist. His flesh began to throb, his forearms to burn, and he was glad he couldn't see the scale pattern in the gloom. The stinging flowed up his arms and over his chest, and at the same moment a chorus of murmurs flooded into his mind.

Who's there? Who disturbs the billabong? Who touches the black shaman's thread? Who? Ned shook his head, trying to rid his mind of the voices filling it. *Who comes seeking the Rai? What skin group? Who follows the black one's cord?* Ned let go of the line and the voices immediately ceased. Something bumped against his leg in the dark water and he shimmied away, grabbing the line again. *It's a man, see? Snake clan, but not initiated. How does he see the cord? Who?* More whispers flowed into his brain.

Controlling his terror, Ned walked forward, following the thread hand over hand in the dark, pulling himself along through the resisting water. The voices continued to murmur in his ear, but presented no corporeal form. Then he felt a shock along the line, an energy wave that touched his fingers and curled around his wrists. Breathing hard, Ned held onto the line and waited. Another pulse came down the line; something was connecting to him, holding him.

Gray light trickled into his field of vision, barely revealing a lagoon surrounded by willows trailing their long hair in the stream that fed it. The cord led him out of the water and onto a gray mudbank. Ned slipped and fell in the muck, but did not let go of the line. In fact, he realized, he couldn't let go if he'd wanted to—the coils of energy glued him to the rope of light.

It led him over the bank and into a thicket of trees. Even though it was now light enough to see where he stepped, he realized there were no colors. The cord in his hands pulsed red-gold, but everything else in this silent world was painted in shades of gray.

The thread pulsed again, with an electric shock that clacked Ned's teeth together. Directly ahead stood a conical hut of bark or grass, with a dark entrance about three feet high. The cord disappeared into it. A guttural voice from inside the hut broke the silence.

"Who's there? Lacy?"

Ned shivered at the sound of that dead voice. He tried with all his strength to free his hands from the cord, but he was held fast.

"Don't struggle," croaked the voice. "Come where I can see you."

Against his will, Ned followed the cord to the dark mouth of the hut and stooped to enter. Inside it was almost as dark as the billabong had been when he'd first been pulled in. Ned's mind was reeling, flashing back to his hotel acid trip, and yet knowing this was far worse than any magic carpet ride he might take.

"Are you my son?" the voice repeated.

"I'm Ned." Shivering, he saw that the quivering thread of light he'd been following terminated in the solar plexus of a shriveled, blackened humanoid creature squatting on its haunches. "Just Ned," he breathed, as if saying those words could somehow retain him his humanity in this dead world.

"You're not my son. What are you?" The voice cracked. "Are you one of them?"

Ned could barely speak. His will to live, if in fact he had ever been alive, faded into a gray fog of despair. "I don't know who you mean. Where is this place?"

"You found my cord. How did you do that if you're not my son? I commanded my son to find me, but you came instead. How?" The burned creature hopped toward Ned.

Ned was shaking from head to foot, his breath frozen. He was vaguely aware of a rustling outside the hut, and then suddenly his hands snapped free of the line. The blackened figure screeched and lunged at him, howling in hoarse yelps. Ned scrambled backward, digging his hands and feet into the gray dirt floor of the hut. He kicked at its face and connected, sending it flopping backward. On his hands and knees, Ned thrashed his way out of the hut and scrambled a good ten feet from the entrance, where he collapsed, gasping in shallow, panicked gulps like a fish stranded on a riverbank. He struggled to breathe, this gray world barely holding enough oxygen to inflate his human lungs.

More rustlings behind him. Ned turned and saw dozens of silvery ovoid shapes, some the height of children and others tall as trees, emerging from the thicket, forming a wide ring around the hut. They extruded limbs of light toward each other, touching and withdrawing, as if passing information all around the ring. The murmuring of soft voices invaded Ned's head again. *He followed the black one's cord. See? Snake clan markings. Is he a karadji?* Ned took a step toward them, and the ring retreated. *His sight is dim but he touched the Great One and rode on her back. How? We are the Rai. Who comes to us, with shaman's markings but with no knowledge?*

"Come back here!"

Ned whirled around and saw the owner of the umbilicus emerge from the hut on spindly legs. It was nearly as tall as himself and might have been a man once, but now it was just a scorched, blackened shell of a body.

See? The black shaman comes out. He sends his spirit-cord out, seeking, but the Wandjina cuts him off. The orbs touched one another and hummed with their spectral voices. *Namarrkun lays him low. He's cursed, that one. The Rai can't help him.*

The burned creature tottered toward Ned. "You're not my son, but you found my spirit-cord. How did you do that?" it growled. "Have you got my book? Answer me!"

"That notebook is *yours*?" Ned's mind was blown. No acid trip could ever compare to what was happening to him here in this shadow world. His only thought now was to get out of this place and back to his waking life, assuming it still existed somewhere and that he would be sane when he found it. He was going to warn Cecil about the notebook and force him to get rid of it. It contained a portal that Ned had no intention of leaving open if he could ever get back.

"Where is it? Who has it?" The creature was screaming now and seemed to Ned more pitiful than terrifying.

It stamped its ruined feet and hopped about in front of the hut in a rage, but came no further than a few feet away from the hut. Then Ned understood—the hut was its prison. He turned toward the silvery orbs of the Rai.

"Why is he here? Is he trapped here for some reason?"

Not properly initiated. Tried to make the spirit-journey, but his eye sees only darkness, came the voices into Ned's mind. *The Rai can't help him.*

Ned pressed his hands to his chest, and saw the scale pattern pulsing dark against his gray skin. "I'm a human, I don't belong in this world. How can I get out?"

The ovoids rustled against each other. *Look there. Taipan's skin group, that one. Snake clan mob. That one been marked, but doesn't understand. Sees, but doesn't see. The Rai can't help him until he sees.*

Ned walked toward the ring, and it opened to let him pass.

"Curse you, come back!" shouted the prisoner.

Ned stretched his fingers toward the closest of the Rai, but it shimmered away just out of reach. "Why can't you help me? I want to go back the way I came, just show me how."

Can't go back that way. The black one's spirit-cord only leads to him.

The orbs followed Ned down to the lagoon's edge. He stared at the still, metallic surface of the dark water, chewing his lip. There had to be a way, because he was damned if he was going to stay trapped here for rest of his life, or death.

"I didn't get into this world by hanging onto that guy's cord or whatever. Something came up under me and threw me in. What was it?"

The Rai flared in agitated ripples, their voices flooding Ned's head with a cacophony of sound. He thought in a panic that his brain was about to split, but then, slowly, the murmurings resolved into a chant, rising and falling with his own breath. Ned opened his mouth and the words flowed out of him as they flashed in his mind like sparks popping in a bonfire:

Great Snake, Jarapiri, Sky Home mob, make the bridge
Taipan mother, dig the pond, plow the gorge
Great Snake, Jarapiri, bring the rain, flood the land
Taipan mother, blood of life, bring the sun

Ned knelt down, his knees in the water. The Rai clustered close around him, pulsing bright silver in the gloom. He felt in his jeans pockets and found his pocketknife. Opening it, he pressed the point into his wrist and let the ruby drops fall into the water. Shivering in body and soul, he waited for the Ancestor to appear.

She came in great heaving swells of river water rushing up the canyon, flooding the billabong and sweeping Ned away like a twig on the tide. Scales the size of boulders rippled past his face, tossing him on the flood, a pebble scoured up from the river bottom. Swept along the crest of the torrent, Ned gulped air and clutched a scale of the Rainbow Serpent's hide as she dove.

Lungs bursting, Ned opened his mouth and breathed water and, surprisingly, did not die. He pondered the fact, found it meaningless, and let it shed away. He let go of the Ancestor, and perceived her undulating body to be two serpents instead of one, twined and wrapped tightly around each other in an endless rippling coil, the spiral of life.

A roaring of mammoth waterfalls filled his ears and deafened his mind as the identity known as Ned ceased to be. He was a speck of sand deposited on an ancient beach, left to bleach in the unrelenting sun.

Ned opened his eyes. He was lying on the floor of an old woman's bedroom with the night stand lamp knocked over, hanging just inches from his face, shining in his eyes. He rolled over onto his stomach and lay still, waiting for the rolling, coasting sensation underneath him to subside. He felt vaguely seasick.

Lifting his head, he saw with relief that all was as it should be. The floor of Yula's bedroom was firm under his hands, his clothing was dry, no voices in his head. Ned rolled onto his butt and sat staring at the floor. He considered the possibility that he'd just had the worst acid flashback of all time or that perhaps he had finally gone completely mad. Either way, he was not opening that notebook again for any amount of money. He picked it up by the corner and dropped it into the strongbox, which he closed with the tips of his fingers and put back in the drawer.

He pushed the drawer closed with his foot and went to sit on the edge of the bed, filled with despair. Maybe he should just end it all right here. His fingers strayed to the knife in his pocket, fondling the top of its sheathed blade. As he let his breath out, an infinite sadness swept over him, and he would have wept like Gloria, mourning for her lost place in the world, if he could have summoned the tears. But all he could do was sit on the bed with an ache in his throat and a constriction in his chest. Without thinking, Ned placed both palms over the spot and pressed them tightly against his body, just above the navel.

"Snake mother, protect me," he whispered and closed his eyes. He lay back on the coverlet, listening to his breath, ragged at first, then smoothing out. At last, he slept.

Chapter 12

April 1965

Ned woke to timid knocking on the bedroom door. He sat up, realizing he'd slept in his clothes and then gradually remembering why. His body felt like it had been run over several times by a manure truck.

"Ned? Would you like to have breakfast?"

Ned dragged himself to the door and opened it a crack. Cecil, dressed in his uniform of a white shirt and black trousers, waited with hands clasped in front of his chest. He looked at Ned with some alarm, but didn't ask whatever he was thinking. Ned knew he must have looked like all hell, but that was nothing compared to his current mental state.

"Are you hungry? I have to go check on some church property that got damaged in last night's storm, and Estell has gone to walk Pearl to school, but there's red-eye gravy and biscuits and coffee on the stove in the kitchen. Please go help yourself."

Ned cleared his throat. "Thanks, I will. But how long are you gonna be gone? I got some new questions for you, and I can't leave till I get answers." Ned thought he saw a look of panic flash in Cecil Rider's liquid brown eyes.

Cecil ducked his head. "I'll come back as quick as I can," he said, and hurried out the screen door.

Ned went to the kitchen, filled an empty plate, lit the gas under an aluminum coffee pot, and waited for steam to come out of the spout.

Pouring a cup, he sat down at the table and finished his meal in just a few minutes. Sipping at the cup, he tried to untangle what he'd learned since coming back. Some of it was new to him, and some of it tallied with what he already knew. He knew, for example, that his father's birthday was September 8, but he hadn't known until now the actual year of birth. With that knowledge he was able to do the math and quickly figured out that his father had been forty-two when he'd disemboweled himself on his birthday with a fish-gutting knife. Ned had been five.

He'd known all too well about his father's fits, and Cecil confirmed for him that Lacy had always been that way. Damaged from birth, it seemed, but born to whom? Someone whose farmhouse was crushed in a monster hurricane at the turn of the twentieth century. That was the most frustrating thing of all: knowing the site was probably somewhere in the county, but having no way to find it. Perhaps most mystifying, however, was how their child had come into the hands of Yula Rider, who was black, when clearly they weren't. At least not entirely. Lacy was a mixture of something, but the components were anybody's guess.

Cecil had also acknowledged knowing his mother and had explained a little better how the couple had ended up in the swamplands, isolated from the rest of the community. His mother's family was no mystery. They were the worst kind of trash and the few times she'd dragged him along to see them, he'd stayed out in the yard with the dogs. Seasonal laborers, they'd moved on long before Ned had made his own break for freedom.

Ned frowned. All of this was skirting around the main thing he wanted to know: what the fuck was this terrible seer's curse he'd inherited from Lacy. Above all, though, he wanted to know how to make it stop.

The awful thing was, Ned knew he'd gotten the most important piece of the puzzle last night, although it scared the bejeezus out of him. He was going to have to question Cecil about the strongbox, which meant admitting he'd pilfered through the contents of Grandma Yula's dresser.

Ned gulped the rest of his coffee and went back to the bedroom. His clothes from last night had dried, so he rolled them up, stuffed them into his pack, and pulled out clean socks. His desert boots were still a bit damp, but what the hell—it was wear them or go barefoot. With his pack squared away and ready to hit the road, Ned sat down to wait.

Before long, he heard the screen door bang and footsteps coming down the hall. Cecil appeared in the doorway, his dark face glistening with sweat.

"Everything okay?" Ned inquired, his tone neutral.

"Yes, thank the Lord. Lightning strike. The wood under the eaves was smoking when the fire department's water tanker got there, but it got saved in time. The old church, I mean, not the new one."

He came into the room and sat down on the edge of the bed, folding his hands over one knee. "What was it you wanted to ask me?"

Ned jerked his head toward the dresser. "What's in that strongbox in the bottom drawer and where did it come from?"

Cecil stared at the dresser. "How would you know about that?"

"Well, obviously, I looked."

"Why?" The pastor's voice was nearly a whisper.

"Because I'm a nosey bastard, and I want to know where I came from. No, I *have* to know."

"There was no need to pry, Ned. I told you I would try to help you find out whatever we could about poor Lacy."

Ned looked at him straight on, his thoughts murderous. "Is that notebook thing part of what was wrong with 'poor Lacy'?"

"I don't believe so. It never belonged to him."

"But what is it?" Ned knew he was prying beyond all propriety now, but he didn't much care; he could be as stubborn as a pit bull clamped onto somebody's ankle if that's what it took. That notebook had linked him to a bad place with creatures that seemed to think he should know something he didn't.

"Where did you get it from?" He was unpleasantly familiar with backwoods spellcasting, and it occurred to him that maybe Granny Yula had been a swamp witch herself. Was the book hers?

The Reverend Rider sat for several moments without saying a word. Ned was prepared to wait him out, even if it took all day.

Cecil's face became drawn and sad, and Ned feared he was about to cry right there in front of God and everybody. Instead he said, "The strongbox and its contents belonged to my father. He stole them from their original owner, a man named Cadjer Harrow, a foreigner with a questionable reputation who founded the church of which I am now pastor. Shortly before my father died, he wrote to me that he thought he was being haunted by the ghost of that man, for stealing the box and using the money many years later to finance the beautiful church building we enjoy now. Is that what you wanted to know?" He continued to stare at the drawer, as if he could see inside the strongbox.

"That must've been a shitload of bucks," said Ned.

Cecil nodded. "He told me how much, but I forget. That was so long ago."

"I didn't take any of it," Ned added.

"I'm sure you didn't," Cecil said, finally looking up.

"Reverend, have you ever looked through that book?"

"It's just church records, isn't it? And some heathen-looking scrawls in the back."

"Yeah, about those heathen scrawls. Have you ever touched 'em?"

Cecil cocked his head, as if he hadn't heard right. "No, I haven't. Why?"

"Because I did and I ended up somewhere that's not here, that's why. Someplace with ghosts that seemed to think they know me and some horrible burned-up guy who was their prisoner."

Cecil rose to his feet. He mopped at his forehead and neck with his handkerchief. "I never honestly believed my father's story. I just assumed it was his guilty conscience making him imagine such ... terrible things. But now I don't know." He bowed his head. "I don't want to know."

"Sorry, Rev, but I do." Ned gripped the arms of the rocking chair. "Those snakeyes you thought you saw in the kitchen? I been seeing them all my life, if you really want to know. Oh, sorry, you don't want to know. It's not a fun trip; in fact, it makes me crazy. That's why I came back, and you've helped me some, but not as much as I need."

Ned got up and watched with some satisfaction as Cecil backed away. He couldn't entirely hold back the urge to scare the old fucker, because he was scared shitless himself and it wasn't so bad if you spread it around.

"What else can I do?" Cecil opened his palms.

"I need you to drive me somewhere." Ned hoisted the strap of his pack over one shoulder and headed for the bedroom door.

He clomped down the hallway, his stride outpacing the smaller man, who followed at a safe distance.

"How far do you need to go? Estell's liable to pitch a conniption if she comes home and nobody's here." Cecil hurried after him, down the porch steps and out to the old blue-and-white Ford Fairlane parked beside the house. Ned slid into the passenger seat, arms crossed tightly over his chest, eyes closed in a tight squint.

"Ned? Are you sick?" Cecil put a trembling brown hand on Ned's shoulder.

Ned bit down on the pain flickering over his arms and chest. "Just start driving. I need to go back to where those guys found me, the ones that brought me to you way back then."

"You mean the National Forest. That's about fifteen miles west."

"Yeah, if you wouldn't mind." Ned gave him a tight smile.

Cecil sat quietly for a moment, whether gathering his wits or praying for swift delivery of his passenger, Ned couldn't tell. Then he put the key in the ignition and started the car.

They drove in silence, planted pines with their palmetto understory rolling by on both sides of the state highway, until they reached a fork that led off the paved highway onto a wide gravel and sand road used by the U.S. Forest Service. For about five miles it was well maintained, running straight as an arrow through sparse flatwoods of tall, thin slash pines and graceful fringe trees just coming into flower along the shoulders of the road. Their masses of drooping white petals like showers of snowdrops brought Ned an unexpected pang of nostalgia; they were an artifact from his childhood.

Soon they reached a narrow bridge on concrete pilings. It crossed steep banks containing barely a trickle of tea-colored river water, and beyond it the road forked again, with the left-hand branch becoming a two-run sandy track leading into the non-public area of the National Forest.

"You can let me off here," said Ned.

Cecil brought the car to a stop just beyond the bridge. "Are you sure? You don't look so good, son."

"I'm all right. I gotta go back, is all."

Ned opened the passenger door and got out. He slid his arms through both straps of his pack and hefted it into place on his back. "Thanks for everything, man, I really mean it." He turned to walk away.

"I don't feel right, just leaving you here," Cecil called.

Ned started walking. The car cranked behind him, but not until he heard it heading away from him on the gravel road did he turn and look. He didn't expect to ever see the Reverend Cecil Rider again, so there was no use asking him to wait.

The sun was cresting the treetops, heading toward noon. He trudged forward, watching its progress over the trees and keeping a lookout for the first of several landmarks.

This part of the trail unrolled in a fairly straight line through higher ground where sassafras, wild persimmons, dogwoods, and black cherry trees rubbed shoulders with the more common pines that stood knee-deep in gallberry bushes and bright green palmettos. Early spring wildflowers that Ned hadn't seen in years carpeted the sandy ground and filled the shallow ditches on both sides of the trail.

After twenty minutes of steady walking, he spotted a grassy track to the right and beyond it a pinestraw-covered clearing. In its center stood a monument to the god of hunting: two ten-foot-high poles connected by a steel crossbeam with heavy-duty cable winches affixed to both uprights. Instructions for hoisting your carcass and disposing of the waste remains in large covered garbage containers nearby were posted on a tree. Ned stood on the spot where he'd been found so many years ago and tried to remember his rescue. He'd been told about it during his recuperation, but the memory of it was lost.

Satisfied that he was headed in the right direction, Ned went back to the sandy track and kept walking. He consulted Grant's watch and guessed that it might be another forty-five minutes before he reached his second landmark, a stand of hardwoods, mostly oaks and maples, on the eastern side of the trail that reached higher and thicker than the surrounding woods. The center of this grove of ancient live oaks was where the house had stood. Further into the woods beyond the homesite, the ground dipped again, becoming a lowland swamp full of titi thickets and standing water where gator holes could swallow a man up to his waist.

Not far beyond the pine, Ned spotted the overgrown meander of a trail, and farther down it, a stand of old-growth oaks. Heart beating, he stepped into the tangle of ilex, a native holly that could rake your skin raw if you weren't careful. Ned pushed through dense clumps of sparkleberry bushes with tiny white flowers bright against glossy green leaves, trying to keep the faint trail in sight. It looked vaguely familiar, but he spent the next half-hour unsure if it was the route to the house he'd been born in. The sun was starting to cast lengthening westerly shadows when at last it began to feel right in a way that only memory could produce. He quickened his pace, pushing through the underbrush, reliving in his mind that panicked, mad dash that had sent him running down this same trail years ago with snake venom pumping through his veins.

Slowing to a walk, Ned began to look for the oak grove off to his right, and shortly, he found it. There was no mistaking the site because there were his initials, N.W., carved into the skin of a sentinel oak whose massive branches now nearly touched the ground. Heart pounding, he stepped around it into the cool woodland shade.

Stumbling forward through catbrier thickets, Ned searched for signs of the house foundation, but all was overgrown with trees that had been knee-high in his childhood and were now taller than his head. Ned was hot and insect-bitten, but not about to rest when he was this close.

He'd hoped to find some remains of the house, but with every stubbed toe and scratched ankle it seemed less likely. Tripped by a vine, he fell forward, hands splayed out in front of his face. They touched something jagged and hard. Scrambling to his knees, Ned saw a pile of limestone rocks, one as large as a car tire, covered by creepers and ferns. He pulled the vines away, revealing a familiar display that brought years of terror and pain and heartsick yearning back in a flash. He'd piled those stones in place himself, with his mother's help. They covered his father's grave.

Ned took a deep breath and sat dry-eyed, just listening to the deep quiet that descended. In early afternoon sunlight, the grove of ancient oaks drowsed in silence except for an occasional whisper of breeze over the glade.

Finally, Ned stood and faced southwestward away from the gravesite. He now knew exactly where the remains of house ought to be, and within minutes he found the charred timbers hiding under sprays of wild lobelia and daisy fleabane, the blackened rippled wood a sharp contrast to the whites and pale lavenders of the tiny flowers. He walked the perimeter of the foundation with care, looking but not touching. It was easy to see where the main walls had been; they'd fallen inward, forming a large blackened rectangle several layers deep. He found no sign of furniture or other household objects in the debris. Had the fire been hot enough to reduce everything inside to drifts of ash and melted glass? He assumed that any human remains had long since been disposed of by woodland scavengers. A shiver passed over him at the thought, and he stepped away from the house.

Pushing through a waist-high stand of wild grapes toward what had once been the front yard, Ned was heartened to find the area still canopied by three massive live oaks so old their long weathered limbs sprawled away from their gnarled trunks in impossible twists and spirals of living driftwood. The limbs of the three patriarchs were so thoroughly interlaced that in summer, when they were in full foliage, a boy could stand underneath them in a light rain and not get wet.

He chose one whose massive roots formed a kind of bench and settled himself against its aged trunk. Taking his sketch pad and a box of drawing pencils out of his backpack, Ned wiped sweat out of his eyes. He felt hot and ice-cold at the same. One quick glance showed him what he feared—the scale pattern had intensified. Now it was dark green-gold and shimmered with its own faint radiance.

For a moment Ned forgot his immediate purpose and gaped at the markings. He'd gotten so used to them over the years that they no longer gave him the willies when he saw them, but now, here in this place of violence and terror and death, he was frightened to his very soul.

Ned licked his dry lips and put the sketch pad in his lap. He pulled out a pencil, touched up its point with a sharpener, and then held it lightly in his fingers, just above the paper.

"Draw me the magic," he whispered.

Chapter 13

April 1965

Ned sat still as stone, barely breathing. His pulse pounded in his wrists and neck as he waited. He hadn't done this in so long, he wondered if it would even happen.

The air inside the grove was perfectly still, the surrounding woods holding its breath. A sliding, skittering noise passed through the underbrush behind him, and a shudder went through the ground, not unlike the minor earth tremors he'd felt in his years living on the west coast. Ned moistened his lips. His hands were trembling, but he sat unmoving.

Twigs snapped and leaves rustled off to his right, as if a large body had intruded itself into the tangle of Muscadine. The ground shuddered again, and Ned could hear breathing from some large creature just behind him. Shivering, he kept his eyes focused on the paper, and his hand began to move.

He now understood, from having encountered a fair number of psychics and seers during his stint in San Francisco, that what he was doing was a form of automatic writing, or in his case, drawing. He was channeling something, to use the terms of the trade. Just what that something was, he'd been afraid to ask when he was small, but now that he had a better idea of what it might be, he was even more fearful.

He felt the serpentine presence filling him up, flowing down through the top of his head, through his neck, down his shoulder, along his right arm, and into his hand as it gripped the pencil. Ned had stopped breathing as his consciousness stepped aside, curling itself up, suspended in a hazy ball of Ned-ness. An alien presence poured into his mind and moved his body, drawing a design he had sketched before, but not in this much detail. He watched, detached, as the image unfolded, black lines on white paper, flat and yet somehow three-dimensional.

It was an elongated oval, leaf-shaped, yet rounder and heavier, if an image could have weight. The pencil point shaded the edges of the oval and stippled the surface, and he began to realize it was a stone, shaped and carved to a specific purpose. Over the surface of the stone designs emerged as Ned's hand moved over the paper, drawing the images with deft, sure strokes. Double serpents in wavy parallel lines ran up one side of the stone, over the top, and down the other side, forming an elongated U. Inside the top of the U floated seven tiny spirals. Under them was crouched a dog, teeth bared. Abstract designs filled the space at the bottom of the stone, along with several sorcery symbols to protect the stone from theft or destruction. As soon as all the elements of the design were completed, Ned's hand went limp, and he felt the presence flow out of his body like air out of a balloon.

His body convulsed and spasmed from the retreat of the invading presence. He'd sensed it dampening its energy field just low enough to wear his human suit for the minutes needed to draw the picture. His arms glowed olive green with a faint golden sheen, and his entire torso itched beyond endurance. Pulling up his T-shirt, he saw with a shock that his shoulders and chest were covered with the scale design. More frightening, however, was the faint glowing umbilicus that emerged from his body just above the navel and stretched out horizontally in a thin shimmering line. It undulated slightly in the patches of sunlight, as if responding to unseen vibrations. Transfixed, Ned saw that it floated over the destroyed house and vanished into the trees beyond.

The pencil and paper fell from his hands as Ned sat slack-jawed, staring with unblinking eyes along the sightline of his spirit cord. Voices murmured in his head, one of them elevating to a loud honking-hiss that made his blood run cold. But at that moment he was beyond moving or seeing; he simply registered the sound in his mind and let it pass through him. The landscape around him was fading.

Ned realized with a jerk that he was no longer sitting, but standing, looking down at his stupefied body as it slumped against the tree trunk. The glowing spirit cord emanating from his solar plexus flowed through his standing body, and when he stepped away toward the trees, the thin glowing line reeled out as if he were a fish on a line.

As he went toward the heaps of charcoal that had once been a structure of pine and oak, he sensed several presences occupying the burned space. Ned passed through them, only peripherally aware of their waves of rage and sorrow momentarily directed toward him. The shining line continued to stretch out from his body as he advanced into the trees where the sunlight faded into black night.

Ned emerged from the grove of oaks into a landscape of red cliffs and wind-sculpted monoliths, their tortured shapes the product of eons of weather chewing and gouging at their sandstone surface. The night sky was lit by an enormous bonfire that flared like an earthbound sunspot, its bright tongues of flame arching and falling in a shower of sparks back into the pyre of brush and the trunks of trees. A ring of dancers, all wiry brown men at least ten feet tall with painted bodies and tasseled headdresses painted in symbols of smoke and clouds, shuffled, leapt, stomped, and twirled with rhythmical precision. Ceremonial smoke bathed the dancers as the bonfire blazed up higher than their heads. Clack-sticks and the low drone of a didjeridu sounded in his head and resonated in the marrow of his bones. He wasn't simply surrounded by the sound; he had become the subsonic tone that rose and fell and yelped like an animal.

The sound rumbled along the ground and toppled a couple of the sandstone monoliths, but the dancers continued to jump and leap, oblivious of their surroundings. Ned felt the bones of the earth splinter and separate as the tone cleaved the elements that held their shapes together. And then, a monstrous dingo, taller than the dancers and transparent enough for Ned to see the outlines of the bluffs behind it, burst through the ring of dancers. One great leap and it landed in the bonfire, scattering coals. The Dingo Ancestor snapped at the flames with red-stained fangs, allowing itself to be consumed by the fire until there was nothing but a glowing lump of rock where it had crouched.

The dancers stopped as one body. The tallest with the highest conical headdress stepped forward and reached out with both hands, retrieving the object from the coals. He turned to the group and held up the talisman for all to see, proclaiming in a high voice words of wisdom for the witnesses of the miracle that had just taken place. Although Ned could not fathom their language, an understanding of the event flowed into his mind. The Dingo Ancestor had given his clan group a sacred *tjuringa* to take back to the human world for their safekeeping. And he knew without seeing it what images were engraved on its surface.

Suddenly, he felt a sharp tug at the spirit cord connected to his solar plexus. Without warning, his consciousness began to slide along the line like an electrical impulse and, picking up speed, it landed with a jolt back in his body. Ned toppled over and lay on his back, staring up into the flaming red eyes of the most hideous dog-shaped creature he could ever have imagined. It did not have the majesty of the Dingo Ancestor he had just seen, but was instead a travesty of that one's beauty, a horrible lower-world mockery of a celestial archetype.

"Die!" it demanded in a guttural voice that was not quite growling and not quite speaking.

"Gahhhhhh!" Ned rolled away from the beast and scrambled to his feet. The dog-creature leapt at him again, crashing against one of the massive oaks as Ned fell to the ground. Propelled by terror, Ned ran headlong into the thicket containing the charred timbers of the old cracker cabin, falling to his knees in a shivering, shaking crouch, waiting for death to strike. Instantly, he was surrounded by shrieks and the sound of timbers falling and fire crackling. The demon-dog turned and lifted its bloody lips over its teeth, questing and tasting the air. Then to Ned's horror, he watched it stand up on its hind legs and slowly stretch into a blurred humanoid shape. The more it went vertical, the less defined its outline became, much the way Ned might have blended the edges of a charcoal drawing with his fingers.

It was now as tall as the overhanging limbs of the oaks, looking around with a small bulbous head whose only distinguishable features were two white-ringed, lidless eyes. Then it turned in his direction and spoke in a familiar voice.

"Neddy, my boy. Why are you hiding?"

Ned clapped his hands over his ears, but the hateful voice continued.

"Come die like a nice boy. Come, Neddy."

His chest pounding almost beyond endurance, Ned cowered on his knees, clutching his chest. Was he having a heart attack? The pain was unbearable.

The loathsome man-thing was coming toward him, a black smudge against the tree canopy. But then it began to gibber, losing its voice and lapsing into something more closely resembling an animal's howl.

"Nonono, not yet, noooooooo!" Then it was gone.

Absolute silence filled the clearing. Lifting his head in spite of the excruciating pain in his midsection, Ned scanned the trees and underbrush for movement or sound, but the forest was as still as when he'd first sat down. Ned confronted the evidence of his watch and realized, stunned, that several hours had passed. His chest hurt so much he thought he might pass out.

"No proper Senior Knowledge-man bin jump back in his body like that." The reproving voice in his head was the other one, the one that held the terror at bay. "You can follow the spirit cord out like a proper initiated man, but you can't find your way back in without nearly killing yourself." The voice cluck-clucked its disapproval.

Ned crawled out of the thicket and collapsed beside his sketchpad, staring at the drawing. "What's that thing?" he gasped, fighting for breath.

"Dingo clan *tjuringa*," said the Taipan Ancestor. She slithered across the clearing toward Ned and rose up in front of him, her smooth olive-golden body gleaming in the afternoon sun.

The constriction in Ned's chest was easing, and he dragged himself, shaking, to the spot where he'd leaned against the oak. The giant snake looked real, but he was damned if he was going to reach out and touch it to make sure.

"It hasss to go back," she hissed, swaying much too close to his face. Ned saw bright dots in front of his eyes and felt the ground tilting underneath him. He clutched at the tree roots, thinking if he could just hold on, things might snap back to normal in a minute or two. But the ground continued to ripple like the waves of an earthquake, and the glittering eyes of the taipan held him breathless.

"Back where?" He could barely get the words out.

"Sacred place, Dingo clan cave," said the Ancestor.

Tears of frustration pricked at the corners of Ned's eyes. "Why fucking *me*?"

"Got to be you," said the taipan, "unless you bin want to father yourself a child and pass the job onto it."

"W-what?" Ned buried his head in his arms to escape those dreadful slitted eyes.

"Shhhh," said the snake, flowing in a liquid motion over his leg and up his body to his shoulders, then around until her head came up behind him and rested in the nest of his hair. "Take up your drawing tool," she said. "Big boss Wandjina says I'm to show you."

Trembling in bone and sinew, Ned picked up the pad and pencil, and began to draw, slowly at first, and then more rapidly as the familiar channeled energy took over his muscles and tendons. Quickly, he sketched a high bluff with a cleft in its side, partially hidden by windswept crooked trees. A distinctive rock formation marked the base of the split in the cliff, and water flowed past it, although the source of that water was hidden.

Then he folded the page back and began a new drawing. A woman's face took shape, small-featured and comely with long hair whipping in the wind. Behind her appeared palm trees and the façade of a building with decorative tiles in Moorish, Egyptian, and Italianate design. As before, Ned's hand then went limp, and the pencil fell to the ground.

The Ancestor retreated, leaving Ned completely alone in the sand and roots of the giant oak, with mosquitoes feasting on his face and arms. The sun was slipping low over the trees, the light fading into gathering gloom under the oak canopy. Ned stared at the woman's face. He would have to go in search of her, he knew that much. But where she was, and what he would do when he found her, he had absolutely no clue.

Chapter 14

July 24, Sunday—Present Day

Margaret settled into the computer chair and logged onto the Internet, surfing quickly to her favorite forum. She still had a couple of hours before they were supposed to leave for camp, and she wanted to post her gone-for-awhile notice in the Absences thread just in case she ended up being Internet-deprived for over a month.

For the duration of science camp, she would be living with three other girls in a dormitory on the university campus, in a "quad suite" consisting of two bedrooms, a communal bathroom, and a kitchenette. She was friends with two of the girls assigned to her group, but the fourth was from out of town. Margaret hoped she was cool and would fit in. If not, well, they would deal.

She slipped her favorite anime soundtrack into the computer's CD player, put on her headphones, and typed GOKU into the user-name field and then typed her password, *shikigami*. Margaret sighed. She wished she had a real *shiki* of her own to command. It would be the bomb to be a genuine *onmyouji*, a Japanese sorcerer, who could conjure up the magical dragon servant just by folding a piece of paper and chanting sutras over it.

She looked to see who was online. The usual suspects were logged on: Ryoga, a board moderator, plus Inu-luvver, Hellboy2, Muraki's Lair, NekoMania, and Kinigar.

Margaret grinned. She'd gotten pretty friendly with most of them and had been a member of the forum long enough now to have posted over five hundred messages, which gave her non-noob status and a couple of stars by her handle. Although she posted in half a dozen Internet forums, she had a comfortable sense of belonging in this particular one. It was hard to say why; it was the typical mix of pop-culture-addicted teens and twenty-somethings, with a smaller sprinkling of older weird-but-cool members, if you were to believe their profiles, which one always took with a grain of salt. But there was a slightly more intellectual, slightly less confrontational tone to this board that Margaret liked. Overfiend, the forum's founder, enforced the rules with a twisted but supportive vibe, and the members followed his lead.

First, she scanned the threads where she had last posted, checking for responses. There were new posts to a topic called "Have You Ever," started by Kinigar. It was one of those "what's the strangest thing you've ever done" type of thread, and she'd written that she'd once had a Dreamtime monster called a Quinkan living in her closet. Nobody took her seriously, of course, although most of them wanted to know what she'd been sniffing.

Her experience with the creature wasn't exactly like calling up a *shikigami*, but it was pretty freaking close. Sometimes when she thought back, it seemed like just an eyelid movie and not something she'd actually seen in real life. Other times it still creeped her out.

She checked her PM box and saw the icon blinking. Kinigar had sent her a message. The subject line simply read "Heya." She'd gleaned that Kinigar was a male from numerous other posts he'd made—statements like, "I'm the only guy in my class who reads slash fanfics." He posted a lot ("Postwhore" was the tagline under his avatar) and was fairly popular on the board.

She clicked open the message and read, "Sooo, u met any shapeshifters lately? Seriousleh. Did u really? XD, Kini."

Margaret chewed her finger, and reread the message. Epic WIN. A guy she sort of admired had taken her post at face value. She read his message again, trying to decide if there was any sarcasm or hidden agenda she wasn't seeing. It seemed straightforward, and he'd signed it XD, an emoticon for a big grin, so she hit REPLY and typed: "No I have not seen any lately. Once was enough, ya know? *shudders* Have u? heh heh, Goku."

After hitting SEND, she clicked on Kinigar's profile, more curious about him now that he'd PM'd her. His profile page opened, displaying his avatar pic, a wildcat's face in full white-fanged snarl. Reading his stats, she saw that he was sixteen if his birth date could be trusted, and that he was into "skating, swimming, Scandinavian Goth music, manga and anime, sci-fi, horror, cosplay, animals (especially cats), and computers," which sounded pretty compatible with herself. She smiled and read on. He listed his personal e-mail address and Instant Messenger ID, and his location. Margaret stopped reading. She couldn't believe what she was seeing. His location was listed as Bondi Beach, Australia. Kinigar was an Ozzie.

She immediately hit PM again and typed a new message to him: "Kini, where in Oz is Bondi Beach? How long have u lived there? What do u know about the Dreamtime? Were u hinting about something? Wanna share? *glomps and hugs you* Goku"

Margaret's chest was thudding. She wondered what he would make of all those questions and if he would be put off. She wasn't stalking him, after all, it was just that she was so shocked to find somebody from Australia actually responding to her shape-shifter post. She really, really hoped he wouldn't just blow her off and not answer. With a click she returned to the regular forum thread and looked to see if he was still logged on. Disappointed, she didn't see his name in the list. Now she really needed a reason to get back on the Internet tomorrow or the next day, to see if he'd answered. Camp could interfere with that because she didn't have a laptop, and she knew Judy and Lissa didn't either. Maybe the other girl in the quad would come through.

* * *

"Hey, Margrits!"

Judy and Lissa came through the doorway of one of the bedrooms in their quad suite. Judy gave her a bear hug. "You're late, so we went ahead and took this room. You and the other girl can have the front one, hope that's okay."

Margaret shrugged. "No problem. I'm late 'cause Mom and Nik are still trying to find a place to park. They let me off at the dorm front door." She looked around. So this was what college dorm life was like.

During the university's summer break, Science Camp took over two floors of a co-ed dorm, housing boys on the third floor and girls on the second. The quad suites accommodated two pairs of roommates, who would share a bathroom (shower, no tub) and a tiny kitchenette that held a pantry, half-fridge, sink, and microwave oven. The main access doors for each suite (she'd counted eleven before finding the one assigned to her) opened onto a hallway that ran the length of the dorm.

Margaret went into the front bedroom and took a look around. If you split the small room down the middle, the halves were mirror images except that one wall had the door to the short hallway inside the suite and the opposing wall held a window to the outside world. Otherwise, both sides of the room had a single bed on a heavy wooden frame pushed into a corner, a small student desk with two drawers at the foot of the bed, and bookshelves bolted to the wall over the bed and desk. A computer desk with Internet hookup took up the space against the wall between the two beds. Two floor-to-ceiling locker-type wardrobes filled in the wall opposite the computer desk. The room was spare and utilitarian, but Margaret had to admit it was a pretty efficient use of a small space intended to accommodate two people and all their belongings.

Nik poked his head in. "Is this your room?" He put Margaret's suitcase and a cardboard box of books down in the middle of the floor. Alice squeezed past him and put her arm around Margaret's shoulders.

"Hi girls, how's everybody? Getting settled in?"

"Yeah, it's all good." Margaret allowed herself to be hugged in front of her friends. She was feeling jittery and nervous, but excited. This was different from the other camps she'd attended. It was like being in college for five weeks.

Alice kissed her on the cheek. "Have fun, then. I've got the dorm phone number, so I'll check on you in a few days and see if you want anything. Call us if you need to."

"Bye, Mom. Thanks, Nik." She was mentally nudging them out the door.

As soon as they were gone, Margaret joined Judy and Lissa on the floor and pulled out the quad assignment info sheet.

"Wonder where our other quad-mate is," Judy said, looking the page over.

"What's her name?" Margaret asked.

"You're gonna love this: Thomasina Redfern, from Orlando."

"No way anybody has a name like that. You made it up, right?" They were all laughing.

"Sounds like Thumbelina. I bet she's some stuck-up rich kid." Lissa made a face.

"Epic FAIL!" said Judy. They started cracking up.

Margaret was twitching. "I hope not. I gotta live with her for five weeks."

"She's the oldest, too," Judy said, looking at the info page. "She's fifteen. Me and Lissa are fourteen, and Margrits is the baby." Sixteen was the age cutoff for Science Camp participants, with the youngest being twelve; most of the college-student counselors were nineteen and older. Margaret noted that the one assigned to their quad was a Biology major named Melissa.

"Who's a baby? I'll be fourteen in two weeks," she protested.

Lissa popped the top of an orange soda and passed it around. "Maybe we should go up to the boy's floor and have a look around."

Margaret giggled and poked her. Then she noticed someone standing in the doorway.

"Hi guys, Tom here," said a husky voice.

Margaret did a double-take. The girl leaning against the doorframe was tall and thin, with jet-black hair cropped short around her neck but slightly longer in front and fringed bangs that fell over her eyebrows. Her pale face was made up with heavy black eyeliner and dark purple lipstick. Both ears displayed a row of silver studs, graduating in size. There was a matching stud in one nostril. She was dressed in a skimpy black camisole top, hip-hugging jean that showed off her belly button, black platform flipflops, and silver toe ring. But the coolest thing of all, the thing that Margaret couldn't stop staring at, was a black widow spider tattooed just under her left collarbone. She had an iPod bud in one ear, with the cord running down to an armband pouch holding her Nano, which probably held thousands of death-metal songs Margaret wasn't allowed to listen to. She was, in fact, the flesh and blood manifestation of all their Goth-princess fantasies.

"So, which one of you guys is my roomie?" she said, removing the bud from her ear and tucking it into the armband. She bent down and dragged a heavy Army-surplus duffle bag into the room.

Margaret raised her hand. "Me."

"Cool. Who're you?" Tom was looking at her, sizing her up, or so it felt.

"Margaret."

"Got a nickname or do they call you the whole thing?"

"Margrits!" the other two chorused.

Margaret flushed to the roots of her hair. She twitched miserably, a red-faced, red-haired flame of teenaged embarrassment.

Tom nodded. "I like. So, Margrits, which bed d'you want?"

"Um, it doesn't matter, I guess." Margaret wished her voice didn't sound so squeaky.

"Right." Tom pushed the duffle bag under the nearest bed with her foot. Then she turned to the group. "Now, let's get this baby up and running."

It was only then that Margaret noticed the briefcase-shaped black bag hanging by a wide strap over Tom's thin shoulder. Her heart skipped a beat.

Tom put the bag down on the bed and unzipped it, lifting out the sleek laptop. She set it down with care on the computer table, pulled a power strip out of the bag's side pocket, and got down on her hands and knees, looking around underneath the desk.

Margaret looked at the other two in silent glee as Tom found the power outlet and plugged in.

Standing up, Tom powered on and typed in her password. "If you guys ever want to, like, check your e-mail or something, just let me know."

Margaret could scarcely contain her joy. Not only did she have the coolest roommate at camp, she had unfettered, unsupervised access to the Internet and, most important of all, to Kinigar.

Chapter 15

May 1968

Suzanne Blacksburg blushed, her cheeks red as her hair. "He said *what?*"

"He wanted to know if you were unattached—"

"And if you were, did we think he had a chance with you."

Suzanne pushed her sunglasses up on top of her head. "Like hell. I don't even know the guy!"

Bailey shrugged. "So what? He's groovy. I mean, we've been trying to score with him for months, and then you come back to Miami after a year in Paris and he falls ass over teakettle. It's not fair!"

"You might like him," said Paula. "At the very least he'll probably get you stoned."

They were laughing and teasing, but Suzanne heard that note of jealousy buried among the giggles. She'd known Bailey and Paula since they were all children. Living in the same neighborhood and going to the same schools, there wasn't much about them she didn't know. Now in their twenties, they'd all gone off to different colleges and each wore a slightly different veneer, but underneath they hadn't changed that much.

It was a cloudless day in May, and they were all sweating, ambling down Ocean Drive toward the air conditioning and raspberry iced tea of The Rising Sun, a preferred hangout among the hip, those aspiring to be, and those who didn't give a shit.

"Cool of them to send you to Europe as a graduation present," said Paula. "All I got was a car."

"I think my parents would buy me a small country if I would just go ahead and finish," said Bailey. They laughed, threading through the weekend crowd of tourists and locals.

Suzanne scanned the South Beach crowd around them. Mostly young, some white, some Latinos, some in hippie garb, the rest in bathing suits and shorts. It felt strange, being back, after having a foreign perspective for nearly a year. She wondered how involved any of these people were in the big issues of their times, like protesting the war in Vietnam or demonstrating for civil rights.

Hal's last letter to her before her return had mentioned riots in cities around the country in the wake of Martin Luther King Jr.'s assassination, but now, barely a month later, things in her old stomping grounds didn't seem much different from when she'd left. There were peace symbols everywhere, on clothing and posters and rock album covers, but how many people sporting those designs on their shirts and headbands would be willing to take part in a sit-in or risk police brutality for the sake of their convictions? Not many, she suspected.

For a lot of them, she guessed, the transformation was only skin-deep; there was a certain daring about going braless if you were a chick or wearing your hair long if you were a guy, but not as daring as, say, being tear-gassed for your support of the oppressed.

Which was pretty much her assessment of Bailey, who had always been a joiner of that sort. She looked sidelong at her friend, skipping along beside her: waist-length chestnut hair when it was down, no makeup, green tank top, no bra, Indian print sarong skirt with peace-sign button pinned to the waistband, handmade leather sandals, ankle bells, a stack of silver bangle bracelets on both arms, a rope of glass beads and tiny shells around her neck, and long silver dangle earrings with feathers in them. She was the perfect hippie poster child.

Paula, on the other hand, hadn't outgrown her preppie roots and still wore perfectly fitted white walking shorts with a pastel polo shirt and white Keds. Her brown hair was cut short, just above her shoulders. Although her speech was peppered with hippie slang, it was clear she had not embraced the concept of throwing out one's TV or giving up any other creature comforts. Suzanne could imagine Bailey moving into a commune just for the thrill of it, but not Paula.

Suzanne supposed she fell somewhere in between them. In her tie-dyed halter top and hiphugging cutoffs, she revealed more flesh than her mother would have liked, but her rope sandals came from Rome instead of some head shop in the East Village, and while she welcomed the idea of free love, she wasn't too pleased that some head case the others were crazy over wanted to know if she would have sex with him, for god's sake. Even if he was groovy.

Paula pushed open the Rising Sun Café's glass door, painted from top to bottom with primary-color psychedelic designs. "Merciful air conditioning," she said, looking over the crowded room. The others squeezed in behind her, where they waited to be seated.

The café was full and a hive of activity and noise, as usual. The Sun, as it was known to regulars, resembled a diner but carried on its business more like a Viennese coffee shop crossed with a vegetarian soup kitchen. Everyone from celebrities to campus radicals to sunburned tourists drank its espresso and ate its Jarlsberg omelets and hummus sandwiches with refillable homemade vegetable soup at all hours. Background music could range anywhere from John Coltrane to Ravi Shankar or The Grateful Dead.

The servers, in their black pants and black T-shirts with the orange and red sun logo over one breast, were quick on their feet and efficient, and familiar with the patrons in a cozy sort of way. The Sun had opened shortly after she'd left for Paris, and this was just her second visit since returning. It had not taken Hot-Waiter-Man, as her friends referred to him, very long to single her out.

"Warm enough for you ladies today?" he said, handing the menus around.

"It's cool in here," said Bailey, letting her long hair down and smiling at him in a way that made Suzanne cringe and want to kick her under the table. Paula giggled an octave higher than normal as she took the menu from his hand. To his credit, he seemed not to notice as he took their orders. Suzanne sank down in the booth.

"And you?" he said, making direct eye contact with her.

Suzanne returned his gaze with what she hoped was a no-nonsense expression.

"One Bavarian crème and a cappuccino."

"A lady with a sweet tooth," he said, writing on his order pad. She watched him angle his slim body through the press of patrons and waiters balancing trays on their arms, heading back to the kitchen.

"What did I say?" Bailey could barely contain herself. "Does he have a fine ass or what?"

Suzanne slouched back in her seat, looking at them. "Would you two just chill out? Yes, he's nice looking, but Jeez, so are a million other waiters in this town."

"You just don't appreciate a beautiful man when you see one," Bailey said.

"I saw plenty of beautiful men in Rome, but I didn't try to pick any of them up."

"Well, why not? I swear, Suzanne, you disappoint me. You should have been with me and Daniel when we went to San Francisco last year. Summer of Love. Now, *that* was a blast. That's where I got these." Bailey jingled the bracelets on her wrist.

"Here he comes again," said Paula. "Hey, did you see *that*?" They all turned to look. "That other waiter just patted Hot Waiter Man on the butt!"

"Far out!" exclaimed Bailey. "Even other guys are into him."

"You guys are too much," said Suzanne, as she watched him navigate the crowd with their drinks and desserts on a tray. He deftly placed each order in front of the right person, and next to Suzanne's pastry and coffee he set a small glass dish of cherries.

"I didn't order this—" She looked up at him, startled.

"A little something extra, for the pastry," he said and smiled. Before she could protest, he had disappeared into the crowd.

"See?" Bailey was pouting. "As far as he's concerned, we're in nowheresville. But for you, he brings cherries."

Suzanne popped one into her mouth. "I'll let you know if he's any good," she said.

"We hate you," said Paula.

They talked and finished their food to the last crumb, and after a while Hot Waiter Man returned, squatting down on his haunches, so that he could lean his elbows on the table as he sorted through his handful of checks to find theirs.

"So how was everything?" he asked, smiling all around.

"Tripping," said Bailey.

"Delicious, as always," Paula added.

"To be honest, I had a better one of these in Marseille," Suzanne said, touching her empty pastry plate with her fork, "but this one was good, too."

"Uh oh, I'd better not tell the chef," he said and stood up, leaning across the table to hand out their checks, and although he didn't touch her, Suzanne was acutely aware of how close his left hip was to her shoulder. She also noticed that his arms had the strangest tattoos she'd ever seen. Maybe he was more interesting than she'd first thought.

When he handed the check to her, it had another smaller card on top. He gave her a wink and quickly walked away. On the card was his photo and a name: Ned Waterston, Artist for Hire. She stared at the card. So Hot Waiter Man had a name. She turned the card over and saw that he had added a note in tiny crimped handwriting.

Both the other girls were leaning over the table.

"He passed you a *note*? I'm going to freak out right here!"

"Read it!"

Suzanne tucked the card into her purse. "He wrote, 'Make love, not war.' Satisfied?"

"We hate you," said Paula.

After they'd paid their bills and wandered along the beach till well past noon, they said their goodbyes, Bailey and Paula driving away in her new Thunderbird. Suzanne, standing by the open door of Hal's Cadillac that she'd borrowed for the day, waved to them and waited till they turned the corner. Then, instead of getting in, she shut the door and locked it, and headed back down the block toward the Sun. As usual, there was a crowd lingering around the entrance, either waiting to get in or just talking and hanging out. She quickly scanned the faces and didn't see him, so she sat down on the sidewalk and leaned against the wall of the building. Fishing around in her purse for the card, she found it and read the note again. What it really said was, "I get off in an hour. Meet me out front?"

So here she was, waiting out front for a complete stranger who might be a really nice guy, but might also be some crazed dope fiend who would drag her into a darkened alley and do God knew what.

"Hey, you did show up. Way out." The man named Ned reached his hand down and helped her up. "What's your name?"

"Suzanne Blacksburg," she answered, ignoring all the warnings she'd ever had pounded into her about giving her full name out to guys she didn't know. "Um, what did you want?"

Ned smiled. "Just your company. The first time I saw your face, I felt that you were someone special."

"Boy, that's an old line."

"It's not a line. It's the truth." She could see that he was serious, no smile this time.

"My two buddies are nuts over you, why not one of them?"

"You mean the hippie chick and the prep school princess? Definitely not my bag."

"And I am?"

"Most definitely you are." Ned slid his arm around her waist and started walking away from the restaurant. He'd changed out of his waiter's uniform and now wore a faded work shirt and jeans with holes in the knees. In his free hand he carried a small gym bag, which she assumed contained his waiter's uniform.

"Hey, want to get stoned? I live just a couple of blocks away. I'm not holding, but Crash won't care if we raid his stash. Come on up to my pad, and I'll show you my etchings."

That was so corny it made her laugh. This Ned person seemed nice enough, and he was really easy on the eyes. He was smiling at her, definitely hustling her, but Suzanne hardly cared; she was charmed.

"What're you thinking?" He looked at her with his funny yellow-blue eyes.

* * *

"I don't even know you. Where are you from?" she asked as they walked arm-in-arm across the empty street toward a row of older hotels that weren't undergoing restoration like the flashier ones near Ocean Drive.

"Here and there."

"No, I mean originally."

"I lived in San Francisco for awhile."

"I'd love to go there. Bailey and her boyfriend drove across the country last summer just to see what it was all about. "

Ned chewed at his lip. "I was there before it was cool. Left about the time it was getting too popular."

"I still wish I could see it. What did you do there? Sorry if that's too nosey. I'm just curious. I like to travel and see new places."

He gave her a squeeze. "I was a street artist, doing quick sketches of strangers and sometimes telling their fortunes. I quit doing that after awhile though; it was starting to weird me out."

Suzanne stopped walking. "Wow, are you psychic?"

"Naw, it's just part of the act. I'm really a hustler."

"You are that," said Suzanne. She was smiling.

They walked for another block, and then Ned aimed across the street to the entrance of a fading pastel pink hotel.

"Get that look off your face," he said. "It's a residence hotel. People live here permanently. It's not a flophouse."

"Oh. Like an artist's colony or something," she said, looking up at the frosted glass blocks that framed the entrance.

Ned led her inside where it was cool and the décor sea-green. She was relieved to see that the lobby was reasonably respectable, and there were no obvious dope dealers hanging around. She began to relax.

Ned steered her across the lobby to the elevators. As soon as the door clacked shut and the cab lurched into motion, Suzanne panicked again and wished she hadn't come. But now, she had gone much too far to retreat.

They stopped at the second floor, and Ned led her down the hall. By the time he got his key in the lock and the door to the apartment open, she was playing out several possible scenarios in her mind, none of them good. Here was her chance to sample the free love and recreational drug scene she'd believed people had a right to enjoy, and instead she was looking the place over for an escape route.

The door opened into a tiny sitting room. From there she could see a kitchenette and two bedrooms of roughly the same size. "That one belongs to Crash, my suite-mate. This one's mine." Ned went to the room straight ahead and she followed.

"Have a seat," he said, gesturing to his mattress. It sat in the center of the bedroom, flat on the floor with no bedstead. A tangle of sheets suggested it was the most-used element of the room. "Ah, sorry, it's a mess. I wasn't expecting company."

Ned was just standing there, hands in his pockets, looking at her in a very unnerving way.

"What?" She sat down on the edge of the bed, shoving a pile of *Zap Comix* out of the way.

"Something I never expected to see," he said.

He stepped out of the room, and Suzanne took a closer look at his surroundings. Ned's bedroom was mostly empty of any real furniture, the main pieces being the mattress and a precarious set of bookshelves against one wall. Albums by the Doors, Cream, and Miles Davis littered the floor among discarded pizza boxes, random shoes, socks, and whatever he'd apparently worn and peeled off. At least, she noted, there didn't seem to be any women's clothing in evidence. The room had no seating except for a small folding chair next to a card table where all his art supplies were spread out.

A full-sized black-light poster of Jimi Hendrix took up most of one wall and an Indian mandala print covered the one opposite. But on the wall with the single window, she saw nearly a dozen drawings and watercolors pinned or taped in a mosaic of color

"Toke?" he said, returning with a lighted joint between his fingers. He inhaled deeply and sat down beside her, and then held the joint to her lips.

Suzanne inhaled slightly, just enough to be polite. She wasn't a total novice where pot was concerned, but she wasn't a pothead, which this Ned person clearly was.

"Just so you know, I didn't come up here to get high and have sex with you," she said, blushing.

Ned let out a laugh and fell back on the bed. "Well, I'm glad we got that sorted out." He continued to laugh, watching her with an expression she found more than disturbing.

Then he sat up, the laughter in his eyes gone. "I didn't bring you here for that, groovy as I'm sure it would be. I wanted to show you something."

He got up and went to a packing crate that held a jumble of books and file folders. He opened a folder and pulled out a piece of paper torn from a spiral sketch pad.

Suzanne caught her breath as she took it from him. It was an amazing likeness of her own face, with this very hotel sketched in behind her. Her face went slack-jawed.

"How ...?"

"Yeah, that's my question, too. I drew that picture a couple of years ago, before I even knew where Miami was on the map. I've been looking for you, Suzanne Blacksburg, ever since." He sat down on the floor beside her feet.

"I don't believe this." She stared at the drawing, trying to make it look like somebody else.

"I would never have known where to look if it hadn't been for the hotel in the background," he said. "Took me a couple of years bumming up and down the Florida coast, but as soon as I saw it, I knew this was the place. Since then I've just been waiting, and hoping, for you to show up."

She put the paper down beside her and looked at him carefully for the first time. He was older than she'd thought, with creases around his mouth that gave his face character. Suzanne realized her palms were sweaty. "Well, now that you've found me, what happens?"

"Right on, now we're getting somewhere." He smiled again, and the stress lines went away. "You asked me if I was psychic." He paused, and she waited. "I get … visions, sometimes, when I draw or paint. I channel images of places and things that make no sense to me."

"Well, yeah, mind-expanding drugs'll do that for you."

"No. I'm straight when this kind of thing happens, with one exception."

Suddenly Ned grunted, apparently in pain. Suzanne was shocked to see that he was trembling.

"Um, Ned, what's the matter? Are you sick?" It couldn't have been the grass, because she'd taken a decent hit and felt fine. She knelt down on the floor beside him.

"What's wrong?" And then she screamed out loud, falling backward away from him. He had looked up at her with reddish-yellow cat's eyes and a hideously contorted face that resembled something vaguely serpentine. She blinked and looked again, but now he seemed normal, although his attractive features were bathed in sweat. He was shaking all over.

"Help me, Suzanne," he said hoarsely. "I think you're the only one who can."

Against her better judgment, she knelt beside him again and put her arms around him, the urge to protect stronger than her urge to flee.

"If I can, I will," she said, wondering what door she had just opened.

He slid his arms around her waist and held tight. She squeezed him back and wondered what the hell was that look she'd just seen, a pot hallucination? Suzanne considered herself a rational, fairly self-confident person who was independent and not afraid to go places and do things on her own, but this was nothing she had any experience with.

"Promise you won't leave me," he said, his face buried in her hair.

"I promise." A shiver skittered over her shoulders and up her neck as she held him. The grass must have been stronger than she'd judged, making his touch seem both warm and cold at the same time. Was he fevered?

Suzanne gently rubbed the muscles of his back, which did not give an inch. There was no extra fat on him, no pliant cushioning. He seemed hard traveled, with few possessions, if this room was an accurate indication. And here she was, cradling him in her arms, as if they had been together forever.

Bailey and Paula would have had their minds blown if they could've seen. Hal certainly wouldn't approve, and she supposed her parents wouldn't either, but she knew instinctively this was not a moment that would be shared with anyone. Maybe not ever. For better or worse, she had stepped off a cliff with a complete stranger, without even looking to see what lay at the bottom.

Chapter 16

August 5, Friday — Present Day

The lights in the Hardison Museum's Learning Center auditorium came up a bit too abruptly. Alice yawned and rubbed her eyes.

"Hey there, wake up." Hannah nudged her shoulder.

"Thanks, I was losing it." She stood up and yawned again. "I hope I didn't snore." She'd been anticipating Fjodor's presentation all week and couldn't believe she'd zoned out through most of it.

Fjodor Kamensky, paleozoologist and the museum's Natural Sciences Curator, was newly returned from his sabbatical, during which he'd been researching mammoths in Iceland and Siberia, and it was his slide show that had put Alice to sleep.

Hanna poked her in the ribs. "Here comes your friend."

Milton Crouch was headed down the aisle toward them, waving.

"Hey, Alice, I got something for you."

"What would that be?" She gave him a half-smile. He was dressed in his usual baggy khakis, rundown deck shoes, and polo shirt. This one was red.

"I know you're interested in that old church, so I xeroxed some stuff for you from my personal clippings file. Folder's on my desk ... wanna come get it?"

In spite of her renewed resolve to never, ever, get sucked into anything having to do with the First Church of the Heavenly Powers or whatever the hell it had been called, Alice found herself saying, "Thanks, I will."

"Super!" He lumbered off in the direction of the elevators and she followed, determined to take a quick look at his stuff and go back up to her office without it.

In the basement, Alice followed Milton through the Conservation lab double doors and back to his desk. He was still situated against the wall behind the receptionist.

"When's Shelton going to find you a proper office?"

Milton laughed like a dog barking. "Oh, he's been trying to get me to move upstairs, but I told him I like it down here where the real action is." He indicated the tank room where shipwreck cannons lay submerged in water, waiting to be cleaned and preserved. Then he picked up a manila folder from his desk and handed it to her.

"So, whattaya think?"

Big old sloppy dog, trying his best to please. If he'd had a tail it would have been wagging in huge loops around his backside. Alice took the folder. Opening it, she caught her breath. The headline on the first page read, "Rural Church Hit Twice by Lightning."

She skimmed the brief article for details, reading that the empty building had been struck along its tin roof on two separate days during a spate of thunderstorms in April of 1965. Firemen had arrived just in time to make sure the flames did not eat further into the structure. There was also mention of the property being owned by St. Christopher's A.M.E. church. Alice turned to the next page.

The second clipping was from early 1945. Its headline was more disturbing: "Pastor Killed in Construction Site Accident." Two small photos accompanied the story; one showed the partially finished stone façade of the present-day St. Christopher's church, and the other was a studio portrait of a grim-faced black minister. The article described how Antoine Rider, pastor of the church in the photo, had been standing under a scaffold that held a large quantity of bricks and building stone. Although no one had directly witnessed the event, it was surmised that one end of the scaffolding had given way, dumping the load of building material down onto his head, crushing his skull. Alice put her hand to her mouth.

"Pretty strong stuff, huh? And there's more," said Milton, his eyes watching her a little too eagerly.

"But this happened on the new church property, not the old," said Alice, trying to connect the dots in her head.

Milton shrugged. "Yeah, but it's the same congregation, right?"

Alice looked back to the last sheet of paper.

"That one there's the clipping I told you about. Remember? The whacked-out guy who built the old church in the first place? A bad luck customer from the get-go, if you ask me."

Alice felt a familiar shiver of fear running under her skin. The clipping from the *Massalina Countian* was dated Monday, February 19, 1900. Her brain was telling her to stop right now, but her eyes were scanning the page, looking for the name of the demon, and there it was: "... the Reverend Cadjer Harrow, founder of the small church on Old Sawgrass Road, was found dead on Sunday evening inside the church." Hopelessly hooked, she read on.

This was not his obituary, which she'd already found in the library folder material that had once belonged to Cecil Rider, but rather an article written the day after his death. "... Harrow was found dead on Sunday evening inside the church along with his deacon, Jefferson Rodney Lathe, of Massalina County. According to witnesses who found the bodies lying in the church belfry, they appeared to have been hit directly by the lightning strike that entered the bell tower and split the bell during thunderstorms that rumbled through the area on Sunday. Burial plans for Rev. Harrow will be announced by the Tanner family, with arrangements through Patterson Undertakers."

"Who's the Tanner family?" Alice asked, looking up.

Milton shrugged. "Dunno. How are they mentioned?"

"They made the funeral arrangements for this Reverend Harrow. Were they relatives or something?"

"Easy enough to find out, I betcha," said Milton. "I can look, if you want."

Alice felt prickles along her scalp. "Would you? Just as a matter of curiosity."

"Sure!" Milton's tail was wagging again. "I got friends in the Historical Society who could probably show me which county records to pick through."

"Really? I'd be curious to see what you can dig up." Alice was kicking herself. "Well, I have to go. I promised Fjodor I'd stop by and discuss mammoth hunting."

"He's amazing, isn't he? That must have been a fun adventure he went on."

"Fun. You bet. Thanks for these." She waved the folder toward him.

"No prob. I'll get back to you on the Tanners."

Alice nodded and was out the door in a dozen steps.

Holy hell, what was she doing? This was insane, mucking around in Harrow's past again. She'd hoped he was gone forever, swept away to wherever by Namarrkun in that mind-numbing act of retribution that had sent her out of body and out of her mind. It had taken weeks afterward to pull herself together, with the support of Margaret and Nik. Bless Shelton for giving her a leave of absence. As the museum boss, he knew she was having emotional problems of some kind, but that was all.

Going out of the country with Nik and away from anything connected to Massalina County or Aboriginal Australians had been the best medicine of all, as it turned out. Nik's parents knew nothing of Alice's difficulties, but they were friendly and more than a little curious to meet this divorced woman who'd snared their unmarried son. The only downside of the trip had been leaving Margaret behind with Alice's sister-in-law, so her schooling wouldn't be disrupted.

So what was she doing, prying into old secrets again? She tucked the manila folder under her arm and caught the elevator going up.

Back in her office, she shut the door and sat at her computer, thinking. Her mind drifted to her mother's funeral, and then to the briefcase of Suzanne's letters, and back to the funeral. And finally, reluctantly, to the hotel dream. Even days afterward she couldn't shake off the dread that filled her whenever she thought of it. Logically, she supposed it was a suppressed reaction to Suzanne's death after the reality of the funeral. The landscape was already in her subconscious from having seen Ned's paintings a few days before. But it didn't feel like only that. It felt real.

Alice closed her eyes and massaged the back of her neck. She was getting a tension headache. Her thoughts were drifting down a dangerous path, beginning to accept the possibility that those places existed, and that Ned had gone there or seen them in a dream state, just the way she had. Alice rubbed her temples. She was losing it again, starting to think the Dreamtime world was real. But how else had the apparition of Harrow gotten into this world and confronted her in a physical body? Accepting that episode as real also meant admitting the Dreamtime Ancestors could come out of Sky Home to retrieve him.

Her mind was fragged. She'd read that Aboriginals believed experienced shamans could go between worlds on errands for their tribes and come safely back to this one. Was it just a mind trip they went on, or something physical, too? Could a person exist in more than one dimension … and why should anybody even think such a thing was possible?

Alice shut her eyes, thinking. Those who tended the sacred sites, the Senior Aboriginal men and women of High Degree, understood how the Ancestors had infused the places of this earth with their presence. What their rock art taught was that there is no separation between the waking world of humans and the Dreamtime realm of the Ancestors who had created the physical world. It was all one to them, a single continuum of existence.

How was Ned connected to all this? And what did that imply for herself and especially for Margaret? She reached for the aspirin in her desk drawer and gulped a few down without water.

Chapter 17

July 1968

Rockets shot up from the beach and burst overhead in a shower of red, white, and blue stars that flamed out over the Atlantic Ocean. On a clear, moonless night like tonight, the effect was dazzling. The City of Miami had spared no expense for its Fourth of July celebration, including live music, street vendors, arts and crafts, and the requisite fireworks extravaganza that was billed as bigger and better than last year's show.

Suzanne remembered coming down to South Beach for the Independence Day festivities every year with her family when she was little and with a gang of friends when she was in high school. But this was the first time she'd sat in the sand on the beach and watched the display in the company of a boyfriend.

Well, she couldn't really call him a boyfriend because she'd discovered that he was nearly eight years older than she. Suzanne frowned, remembering her brother Hal's reaction; he hadn't been happy at all when she'd told him about her new love interest. She'd kissed Hal on the cheek and told him to stop being so critical. Not that it mattered; she would see anybody she wanted, family opinions be damned.

They were two weeks into a relationship, and she could tell that Ned wasn't going away; in fact, he seemed to take it for granted that their attachment was permanent. Such a headlong rush made her uneasy, and she'd said so. He was undeterred. There'd been no further episodes like the one she'd witnessed that first day in his apartment, and she'd convinced herself that what she'd seen in his face was just her stoned imagination at work. All told, things between them had been progressing smoothly, to the naked envy of her friends.

A grand finale of Roman candles exploded, sending multicolored balls and expanding plumes of light high in the sky while set pieces on the ground created fountains of flame and waterfalls of silver and gold in an overwhelming five-minute barrage of light and sound.

The show over, spectators packed up their lawn chairs and wandered back down Ocean Drive while many more stayed on the beach, listening to the music of local bands and taking in the real stars overhead.

"Look, isn't it beautiful? You see the Milky Way!"

Suzanne leaned against Ned's shoulder. They sat quietly, comfortable in each other's company. They had made love for the first time that afternoon, and now Suzanne felt wrapped in that intangible sense of well-being she attributed to being completely in synch, physically and emotionally, with another person.

* * *

Ned put his arm around Suzanne and drew her close. He knew he'd made the right decision about her. But now that he'd found her, what were they supposed to do together, other than the obvious? Her face, in this place, had been sent to him in his trance-drawing state, but what now?

Ned was deep in these thoughts when she'd said something to him about the Milky Way and the stars overhead. It brought him out of his meanderings long enough to note how the sky was dusted with pinpoints of light against a black velvet backdrop. Such a contrast to the lurid colors and surreal cloudbanks that filled the skies of his head-trip art. That art, which his sellers labeled "psychedelic," was a major part of his livelihood, yet it still frightened him in a way that sometimes froze his blood. He thought of the designs his childish hands had made for his mother: suns with hollow eyes, snakes and spirals and braided waving lines, and upside down stick figures with spears and long phalluses, which he hadn't recognized as such until he'd become a teenager. He had no idea what they represented, but she claimed the charms made from ashes of the paper he'd drawn on were more potent than ordinary potions. Ned shivered, remembering.

He was feeling ill at ease, which was a bummer, because he should have been relaxed, with a sense of fulfillment. Suzanne was a fine lay and turned out to be much less inhibited than he'd expected. She was intelligent, worldly, and pretty in a small-boned way. He also realized that she reminded him of Mary Catherine, who'd held him in her circle of warmth while he fought for his sanity on the hotel bathroom floor three years ago. On the surface, life here was good. He had a great crash pad, no debts to speak of, and he'd found a woman he was beginning to think long-term thoughts about. So why did he feel like shit?

"Ready to go back?" he asked, brushing his lips over the nape of her neck.

He liked the feel of her arm around his waist, walking back to the hotel, and he hoped Suzanne regarded him as more than just an exotic fuck buddy. She hadn't been put off by the scale pattern on his forearms, had even claimed they were a turn-on, so why was he so jittery?

"Neddy?" She'd asked him something, but it sailed past him.

"Sorry, baby, I missed that. What did you say?"

Suzanne was looking at him in that direct way of hers. "I just said you seemed spaced out. Are you okay?"

"Nothing a little weed and a back rub wouldn't fix." He hugged her slender shoulders. The thought came into his head that she was so slightly built she could be crushed like a dragonfly. He needed to be careful.

"Well, I can't help with the weed, but I can do the second part," she said, smiling up at him.

She was so pretty, with her red hair and dark blue eyes. He felt a moment's pang. She deserved better. Wherever he was headed, it was gonna be a rough ride. But she'd been sent to him, or he'd been pushed toward her, so there it was. Ever since that one awful moment when she'd glimpsed the demon within, he'd kept a tight lid on his psyche.

When they got back to the apartment, the door of the second bedroom was shut, with a *Better Living Through Chemistry* bumper sticker taped to it.

"Crash is home, I see," said Ned. No doubt some serious acid test was in progress, so he knew not to disturb.

He gave Suzanne a squeeze. "Why don't you get some coffee started while I roll up a few jays. Then we'll have our own private party."

"Okay, just don't start without me."

He watched her heading off to the kitchen, thinking how much he wanted them to be a couple on equal footing and hoping he wouldn't have to keep his secrets hidden from her too much longer. He pulled a baggie from under the mattress and rolled up a fat joint, using all that was left and eating the few seeds that remained.

Ned put *Sketches of Spain,* that strangest of Miles Davis albums, on the turntable. It was perfect—jagged and raw, exactly the way he felt inside. He was living in Edge City, man, and this little domestic dance they were performing was only a prelude to some madness he felt but couldn't see.

Before long, she came in with two steaming mugs. He lit up, and they smoked and drank in silence until the record ended.

"There's something wrong, isn't there?" She was staring at him again, trying to look inside. Ned studied the floorboards.

"I don't even know where to start." He felt the bones of her hand, thin and birdlike. "I'm very attached to you, Suzanne."

"Is that a problem? Are you married or something?"

Ned let out a laugh. "No, baby, I'm definitely not married. Never have been."

She wasn't smiling. "Then what? Is it my brother? He isn't thrilled about us, but so what? I'm twenty-three. I do what I want."

"Your brother is absolutely not my problem. This is." He showed her the insides of his arms, where the scale design was visible even in the subdued lighting of the bedroom.

She touched his skin, running her fingers over the pattern in a way that made him shiver. The scales were dark enough to appear three-dimensional although the skin was smooth to the touch. He'd rubbed his fingers over those designs too many times himself, trying to understand how and why he'd been marked like that.

She was doing it now, rubbing her fingers against his skin, seeking a texture that wasn't there. "I did notice that your tattoos had changed color and thought it was kind of strange. I thought maybe you were having an allergic reaction." She was holding his arm in her lap.

"They aren't tattoos," said Ned.

"Then what are they?"

"What would you say if I told you a snake put them on me?"

Suzanne blinked, but didn't laugh. That was good, because Ned was losing his nerve and had almost decided he'd made a mistake, opening up like that. It was the grass; that stuff was stronger than the last batch Crash sold him.

Suzanne was speaking slowly and carefully, trying, he supposed, to find her way through the cannabis fog to the right words. "I'm willing to believe," she said, "that there could be some level of existence beyond what we see and touch. Getting stoned gives you a glimpse of what that expanded state might be like. On the other hand, I've never had a supernatural experience, so I don't understand how you could've gotten those marks that way. But if you want to tell me how you think it happened, I'm willing to listen."

"Fair enough." So then it all came out—how he'd grown up in a Florida swamp with his mother who handled snakes and that he'd helped her until he'd run away from home at age sixteen, then got bitten by a rattler and recovered without hospital treatment, and when he'd finally come to, his skin had changed from freckled and pale to his current olive complexion with the snakeskin designs. He skipped telling her how his forearms had been previously scarred by his mother's fish-gutting knife. Some day he might get around to explaining that part, but not now. And the exact fate of his mother and what she'd turned into before her death was not going be told to anyone, ever.

Ned got up and retrieved the folder that contained his drawing of Suzanne. "Let me show you this." He handed her another page, and watched as she held it up.

"What is it?"

"Good question. I have no idea, but I drew it the same day I made that picture of you."

"It looks like a native shield. Is it African?"

Ned shrugged. "I drew it in that trance I told you about."

"Drawing the magic," she said softly. "Can you do it whenever you want? I mean, do the spirits or whatever need to be there when you start to draw?"

Ned let out his breath, relieved she hadn't bolted for the door.

"No, I can't, and that's the worst part. I don't know why they come when they do. It's a bad scene. No, it's worse. The first time it happened, I was only a little kid. It scared me shitless, and I didn't even know enough to be *really* scared, because I didn't have any guidelines for a reality check. Now I do, and I know that something about me is really fucked up."

Suzanne was squeezing his hand, her attention fixed on his face. "What's it like, Neddy?" she whispered. "When they come?"

"If I tell you, you might decide Hal's right, that you shouldn't get mixed up with me." Ned tightened his grip. "I'm not a normal person."

"I knew that when I met you," she said.

Ned pulled her close, holding her against his chest, her hair in his face. He'd wanted for years to confess his weirdness to somebody, but he'd never dared before now. He'd danced around it with Cecil Rider, but couldn't give the old man too many details or it would've come out that he'd murdered his mother with a shovel to the head because she'd changed into something that talked with her voice but looked like all Hell. He'd gone berserk and didn't remember the details of how it went down, but in the end he'd stopped the creature and followed his first instinct, which was to burn the house to the ground. It had taken a monumental act of courage to go back there after so many years, but by following that urge he'd been given a vision and what seemed to be a mission. It was that part, figuring out the mission, where Suzanne came in.

"This thing I drew," he said, "it's a magical object, some kind of holy grail. In the trance, I saw how it got created for a tribe by one of their gods. Then something happened to it, stolen or something. But really, I'm just guessing. The snake spirit I channeled said I'm supposed to return it. But how can I return something I don't even have?"

"Why don't you go into a trance and just ask what it is?"

Ned shook his head. "I've tried, and like I said, they don't answer when I do that, or they'll give me some damned cryptic vision like I just described to you." He took a breath. He remembered asking his mother what was wrong with him, but all she'd said was that it was blood magic, which he now understood was probably why she'd wanted to marry his father.

When Suzanne lifted her face, he was tempted to just kiss her and forget about this shit with visions and snake demons, but he was so close to telling what had been withheld for so long that he didn't want to stop.

"Anything else?" Her eyes looked afraid, but he could tell she wanted to hear.

"When I got the snakebite that I told you about, just before I blacked out, I hallucinated a snake goddess or something that talked to me. I don't know if she was real or just in my head, but she told me I had to fix something, find something that was missing. I think she saved me, because I woke up days later still alive instead of dead." He let that sink in.

"Is that what I saw, that first day when we came here—your snake goddess?"

"I don't think so," he said, certain it had been the other she'd seen, because he'd felt its chilling presence along his spine. He felt her stiffen in her arms.

"I don't want anything to happen to you, Neddy. I want to be with you, just like you are now."

Ned too wanted that more than anything, but the odds, as he figured them, were about as good as a dragonfly in the path of a semi.

Chapter 18

August 6, Saturday — Present Day

Margaret, Lissa, Judy, and Tom walked in a clump along the narrow sidewalk leading back to the dorm. The streaks of a salmon pink sunset lingered against the darker backdrop of approaching night.

"Are you really gonna do it?" Margaret asked, walking beside Tom.

"Like, yeah. Nobody in their right mind would turn down a chance to sneak out after hours with Devin." Margaret knew Tom would score major points if she pulled that off. Devin was a wicked mix of computer nerdiness and soccer-player hunkiness, plus he was almost sixteen.

Judy looked back at her. "What're you and Devin gonna do?"

"Something you don't know how to do yet." Tom said this in her typical husky monotone. Tom wasn't smiling, but Margaret could sense the smirk in her undertone. If anything, she was teasing them, making them believe she was more world wise than she might really be. That was just Tom.

Back in the dorm, they congregated in Tom and Margaret's room with sodas and doughnuts from the dorm vending machines.

"Happy birthday," Judy said and hugged Margaret hard.

"Yeah, hurry up and open those presents!" Lissa handed her a wrapped gift and watched with a wicked smile as she tore off the paper. It was *Seize the Night*, volume seven of Sherrilyn Kenyon's erotic Dark Hunter vampire series, which received appropriate nods and nudges as it got passed around.

"See? It's signed!" Lissa found the title page and held it up. "My brother got that at a sci-fi convention he went to."

Margaret stared at the signature, properly in awe. "If Mom sees it's signed by a famous writer, you think she'll let me keep it?"

They all cracked up, and Margaret picked up Judy's package in its red wrapping paper.

"Jude-dude!" She held up the box of chocolates. "Omigod, you are made of WIN!" She took the lid off and passed the box around.

Her mouth full of caramel crème, she opened Tom's gift last. As the shiny black paper and silver ribbon came off, she could see that it was an anime DVD. Margaret stopped chewing.

"*Descendants of Darkness*! Tom-tom, this is beyond cool! I can't believe you got me this!" Tom, whose face was normally a mask of neutral non-expression, was actually smiling.

The others crowded around. "Wow, can we watch it now?"

Margaret was grinning. "We might as well, 'cause there's no way I can watch this at home, especially not with Nik. He'd faint!"

The girls whooped with laughter.

"Can't you just see it," gasped Lissa. "The Nikster discovers yaoi!" Yaoi, the forbidden love of impossibly beautiful men for each other as expressed in Japanese anime, was only one of the things Tom had introduced them to. That would come to a halt once camp was over and Thomasina Redfern went back to her ultra-cool life in Orlando, Margaret knew. But for now, she was determined to soak up every drop of decadence camp had to offer.

"Be sure to give me your emails before we leave," Tom said, "so I can send you links to my favorite online manga reader sites. They have all the best stuff—uncensored peens and everything."

Margaret joined in the squeals. She wasn't entirely sure what a "peen" was, but she hoped it was what she thought. Tom was nothing if not educational.

Tom popped disc one of *Descendants* into her computer, maximized the screen, and they all gathered around as the title segment began to play. They giggled and watched and hit Pause and Replay for over an hour until a knock at the outside hallway door brought a quick silence. Tom minimized the screen, and Margaret got up to let in their quad's camp counselor.

"Hi, girls. Everybody accounted for?" Melissa checked off their names on her clipboard.

"Have a birthday chocolate." Margaret held out the box.

Melissa's hand hovered over the bonbons, dowsing for the right one. "Yum, chocolate-covered cherry. Happy fourteen, Margrits." She gave her a hug and went to the door. "Good night, all."

"Goodnight," they chorused.

As soon as the door was shut, the four of them collapsed onto Tom's bed, consumed with conspiratorial laughter.

"Okay," said Tom. "Let's finish this puppy off. I gotta get ready to go meet Devin."

They watched the end of *Descendants*, and Margaret carefully packed it back in its box. As Judy and Lissa left to go watch *Scream* on Lissa's portable TV, she gave Tom a quick smile and said, "You rule. Thanks."

Tom nodded. "There's plenty more where that came from," she said, pointing to the box of DVDs beside the computer. "Knock yourself out while I'm gone."

"Be careful, okay? I don't want us to get busted."

"No worries. Devin's good buddies with his floor warden. It'll be cool."

Margaret watched as Tom got dressed in full Goth gear, blew her a kiss from purple-tinted lips, and slipped out. Her exit from the main hallway door was so quiet Margaret didn't even hear the latch close.

Sitting alone on her bed, she yawned and opened the book Lissa had given her. She'd only read a few pages into the story when a wood tick fell out of her hair onto the page. Momentarily freaked, Margaret dropped the book. Living in the rural south all her life, she'd grown up with the ubiquitous presence of ticks, but that didn't keep her from being repulsed whenever she found one on her. She must have picked this one up during the field trip to the St. Mark's lighthouse on the coast that afternoon. The woodland scrub surrounding the lighthouse was notoriously full of ticks and redbugs, chiggers to the locals.

She looked under the book, but couldn't find the tiny creature. Mentally running through her vocabulary of curses, she scanned every inch of the bedspread where she'd been sitting. The effing thing had gone invisible. There was no way she was sleeping on this bed tonight until it was found, so she ran her fingers all over her pillows and sheets, but still couldn't find it. Then she spotted the tiny black body crawling up her arm in the slow, methodical way ticks do. She pinched it between thumb and forefinger and forced it onto the surface of the computer desk.

"Die!" she said, and impaled it with the point of a pair of scissors before it could crawl away. Then she brushed it into the trash basket. Unnerved, Margaret put her book away and sat down at the computer. Reaching for the mouse, she felt something brush her hand and thought for a minute she'd glimpsed something fall onto the mouse pad, but when she looked, there was nothing to see.

"Damn tick," she said, hoping it was the only one. Just the thought made her itchy all over.

She quickly logged onto the Internet and went to her favorite forum. Down in the forum stats, where it listed the birthdays for the day, she saw her own handle GOKU, and sure enough, Kinigar had started a "Birthday Wishes" topic for her in the Raves section. She sent him a silent kiss toward the screen. In the Miscellaneous Rants section, she started a new topic called "Ticks—we hates em!" where she described her tick execution and invited anybody else with a tick story to post. She saw that Kinigar was still online, so she pinged him. He responded immediately.

"Happy birfday, Goku! *throws cake at u*" he wrote.

"Heya! Thankees. Remember I told you my roomie here at camp took meh pic with her digital camera? Here it is, shield your eyes." She attached the picture of herself sitting on her bunk, smiling and waving at the camera. "BTW, I'm Margaret in Florida, in the US. Is Kinigar your real name? What does it mean?" She hit SEND.

Margaret counted the seconds, and by the time she'd reached thirty, Kinigar responded.

"Bloody hell Margaret, U R hot. Got any more? Yesh, Kinigar is meh name. The parent's big joke coz we got Aboriginals on my dad's side. Pretty far back I think. My cousin's great uncle is a senior man, u know what that means?"

Margaret read that last part bouncing in her chair. She wrote back as fast as she could type.

"Bloody hell Kini! I do know. Does he cast spells n stuff?"

"Dunno, mate. I never met him. I just heard my aunt talk about him once or twice. But I know a little about some of the stuff they do. My aunt and Mum told me Dreamtime stories when I was little. Ask if u want to know anything. Kinigar is Dreamtime evil cat-man. He's got the head, body, and tail of a cat, and arms & legs of a man. In legends he was bloodthirsty and fearless and all the creatures were scared shitless of him. He was killed by the owl and the crow that tricked him with an ambush. A spark of his body went up to the Milky Way. Another spark flew out and made the native cat. Cool huh? Meh other name is Jason but I dun use it. Kini is fine by me."

As Margaret was reading this latest message, a slight movement in her peripheral vision made her stop and look. She sat quietly, breathing in small shallow sucks of air. Now that she was looking directly at the spot, she could see that nothing was amiss.

She turned back to Kini's message and saw an attachment. She clicked on it, and the image of a tanned teenage boy wearing rumpled khaki walking shorts and no shirt filled the screen. His feet were securely shod in heavy hiking boots with white socks showing over the laced-up tops. A little on the wiry side, he looked to be of average height, at least in relation to the truck he leaned against. He had an open, cheerful face with a shock of blondish-brownish sunstreaked hair that curled over his forehead and around the nape of his neck. Margaret stared and stared. He was too good to be true.

"Kini-kun, is that u? XD!! *pounces on u*" she wrote back.

"Hehe, yesh, that's me next to my dad's truck. Glad u like it. Meh dad's a schoolteacher. It drives him crazy mad cuz I can't spell fer fuk heh heh. It's just me and Dad, since Mum moved out. Dad's girlfriend sometimes stays with us but I dun like her much. Long story, won't bore you. What color are ur eyes? They look black. Mine are brown. Can I call u Mar-chan?"

Margaret was getting all warm and fuzzy inside. The addition of the Japanese name suffix "chan" was the female equivalent of "kun," which she had brazenly appended to the shortened form of his name. Both indicated a playful familiarity with a close friend, but they could also mean endearment, especially when attached to a shortened first name. Were they inching toward a virtual relationship? Margaret felt tingly all over. Something tickled her cheek, and she absently brushed her hair away from her face, reading Kini's message again and soaking up his picture. She would have to get Tom to copy it off on a CD or e-mail it to her so she didn't lose it when Tom went home after camp.

Margaret wrote back: "Kini-kun, what do u know about Quinkans? I want a spell to banish one. Dunt laff, 'K?"

She hit SEND and waited. Behind her, something clearly went bump. She whipped around in her chair, but saw nothing. Margaret held her breath and stared at the back of the room where the closets were. She was starting to get that anxious, hunted feeling she'd had in that dream back in the hotel room in Miami. Checking the time on the computer clock, she saw it was just after midnight. Maybe Tom would come back soon. Tom was so totally unafraid and self-confident, Margaret couldn't imagine her ever getting spooked by strange noises in an empty dorm room.

She glanced back at the computer screen and saw a new message from Kinigar scrolling down the IM window.

"Mar-chan, Quinkans are evil spirits, they lure kidz away from their parents and eat em so they can make more Quinkans. They can sound like the voices of the kidz moms and dads, they can pretend to be anything they want and u cant tell the difference. I heard about em from my Mum when I was a kid, prolly to keep me from wandering away from the house. Seriousleh, they r bad news!"

She typed: "How do u get rid of one?"

"You got to be a shaman to do that," he wrote back. "I bet my cousin's uncle dude could. I could never be a shaman cuz therz no way I'm having me front teeth knocked out or my dick cut on, ya know? No fukkin way! That would really suck. I can't think of anything else at the mo but can ask around if u want."

"Kini, I think there's something in the room with me."

"Mar-chan, r u by yerself? What time is it over there?" She saw he'd appended a question-mark smiley to the message.

Something fell over near the closet on Tom's side of the room. Margaret stood up. This time, she could see that Tom's tennis racket, which had been leaning against the wall, was lying flat on the floor along with the oversized T-shirt she slept in, which had been hanging on the closet door handle.

"What's going on?" Margaret said out loud, not that there was anyone to hear. She walked over to the closets and put the racket back against the wall where it had been, and hung Tom's nightshirt back on the door handle. Her heart was thudding as she touched the handle, but nothing jumped out at her. She went back to the computer.

"Kini-kun, something just made some stuff fall over but when I looked there wasn't anything there. I'm a little spooked. *shudders* wish u were here right now."

Kinigar's response was instant. "u got a cell phone? What's ur number, I'll call u. Was that story u posted about Quinkans for true? Mar-chan i wish i was there with u."

But Margaret didn't read his last message. Instead, she heard the bump again, and this time when she turned around, a shiny black bug-like creature occupied the middle of the room. With revulsion, she realized that it was a tick the size of a mastiff.

It had four pairs of jointed legs, with spurs on the second, third, and fourth pairs. A tough black skin covered its oval mite-like body. The mouthparts consisted of paired anchoring organs, covered with backward-curving hooks like the ones Margaret had seen on large spiders, plus a pair of sharp mandibles for biting and sucking. Its clawed feet scratched over the floor as it slowly and deliberately stalked her, following the scent trail of her exhaled breath and body heat. Margaret scrambled up onto her bed. The arachnid was between her and the door, so making a run for it was out of the question.

It came toward her in a slow, relentless tick mosey. Margaret was about to lose her dinner and tears of fright stung her eyes. She knew what tick bites felt like and how painful it was to pull one off you once it was seized in. Even with tiny ones, those mouthparts went right in and buried the head up to its hard body shell in your flesh. Blow that thing up to this size, and you were looking at certain death.

Margaret was dizzy. The thing had reached the foot of her bed and placed one waving leg over the edge of the bed frame, questing. Slowly it began drawing itself up onto the bedspread, its foot claws grabbing hold of the quilted surface. It lurched forward, its body scraping over the wooden frame with a sickening noise like pieces of Styrofoam rubbing together. Margaret screamed, but her throat, constricted in terror, produced no sound.

At that moment, the door opened and Tom came in. She stared in surprise.

"Margrits, what are you doing standing on your bed?"

"Ohmigod—" Margaret pointed to the end of the bed, at nothing. Suddenly the room spiraled and she fell, cracking her forehead on the bedpost. "Oww! Shit, that hurt!"

She felt Tom's strong, skinny arms pulling her upright. "Hey, are you okay? Lemme see that bump."

"Oww, is it bleeding?"

"Nah, it's all right. Uh, what was up with that little scene?"

"Oh god, Tom, you saved me! That thing was coming up on the bed." She clutched Tom's arm and couldn't let go.

"Like, what thing?" Tom stood up and scanned the room.

Margaret was getting her breath back and touched the rising bump on her forehead gently with the tips of her fingers. "Tom, do you believe in the supernatural?"

"Fukkin-A. Is this place haunted?" She sat down in the computer chair. "Hey, are you online with somebody?"

Margaret saw the IM icon flashing. "Oh, shit yeah, that's Kini. Let me answer him back." Tom got up and Margaret slid into the seat, grabbing the mouse. She scrolled to his latest entry.

"MAR-CHAN ANSWER ME!"

Margaret put her trembling fingers on the keyboard, but couldn't type. Thank god for Tom, who sat calmly on her own bed, watching the screen with a detached expression except for pursed lips, which Margaret noted were devoid of lipstick.

Finally, she managed to respond: "Something horrible was here in my room, but then my roommate came in and it disappeared and she didn't see it at all. So I dun know if it was really there or not. Kini, I think that Quinkan's back. Can u help me? Seriousleh."

"ur sure it was a Quinkan?" he responded. "They hang out in caves and billabongs and places like that, not girl's dorms. Dunt make any sense."

"I'm spazzin, Kini-kun. Wish I could talk to u for real. It's not just me. Last year my mom saw it 2. A horrible black one-eyed dingo. But the Wandjinas came in a storm and we thought they killed it. No laff, this is for true." She hit SEND, and wondered what he would make of that.

"Hey, Margrits," said Tom, reading over her shoulder. "What's a Quinkan?"

Margaret scrabbled through her brains for a quick and dirty answer that would explain a shadowy creature that had probably been around for hundreds or thousands or maybe millions of years. "It's an evil spirit that can shape-shift and sound like somebody you know, so it can lure you where it can grab you."

"Why would it want to do that?" Tom asked.

"To kill and eat you and turn the leftover parts into new Quinkans. It's supposed to like children best. It's also supposed to live in the Australian Outback, but I think it can go wherever it wants."

"Nasty," said Tom. "What does it want with you?"

"That's what I want to know! This thing has been hassling me ever since I was little, mostly in my nightmares, but once it walked out of my closet and talked to me. It talks in Mom's voice, and when it's in a dog shape it has this awful snarly sound. Sometimes it's a lizard. It's just horrible and always threatens to chew me up for dinner. Usually I can make myself wake up, but sometimes I'm just stuck there, watching it drool on the carpet." Margaret shuddered again.

"Ya know, Margrits, I never would have figured you for a spirit magnet. You just seem too … what's the word?"

"Ordinary?"

"Yeah. I think you need to get in touch with your guardians."

Margaret stared at Tom. "My what?"

"Guardians. Your totem spirits. Everybody's got them, but most people don't know what they are. This is mine." She pointed to the tattoo on her chest.

"Everybody has one?"

"Damn straight."

"Hold on a second." Margaret turned back to the keyboard. She read Kinigar's last message: "WTF? U called up the WANDJINAS?? How??"

She responded quickly, typing, "Kini, what's your totem? Your spirit guardian, if it's not a secret."

"No secret," he wrote back. "Native cat, that's mine. He's fukkin awesome. Nobody can see him but me but I know when he's around. Sometimes he's small and sneaky, but when I need him to protect me he's so badass he even scares me!"

"How did you find him? How can I find mine?"

"Just ask it to show itself to yeh. If ur psychic it's easy."

Margaret took a deep breath. She was hatching a plan. "Thanks Kini-kun, gotta go now, but talk to me tomorrow, 'K? *superclingcuddleglomps* BTW, your picture is The Sex!"

"Laters, mate. Yeh sounds okay now, so take care. Tell me about those Wandjinas next time, yah? XD, Kini."

Margaret exited the forum and swung the chair around so that her back was to the screen. "Tom, can you show me how to contact my spirit guardian?"

Tom scratched her head. "Maybe. I can show you what I did. Who knows, maybe it'll work for you."

"Cool. What do I do first?"

"Okay, listen. If we're gonna do this, we gotta do it right."

Margaret was finally feeling close to normal again and leaned back in the chair. "Thanks. By the way, what did you do with Devin?"

Tom's eyes went half-lidded. "Who wants to know?"

"The whole dorm."

"Then the answer is, I been here all night, 'cuz sure as I told one person, some fucktard would hear it and spread it all over." She pulled her duffle bag out from under her bed and scratched around in it, eventually producing a plastic bag containing a dozen or so sticks of incense. She pulled one out.

"Lemongrass. Good for smudging and cleansing a room if you're going to contact the spirits. Which we are."

"You can't light incense in here. Won't it set off the smoke alarm?"

"Yep, it would. So we're gonna go stand in the kitchenette, turn on the oven hood exhaust so it'll suck up the smoke, smudge each other up quick, and then come back here and seal the circle."

"What circle?"

"You'll see." Tom hustled Margaret out the door. No one was in the kitchen, so Tom turned on the hood fan, produced a lighter, and in just a few seconds a thin spiral of very pungent, aromatic smoke rose from the tip of the incense stick. She quickly ran the coils of smoke up one side of her body and down the other, and did the same to Margaret. Then she licked her thumb and index finger and pinched out the glowing tip.

"Awesomeness," Margaret said, wishing she could someday be a tiny percent as fearless and cool as her roommate but knowing it would probably never happen.

Tom dragged her quickly back to their bedroom and shut and locked the door.

She stood in the middle of the room and motioned for Margaret to come stand beside her.

"Now, here's what you do," she said. "Point with your finger and draw an imaginary circle of fire all the way around us. Be sure you overlap the ends to make a complete circle. Try to see it real clear in your mind." Tom did as she had just described, and then watched as Margaret copied her.

"Now, sit down inside the circle."

They sat quietly for a moment. "Ready?" Tom asked.

Margaret nodded.

"In your mind's eye, try to see some kind of reflecting surface, like a mirror or a pool, or even a TV screen. Ask your guardian to show itself to you."

"Okay. Should I close my eyes?"

"If it helps. If it doesn't, don't."

Margaret closed her eyes. She imagined herself picking up a hand mirror and looking at its surface, but all she saw was her own face. No matter what she tried to see, nothing could displace her reflection. She tried visualizing a large projection screen and mentally asking her guardian to appear when she flipped on the projector. The only thing she saw was her own face again.

"Tom, it's not working."

"Give it a minute. I didn't get anything either, the first time I tried. Maybe you're trying too hard. Just relax."

"I'm trying to."

They sat still, waiting and just breathing.

"I don't know how to do this," Margaret complained. "It's just not working."

Tom sat up straight and arched her back, stretching her arms overhead. "Well, maybe your totem doesn't want to show up for some reason. Ask 'em again and just wait."

More silence. Margaret's legs were going to sleep. She decided to try something different, and imagined herself sitting in a bright yellow pool of light. Then she saw her shadow-self get up and step out of the shaft of light, and stand on its periphery, watching as her body sat quietly with its eyes closed. The shaft of light rippled as something came into the spot she had just vacated.

Then Margaret's body opened her eyes and stared at Tom, unblinking.

She heard Tom's voice say, "Is somebody there?" as if from a long ways away.

Margaret's body spoke in a soft voice, lower than her normal register. "We are here."

Tom's voice again. "Who's we?"

"We are the Rai."

Chapter 19

April 1969

Neddy! Please wake up! What's happened?"

Kneeling between the mattress and the chair Ned had been sitting in before he fell, Suzanne lifted his head and shoulders into her lap, dreading that there might be blood. She didn't see any, but he was out cold, and, in fact, his skin was cool to the touch. She pressed her fingertips to his temple and felt a pulse, but he didn't wake up.

"Neddy, please …"

She eased his head down onto the floor and ran to the other bedroom. Its door was closed, so she knocked, hoping Crash was there.

"Crash?" She knocked again. "I need your help!"

The door opened a crack, revealing a pale sleep-fogged face. "Huh?"

"Crash, come help me, Ned's passed out or something. I can't get him to wake up."

"He'll get over it, man. Just let him lie there."

"No, you don't understand, we weren't smoking anything. I was sitting on the bed, reading some of those stupid comics he likes, and he was working on a picture. I looked over at him and he was just staring off into space. I assumed he was just thinking, but then he went limp and fell out of the chair. I can't get him to wake up!"

The door opened a bit wider. "I guess he didn't tell you about his fits, huh? Ned has fits. He passes out, falls over, and then wakes up. That's it."

Crash ran his hands through his tangle of dirty brown hair and yawned. He wore a pair of drawstring karate pants and nothing else. Suzanne realized she'd woken him up, but she didn't care.

"At least help me get him onto the bed. Please." She put her hand on the door so he couldn't shut it.

"Okay, but I'm telling you, he'll come around in a few minutes."

"Thank you." She waited for him to go to the kitchen and return with a glass of water, then followed him to Ned's room.

Crash took hold of Ned under the armpits while Suzanne picked up his feet, and together they half-lifted, half-dragged him onto the bed, which wasn't nearly as easy as Suzanne had imagined—he was dead weight. Crash looked down at him.

"Looks pretty out of it."

"That's what I was trying to tell you. Shouldn't we call a doctor or an ambulance? What if he's had a stroke?"

Crash dipped his fingers in the glass of water and flicked a few drops across Ned's face. Ned twitched, but didn't open his eyes.

"He'll be all right."

Suzanne knelt beside Ned and held his left hand in hers. "He's so cold. God, Crash, what if he dies?"

"He ain't gonna, but call an ambulance if it'll make you feel better. Just give me time to hide my stash."

Ned moaned and Suzanne felt the barest pressure from his hand. She squeezed it and held it to her lips. "Ned, can you hear me?"

* * *

Ned was on his knees in the dark water again, soaked and shivering. His left hand held tightly to the spirit cord that stretched away into nothingness, while with his right he felt around in the water for a thing he'd dropped. It was an oval-shaped stone, heavy and slick with lichens, and it had slipped out of his hand when he'd stumbled over something in the water.

He couldn't remember clearly why he'd been carrying the stone or why he was desperate to find it again, but he could feel a panicked despair constricting his chest. Something terrible would happen if he couldn't find it. Red resin drops slid down the cord, stopping at his hand and forming a translucent pool around his fingers. Ruby tears of the bloodwood tree. They were said to heal wounds and illness, but because of them his grip on the cord was slipping. Ned knew in his soul that if he let go of the cord, he was lost; he would never be able to find his way back to his body in the directionless dark.

A willy wagtail darted past his head and flashed out of sight. He knew about wagtails. They were harbingers of death. The wagtail swooped back into his field of vision, chasing insects unseen, its glossy black wings and back nearly invisible against the gloom of the billabong. Its white belly flashed by his face, and it landed on the spirit cord beside his hand. The bird cocked its head, watching him with tiny bright eyes and fluffing its white eyebrow feathers in avian aggression punctuated by alarmed chattering. It began pecking at the resin, plucking out grubs or something edible, Ned guessed.

He was unsure who'd told him the lore of the wagtail or the origin of *kino*, the sticky red resin of the bloodwood, but it was old knowledge, something he understood with his bones and sinews. Like he understood the stone he'd lost. Fear flowed into him again as he remembered that he'd dropped it in the black water. Suddenly, he felt a sharp stab of pain in his hand.

"Hey you, goddammit!"

The bird had pecked him with its sharp little beak. It pecked again and he recoiled, letting go of the spirit cord, which vanished the moment his fingers gave way.

"Fuck, no!" He stumbled forward in the dark, the water dragging at his knees. Ned couldn't tell if the cord had just lost its luminescence or if it had really disappeared, but thrash as he might in the general location where'd he'd let go, he couldn't find it.

A numbing cold crept into his veins, congealing the blood and slowing his heart. He could barely move, and finally he sat down in the water, his hands limp and floating, ripples lapping at his shoulders. His head fell forward until his face touched the swirling pool. He wondered how long it would take him to drown if he didn't lift his face to breathe. He couldn't remember his purpose or why he'd been so worried over a piece of rock that no longer held any meaning for him. He was becoming part of the lagoon, his consciousness fading, his humanity drifting away in the black water.

Something solid bumped against his shoulder, nearly pushing him over. Ned raised his dripping head and saw the vague outline of a canoe drifting beside him. He touched it with his hands; it was rough, like the bark of a tree. The idea penetrated his brain that if he climbed in, the canoe might take him somewhere. He grasped its curved side and tried to stand, then froze. The canoe was occupied.

A tall, impossibly thin brown man with a wild shock of curly hair that spiraled out from his head like a halo stood in the center of the canoe, an upright spear held in both hands. He stood on one leg, the foot of the other leg resting against the supporting knee. A sounding bone pierced the septum of his nose, and he stared straight at Ned with shining eyes.

"Long way coming," he said, his voice soft and liquid, like streams over pebbles. "You bin no blackfella, but here you are. Where's the clan *tjuringa* you carried?"

"I-I don't know," Ned said between his chattering teeth.

"You bin get in the boat, eh?" At this, a sound began, a single subsonic note held long, then subsiding, then pulsing outward again. Ned knew at bone-level it was the note of creation blown through the first Ancestor's bloodwood didjeridu—the great I AM that sang all the creatures of Earth into life and breath.

"Would you go to the island, then?" The boatman shifted his spear to one hand, put his foot down beside the other, and reached out to Ned. "Say me your name."

Alarm coursed through Ned's body because he knew what the "island" meant. It was the land of the dead.

"I don't want to die." The droning sound coursed through his body, making ripples across the surface of the lagoon. A patina of overtones hung above the anchoring pedal note, dipping in and out, zooming along in synch with the bottom tone and then flying away from it, singing the rock wallaby and the barramundi and the honey ant into the Great Making.

"Well, then." The boatman withdrew his hand. "This poor fella bin lost his cord and his stone. Can't come in the boat and can't go back." He stood impassively staring down at Ned, as if the matter was settled and he had no further duty here.

"Can't you at least send me back?" Ned pleaded, panicked.

The boatman stood still as if carved from the primal eucalyptus, smooth and bronze and shining. The boat began to drift away.

"Wait!" Ned cried out. "Don't leave!" He strained his eyes, trying to see the dim outline of the canoe and its rider as they receded into the gloom. Thrashing about in the water, Ned shouted with all his strength. "Send me back! Help me!"

A murmuring filled his head, voices he remembered from … when? Where? He ransacked his addled memory, looking for the time or place when he'd heard those voices.

Who comes seeking the Rai? What skin group? A voice whispered and curled around his ear like mist.

He met Death but chose not to go, said a second. More joined in, filling Ned's mind with a hushed chatter.

Then he saw them approaching, a throng of ovoid-shaped lights, some tall as willows and others small as an egret. They formed a ring around him.

We are the Rai. Who calls?

Ned stood as straight as he could manage. "My name is Ned."

This name means nothing. What skin group? The voice sounded in his head.

Ned turned around in the knee-deep water. "I don't understand," he said. "Help me."

The tallest of the Rai approached, gliding over the surface of the pool. Amoeba-like, an extension that might be called an arm flowed out and touched Ned on the chest and then on the arms. *Snake clan, Taipan mother,* it said. *You bin marked, but you are not karadji.*

"What's a karadji?" asked Ned, desperate.

Wise man, clever man, one who sees far, spirit-master, one who makes the spirit-journey between worlds, the voices chorused.

"Then it's true, I'm not a medicine man," he said, using his only cognate for what they were describing. "I don't know any magic."

What is magic? We are the Rai. Why did you call?

Ned was shaking worse than if he'd taken too many uppers. He decided to try a different tack. "I lost something in the water when I let go of the spirit cord. It was a sacred stone, a clan stone. Can you help me find it?"

Instantly the circle closed in. *He came for the tjuringa. Open his eyes.*

The tallest Rai reached out again and touched Ned on the forehead. A blinding flash seared through his brain and his entire field of vision went white, like staring into the heart of the sun. And he understood. The Rai were spirit guides who trained and protected shamans on their journeys into worlds beyond the physical. They were life's essence, bodiless, old as Sky Home itself. They came, often unbidden, when a shaman of sufficient power touched the membrane of consciousness that separated the physical world from the beyond. They were the bridge to the Dreamtime.

Blood ties, blood debts, said the Rai. Ned was transfixed, held by the silent struggle inside him and the blinding field of white that obliterated all sight. *Two others we see, fused in the blood. Taipan mother and hungry lurker. One protects, the other kills.*

Ned felt the two as each surfaced in his mind, and he shivered in terror. "W-what do they want?"

One wants justice, the other, freedom. The Rai can see. This is your birthright, told by the blood.

"Then how did this shit get in my blood? Who gave me this poison?"

That one. Your grandfather.

An image of the blackened, burned creature he'd found in the hut of reeds materialized in his mind, and then he remembered. He'd followed its spirit cord right up to its prison on the gray banks of the billabong.

"*He* stole this whatever-it-is? So why can't he give it back?"

The bright form of the Taipan Ancestor materialized before Ned's face. "He can't go back. Can't ever go back. You go back, fix things up."

Ned's head was swimming. "Show me the damn thing, then." Instantly, he saw his own drawing of the leaf-shaped object with the incised symbols. The Taipan Ancestor glistened in his mind, her golden-green scales radiant. "Dingo clan received it, that one from Snake clan mob stole it, hid it. That one," she hissed at him.

"Where does it belong?"

"Dingo clan home!" His two landscape paintings from his early days in San Francisco took shape in his mind.

The Taipan Ancestor vanished, and his head was filled again with the Rai, little whispering bees buzzing from one side of his skull to the other.

Great Snake Galeru weaves the rainbow. Ungar, Wonungur makes the spirit-children. Worombi, Yurlunggur brings the rain. Julungguf, Langal, Mui, Mindi. Taipan Mother brings the flood, bringer of death, bringer of life.

Ned clapped his hands over his ears. "Stop!" Instantly all was silent and he was alone in the dark. He looked down, and stretching out from his solar plexus was the shining ropelike length of his spirit cord. It flowed away from him horizontally in a straight line, undulating slightly like a plucked guitar string.

He placed his hands on it and started walking, imagining in his mind that he was following it back to his body, to his source, to the world where he belonged.

* * *

"See, Suzie-Q, what did I tell you?" Crash gave Ned a pat on the cheek as he opened his eyes. Ned groaned and tried to sit up.

"Wait, let me help you." Suzanne put her arms around his shoulders. "God, Ned, you scared me to death. How do you feel?"

"Like shit, but give me a minute." He swung his feet off the mattress and onto the floor, reaching a hand out to Crash. "Help me up, man."

Crash pulled him to his feet, and Suzanne slid her arm around his waist. They stood, waiting, while he found his balance.

"I seriously need to piss," he said. "I can make it to the bathroom okay."

Suzanne held onto him, helping him maneuver around the bed and toward the door. "Are you sure? You don't seem too steady to me."

"So, man, you want one of us to come in and help you?" Crash cut Suzanne a look, and she gave him back what she hoped was a glare that told him in no uncertain terms what she thought of that idea. He backed away. "Yeah, well, I'll just go back to bed now. Holler if you need me. Which you probably don't. G'night." He disappeared into his room and shut the door.

Suzanne let go of Ned, and he gave her a quick peck on the cheek. "I'm okay now. Don't look so scared."

She was still alarmed at the gray tinge around his mouth. "I'm going to make some tea, then we need to talk."

He nodded and walked away toward the bathroom. Suzanne went into the kitchen, filled a glass teapot with water, and then lit the gas under it. Just as it was starting to boil, Ned returned, looking much better. Suzanne could see that his color was back, and he was smiling at her. He reached for her and held her close. She slipped her arms around him and returned the squeeze.

"What would I do without you?" he said.

"I wonder," she said, her face against his chest. "If it were left up to Crash, you'd be waking up on the floor about now."

"Wouldn't be the first time. He's not the mothering type. But you are, and I thank you for that."

Suzanne turned to the teapot, and poured hot water over herbal tea bags. Stirring in honey and handing a mug to Ned, she headed back to the bedroom.

Sitting on the bed beside him, she watched as he sipped at his tea and shut his eyes. "This is good."

Suzanne frowned. She was hooked beyond hope on this strange man who seemed one moment to have so much promise and the next to be damaged beyond repair.

"Have you ever seen a doctor about those seizures?"

"Can't afford it," he said. "And I honestly don't believe they'd find anything. A faith healer might be more useful." He drank more of the tea, and watched her over the cup. She held his eyes.

"What happens when you black out like that? You didn't go epileptic, you were just out cold. And your skin was cool, too. Do you have low blood pressure or something?"

"Well, there's an excuse I hadn't thought of. Yeah, maybe I do. As to where I go when I'm out, my mind takes its own private acid trip. Sometimes I remember after I wake up, other times not."

"What about this one?"

"I remember it all. Want to hear?"

Suzanne nodded, folding her legs into a more comfortable position. "I want to hear everything."

Suzanne listened, barely breathing, as he related what sounded like a drug-induced nightmare, from finding himself in the water clutching something he called a spirit cord, to meeting Death the boatman, to the moment when his cord returned and showed him the way back.

Suzanne smiled for the first time that evening. "Would you believe, I actually know something that may help. *Galeru* is the Rainbow Serpent, from the Dreamtime. Australian Aborigines believe the Rainbow Serpent is their creator. It's part of their religion. I learned that in my World Mythology class in college."

"Australia," he said, chewing his lip. "I've been haunted, and hunted, all my life with no clue how to make it stop. But at least now I know where to go, thanks to you. I don't know how the bloody hell I'm going to get over there, but I'll figure it out."

It was funny, Suzanne realized, how easily she'd switched from observer to conspirator. If there was any way to help Ned accomplish this task he believed he had to do, she would make it happen. "I have some money. We can go together."

"Your family will disown you, especially your brother."

Suzanne put her arms around his neck and kissed his shapely mouth. "Then let's make it worth their while. Marry me, Neddy Waterston."

He kissed her back. "You'll be sorry, but I accept."

Chapter 20

August 6, Saturday—Present Day

Margaret stood on the edge of the circle of light, allowing the other presence to take over. Although *stood* wasn't exactly right; *hovered* was more like it. She could see the dim outline of her body sitting cross-legged opposite Tom. For all she could tell, Tom appeared unfazed by the fact that some alien consciousness had invaded her roommate's body and was addressing her in a whispery voice. Margaret thanked her lucky stars that she hadn't tried this with anybody else. Tom was way cool and knew what to do.

"Are you Margaret's guardian?" Tom asked.

Margaret watched, fascinated, as her mouth moved and words came out that weren't her own. She could also see that the pupils of her eyes were wide and black as she stared unblinking across the circle at Tom.

"We are … guardians, yes …" The words came slowly, just above a whisper, as if the connection was so far away it could barely be received.

"Are you more than one person?"

"We are … many … you may perceive us as one."

"Where are you from?" asked Tom.

"Sky… Home," came the answer. Margaret understood instantly, but she was pretty sure that wouldn't make any sense to Tom.

"Um, how are you connected to Margaret?"

There was a pause. Finally, the words came slowly. "We are ... searching the vocabulary of this person ... for the words ..."

Tom and Margaret waited as the entity scanned her brain. Margaret sensed a faint tickling sensation in her scalp and face, and hoped it wouldn't make her sneeze.

"This person is ... the end of the long line ... from Snake Clan mother, to black shaman who made the taboo ... to the damaged one and then to this one's grandfather—"

Margaret twitched in her noncorporeal state. That was Ned the spirits were talking about!

"—to this one's mother."

Margaret would've laughed aloud if she'd been able. Tom had asked a metaphysical question about relationship, but the entities had given a literal answer, listing the branches of the family tree.

"Can you protect Margaret from the evil spirit that's been stalking her?"

Another pause. "That one ... cannot be split from the bloodline ... until the taboo is repaired."

Margaret could see Tom's mouth pursing, as she pondered what to ask next. Margaret knew what she would have asked, and luckily, Tom wasn't far off the mark.

"What's the taboo?"

"Dingo Ancestor gift ... taken, misused, lost. To damage a sacred site ... is dangerous ... threatens the living and the unborn, unbalances the order of the world ... it is forbidden. The hungry one, the shadow one, the lurker ... bin fused to the black shaman by accident."

Tom waited in silence, and the Rai spoke again. "We are guardians for those who make the spirit-journey ... we are the Rai, we teach, we guide, we protect."

"What can Margaret do to protect herself?"

Margaret was thinking she needed to tell the Rai to blink her eyes. Nobody could stare that long without blinking. But the next thing she heard made her forget that small discomfort.

"Snake clan descendents ... must take the *tjuringa* back. Dingo Clan needs it ... Wandjina say it bin go back."

Tom asked, "Where is it?"

A long pause ensued. Margaret sensed the strange presence fading and felt a very strong urge to step back into the pool of light.

Finally the answer came, very slowly, in a whisper. Tom leaned forward.

"This body is tiring … we must release it … we do not see place and time as you do … we bin see *tjuringa* energy dim, buried in earth … we see you and this one … small balls of light … we see threads of your lives branching and intersecting with others …" Margaret's eyes closed as she slid toward the pool of light.

Margaret shifted her weight, slowly stretching out her cramped legs. It took her a minute or two to feel firmly seated back in her body. She desperately needed something to drink and could have gulped a quart of juice if they'd had some handy.

"Thirsty," she croaked, opening her eyes.

Tom stood up. "Hang loose." She went out of the room to the kitchenette and returned a minute later with two sodas. Margaret downed nearly the whole can in a single long swallow.

"Sorry I didn't write all that stuff down," said Tom, "but I didn't want to step outside the circle for a note pad."

Margaret put down the can. "That's okay, I remember most of it. What do you think would have happened if you had gone outside the circle?"

Tom shrugged. "Maybe nothing, but I didn't want to chance it. You got some serious mojo happening. How come you never mentioned you could do that?"

"I didn't know."

"So, like, you're telling me this is the first time you ever channeled? Awesome."

Margaret was grinning and trembling slightly, the exhilaration of the experience lingering in her blood like champagne bubbles. "Yeah, it was. Thanks, Tom, I would've been scared if you hadn't been here. I'm not sure I want to do it again, it was a really weird feeling, but it was worth it once."

"What's this Sky Home place?"

"That's like heaven to the Aborigines, in Australia. I learned that from my mom. It's where their gods hang out and maybe people go there when they die, but I'm not sure about that. The Ancestors who made all the land and animals and people went there after it was all done. I gotta ask Kinigar, 'cause he says his cousin's uncle is a shaman, and he knows all these Dreamtime stories. I can't wait to message him about what just happened!"

Tom yawned hugely and stretched. "I'm gonna bag it. Stay up if you want, I don't mind."

"So, like, Tom, did you and Devin ...?"

"Did we do it?"

"Yeah. Did you?"

"I'll tell yah someday."

Tom went to her closet and took her nightshirt off the handle. Margaret couldn't bring herself to tell Tom about the Quinkan pulling it off onto the floor. Just the thought of the form it had taken this time creeped her out beyond anything she'd ever seen it do. She had almost forgotten about it because it hadn't bothered her in so long, but this was far worse than dreams. Of course it would take the shape that repulsed her the most. But she wondered, would it have been solid to the touch, or had it just been an illusion to scare her?

She sat down at the computer. Remembering the few times she'd actually seen the Quinkan in daylight, it had looked pretty damned solid. Then she recalled what the Rai had said about splitting it apart from her, and something about a sacred object being stolen. She really needed to talk to Kinigar again.

She logged on and was overjoyed to see he was still there. What time was it in Australia, anyway? She pinged him.

"Kini-kun! u wont believe what just happened. I channeled some spirits who said they were the Rays or something, from Sky Home!!! What do u think about that? XD M-chan."

"M-chan! Was worried about u." A pulsing heart smiley was appended to the end of the sentence.

Margaret chewed her finger. Kini had just sent her a heart, that same Kinigar whose picture was so cute she could eat him up. She resolved to have Tom take some more pictures to send him tomorrow. She also hoped to God Kini was the real deal and not some hopeless dork masquerading as a hot Ozzie.

Tom returned, gave Margaret a pat on the head, and crawled into her bed without a word. Almost immediately her breathing became regular and deep. Margaret wished she could fall asleep, snap, just like that. It was another of Tom's enviable talents.

A second message rolled in above Kinigar's first.

"How did ur mom call the Wandjinas? she Aboriginal or sumthin?"

"No, long story. Kini, I have so much 2 tell u." She sent him a confused smiley with crossed eyes and launched into the whole long story of Alice and the *Land of Legends* exhibit saga as she understood it. When she told how the Quinkan acted like a sidekick for a demon preacher who threatened to kill her mom, and then how the Wandjinas came to her rescue in the middle of a thunderstorm with an Ancestor called the Lightning Man, Kinigar cut in.

"WHAT THE FUKK??? M-chan, shamans train all their lives to do stuff like that! I dun think u need any help from me!"

"No, see, I do coz I dun understand this stuff. The Rays told me it couldn't separate us from the Quinkan until some Dingo Clan thingy got returned. I hafta figure out what that means." She then described as best she could remember the gist of her channeling experience.

"Does ur mom channel 2? Like, does it run in yer family?" he wrote back.

"I dunno. She has weird dreams sometimes. Like this one she had when we went to Miami for my grandma Suzanne's funeral." Margaret recounted Alice's dream of the black cockatoos with the small black and white bird that chased them away.

"Fukkkkk, M-chan. That was a willy wagtail, u know what that means?? They show up just before somebody dies. Was anybody in that dream besides ur mom?"

"I dunno, just her, I guess. That's all I know."

"This is dangerous shit. Spirits like that show up to meet u when u cross over to the other side, like I mean die. M-chan, I think your mom's in danger or maybe u."

Margaret felt shivery again. She was thinking the same.

"Kini, what can I do?" She doubted those few words could possibly convey the sense of helplessness she felt at that moment.

He didn't reply back immediately, and she wondered if maybe he'd lost his Internet connection. There was so much else she wanted to share with him but hardly knew how to get started. She stared at the screen, her mind a blank.

The IM title bar was flashing again: *Kinigar is writing a message.* She waited, holding her breath. She also saw that there was an attachment. She clicked on it and the image viewer opened, revealing the same wide smiling face of the kid beside the truck, only this time he was sitting in a desk chair in what was clearly a boy's bedroom. An electric guitar on a rumpled plaid bedspread was dimly visible in the background. He was wearing a black concert T-shirt of a German metal band both she and Tom adored.

"Just took this with meh digicam," he wrote. "Print it out and u can have me with u all the time, for protection."

Margaret reread the message several times, feeling a tiny sting of tears under her eyelids. Please, she begged whatever powers there were, let him be real and not some troll pretending to be cool.

She wrote back, typing fast and not reading over what she'd written. "XXXDDD!! ur so freakin hawt Kini. Do you hve a girlfrind?"

He replied immediately. "No. r u taken?"

"No."

"Then I claimz you. *tackleglomps* Ish mine!"

Margaret hugged herself, suppressing her fangirl squee to a mere eep, for fear of waking Tom. She responded, "*claimz u back* Nice Ozzie kitteh *puts a collar on u, drags u away* Hehe."

"Rawr. Send more pix, K?" he responded.

"I will! Kini, what's your full name?"

"Jason K. Trescott. What's yers?"

"Margaret Alice Sullivan. Middle name is my mom's, last name is my dad's but Mom went back to Waterston. I like M-chan best."

"Coolness. Byes for now."

"Laters." She saw his username disappear as he signed off. She yawned and rubbed her eyes, only then admitting how exhausted she was. It was approaching two A.M., according to the computer clock.

Margaret fell onto her bed, too fatigued to even change clothes or go pee. The camp wakeup call would come much too soon, and she had a lot of things to do tomorrow, the most important of which was to find a way to print out Kinigar's smiling face. She intended never to be parted from it again.

But instead of falling asleep, she lay awake, her brain too wired to shut down. It had been a tumultuous birthday, to say the least. Terrifying and exhilarating, but the best part was that plain old Margaret Sullivan that nobody ever paid any attention to now had an official boyfriend who was sixteen, played an electric guitar, listened to Rammstein, and was as cute as a koala bear. He was so made of win she could hardly stand it.

Chapter 21

August 11, Thursday — Present Day

Late summer sunlight pierced the trees off to his right as Nik pounded down the one-mile stretch of Black Creek Ferry Road leading back to Alice's house. He estimated that when he reached the driveway he would have done a forty-five minute jog with a good wind sprint at the end. It pleased him that at twenty-seven he could make a run like this as easily as he had done at twenty.

Dawg galloped joyfully ahead of him, tail flogging the air in wide loops like a canine propeller. Running like this, with muscle and sinew and bone all working as one to propel the mass of his body through space, Nik embraced the runner's euphoria. At these moments, he loved being alive. Not that he would confess such a thing to anyone … it was just a silent acknowledgement. Alice would say he embraced his inner Dawg.

The two of them dashed down the curving driveway to the house, slowing up when they reached the sandy front yard. The bay where Alice parked her car was empty, so he assumed she was still at that meeting of the county historical society she'd been invited to by a coworker. She'd said it might be dark before she got home, in which case he was to feed himself, and she'd eat leftovers when she returned.

With Margaret still at camp, Nik and Alice tended not to make sit-down meals. Thinking of Margaret, he wondered how she was doing. They hadn't heard from her since she'd called to thank them for the birthday gift card to her favorite music store five days ago, but that was to be expected. Margaret was spreading her wings and experiencing some independence, which they both agreed was a good thing.

He walked briskly around the yard, cooling down, letting his breathing slow and his pulse settle back to its normal rate. Dawg immediately began nosing around in the remnants of Alice's summer garden, poking his head into hydrangea bushes before peeing on them and following his nose to the edge of the clearing. Then with a loud yawp he was off into the trees, on the trail of whatever had snagged his interest.

Dripping wet, Nik went up the stairs, peeling off his sodden T-shirt and draping it over the deck rail before going inside. He discarded the rest of his clothes and his shoes on the bedroom floor and got in the shower, turning on just the cold water. He'd adapted somewhat to the hot, humid climate of Florida, but had to admit that the Nordic component of his physiology longed for ice and snow, for freezing cold and whitened breath. He stood under the showerhead with his face upturned to the chilled well water, feeling the heat drain away from his body.

Standing in the shower, thinking, Nik thought about Alice. Six months ago, in Norway and Sweden, she'd been a good travel companion, eager to see and experience whatever presented itself. She'd charmed his parents, proving that he'd been right to insist she come with him on the Mycological foray in Trondheim. When they'd returned home in late February, she'd seemed happy, and healed.

But lately she was more hard-edged and bitchy, cold even, and it was affecting all of them. Frowning, Nik turned off the water and stepped out onto the bathroom rug. He wanted his old Alice back, the one he'd met when he first worked at the museum as a contracted illustrator, but he was beginning to suspect that she didn't exist anymore, that she'd been permanently changed by those experiences she regarded as supernatural.

Whether indeed something unnatural had taken place with her Dreamtime exhibit and her research into local history, Nik couldn't say. She had been fixated on a crumbling wooden church located on a deserted county road about four miles away, convinced something paranormal had taken place there. Nik toweled his body, replaying in his head those scenes from last year … pieces of evidence he still couldn't get his head around, such as the wild dog he'd shot in the eye in the woods beyond Alice's house. It had leaped at him, hit his chest with its monstrous paws, and then disappeared in front of his eyes. He shook his head, spraying water droplets. Then there was that freak storm that had blown through the neighborhood, blasting the front door off its hinges and trashing the living room where he'd found Alice unconscious on the floor.

That event had shocked him and, he had to admit, frightened him on several levels; he'd been alarmed for her safety, but he'd also been unable to rationally construct how the scene of destruction could have come about. Margaret seemed to have no trouble accepting what she claimed was obvious: the Dreamtime Wandjinas had come to rescue her mother, or her rescue had been a by-product of the retribution visited on the phantom preacher Alice believed she'd called from some other dimension into this one.

Try as he might, Nik simply could not accept the notion of anyone being haunted by creatures that manifested from somewhere outside the here and now. He could almost accommodate the notion of consciousness existing beyond the physical plane, but to have it deliberately haunt one's dreams and invoke visions of terror that could cause bodily harm was to admit a universe he'd stolidly denied most of his life. The closest he could get to it was the ongoing scientific discussion of extra dimensions that might resemble membranes or strings or some other construct *du jour*. He could discuss in speculative terms a model whereby planes of these unknown universes might bump up against each other and somehow bleed into one another, but outright belief in the supernatural he held at arm's length.

Alice had said, when she'd recovered enough to try to describe what had happened on that afternoon of rain and shrieking wind, that an Aboriginal god, an Ancestor called Namarrkun, had come down and taken away the vile thing named Cadjer Harrow, a character whom she admitted to having largely invented from a few scraps of nineteenth-century newspaper reporting. She also believed that her own consciousness had been scooped up along with Harrow's and transported out into the cosmos. To the Milky Way. Sky Home in Aboriginal terms, she'd said. These were things he didn't like to think about, which was why he kept up his jogging routine, even on the hottest days of summer: running cleared his mind.

Nik toweled his hair dry and went out into the hallway. He heard Dawg barking outside in a barrage of yipping and yelping punctuated by growls that escalated into alarm barking. Nik wrapped the towel around his waist and looked out the bedroom window to see if anyone had driven up in the yard. Seeing nothing, he went out onto the deck and tried to course the direction of Dawg's incessant yelping. It seemed to be coming from the trees behind the clearing at the back of the house.

He knew that he needed to get dressed and go check on Dawg, but his thoughts kept returning to Alice and the events of last year. As much as they had all tried to settle back into a pattern of normalcy, tacitly agreeing to carry on as if nothing had happened, he still thought about those fear-filled months all the time and assumed both Alice and Margaret did as well. How could they not?

So, it bothered him that Alice had gotten involved with the history of the church down the road again, because it seemed clear to him that had been the origin of her problems. For whatever reason, she'd begun to imagine seeing characters from an aborted novel she'd been researching and hallucinating spectral visitations. These delusions had temporarily driven them apart, and it was mainly his concern over her physical safety, and Margaret's, that had brought him back. But once he'd come back, he made a commitment to stay, because for that brief time when they'd been separated, he'd found himself surprisingly lonely.

He firmly believed that for a couple to make it together, they should support each other through whatever crises might occur in their lives. But in this case, the problem was that although he felt competent to physically protect the property and make sure Alice got proper medical attention when she'd been mauled by the feral dog, he'd been unprepared to help her in the way she'd obviously needed most: confirmation of the unreal.

The dog attack, however, had been real enough … at least, her injuries from it were real. She had a torn coat and a dislocated shoulder to prove it. And his own chase of the beast and confrontation down by the pond in the woods had certainly been real. Remembering that encounter brought his focus back to the edge of the trees where Dawg continued to yelp. Nik could just make out the movement of his tail and rear end near a fallen beech just off the beginning of the footpath.

"*Hej*, Dawg!" Nik whistled sharply and the barking ceased. Dawg came trotting into the yard, his head up and tail beating his hindquarters. Even without his glasses, Nik could see that Dawg's fur wasn't bristled, so whatever had excited him didn't appear to be threatening.

"Wait, Mutt-butt," he called, using Margaret's favorite nickname. "I'm coming there in a minute." Dawg danced around the yard, seeing his master leaning over the rail, and then he bounded off into the woods again. Soon Nik heard his yipping resume with renewed excitement.

Nik went to the bedroom and found a clean T-shirt and jeans. Normally, with the weather so hot, he would have opted for gym shorts, but if he was going to have to go into the woods he wanted his legs protected from briars and biting insects. He found a clean pair of socks after much rummaging in the bottom dresser drawer that Alice had allocated for his use, put his running shoes back on, and tossed his sweaty jogging shorts and socks on top of the towering mound in the corner hamper. Between Alice and himself the pile grew at an alarming rate; one of them would have to break down and do the laundry soon.

Putting his glasses on and tying his wet hair back with a shoelace, Nik headed out the front door and bounded down the steps. He was thinking of the ways in which he and Alice complemented each other when she was happy and things were going well, which only contributed to the glum feeling that a lot of what he enjoyed about their being together had been quietly eroding. Things weren't right, but he was at a loss as to how to fix whatever it was.

He knew that Alice fit most of the things his parents would wish for him: she was attractive, intelligent, educated, professional. But maybe not young enough; they would want grandchildren that were Nik's own blood, not adopted from a former marriage. Of course, they would never say that to his face, but the thought would be there.

Some of this was bound to come to a head when he graduated, which wasn't that far away now. He had already started sending out employment query letters both in the U.S. and abroad, with the help of Stuart Eisner, his major professor, and if he got a good offer in Sweden, chances were that he would take it. He had his own fantasies of how he wanted that to play out, but without Alice's cooperation, making it happen was questionable. If she chose to stay here because of job or friends or whatever reason, it wouldn't deter him from taking an offer if it seemed good enough. That would likely mean seasonal visits to keep their relationship going.

He walked around the corner of the house to the back yard. Dawg burst out of the woods, ran circles around his master, and made a few perfunctory leaps in the air in front of Nik to be sure he had his human's full attention.

"*Lägg av*, cut it out already!" Dawg sat down, but it was clear he could barely contain himself.

Nik surveyed the perimeter of the clearing and the opening into the trees where the path began. "So, what's this thing you want so much to show me, eh?"

He reached down and scratched Dawg around the ears and under the chin. A small round object fell off into his hand: it was a tick, bloated with blood. In late summer, that was to be expected; they were everywhere.

"Time to get you a new flea and tick collar, I see," he said to Dawg. "Another reason I can't let you in the house, old pal."

Nik held his palm open, dispassionately observing the unwieldy creature trundling slowly across his hand, its body so swollen that the head was all but invisible. He fully intended to kill it because he didn't want more of them proliferating in the grass around the house, but it was interesting to him from a purely biological standpoint to identify what type of tick it was and observe how it moved.

Finally, Dawg could restrain himself no longer and leaped up, dashing down the trail. Nik crushed the tick between his shoe and a rock at the edge of Alice's butterfly garden and followed. He could see Dawg crouched down in the leaf litter just off the path, clearly pointing at something in a hole under the fallen beech. The massive trunk had been there for several seasons and its gray skin was peeling up, making a home for beetles and other things on the raccoon menu, like the row of *Pluteus cervinus*, the deer mushroom, marching in a neat row along the eastern-facing side of the tree. The sizeable excavation underneath the trunk suggested armadillos.

"What do we have here?" Nik said aloud. He whistled and called Dawg to him, holding him in check, and squatted down, not too close, to see if he could glimpse what was under there. If a rattler or a moccasin, he certainly didn't want to be within its strike range.

Balanced on his haunches, Nik waited, perfectly still, for some minutes just watching and listening. And then whatever was under the log made a distinctly animal sound.

"Not a snake," he said. It was probably some hapless raccoon or opossum that had sought a place safe from Dawg's chasing instincts.

He stood up, pulling Dawg away from the tree. "Follow with me. Let's just leave the poor creature in peace." But then, it made a distinctly feline sound, a sort of mewing that sounded quite pitiful. Nik stopped in his tracks.

Going back to the hole, he got down on his hands and knees and tried to get a better look. It was impossible—the creature was wedged in too far to see.

Nik stood up and went quickly back down the path to the house. Opening his truck, he retrieved a flashlight and shut Dawg in the laundry room. Dawg protested, whimpering and scratching at the door, but Nik was unmoved. "Back in a minute, old pal. I just need to see what you've got cornered."

He ran up the steps and went to the kitchen. In the refrigerator, he found the leftover grilled grouper from last night's supper wrapped in plastic. Breaking off a small piece, he hurried back downstairs.

Crouching in front of the hole, he put the fish on the ground and waited. Before long, he saw movement and heard a scrabbling as the creature maneuvered itself out of its hiding place and into the daylight. It was a cat, so thin as to be skeletal, with long matted gray-white fur. It began to gnaw the piece of fish with a fury, by which Nik could tell it was starving. Then he observed that one of its front legs dangled limp from the shoulder as it hunkered over the food.

Looking more closely, he also saw that part of an ear was missing and there were other healed scars on its body. A dog had probably mauled it. And then, when he finally realized what he was looking at, he could not believe his eyes.

"*Satan och helvete*," he whispered, "Holy Hell."

Alice pulled up under the house just after sundown and was surprised to find Nik's truck gone. Usually he was home every evening unless there was some university function he needed to attend. His dissertation deadline was looming, and she'd pretty much let him take over the spare bedroom, turning it into his study. He often worked late into the night, sorting through slides for his field guide and writing up the ones selected. He still taught a few classes as a graduate assistant to keep his university stipend, but he was in writing mode now and rarely had time for anything else. Since this was Thursday, she knew his classes were over at noon and that he should have been home this late in the day.

Then she heard Dawg barking and whining, but didn't see him anywhere. It took her a moment to realize he was shut up in the laundry room.

"Dawg! Who put you in here? Did Nik go off and leave you? Bad man!" she exclaimed as Dawg embraced his liberator with a wet sloppy kiss.

"Yuckkk! Stop that!" Alice wiped dog drool off her cheek. "But really, where's your sorry master, eh?" Dawg bounded away to the edge of the woods, nose to the ground, but then came trotting back, apparently not finding what he was after.

Alice was shaking her head. "I don't get it," she said as Dawg galloped up the steps ahead of her.

Reaching the landing, she was surprised to find the front door unlocked and a note written in haste taped above the doorknob: GONE TO VET. RAINE'S CAT IS FOUND!

How was that possible? She couldn't even begin to imagine. Late last year, on Christmas Day to be exact, Nik had discovered the grisly remains of Raine's other cat, Tux, mauled by a wild dog, the same one, it was assumed, that had attacked Alice on the stairs of her house one dark night a few weeks later. When Sesshomaru, Raine's white Persian, disappeared, they assumed he'd met the same end, and although they'd all searched the surrounding woods for months, the body never turned up.

"Well, I guess that explains that," she said to Dawg.

Alice was about to give Raine a call to see what she could find out when Dawg's head went up and his tail went into action. Then she heard Nik's old truck chugging down the drive. She went out onto the landing and waited for him.

"Hey, I found your note," she said, as he came up the stairs. "Sesshomaru's still alive? That's amazing!"

"*Ja*, I thought so too. When I first saw him, I wasn't so sure it was a cat, even, he was so emaciated. I called Raine and went straight to the vet. She met me there."

Alice followed Nik inside. "What did the vet say?"

"She thinks they can save him. He had a lot of old wounds on him, and one leg had been dislocated and broken. He's been dragging it around useless. It's anybody's guess how he's been able to catch or find enough food to stay alive. One would think he would have gone home when they were looking for him all that time."

"I've heard about that kind of thing," Alice said. "Cats aren't like dogs, y'know. Injured or highly frightened cats will hide out and not come to anybody, not even their owners. They can get in such a state that they actually forget where they once lived. Cats that have been missing for months are often found not far from their owner's home."

Alice pulled a bowl of tuna salad out of the fridge and set about making sandwiches. "Are you hungry?"

"Ravenous."

"Me, too. This won't take a second."

"How was your historical meeting?"

"Very interesting. I'll tell you after we eat."

Nik slid into his usual chair at the breakfast nook. Alice noted that he sat quietly, just watching her. Finally, she could stand it no longer. "Something on your mind?"

"Just thinking."

"About what?"

"What will we do, you and I, at the end of the year, when I graduate?"

Alice stopped painting mustard on bread slices and turned to face him. "I don't know, I haven't thought that far." Which was a lie, but one she hoped would fend off a discussion she'd been dreading. Change was always unsettling to her, and this impending shift in their arrangement made her queasy.

"I have," he said, "and the fact is, the only option that lets me stay here in town is to get funded for a post-doc."

Alice glued the pieces of bread together with a wide swath of tuna salad. "How likely is that?"

"About zero. Not that the department wouldn't like to keep me around, but there's no money available, at least in my field. I might finagle something in Microbiology since it was my undergraduate major, but again, it's a long shot."

She put a plate in front of Nik and sat down with one of her own. Suddenly, she didn't feel much like eating, but took a perfunctory nibble. "I assume you're sending out query letters. Where to?"

"In the U.S., to Penn State, University of Wisconsin, Oregon State University, Washington State University."

"All cold places."

"Well, that wasn't a criterion for choosing."

Alice could feel her good mood evaporating. She wanted to share the fascinating lead she'd gotten from Milton and the historical society people about the Tanner family and their connection to the old church, but now it seemed unimportant. "What about places abroad?"

Nik shifted in his chair. "There are strong mycological programs at the University of Tübingen in Germany, the University of Oslo, and the University of Copenhagen's Botanical Institute. I might also try for the CBS—that's an important center for mycological research in The Netherlands."

"What about Sweden?"

"I've written to the University of Göteborg, and the Department of Forest Mycology at the Swedish University of Agricultural Sciences in Uppsala. And, of course, the Swedish Museum of Natural History in Stockholm."

"Your parents would love that."

He nodded. "So they would."

"What about you? What would make you happy?"

"I—"

The phone rang, cutting off whatever he might have said. Alice cursed to herself and caught it on the next ring. "Maybe it's Raine."

"Hi, Mom." Margaret's voice was upbeat.

"Oh, it's you, Munchkin! How's camp?" She smiled at Nik and mouthed 'Margaret' at him. "Hey, you won't believe this, Nik found Sesshomaru!"

Margaret whooped through the receiver. "Wow, that's the bomb!"

"I don't know the specifics, Nik was still at the vet with him when I got home. I can call you back or e-mail you once I get the details from Raine. It's the best news I've heard all week. So, is everything okay there?"

"Killer. Would you tell Nik that our butterfly project got an Honorable Mention in the camp-wide competition?"

"That's great, Munch—eh, sorry. I really am trying to break myself of the habit. I know you hate to be called that now. Anyway, I'll let you tell him yourself. Hang on." She handed the phone to Nik. "She's got something cool to tell you."

Nik took the phone. "*Vad?*"

"*Hej*, Nikster! Our neighborhood butterflies catalog got Honorable Mention. Isn't that great?"

"*Ja, det var kul.* Very nice."

"And my roomie Tom got Third Place for her thing on America's Top Ten Worst Hurricanes. And guess what, Mom's birthday is on the same day as the Galveston Hurricane of nineteen-hundred—September the eighth. The Galveston hurricane is number one, at the top of the list. It's the all-time worst."

"That's auspicious, in a disturbing sort of way."

Margaret started laughing. "Yeah, kind of suits her."

"I'll be sure to tell her."

"Tell me what?" Alice cut in.

"Your upcoming birthday coincides with the most devastating hurricane in U.S. history."

Alice groaned. "Figures."

"Have you made some good friends, then?" Nik said.

"Oh god, the best. Well, anyhoo, I just wanted to tell you about the science project. *Tack så mycket.* Did I say that right?"

Nik smiled. "Perfect."

"Okay, then. Laters. Say bye to Mom for me."

"Right. Margaret says 'bye.'" He handed the phone back.

Alice hung up the receiver. "You're really good with her."

He shrugged. "She has a lot of potential, you should be proud of her."

"I am. But …"

"But what?" Nik was looking at her with that passive ice-blue stare she found sometimes intriguing but mostly squirm-inducing.

Alice looked away. "I worry about her. I worry that I may somehow be the cause of that thing that turns her dreams into nightmares. I worry that … forget it. The whole thing just makes my head hurt."

"What were you going to say?"

"You really want to know?" Alice could feel the blood draining from her face. She'd vowed never to have this conversation again, yet here she was, diving in. "I'm afraid for her safety, and mine, and anybody who's close to us, like you."

"You don't need to worry about me—"

"But I do! Nik, I would die if anything happened to you!" Alice bit her lip and waited. If that didn't get a reaction, nothing would.

Nik leaned across the table. "I'm not worried for myself. But I don't want you, or Margaret, to live in fear. Wouldn't you like to live somewhere different, someplace completely removed from all this history that causes you so much angst? Stockholm is beautiful, winter or summer."

"What are you saying?"

"I'm saying that, if I can get a good position early next year, we should all move together. Just consider the idea, will you?"

"Move together, how?"

"As a married couple with a child."

"Nikolas Thorens, was that a proposal you just sailed past me?"

Finally, he smiled with his whole face. "Yes, it was."

Alice licked her lips. "I have a lot of ifs … like, if I didn't have a kid in school, and if I weren't well-employed in a job I love, I'd say let's do it tomorrow. Elope and get the hell out of here. But—"

"Shh. Just give it some thought."

"I will. I promise."

Chapter 22

August 12, Friday—Present Day

Alice woke just after dark from a nap she'd only intended to take for ten minutes before confronting the task of making Friday night supper for herself and Nik. Instead, she'd been asleep for nearly an hour, which wasn't surprising, really. She'd been walking around for days with that numb, sleep-deprived feeling that typically set in when she couldn't get through the night without waking up every five minutes. It was as if some virus security system in her brain went into action whenever something potentially harmful tried to load itself, blocking the dream and waking her up. Some nights she couldn't fall asleep at all.

Feeling groggy and out of sorts, she sat up and hung her feet over the side of the bed, trying to get the cobwebs out of her brain. Maybe if she got in the shower, it would wake her up properly. Then she might be more willing to go stand in front of the pantry waiting for inspiration to strike.

She pulled off her shirt and shorts and shuffled out into the hallway, and then noticed the light was on in the bathroom. The door was open, and she saw that Nik stood naked, staring at his face in the mirror over the sink. In one hand, he held his ponytail in a tight wad and in the other he adjusted his grip on a pair of scissors.

Alice bolted down the hall, as it dawned on her what he was about to do. "Stop! What the hell are you doing?"

Nik lowered the scissors, turning toward her voice.

"It's getting long. I thought maybe I would cut it before getting in the shower."

Alice crammed herself into the tiny bathroom behind him. "Good God, don't do that!"

He looked at her sideways. "Why not?"

"Because … long hair on men is sexy, that's why!" she said, blushing, her secret fetish revealed.

"Ah. If I cut my hair, I lose my sexual prowess, eh? How biblical." He was almost smiling.

Alice put her arms around him and pressed her cheek against his back. "Please don't cut it."

"Just for you, then." He put the scissors back in the medicine cabinet and let his hair fall loose. It brushed across Alice's face.

"Mmm." She squeezed him and slid her hands down.

"You want to do that in the shower?" he said, turning around.

"Sure, why not? But I can't picture how we're gonna do it standing up."

Nik traced the line of her collarbone with a fingertip. "I can pick you up."

"No way."

"You're not that heavy," he said, stepping behind the shower curtain with its cascading ferns and hummingbirds.

Indeed, thought Alice. "Swedish studmuffin," she said aloud.

"*Vad?*"

"I said, we can even leave the door open."

His response was drowned in the sound of rushing water.

Alice dropped her underwear to the floor and stood for a moment, seeing his form through the shower curtain and feeling that momentary flush of excitement she remembered from the first time she'd stayed overnight in his apartment while Margaret visited her grandmother. That was over two years ago. They'd been through a lot since then.

She pulled the curtain aside and got in behind him. Immediately, sprays of water hitting his shoulder glanced off at just the right angle to hit her in the face. Blinded and spluttering, she ducked under his arm. So much for romance.

"You sure about this?" she said, wiping water out of her eyes.

Nik was grinning evilly, something she didn't see every day. He reached for her with soapy hands.

At that moment, the phone rang. And rang.

"Double damn!"

"Just let it ring," said Nik. "If they leave a message, you can call back. If they don't, eh, who cares?"

"You're right. Hell with 'em."

The phone rang a few more times, and then a male voice mumbled something she couldn't hear.

She also thought she heard a noise out in the hallway, like something bumping against the wall. But then Nik slid his arms around her and she forgot all about noises in the dark.

* * *

It was nearly eight-thirty by the time Alice dressed, dried her hair, and wandered into the kitchen in search of food she could put together without much effort. Only then did she remember that someone had called and left a message. She punched PLAY beside the flashing message light and recognized the voice at once.

"Alice, dear, if you could call me this evening, I'd appreciate it. I need you to sign some papers authorizing you as a guardian for Margaret's trust that your mother set up. This weekend, if you could. I'd like to get this settled as soon as possible." There was a pause, and then he added, as a seeming afterthought, "I've got a buyer for Dunescape and should be moving out very soon. I feel uneasy here now, without Suzanne, and, well, just please give me a call. Thanks, dear."

"That sounded like your uncle," Nik said, opening the fridge and pulling out bread, a block of Jarlsberg, and a mostly used-up jar of spicy brown mustard. Alice watched him, dubious.

"Whatever you're fixing, I think I'll pass. And yes, that was Hal. Wants me to drive over tomorrow to sign something to do with Margaret's trust fund. He's sold Dunescape and sounds like he's ready to get the hell out."

"To where?"

"Back to Miami, where his old friends are. When we were there for Suzanne's funeral, he said something about finding a place in Coral Gables. I think that would suit him."

Nik completed his sandwich and sat down at the table. "What about the old dog?"

"Oh, I don't think Hal could be parted from Carlisle. I assume they'll move together."

"That was good of your mother to make a trust fund for Margaret."

"Yeah, it sure was. I never had a clue she'd done such a thing. You'd think that if somebody set aside that much money for your child they'd tell you, wouldn't you? Controlling bitch."

"But—"

"I know, I know. Whatever I think of her personally, I'm glad she did it and I thank her for it. It means Margaret can go to college wherever she wants."

"When can she draw on the money?"

"I don't know, but I'll find out in a minute when I call Hal back. Want to drive over with me tomorrow?"

Nik shook his head. "I need to work on the dissertation." Alice watched with horror as he opened a can of sardines to go with the sandwich.

She took a banana from the fruit bowl on the kitchen counter and reached for the phone. Settling onto the couch, she dialed Hal's number, and was a little surprised when he answered on the first ring.

"Hi there," Alice said. "I got your message."

"Alice." He sounded relieved. "I hope it won't inconvenience you to make the drive over."

"No, no, I'd be happy to. I could finish going through Suzanne's things, too. I was thinking I could drive over tomorrow afternoon and spend the night, and then come back on Sunday."

"That would be perfect." Hal's voice was breathy.

"Hal, are you feeling okay? You sound a little short-winded."

"I think it might be the stress of these past weeks. My heart has been giving me a bit of difficulty, but my doctor didn't seem overly concerned when I went to see him yesterday. I have new medication, and it's helping." He paused. "It's just so lonely here without her. Carlisle and I commiserate with each other daily."

"I'm sorry," Alice said, knowing there wasn't really anything she could say to make things better. She was thinking about the letters he'd given her, and how hard it must be for him to let Suzanne go.

"Hal," she said. "I know you didn't think much of him, my father, but …" There was so much she wanted to ask about that, but wasn't sure how far she could push without upsetting him.

"That is putting it mildly, I'm afraid. The truth is I loathed him."

This wasn't quite what she'd expected to hear from her uncle, a man who, as far as she was aware, rarely spoke ill of anyone and never admitted aloud to hating someone. It was out of character.

"I don't know what kind of image of him you must have fashioned in your mind," he continued, "having nothing to go on, which I apologize for, but I hope you will understand that my reasons were to protect your mother.

She was very dear to me, and I couldn't abide the fact that she'd been taken in by him."

"Taken in, how?" Alice's defenses were up. Her idealized notions of her father were threatened, but still, she wanted to finally hear Hal's whole story if he was willing to tell it.

"You mother would never admit it, before or after their disastrous trip abroad, but I remain convinced to this day that he was a con artist who married her as a way to get to Australia for whatever nefarious scheme he had going. Perhaps he was running from the law. I couldn't find any direct evidence of that, but it is the only explanation that makes sense."

Alice was silent, hurting inside as her father morphed from talented artist and world traveler to criminal low-life scum who preyed on wealthy women.

"Do you think he loved Suzanne?" she asked finally.

"I honestly cannot say. I believe he used her in numerous ways, not the least of which was to empty her entire savings account just before they took off for Sydney. I also know that he was a well-known pothead and that his roommate dealt drugs. It was an environment completely unsuited for Suzanne, and I think," he paused again for breath, "had she not met him, she would have gone on to have a distinguished career as an interpreter or translator, possibly in the diplomatic field. That was her intention when I helped pay for her trip to Europe after college."

Thinking back, Alice could almost imagine Suzanne having a career like that. Her mother had always been so precise in her own use of the language and took great delight in pouncing on anyone who misused or abused it.

"I'll tell you something I've never told anyone," Hal said. "I met with him, just once, and offered to pay him to leave town, no questions asked. He refused me, and took such offense that I thought he was going to strike me, but he controlled himself. I guess he supposed that a much larger amount was to be had by marrying my sister and taking everything she owned. I know they must have sold or pawned some of her jewelry when they were close to running out of money. Her wedding band was all she had with her when I flew out to Queensland to get her. Needless to say, she ceased to wear it after her recovery."

Tears stung Alice's eyes. This wasn't the family history she wanted. She hated what Hal was telling her because it made them all sound so mean-spirited and deceitful. From the kitchen, Nik was watching, a concerned expression on his face.

"What were they doing over there?" Alice asked, when what she really meant was, how did my father die?

"No one is certain," Hal answered. "You mother was fairly incoherent when she made it back to a civilized town with her Outback guide. For my part, I felt that it was a lucky stroke to be rid of Ned Waterston, and that I'd got my Suzanne back, but she carried on her mourning for him beyond all bounds of sanity and decency. When it became evident that she was pregnant, I began to hope that the child—you—would bring her out of it and give her something to focus her love and attention toward. But, as you know, that did not happen."

"No," said Alice in a small voice, "it didn't."

"I never thought she would push you away so terribly," he said. She could hear conciliation and sympathy in Hal's voice, but there was something else as well. A plea for forgiveness? It was too damned late for that, she was afraid. Instead of breaking into tears, which she'd been close to a moment ago, her mouth set itself into a hard line and she gripped the receiver. Anger was closing itself around her heart, condensing remorse and sorrow into a bitter fist. She bit back the hateful things she wanted to shout over the phone. *You spiteful, selfish old man, how dare you judge my father and how dare you keep my mother all to yourself! What are you, some kind of pervert?* Instead, she said, "I see."

"She attempted suicide twice, barbiturate overdose and something a bit more violent, but she wasn't fated to die, or perhaps to look at it another way, you were destined to live. I tried to fill the void for you while you were young, so you could have some taste of what a parent's love might be like."

Alice ground her teeth, recognizing that he might also have wondered what it would have been like to share a child with Suzanne. She suddenly felt used beyond repair. "What exactly was your relationship with my mother?" she asked bluntly.

There was a painful silence on the line. In the corner of her eye she saw Nik come over and stand beside the couch.

Finally Hal spoke, his voice old and frail. "I loved Suzanne desperately, in every way the human heart can imagine, but our relationship was completely platonic. So, was all my dealing with her and the man she married totally self-serving? I don't know anymore. At the time, I felt only righteous fury that her life had taken a wrong turn. I might add that I was not alone in that assessment; our parents felt that way as well."

"Would he have loved me, I wonder," Alice said, mostly to herself, "if he had lived?"

"I can't answer that." Hal fell silent, breathing heavily.

The sound was painful in Alice's ear, and she held the receiver in her lap for a moment.

Nik touched her on the shoulder. "Is it okay?"

She nodded and put the receiver back to her ear. Hal still wasn't talking, but she could hear Carlisle barking in the background.

Then Hal coughed lightly. "Excuse me, dear, if I'm permitted to still call you that. I need to go see what Carlisle's making a fuss about. Will you please come tomorrow?"

"Yeah, I will. Count on it," she said, thinking how she was going to enjoy a face-to-face confrontation in which she would ask all the questions she'd sat on for years until she got answers she could live with. She punched the phone off.

She reached up and took Nik's hand, pulling him down beside her.

He adjusted his glasses. "What was that all about, or should I not ask?"

"You should ask, and if you're really serious about marrying me, you deserve to know."

He put his arm around her, and she settled against him, fitting into the curve of his side. Comforted, Alice told him word for word, as best she could remember, everything Hal had said, coloring the story with her growing resentment and anger.

"What do you think?" she said at last.

"I think this. It must have been as hard for your uncle to carry his secrets around with him so many years as it was for you not to know them."

Alice chewed on that for a moment, knowing what he said was true. Suddenly she felt embarrassed at her selfishness. "Thanks for the reality check," she said.

"You're welcome."

"You cut right through the bullshit to that little grain of truth the rest of us are trying not to see. That's exactly what I love about you."

"Ah, so you *do* love me."

She collapsed against his chest. "My secret is out!"

Nik held her with both arms. "You may confess your undying love for me again, if you like. I don't mind."

Alice burst out laughing, her evil mood dispelled. "Iloveyouiloveyouiloveyou," she said, and the best thing was, she really meant it.

* * *

Late that night, they lay on their sides like spoons, her back pressed against his front. His quiet breath rising and falling slowly just behind her ear let her know that he slept deeply. His left arm lay heavy across her ribcage. Alice dozed, completely relaxed and feeling like she might actually drop off to sleep with no difficulty. Random images floated across her mind, harmless eyelid movies of the day's events and things she planned to do tomorrow in Gull Harbor. She thought about Margaret's last day at camp and hoped she wouldn't mind being picked up by just Nik while Alice went to take care of business with Hal. It sounded like she was having a wonderful time, making friends and going on field trips and such.

Alice yawned and snuggled against Nik. There was no place in the world she'd rather be at that moment. Images of her trip to Sweden glided idly by, and she slipped off into a dream of Stockholm covered in snow. Flakes fell in white powdery drifts, covering houses and streets, canals and ships at anchor, islands and ruins of castles. Everywhere, as far as she looked, was a vast expanse of featureless white.

And then the snow began to melt, turning to streams and rivers, flowing through deep canyon walls, becoming a torrent and eventually reaching the sea where it beat its breast against jagged rocks high as pointed cathedrals. It roared in her ears, and she realized the sound wasn't water flowing, it had a hollow, crackling sound that wasn't wet at all. Something was burning. A building of some sort was engulfed in flames, roaring and booming, with whistling cinders flying away from the conflagration like tiny Roman candles. She watched the wall as timbers fell, sending flames up into the sky twice as high as the roof would have been.

The heat on her face was becoming uncomfortable, and she floated back from the site of the burning, watching transfixed as flames ate the remaining outline of the building. And then, a movement near the edge of the fire caught her eye. Something was crawling away from the inferno. She tried to see what it was, but couldn't. Was it an animal? Someone's pet, perhaps, trapped in a burning house, or a man, blackened like charcoal? Alice screamed in her dream, and woke up.

Nik coughed in his sleep and rolled over. Alice sat up, shaking, her heart racing. She shook her head, trying to get the horrendous image out of her mind. Finally, she lay back down, but the nightmare had poisoned her sleep. She lay awake the rest of the night, watching for the first gray signs of sunrise through the bedroom window.

Chapter 23

May 1969

"Until death us do part," said the minister of the Universal Love Church. With his thin beard and shoulder-length brown hair, he resembled a modern-day Jesus in love beads.

"Until death us do part," repeated Suzanne.

"Mr. Waterston, you may kiss your bride." The minister, clad in a flax-colored gauze shirt and loose-fitting Yoga pants, folded up his printed copy of the wedding ceremony and beamed at Suzanne, Ned, Bailey, and Daniel, his job completed. Ned didn't particularly care for the way this so-called hippie minister looked him over; he'd seen that look too many times not to recognize it for what it was.

Ignoring the self-appointed Reverend Lotus Blossom, Ned took Suzanne in his arms and kissed her deeply. The Italian Renaissance shell-lined grotto, one of the best photo-op spots on the grounds of Miami's Vizcaya Museum, had been her choice for the wedding. She wore a white Mexican wedding dress, ankle length and embroidered with flowers. Her flame-red hair falling over her shoulders and across the lace bodice of the dress was possibly the most beautiful thing Ned had ever seen.

He wore his best clothes, consisting of the same shirt and pants he'd worn when he'd met Grant, an encounter that had turned out to be incredibly fortunate for him. He hoped this thing he'd just done would be equally lucky.

"Let me see," Bailey was saying, taking Suzanne's hand and reaching for Ned's. They both now wore slim gold wedding bands.

"Eighteen-karat red gold," said Suzanne. "I got the date engraved on the inside. Almost a year to the day since we first met."

Ned allowed himself a brief smile. In the formal gardens just beyond the hill where the shell grotto lay in cool shade, the sunlight was bright and unrelenting, exposing to the world that Ned and Suzanne had joined their lives, for better or worse.

Ned held Suzanne close, contemplating the enormity of the moment and, at the same time, its utter artificiality. But rituals carried their own energy wave that could influence events, or so his mother had said. He hoped in this case it was true. The wedding ceremony had been for Suzanne, but it was also his private plea for good luck. In any case, he liked the way she looked in her lace dress. Her hair smelled like strawberries.

Suzanne had been living with him for the past six months, as the struggle with her family over her "hippie boyfriend" became increasingly heated. He knew Hal had done some checking up on him because Suzanne let it slip that Hal was concerned about Ned not having a birth certificate or a driver's license on record anywhere. Although he did have a Social Security number, apparently that was not enough to satisfy Hal, who disliked him intensely.

The need for documentation was another way in which Ned's acquaintance with Grant had turned to his advantage. Before Ned took off across the country, Grant had helped him obtain a California ID card using a baptismal certificate from a church in San Francisco who'd taken Ned's statement of his birth date at face value.

How many strings Grant had pulled to make it happen, Ned didn't ask. His instinct told him the less he knew about Grant the better. It had required more than a single visit to Grant's hotel room, but Ned judged the benefit to have been more than worth it. The California ID card and baptismal record had been enough to get him a Social Security number, which he hoped would be enough to get him a passport. By Thanksgiving at the very latest he hoped to have it in hand, and the fact that Suzanne insisted on making the journey with him was the thing that enabled him to make it at all.

"Fantastic!" Bailey exclaimed, staring at Ned. "What a total gas!"

"Yeah, far out. Australia, man, that's like on the other side of the world." Daniel looked from Ned to Suzanne with pot-glazed eyes.

Suzanne was laughing. "The landscape should be a trip all by itself."

"Wow, when are you going?" Bailey seemed more amazed by their honeymoon plans than anyone.

Ned shrugged. "As soon as we have enough money saved." A shadow crossed Suzanne's face but to Ned's relief she kept her mouth shut. He'd not wanted it made common knowledge that they were bankrolling the trip with her money. "I think we're done here," he said, guiding her away from the grotto and toward the parking lot.

"Abso-fuckin-lutely!" trilled Bailey. "C'mon, Daniel, let's leave the newlyweds to their own devices." She linked arms with Daniel and the minister, skipping over the parking lot gravel.

Ned suddenly wished them all gone with a vengeance. He was through playing at pretenses and wearing a mask of civility that he didn't feel. And something was scratching at the inside of his skull, wanting out.

* * *

In the apartment, Ned lay back on the bed, trying to unclench his stomach. He could almost feel the liquid darkness creeping in from all sides, telescoping his vision of the room and his new bride.

"Ned, are you there?" She was bending over him, no trace of a smile on her pretty face. "Neddy, don't fade out on me." He could feel her rubbing his hands.

He opened his mouth, but there were no words. There was only a nauseous hiss in his ears and a cold, reptilian slither of a consciousness invading his mind. There was no other way to describe it, that insidious taking-over by the bilious hunger of a presence that had been with him from the beginning. Ned fought for consciousness, but the other was more determined, its purpose more focused. His eyes rolled back in his head and the world around him dimmed as he heard Suzanne's pleading voice far, far away, begging him to come back. But he couldn't do that because his essence had already begun its journey through the wormhole that led to the wasteland where the blackened man-shell crouched in its wretched reed hut by the gray banks of the billabong in the place between.

Chapter 24

August 27, Saturday—Present Day

Nik watched the sky. It was reinventing itself by the minute, with two discernible layers forming and reforming. He understood how it worked—damp, humid air from the Gulf of Mexico was bumping up against a front of cooler upper-level winds. A major summer thunderstorm had been brewing for the past hour, and now it was rapidly morphing into a supercell. High above, cumulo-nimbus mountains piled up toward the southwest, darkening the sky and blocking the late afternoon sun. Closer to the ground, long streaks of gray storm scud raced along the wind as it gusted over the treetops. The massive cloudbank moved more slowly, trailing long streamers that reached from its underside toward the land. Nik stood in the parking lot of the university's science complex watching with fascination as the elements made mischief overhead.

He knew that these hot, humid late afternoons of summer bred conditions just right for supercell formation, which in turn spawned flooding rain, hail, violent downdrafts, and tornadoes. He also knew that the flanking column of updrafting air would feed the supercell for a number of hours, during which all manner of extreme weather was likely. He wondered what they would get today. The darker base of the cloudbank lit up momentarily, as if in answer, as a twisting neon tube shot downward. The following thunderclap came ten seconds later, by which he knew the rain would move in shortly.

It was barely five in the afternoon, but already campus streetlights were coming on as the dark closed in around wide, slate-colored curtains of rain visible from miles away. He hoped Margaret would be ready to leave before the torrent hit. With her boxes and suitcase stowed on the floorboard and seat of his ancient truck, he waited for her to say her final goodbyes to counselors and friends. He also hoped Alice wasn't driving through any of the looming storm. She'd gotten a late start heading over to Gull Harbor to help Hal close up the house as he prepared to move back to Miami. Her car, a low-slung Camaro in the old 90s body style, wasn't designed for heavy rain and deep puddles, but the storm looked to be far enough south that the route to Gull Harbor might not be in its direct path. He hoped she would remember to call him as soon as she was safe inside the house with Hal and Carlisle.

At that moment, Margaret emerged from the dorm arm in arm with a tall, thin girl whose jet-black hair obscured most of her face.

"Nik, this is my roomie Tom. Tom, this is Nik."

"*God middag*," he said, knowing he was on display. "Good afternoon."

"See, isn't he cool?" said Margaret, still clinging to the arm of her girlfriend.

"You're from Sweden?" asked Tom.

Ned nodded. "Stockholm."

"My great-granddad's from Norway. He's blond and blue-eyed, like you," Tom stated. "My mom's a Gypsy. That's why I have black hair. Your hair's really long for a guy." She was looking him over in a frank way that made him distinctly uncomfortable.

Nik shifted his feet, wondering what to say. He wasn't used to having teenage girls check him out like that.

"Was camp successful, then?" he asked, and they both broke into a cascade of giggles.

"You could say that," answered Tom.

"Um, Tom got third place in the camp science fair," said Margaret. "Nik's a mushroom scientist," she said to Tom.

Tom's eyebrow went up. "Ever eat any funny mushrooms?"

Nik smiled and shook his head. "Sadly, no."

"Is that your truck? It's wicked cool, like a train wreck on wheels," Tom stated, with what sounded like approval, although Nik couldn't be sure. Margaret was hard enough to read, but this girl was beyond him.

"It's fun to ride in, especially on dirt roads and through the woods," said Margaret. "My mom has a Camaro, and she won't let anybody else drive it."

"I wouldn't either," said Tom, nodding.

Thunder boomed in the distance, and the first few raindrops pelted their faces and the hood of the truck with fat plops.

"We'd best get this scrap-metal heap on the road," Nik said to Margaret, opening the truck door to get her moving.

Tom hugged Margaret and kissed her full on the mouth. Margaret blushed as red as her hair.

Nik raised his own eyebrow.

"E-mail me," said Tom.

Margaret waved as Tom walked away to join other campers straggling into the parking lot. "It's not what you think. She helped me out a lot, so we're really close."

Nik noticed that Margaret cut her eyes away. There was something she wasn't sharing, but it was not in his nature to pry, so he let the moment pass.

"Where's Dawg?" asked Margaret as she climbed into the truck.

"I left him sleeping on the deck. He was so hot his tongue was hanging out this far." Nik gestured, making Margaret laugh.

"He's so funny. I love Dawg. *Hund*, right?"

"*Ja*. You're picking up a Swedish vocabulary pretty fast."

"Well, I wanna know what to say when we go there."

Nik blinked. While he and Alice had been inching in slow motion toward a decision about where they were headed as a couple, or as a family, Margaret seemed to have leapfrogged ahead of them and was already making plans for life abroad.

"What'll we do with Dawg, though?" she asked.

Nik turned on the windshield wipers as he navigated the traffic around campus and headed out toward the state highway that would take them into rural Massalina County.

"It depends on how long we stay." That was, of course, the heart of the question. He was hoping to land a permanent position, likely in Sweden, after his doctorate was done. Alice would have to decide if she and Margaret would move with him or just visit and come back.

His thoughts kept being pulled back to Alice. He knew she'd made the drive to Gull Harbor alone any number of times, but it still made him uneasy to think of her on the highway by herself in potentially dangerous conditions.

They rode a few minutes in silence, listening to the thump thump of the wipers. "When's Mom coming home?"

"Tomorrow. I believe she said she intended to be back by mid-afternoon."

"I want to tell her about Kinigar. He's just the coolest. And he's not a stalker, like she thinks."

"She just wants you to be careful."

"I've seen his picture. He's this really cool sixteen-year-old high school kid from Sydney, and I like him a lot."

They drove in silence for a while, watching the rain sweeping in over the highway and listening to it beating down on the roof of the truck. Nik could tell from the occasional pull on the steering wheel that some of those gusts were pretty strong. He was glad Margaret didn't seem to expect him to chatter away in meaningless talk because navigating in the sheets of rain was taking his full concentration. So much so that he almost missed it when his cell phone emitted a faint monotone beep. He pulled onto the shoulder of the road and stopped the truck, removed his cell phone from its belt holster, and flipped it open.

"Hello?" Nik expected to hear Alice's voice, but instead a strange man with a pronounced Southern accent asked for a "Mister Thorens."

Nik identified himself and listened with dread as the man explained that he was Deputy Sheriff Crowder and was callin' on behalf of a young lady named Alice who was in a bit of difficulty and needed him to come right away, seein' as how there was no next of kin she could call.

"What's happened?" Nik heard himself ask. His mind was falling over itself, imagining any number of possible scenarios, but none of them were what Deputy Sheriff Crowder described over the phone.

"Yes. I'll leave now, but it'll take me about two hours to get there. Please tell her I'm on my way." He clicked off and replaced the phone in its holster.

Margaret was staring at him with wide eyes. "Mom?"

Nik watched the pounding rain, his stomach in knots.

"Alice is safe, but Dunescape has burned to the ground."

Chapter 25

August 27, Saturday—Present Day

Putting her Camaro on cruise control, Alice settled back against the padded seat and took her foot off the gas. Traffic was light on the main highway heading toward Gull Harbor, and it appeared she would make good time getting there.

The sky off to her left looked troublesome, with cloudbanks massing and darkening near their base. She'd come through a couple of thundershowers about thirty miles back, but none had lasted more than a few minutes. Although the sky was heavily overcast, she was still hoping to pull out from under the rain altogether by the time she got to Hal's.

The more she thought of Hal, the more pissed she felt about the way he'd kept her in the dark all these years. She supposed she should be grateful he'd parted with the briefcase and its cache of letters, but the whole deception while she was growing up just wasn't right. Plus, she was truly dismayed at the unsavory whiff his obsession with Suzanne left in her mind whenever she thought about it, which was a lot these days.

Had Suzanne been aware? It was hard to imagine that she couldn't have copped a clue somewhere along the line, but if she'd known, it was even harder to imagine her living under the same roof with him for so long.

"Shitfire," she said, shaking her head. None of it made any sense.

It also made her more determined than ever to play her relationship with Nik as straight as possible for Margaret. No hidden agendas or secret plans. If her daughter wanted to know what was up, they would tell her.

Crossing the railroad tracks at the intersection of the state highway running north-south, she checked the time: 5:45. She would reach the driveway at Dunescape in another hour or so, depending on the traffic. Heading south, she eased into the steady stream of cars aimed toward the beaches along the Gulf coast.

She hoped Margaret wouldn't mind just Nik picking her up on the last day of camp. Alice had hoped to chat with the counselors and Margaret's girlfriends to get a measure of how well the session had gone and whether it was worth investing in next year. Hard to imagine it wouldn't be, given the opportunities it offered to the students chosen to attend.

Her mind coasted back to the museum and the *Legends* introduction. One sentence she'd written about the senior men and women stuck in her mind: "The seer's path would be seen as wisdom by some and madness by others." That got her thinking about Aboriginal shamanism in general. Gifted individuals were obligated to make spirit journeys for the benefit of their tribes. Would we label them crazy by modern standards? Maybe there were modern-day shamans who practiced ancient arts when no one was paying attention. She wondered if she knew anyone who might qualify, and immediately the image of mild-mannered Cecil Rider came into her mind. That surprised her at first, but the more she thought about it, the more right it seemed.

It was clear the Reverend believed that Cadjer Harrow, who'd founded his tiny rural church in 1894, had returned to the corporal world and that she was somehow responsible, with her snooping around and digging up secrets he thought he'd buried. She remembered with a twitch of fear that she hadn't done the one thing he'd demanded: destroy Harrow's notebook. As an historian and collector of artifacts, she just couldn't bring herself to do it, even though she had thought about it many times.

Alice's right front tire rumbled onto the shoulder of the highway, and she jerked the car back onto the road. Damn! She needed to stop daydreaming and pay attention. She was still driving through intermittent gusts of rain but could see patches of late afternoon sky ahead. By the time she got to Gull Harbor, the storm should have done its worst and moved on.

She thought of Ned again and began to fantasize that he'd gone to Australia with Suzanne on a shamanic mission. The idea was pinging something in the back of her mind, a memory of something, but she couldn't get to it. Her brain was so sleep-deprived these days that she sometimes felt like an Alzheimer's patient, searching for words in a vocabulary that was long gone.

With any luck, she might be able to get some sleep at Dunescape tonight. She hadn't bothered to pack an overnight case, figuring she could just wear the same tank top and cutoff jeans she had on now back to Magnolia tomorrow. Her toothbrush and a change of underwear were in a plastic bag on the seat beside her. She'd just help Hal deal with Suzanne's things and then he could sell Dunescape and go back to his cronies in Miami.

Evil sonofabitch, deceiving her all those years. Well, she was going to make him open up all the dirty laundry, hidden agendas, buried memories, and leftover secrets still squirreled away. He might even redeem himself a little. She'd give him that option, at least.

* * *

Tires crunching on shell and gravel, Alice pulled into the driveway at Dunescape right at dusk. Shutting the car off, she heard Carlisle barking. That was odd. Not that he was barking, because he always sounded the alarm when people drove up in front of the house, but that he was loose in the front yard. Suzanne would have never let him outside like that by himself.

"Hey, big fella," she said, calling to him as she got out of the car. "What are you doing outside?"

Carlisle continued to bark nonstop, jumping in little hops around a clump of weeds and grass beside the front steps, completely ignoring Alice.

"Hey, buddy, I know you're mostly deaf, but, HEY!"

Unable to get his attention, she shut the car door and walked toward him, then froze in midstep. Even in the fading light, she could see what the dog was fixated on: the characteristic tan and dark-brown scale pattern and large triangular head were unmistakable. Carlisle had cornered the longest Diamondback rattler she had ever seen. A heavy-bodied snake under any conditions, this one was massive, with at least twenty rattle segments on its loudly buzzing tail tip. The biggest ones she'd seen in captivity were around six feet, and this one was easily that or more.

"Carlisle! Come here!" she screamed.

Having read that rattlers were sensitive to vibrations through the ground, she was afraid to move any closer, but she had to pull Carlisle out of the snake's strike range, which for the Diamondback was more than half its body length. Alice had seen enough nature programs on television to know the basics, and she'd read up on snakes when she'd moved to the Florida woodlands. Occasionally, she'd found their calling cards, discarded molts of skin turned inside out, in the garden or along a trail. Now, everything she'd ever learned and feared about the Eastern Diamondback was materialized there in front of her.

The snake was coiling and recoiling in mesmerizing loops near the steps, hissing and rubbing its rough, ovoid-shaped scales together as its rattles buzzed an agitated warning. Carlisle barked in sharp bursts, feinting in toward the snake with little snaps of his long muzzle and then dancing away. Unlike western varieties of rattlesnakes, the Eastern Diamondback typically did not make repeated quick strikes at its prey, preferring instead to size up the target and deliver a single lethal blow, a tactic Alice hoped would give her a quick chance to dodge in, grab Carlisle by his collar, and drag him away before it decided to strike.

Breathing in short gasps, Alice took a step forward, and the snake raised its head several inches higher.

"CARLISLE you fucking mutt, come here!" she screamed, again with no effect.

Taking a deep breath, Alice rushed in, reaching for the dog just as the rattler uncoiled. Carlisle jumped in the air, and Alice saw in a flash the curved fangs unfold and thrust forward in its wide-open jaws as they flew past her face. She screamed as the rattler's jaws fastened on Carlisle's neck, and both fell flopping on the ground at her feet. Without another thought, she punched at the snake's head, screaming and kicking at its body. It released the old hound and, with a swish of scales in the grass, disappeared under the house.

"No, NO!" Alice was beside herself, holding Carlisle's head as his tongue lolled out. He was panting fast, his front feet jerking as the venom coursed through his carotid artery. Her face bathed in sweat, Alice wiped away tears and dashed up the porch steps and into the house.

"Hal! Carlisle's been bitten! Hal, we have to get him to a vet!" She stood in the living room for the briefest of seconds, waiting for an answer. Where was he? The room was shrouded in darkness, the final rays of sunset obscured by thunderclouds. Fumbling around for the wall light switch, she clicked it on, but nothing happened.

"Hell!" Alice felt her way to the kitchen and looked through the window toward the neighbor's houses; all were dark, which meant the storm must have knocked out the power. She had no idea where Hal and Suzanne kept their flashlights, but she did remember that there was an oil lamp shaped like a dolphin on a shelf near the sink. She found it and the box of matches beside it, then by its flickering light she went to the kitchen phone and paged through the phone book, looking for animal hospital listings. She found several, including one with a circle drawn around it, which she assumed must be a vet Suzanne had used. She called, but got their after-hours message advising her that they were closed for the day.

Fighting back tears, Alice picked up the lamp and went back into the living room. "Hal? Are you here?"

A muffled voice came from upstairs, where his study was located. "In the bathroom … down in a minute."

"There's a huge rattler under the house! It bit Carlisle! I think he might die …"

Alice put down the lamp and went back outside to the old hound lying flat in the sandy yard. It was almost dark now; the rain had stopped, and a stiff breeze was blowing the shards of clouds away toward the northeast.

She bent down to lift Carlisle's torso, and his head fell back. "Don't die on me, dammit," she cried, massaging his chest, but she knew he was gone.

Stricken, she sat down on the wet ground and pulled him into her lap, holding him tightly against her face. All her grief and anger and sense of loss and loneliness tied to Suzanne and her poor old dog poured out of her in wracking sobs, raking her throat and blinding her eyes. Alice cried as she had never cried in her life, with complete abandon and a sense of desolation that went far beyond the death of one dog. The pain in her throat and chest left her breathless, and yet she couldn't stop.

Gradually coming to her senses, she wiped her eyes and smoothed Carlisle's silky fur, wishing him farewell. She laid him carefully back on the ground, and went to face Hal. This would be a blow to him as well, since he'd planned on taking the dog with him to Miami.

She hurried back inside, wary of what lay under the porch steps, and picked up the oil lamp; it cast long misshapen shadows across the living room and over the stairwell.

"Hal? I-I'm sorry…" she called toward the stairs.

She waited, but there was no answer. What on earth, didn't he even care about his damn dog? "Hal, this is Alice. Are you all right?" More silence.

Then she heard his muffled voice again. "Alice? … not feeling well … power's off. Could you come up and help me?"

"What's wrong? Should I call nine-one-one?"

"I need your help to get down the stairs."

"All right, I'll come up, just sit tight." Alice frowned. She heard a thump upstairs and what might have been a couple of shuffling footsteps. That was worrisome. Hal wore a pacemaker and had weathered several past heart attacks. She imagined the worst.

Because Hal's study was basically a conversion of the attic space, the stairs went up at a steep pitch to a landing that opened onto one large room. Under the slanted ceiling its single small window looked south toward the Gulf. Shelves and storage cabinets lined the walls to left and right as one stepped off the stairs up onto the attic floor.

The area near the window contained comfortable furniture suitable for a man's study. Sturdy desk, storage credenza doubling as a computer desk, lateral file cabinet, and bookcases, all in polished cherry. The few times Alice had been up in Hal's study, it had seemed a lamp-lit, cozy place redolent of leather and pipe tobacco, mixed with other smells coming from the home improvement supplies stacked in boxes and cans in the storage areas. Some pine paneling had been installed on the south wall, but the work was unfinished and building materials lay stacked up to the low end of the ceiling.

Alice came up the narrow stairs, watching her step in the yellow lamplight, not knowing what she might find. If Hal were ill or actually having a heart attack, there was no way she could get him down the stairs to the car. She'd have to call paramedics or the sheriff's office to transport him to a hospital. Gull Harbor wasn't strictly rural, but it was beachfront property and sparsely built up in the area where Dunescape and other large vacation homes nestled among the sand hills. It could easily take an ambulance or other emergency responder twenty to thirty minutes to get to them.

Reaching the top of the stairs, Alice could see nothing amiss. She stepped onto the attic floor and looked across the room, holding the lamp up above her head.

Her uncle's desk chair was empty, but he might be in the bathroom. She walked across the darkened study and knocked on the closed door. "Hal?" she said softly. "Are you in there?" The door swung open at her touch, and when she held the oil lamp up high, she saw that he wasn't there, either.

Slowly, Alice's shocked brain worked its way around to the realization that Hal couldn't have called down the stairs to her because clearly he wasn't here. But something had spoken to her, and she was beginning to suspect. Her blood ran cold as she looked around the attic, with its sloping roof and shadowy shelves. She was shaking, wondering where the damned thing was hiding.

She went back to Hal's desk and saw a large envelope with the Gull Harbor Regional Bank logo in the corner and Alice's name in Hal's handwriting across the front. She reached for it, folded it once, and tucked it into her back pocket.

Then Hal's not-quite-right voice spoke to her from the shadows just beyond the stairs.

"Dear Uncle Hal is indisposed, I'm afraid. He didn't like my new look, scared him to death, quite literally. Didn't even have to touch him. He wasn't edible, either, too old and shriveled for my taste." A shuffling, bumping noise came from the area beside a stack of boxes containing the plastic branches of Suzanne's dismembered Christmas tree.

"I sent a friend to deal with the dog. Did you find him, I wonder?"

Alice ground her teeth. "You know I did."

A shape darkened the space at the head of the stairs, and she caught her breath.

"Shall I show myself to you? The lovely Margaret didn't much care for this form, but it didn't frighten her quite as much as it did the old man." The voice had taken on a dry, papery sound with an unpleasant click at the end of each word.

Alice was shaking uncontrollably, trying to collect her wits. She knew that blind panic wouldn't save her, but the shape-shifter's mention of Margaret shocked her nearly senseless.

"Why do you want to harm us? What have we ever done to you?" Alice asked, her voice breaking.

"Well, mate, that's the big question, innit?" said the voice, adopting an Aussie accent on top of its clicking squeak. "Y'know, I thought Black Harrow would straighten things out once you opened the door for him, finding his book of spells and all that, but look what happened—whole freakin' Sky Home comes calling. Now you can't even find a smear of him on the landscape. What Margaret would call epic failure, I believe. His fault I'm stuck between here and there, and now, of course, it's yours."

"H-how?" Alice said. Her eyes searched the area of the desk and credenza for anything that might serve as a weapon. Hal's ornate letter opener lay close by, but Alice had no intention of getting close enough to the creature for the sharp point to do any damage. The only thing available was the oil lamp in her hand, and a straw wastebasket full of crumpled papers, plastic bags, and an empty Kleenex box.

"How indeed. You figure out how to be a proper shaman," the voice rasped from the shadows, "and release me. I'll be gone right smart. If not, well …"

A shiny black insect-like leg stepped out of the dark into the pool of light. Something vaguely spider-shaped, but flatter and nastier, was emerging from the shadows, its tough chitinous abdomen scraping against the floorboards and humping along like a Galapagos tortoise. Alice saw the barbed mouthparts on its head in the lamplight and nearly blacked out. In that same moment, white-hot pain lasered into her ankle and up her right leg. The barb has speared through her right ankle, hooking her fast.

Dazed, Alice fell to her knees, too traumatized to even scream. The tick-Quinkan slowly pulled her leg out toward its swaying body. Finding her voice, Alice shrieked her throat raw and rammed the lamp down into the trash basket, setting the dry contents on fire within seconds. Blind with pain and terror, she hurled the burning wastebasket directly at the head of the shape-shifter. It flinched just long enough for her to rip her foot free and career past it to the stairwell. In a daze, she stumbled down, losing her footing and nearly falling before she reached the bottom. Scrambling to her feet, she limped toward the porch, her entire leg numb and mostly useless.

She pushed open the screen door in the dark, but then froze. The buzzing rattle of the Diamondback was somewhere just in front of her. In the light of the rising moon, the rattler was barely visible, but Alice could make out its raised head, tasting the air with its tongue. Then it struck at her, but not far enough to connect; instead, it seemed to be herding her back toward the stairs. Undulating in liquid s-curls, it came over the doorstep and into the house.

"Hell no you don't, you sonofabitch!" she yelled, falling over a coffee table in the dark. Unable to see the snake, she coursed the sound of its buzzing tail tip, and scrambled away in the opposite direction.

Suddenly, an explosion sent flames billowing down the narrow stairwell in a sudden wall of heat and smoke. Stunned, Alice felt her way to the kitchen, emerging out onto the back patio, where she received another shock. Hal reclined in his patio chair, clutching his shirtfront just over his pacemaker. His other hand hung limp at his side, his tumbler of whiskey shattered on the terrazzo.

"Uncle Hal?"

Alice touched his shoulder, and then fell back in revulsion, tripping and dragging her injured foot. Harold Blacksburg's corpse wore the horrified expression of a man who has looked at a walking nightmare.

Above and behind her, Alice heard window glass breaking and turned in shock as flames climbed into the air, painting the roof red. Then she remembered that other things besides Christmas decorations were stored in the attic: several kerosene heaters and jars and cans of paint, acetone, and other flammables packed in boxes under the eaves. An old gas heater connected to the same line that fed the stove in the kitchen had been installed on the wall behind Hal's desk. It must have been the source of the explosion.

Smoke and flames burst out of that single window, and then she heard a heavy, rumbling crash, as parts of the second floor gave way. Fire licked along the eaves of the back bedroom that had been Suzanne's—soon the entire wooden frame of the house would be completely engulfed. She could only hope it had snuffed the Quinkan and its serpentine accomplice before it could escape to wherever it went when it shifted bodies.

Alice stumbled to the front yard where Carlisle lay like a sleeping watchdog in the moonlight, highlighted now by leaping flames orange against the sky. She made it to the car and retrieved her phone, then punched in 911 with trembling fingers. After she had given the address and a general desperate statement about fire and death, she dropped the phone, exhausted.

Alice knelt on the ground, her head swimming. In the haze of timber smoke filling the yard, it was hard to breathe. Putting her hand on Carlisle's silky coat, she lay down beside him and shut her eyes. The roar of a forest fire played at the edge of her consciousness until she slipped into a pool of black silence. Then the disturbing noise went away.

Chapter 26

December 1969

Early morning sunlight streamed over Suzanne's shoulder, falling on the hotel's ivory letterhead where she'd written the date, December 11, 1969, and the salutation, *Dear Brother*. With the city phone book balanced in her lap as a writing desk, she chewed the end of her pen and thought about how to frame what she wanted to say. She could be conciliatory, or cheerful and informative, with a dash of local-color sightseeing info. Or she could be honest and try to describe why they were here in Queensland, in this place called Townsville on the eastern coast of Australia, and what she was feeling at the moment.

Through their hotel room window Suzanne saw bright blue sky and the gently waving tops of palm trees. Townsville was tropical and, at this time of year, warm and humid, so similar in look and feel to Miami that Suzanne was flooded with a momentary wave of homesickness. She loved travel and strange new places, but this wasn't a honeymoon; they had a dangerous trip ahead, with a questionable outcome. Traveling up the coast toward Queensland, she hoped they were heading in the right direction, but there was no way to be sure: Ned was following his instincts and the voices in his head, which she couldn't hear and didn't trust.

She looked at Ned, deeply asleep in the double bed, his mouth slightly open and arm flung back over his head. He was so beautiful to her when he lay like that, serene and undisturbed. It was a shame he couldn't just be an ordinary good-looking guy with a rather peculiar past. But that childhood, she now knew, was part of what kept him from ever being ordinary.

And she held no doubts at this point about his being truly hounded by demons or something unnatural. At first, she'd tried to rationalize his seizures as physiological and his visions as psychological, but after moving in with him, she'd seen enough to be convinced there was something that wasn't just the effects of too much Acapulco Gold. She'd seen an alien presence in his eyes when she was straight and sober, and it had rendered her speechless. But it had not scared her away; if anything, it made her more determined to fight for him and win against whatever was trying to ruin him. He was hers now, and when she dug her feet in, Suzanne could be surprisingly stubborn.

Sighing, she put the letter aside and stood up, stretching. Her white satin nightgown slid softy against her skin in folds of molten silver, the scalloped hem pooling around her ankles. The peignoir set was an interesting combination of tastes in which the elegant simplicity of the gown with its thin shoulder straps and straight lines was eclipsed by the elaborate lace insets and pink and white roses appliquéd across the shoulders and down the breast of the matching robe. It must have been expensive as hell, and she dutifully wore it because Bailey and Paula had given it to her with such enthusiasm.

For her own taste, Suzanne would have been more comfortable sleeping in one of Ned's well-worn T-shirts or nothing at all. She looked at him again and was tempted to crawl back under the coverlet and fit herself against his side. She loved him intensely. They were two against the world, bravely facing the unknown. What romantic rubbish, Hal would have said. What they were doing was completely mad and driven by much baser intentions than high adventure and heroic battles. Plus, it was costing them a lot of money.

Suzanne worried about that. She had emptied her bank account so they would have cash for the trip, and the big purchases like the Qantas flight from L.A. to Sydney, and from there to Brisbane and on to Townsville, with the requisite hotel rooms, had all gone on her credit card. It had a high credit limit, thanks to Hal, who'd presented it to her for her trip to France, but she knew they couldn't keep using it indefinitely. Soon it was going to hit the wall. She hated taking advantage of Hal's generosity, but the trip was Ned's salvation, and there was no other way to make it happen.

And so here they were. She'd convinced Ned that it would be better to rent a vehicle and drive the rest of the way from Townsville up toward Cairns and smaller towns northward. Suzanne loved to drive and was not the least bit intimidated at the prospect of getting behind the wheel of a Land Rover, even if it was located on the wrong side.

Ned moaned in his sleep and rolled over. She stood by the bed, looking down at him. Over the months of their courtship and especially after the wedding, he'd given her pieces of his history, little by little, stoned and not stoned, so that she figured he'd now told about as much of his twisted tale as he was able to share. For the moment, she was content to think she understood him better than anyone.

His mother had been one nasty piece of work as far as Suzanne was concerned. Physically and mentally abusing a child that way, it was unforgivable. Who wouldn't have nightmares? If Suzanne and Ned ever had children, she was going to make certain they never doubted, even for a second, that they were completely loved and wanted. Suzanne smiled to herself; her period was late, and although the disruption of her menstrual cycle might be caused by the stress of travel, it could also mean something else. She hoped Ned would be pleased if she turned out to be pregnant.

After they got this business with the lost totem thing taken care of, they might even want to settle in Australia. So far, she liked what she'd seen, especially here in the northern tropics. She could get a job teaching or something related to languages, and Ned could become a famous artist. Their children would be comely and intelligent, and take on noble causes like fighting for Aboriginal rights and protecting the Queensland rain forest. It was a wonderful fantasy, and might even come true if they could chase Ned's Furies away. Suzanne sat down on the bed beside him. That was a monumental *if.* Thinking about it pulled her back to the list of things needing to be done, like finding a rental vehicle and making preparations for the next leg of their journey. Ned moaned again.

She stroked his arm. "Neddy? Are you awake?"

Ned rubbed his eyes and sat up. "Sort of."

"It's a beautiful morning. Want to go walk along the beach before we try to get any business done?"

"What time is it?"

"Um, eight-thirty-ish."

Ned fell back on the pillows. "Too early." He patted the mattress beside him. "Come back to bed, m'love."

Suzanne was sorely tempted, but she knew if she gave in, it could be noon before they got out of bed, which might delay everything for another day. She leaned over, kissed him, and wriggled out of his grasp.

"Well, I'm going for a quick walk. Sleep in if you like, and when I get back we'll call around for a vehicle."

Suzanne got dressed in shorts and a cotton shirt, pulled her hair up into a high ponytail, and stepped into a pair of flip-flops. Then she stood with her hand on the doorknob for a moment, debating whether to leave him alone.

Ned lifted his tousled head. "Wake me when you're back." He buried his face in the pillow.

Suzanne shut the door quietly behind her. She felt a little uneasy, leaving him like that. His physical and mental well-being fluctuated, often without warning. Ned seemed to be following some homing instinct that felt "right" when he was on target and "muddy" and confused when he was off. She had the image in her mind of an old-fashioned dowsing rod questing for hidden waterlines running underground. Neddy was like a human dowsing rod, pointing toward something invisible, yet becoming more convinced of its presence the closer he got to it. Like the dowser, he was after a source; he was convinced that if he could get back to the locus of the original wrongdoing, the place where this dreadful taboo surrounding the stone had taken place, he could somehow make it end. Chewing her lip, Suzanne hesitated, then stepped out into the bright sun flooding the street.

The lodge was within walking distance of the shoreline, and it wouldn't take her long to reach the beachfront walkway known as the Strand. Suzanne headed down Fryer Street toward the winding beachfront esplanade where it seemed at least half the citizens of Townsville took their morning constitutionals. Wandering along the Strand with the deep azure waters of Cleveland Bay, and beyond that the Coral Sea, off to her right, Suzanne thought about what they might be facing once they got to wherever Ned felt was their destination. He'd tried to do a trance drawing the first night they'd come here to see if he could make an actual map, but no connection had been made.

But last night was a different story, when he'd jerked awake in a cold sweat, trembling from the visitation of his taipan guardian, as he'd begun to call her. Suzanne wasn't fond of reptiles, and it made her squirm just to hear his recount of the dream where the golden snake-woman had whispered in his ear, tasting his cheek with her forked tongue while keeping that terrifying other one away from him. Despite this fear, Suzanne understood that Ned's love/hate relationship with serpents was what powered his visions, which they now needed if there was to be any chance of ending this inherited saga.

What had really convinced them they were on the right track was the white-haired Aboriginal man at Nielson Park beach in Sydney who'd taken one look at Ned's drawing of the sacred stone and told them not only what it was and what sort of clan it likely belonged to, but also why it was such a powerful object and that Ned would do well to fold up the picture and keep it in a private place. Persons were obliged to be speared for displaying another clan's *tjuringa* in public, he'd warned them. If someone had in fact stolen it, he'd said, it would mean the greatest of calamities for the one who was the thief as well as the people from whom it had been taken.

From then on, Ned had been more careful about showing the drawing around, instead asking people if they'd seen the landscapes in his other pictures. That was when he'd found out about the Foundation of Aboriginal Affairs on George Street. More than a few people had told him to go there if he wanted to talk to some real Aborigines. Suzanne had decided to stay behind in their Sydney hotel room while he went alone to check the place out. With her pale skin and Anglo features, she had been pretty sure her presence wouldn't have helped his cause all that much.

Walking down the Strand with its dazzling blue sky overhead and scent of flowers on the breeze, she remembered the waves of anxiety she'd endured that night, sitting alone in a hotel room in a strange city halfway across the world from home, not knowing if Ned had found this notorious Foundation or gotten into any trouble. As the hours ticked by she began to rehearse in her mind what she would do if he didn't return, and even went so far as to look through her passport to find out what one should do to report missing foreigners. She tried not to think about the possibility that she could be stranded in this place with no way to find her husband of just seven months, but as it got later and later, with still no word from him, she'd begun to think the worst. Even a short burst of tears did nothing to relieve her rising panic.

Finally, toward dawn, she'd heard the door unlock. It was Ned, so excited he couldn't sit still. He'd seemed oblivious to her tearful state and sat on the bed trying to tell her about the trio of young Aborigines he'd met loitering outside the converted funeral parlor that served as Foundation headquarters. They'd been predictably suspicious of him, but when he'd shown them the scale markings on his arms and told them he had a taipan spirit totem, and that he was from the United States and had been on the fringes of the nascent Black Power movement in San Francisco, they'd decided to call him Brother. Back at the Foundation they'd introduced him to an elder whose black eyes had stared at Ned for several uneasy moments and then contemplated his pictures for a solid twenty minutes before he was prepared to share what he thought about them.

Eventually, once he'd sorted out how Ned was to be properly addressed, which he decided was "brother of these three," he advised Ned to head up the coast to Queensland and look around in the sandstone tablelands and wilderness gorges, especially in the Laura River area where there were many escarpments with caves like that picture he'd drawn. But he also warned that Ned might want to have a guide with him who knew how to avoid the Dangerous Places. Ned told her, laughing, how he'd suppressed the urge to tell the old man that he didn't want to avoid such places—he was specifically trying to find one.

His new Aboriginal friends had been kind enough to return him to his hotel and wish him well on his journey. All that took place nearly a week ago, and now here they were over a thousand miles up the coast, still following the pull of that invisible spirit-line back to … where?

Ned seemed convinced that the sacred site he needed to find was somewhere in the rock-strewn landscapes of his artwork, hidden among all the rock shelters where Aboriginal ceremonies had taken place over the centuries. Caves filled with Dreamtime rock art were the most likely, they'd both agreed, and locals had confirmed there was a lot of it in the area from Cairns to Cape York. So they'd headed north.

Anxious, she turned around and headed back to the lodge, kicking herself for leaving Ned alone for even fifteen minutes.

By the time she reached Fryer Street again, she was hot and sweaty. The hotel parking lot was empty except for two men standing beside an old Land Rover, talking and laughing in what her Southern friends would have called a "good old boy" way. She pegged them for locals, in their T-shirts, work shirts, khaki shorts, and hiking boots, until she realized one of them was Ned. He had taken so immediately to local culture she hadn't even recognized him.

"Ah, here comes the love of my life," he called as soon as he spotted her. "Ollie, meet Suzie, my wife."

Suzanne smiled at the stranger, wondering what the hell Ned had gotten them into now. To her, Ned said, "Suzie, this is Ollie Barnes, and he's driving us all the way to Cooktown."

Over a dinner of Spanish mackerel and mangoes at a packed bar & grille, Oliver Barnes, mechanic for hire and otherwise jack of all trades, brushed his sun-bleached hair out of his eyes and explained himself.

"When I was havin' a bit of a chinwag with your hubby here about Land Rovers and such, I mentioned that I'm headin' up to Cooktown to check on my mum who's not been well this past year," he said, between bites of a salad the size of small gardens. "She lives by herself and it's just me that looks after her."

He uncorked a bottle of rich, fruity wine. Shiraz that appealed to Suzanne. She resisted the urge to gulp it down in a couple of swallows.

"As I was telling him," Ollie said, refilling her glass, "I've been keeping that Land Rover humming for the last ten years; she'll go anywhere. There's nawt mechanical I wouldn't have a stab at. Fair dinkum, that is! You can take it to the bank."

Suzanne looked at Ned, wondering how much of their mission he'd imparted to the enthusiastic Mr. Barnes whose gray eyes twinkled with mischief under his sunburned squint.

"I explained to Ollie that I'm doing illustrations for a book," said Ned, turning his eyes to her. "We're researching Aboriginal rock art, especially anything to do with sorcery and magic."

"Plenty of that around," said Ollie. He bit into a sausage roll and nodded cheerfully. "The start of the Wet's not the best time of year to be going walkabout, y'know. Much better if you'd come in June."

"Sorry, that couldn't be helped. Our schedules just didn't work out for any other time of year," Ned said. Suzanne was again struck by his ability to lie so glibly on the fly.

"Do you think the roads will be passable?" she asked.

"What roads?" Ollie chortled. Suzanne blanched.

"Hey now," he said, patting her on the shoulder, "y'just need the right equipment, vehicle, guide, and provisions, that's all. I wouldn't advise the two of you to just take off into the never-never by yerselves, obviously."

"What *would* you advise?" she asked.

"That you hire me to be your driver, tour guide, and bush tucker expert," he said grinning. "I was born in Cooktown and know a lot of places along the rivers—that would be the Palmer and the Laura—what nobody's ever seen. At least, no white bodies." He was chuckling, leaning back in his chair. Suzanne smiled; she wanted to trust him, and she was pretty sure that Ned already did.

She searched his face. "So, Ollie, do you think you can take us around to some of these sites, and, um, keep us out of trouble?"

Ollie folded his hands over his flat stomach. "No worries, mate, she'll be apples all the way."

Suzanne assumed this meant something to the effect of hunky-dory. She was warming to him and was beginning to think his sudden intrusion into their saga was a stroke of good luck. It was easy to see that Ned had bonded with him and was relating to him like a long-lost friend.

Ollie turned to Ned. "About that rock art, what kinds of sorcery pictures are you keen on, mate?"

"Well, we're hoping to find images of dingoes and serpents, and maybe evidence of curses or magic spells, anything that would make the book dramatic and exciting."

Suzanne bit her lip. "When are we talking about leaving?"

"As soon as we can," said Ned.

"Then tomorrow morning we'll have a cuppa and just get on with it. I was getting bored around here fixin' Kombis and Rovers. Looks like you blokes have something far more interesting on the barbie. So I think I'll just help you out, for an appropriate fee, of course. An experienced guide like meself can't be had for free. We can stop over with my mum up in Cooktown; she'll be glad for the company. Just don't let her overfeed you."

"Cool, man, er, mate. You're a life saver," said Ned, and Suzanne could tell he meant it.

"Thanks, Ollie. Really," she added.

"No worries. It looks like your little trip is right up my alley."

She wondered, though, how much of Ned's story Mr. Oliver Barnes was buying. He seemed like a character who'd heard it all and then some, and she couldn't see them fooling him for long.

She sighed and held her wine glass out for a refill. It really didn't matter what he believed or didn't believe, as long as he could get them where they needed to go, and from the way he talked, he seemed plenty capable. Perhaps a little luck had crossed their paths, after all.

Chapter 27

December 1969

Sunset over the Endeavour River at Cooktown was as beautiful as Ollie's mother had promised. Ned reached his hand out to help Suzanne onto the grassy hilltop where they had a spectacular lookout over the river's mouth. Across the water, rocky outcroppings protruding from tree-covered hills.

The silver-gray water was dappled with an archipelago of green-topped islets. Across the inlet, hills became a silhouette against a gray and yellow sky. Just below curdled clouds, the sun shot through in a dazzling spotlight of lemon-white, reflected as a single bright patch on the slumbering water. Ned and Suzanne stood arm in arm, watching the tiny spits of land turn black in the fading light.

"Worth the whole trip so far," Suzanne remarked.

Ned pulled her close. "Better than anything I could paint."

The warmth of her shoulder against his chest and her hair brushing his face calmed the tumult inside. He felt in range of the target now, his nerves so jumpy he could barely sit still. But standing here, surrounded by rocks and trees and water, Ned enjoyed a quiet moment's respite.

The bones of the continent and the deep azure waters of the Coral Sea were vastly more ancient than the settlement Captain Cook had founded here in the 1700s. Ned felt that antiquity through the soles of his feet as he walked barefoot over the grass and rock. Something inside him was trying to reconnect to the land.

"Suzie? Are you sorry?"

"What? Of course not." Suzanne was looking up at him. "I wouldn't be anywhere else on earth right now."

Ned closed his eyes. "I mean, are you sorry you met me? If things don't turn out all right, I apologize now for ruining your life."

"Stop," she said. "We'll do what we have to do, and then we'll go home. Or who knows, maybe we could even settle here."

Ned gave her a squeeze. "Trippin' idea, a landscape painter wouldn't hurt for subject matter here, would he?" He encircled her in his arms. "Sydney would be cool, too."

"Brisbane," she said.

"Cairns."

"Townsville?"

"Alice Springs."

"Hey, we didn't go there."

"I know, I just like the sound of the name."

Suzanne was laughing now, and Ned's heart felt lighter. It soothed his soul when she laughed.

"We could name our firstborn Alice," she said, grinning.

"Whatever you like," he responded, playing along. She hugged him back with more warmth than usual, which made him wonder. This was the calm before the hurricane, the remaining moments in which you could gather your belongings and strap yourself in before all hell was unleashed. He was being pulled strongly now and felt certain that somewhere down one of those four-wheel-drive-only tracks of the Outback his nemesis waited.

When they reached Mrs. Barnes' small cottage, Ollie met them at the door.

"I was about to come looking for you two," he said, running rough fingers through his blond hair.

Ollie's mother, a short, squat woman whose gray-brown hair was pulled tightly back from her face and snagged with the claws of a pink plastic hairclip, beckoned them out to the tiny screened back porch. "Have a stubby before dinner," she said, handing out short bottles of beer from a portable cooler. "But only one each, mind," she said, "coz yer might want to take a few with you. How long did you say, lurv?"

Ollie chugged at the bottle and wiped his mouth on the tail of his camp shirt. "The Rover's fueled and ready and all the camping gear's stowed. I think if we leave early in the morning, we could get into the Outback past Laura by sundown, camp on the river and then spend a day or two muckin' about, and then a service stop in Laura or Lakeland on the way back. So, on the outside of four days all told, assuming we don't get stuck or flooded and have to dig ourselves out."

Mrs. Barnes nodded. "Sounds 'bout right." She reached out and patted Ned on the knee. "You blokes have a safe trip, and I'll be lookin' fer yeh 'bout this time next week, if Ollie here does his job right."

They were up early next morning, and although Ned felt an urgency to be off, Ollie's mother refused to let them get away without a hearty breakfast of fried eggs and tomatoes, avocado slices, spicy potato salad, and just-baked scones with ginger jam.

When they were finally ready to leave, she followed Ned and Suzanne outside and stood with them on the front stoop of the cottage. A bougainvillea heavy with dark salmon-pink clusters covered a trellis over the doorway so that everyone except Mrs. Barnes had to duck under its thorny arms to come out. It had rained that night, and the yard was dappled with puddles. Droplets of water sparkled all over the garden in the morning light.

"I wish you wouldn't just blow through like this," Mrs. Barnes said. "I hardly get used to seeing Ollie and then he's gone again." She swatted his backside and grinned with gold-rimmed molars. Ned watched her, amused. There was a bit of the pirate about her, and it wouldn't have surprised him to learn that Ollie was descended from the late Captain Cook's privateering stock.

Suzanne handed Mrs. Barnes a blue aerogramme. "Would you mind posting this for me? It's to my brother Hal back in the States."

"No problem, luv." Mrs. Barnes gave Suzanne a final hug and pocketed the letter. Ned let his breath out. He truly hoped they would all be standing here like this in the sunlit garden with Ollie's mum sometime next week.

* * *

By ten o'clock, they were rumbling along a fairly well-traveled road toward a town called Lakeland that Ollie described as a service town, which meant a place where they could buy petrol, tinned food, and ice, and replenish their water supply. It would be their last stop along the Peninsular Development Road, which led toward an even smaller service townlet called Laura, but Ollie planned to drive them off into the bush before they got that far.

When they pulled into Lakeland, Ollie parked the Land Rover in the shade of a large mango tree just off the road.

"Alrighty, mate, let's have a look at that drawing of yours again."

Ned rummaged in the zippered side pocket of his backpack and pulled out a folded sheet and gave it to Ollie, who flattened it out and studied it silently for a moment.

"You got me up a gum tree on this one," he said, fingering Ned's pencil sketch of the cleft in the side of a bluff with a unique grouping of boulders beside it and pooling water at its base. "I've never seen this particular formation in my rambles, but that's not to say it ain't there, 'course. You're certain it's in this area, are you?"

Ned nodded. "The guy I was telling you about at the Foundation told me it looked like a bluff in the Outback where Aboriginal people once lived. He said the closest town was a place called Laura."

Ollie scratched his head and replaced his hat. "Well, who am I to second-guess an old doctor-man, hey? Let's see those two color ones."

Ned unfolded the two watercolor paintings.

"Obviously, it's a plateau at the top of a gorge, but which one I dunno. And where'd you say you got these directions?"

Ned hesitated. "From the person who wants the book illustrations. Sorry, he couldn't give me names."

"Tell you what," said Ollie, handing the pages back to Ned. "I know where the major site clusters are, so I'll take you to the closest one. It's a couple of hours walk from a campsite I know about. If you're lucky, we might even stumble onto your spot somewhere down river where there's some high sandstone bluffs I haven't explored yet. Understand, this area is riddled with sacred sites and ceremonial caves. Not too many people know about 'em yet, far as I can tell, 'cept for locals like the old stringybark fellas who showed me where to find them. The people who made those places have been gone so long nobody remembers who they were."

"I'm sure this is the right area," said Ned.

"And how d'yeh know that?" Ollie was looking at him through narrowed eyes from underneath the brim of his hat.

"It … feels right."

"Well, yer the bloke's paying the money, so if it feels right to you, we're off."

Ned shot a look at Suzanne in the back seat, but her mouth was set in a tight line and her eyes revealed nothing. He knew she was resigned to go along with him wherever this wild goose chase took them.

Ollie's short-bodied Land Rover was loud and hot, and its stiff shocks registered every pothole and ripple in the dirt and gravel road heading away from Lakeland. It was a jolting, bumping ride that took some getting used to.

Sitting in the front passenger seat, Ned gritted his teeth and endured it; he hoped that Suzanne, strapped in behind them, wasn't too miserable.

In fact, she turned out to be a real trooper, as Ollie observed when they'd left the main road and turned onto a deeply rutted track that climbed up and down through rain-forest ferns that covered the steep embankments of the trail. Occasionally the narrow road opened out into stands of native bamboo higher than a man's head. Melaleuca filled the banks of creeks, their twisted misshapen trunks hemming in the Rover and scraping against its roof as it splashed through shallow watercourses. Often one side of the track would be washed out lower than the other so that the Rover leaned precariously, its tires chewing rocks and damp earth before righting itself again.

They crossed their first seriously flooded section of road by early afternoon.

With his wide-brimmed felt hat crammed tightly down on his head, Ollie charged cheerfully into the narrow stretch of tea-colored water. It crossed the rough track that had been wandering through eucalyptus trees and a vine thicket understory.

"Hullo," he said, "bit deeper than it looks," as water curled past the tops of the wheel wells. The Rover climbed out of the pool none the worse for wear and lumbered forward, its oversized tires grabbing at the rocks and sand of the makeshift road.

"That was fun," he said, grinning at Ned. "Maybe we won't have to run a banker."

"Do what?" Suzanne yelped from the back seat.

"Ford a flooded river. Still a bit early into the Wet, not too much rainwater fillin' the rivers yet. We could get lucky."

"I thought you said these sites you wanted to show us were accessible," Ned said, between jolts.

"They are, mate, but you gotta be willing to do a bit of work to get there. It's not like it's a national park or anything."

"Who exactly owns this land where the sites are?" Ned asked. "Are we going to be trespassing?"

"Old cattle station," Ollie responded. "Nobody on it nowadays that I know of. Dunno who owns it, on paper. The Aboriginals who had it first got killed off and driven away during the gold rush back in the last century. I got some bushie friends who showed me a couple of sites, and then I found more on my own. Fulla sandstone shelters and caves with rock art like you're looking for—sorcery stuff," he said, taking his eyes off the narrow track and looking at Ned with an unreadable expression.

"Good." Ned stared back at him. "That's what I'm after. Getting us there is up to you."

"Righto!" Ollie gunned the engine, propelling the Rover with a leap forward and careening around a sharp bend in the track.

They drove in much the same manner for over an hour, while Ollie kept his eye on the Rover's odometer and a large compass affixed to the dashboard.

"Should be coming up on a river crossing soon," he said, breaking the silence. "Let's see what we get."

He navigated the Rover up a slight rise thick with myrtles, then lurched sharply down and skidded to a stop. A narrow log bridge slightly wider than a four-wheel-drive vehicle stretched over the swollen river, but most of its planks and support trestles were below the surface of the water. As Ollie got out and walked down to the pebble-strewn waterline, Ned reached back to take Suzanne's hand.

"He'll figure something out, don't worry."

"I just hope we don't have to swim across," she said, giving him a half-smile. "Isn't Australia supposed to be croc-infested?"

"Yeah," said Ned, looking back at the river. He was reminded of rivers and ponds near his mother's homestead that you wouldn't go swimming in on a bet. He'd actually confronted a small gator crossing a trail in the river floodplain when he was a child. It had taken one look at him and galloped off into the titi as fast as its stubby bent legs would carry it. He'd laughed at the time about how it had been more frightened of him than the reverse, but remembering that event now, he wondered what it had really seen when it looked at him with those yellow eyes.

They watched as Ollie sat down on a nearby boulder and took off his boots and socks. Then he stepped onto the first couple of logs where the water was even with the bridge mounts. The further out he walked, the deeper the water rose as the bridge sloped downward, up to his ankles and then to mid-calf. He waded out to the middle of the river and turned around. The water was nearly knee-high and the bridge itself was completely invisible. Ned watched him coming back toward them, trying to read the expression on his face.

"I think we can have a go," he said, picking up his socks and boots, and sitting sideways on the driver's seat to put them back on. "But I need one of you to walk out ahead of me so I don't run off the edge. If you look down, you can see the bridge under the water. All you have to do is walk backwards down the center of the span and keep a watch on my tires. Are you game?"

"I'll do it," Ned said, unlacing his desert boots.

"Are there crocs in the water?" Suzanne asked.

"Could be, and snakes, too, so look sharp," Ollie said.

Ned put his shoes in the passenger seat and walked down to the river. He stopped for a moment and considered the dark water swirling under and over the structure, then waded out onto the bridge. The sodden logs were slippery, and not as close together as he'd like, but he forced himself to look down. Indeed, like a ghostly image, the bridge was visible under his feet. He walked out a bit further and then turned to face the Land Rover. Ollie engaged the clutch and eased forward, tires slipping a little on the muddy incline of the bank. Ned held his breath until the front wheels were firmly on the bridge. Ollie gave him a thumbs-up and began inching forward. Ned began to back up slowly, keeping his footing dead-center of the track so Ollie could line the Rover up in a straight shot across.

The seconds ticked away in slow motion as Ned backed carefully over the bridge. Flies swarmed his sweating face, but he ignored them. At the midpoint, water was licking the Rover's undercarriage, but it was clear Ollie's nerves were made of stainless steel as he kept the vehicle moving at a steady crawl. Ned gripped the bridge with his toes and felt a flood of relief as the water level against his legs began to drop. Then he saw an undulating shape below, darker than the blue-brown water, and knew at once that it wasn't a crocodile.

The shock was so sudden that he nearly lost his footing. Slipping to his knees, he grabbed the edge of the bridge and hung there a moment, not daring to breathe. He could see the serpent's head angled up toward him and saw immediately that it wasn't his taipan guardian. It whipped the water just below his feet and sank out of sight.

Ned's heart was beating so hard his chest was in pain, but he stood up, regained his footing, and continued to walk backwards, feeling the water drop to his ankles, and then at last he was on the solid bank. The Rover followed on, and Ned stepped out of the way as it clawed at the bank, digging in for a heartstopping moment, and then catching on rock beneath the sand and jumping forward a few yards. Soon they were all standing at the top of the bank, gasping and soaked in sweat, looking back at the submerged crossing.

"Good onya, mate!" Ollie exclaimed in a flash of teeth, white against his flushed face. He slapped Ned on the back and went to inspect the Rover.

Suzanne clung to Ned, smiling, but visibly shaken. He put his arm around her shoulders. "You all right?"

She nodded, mute.

"Snake under the water, right by my foot," he said.

Suzanne tightened her grip on his arm. "So that's why you nearly fell," she said. "We thought you'd tripped."

"It showed itself to me, deliberately."

"A dangerous place ..." said Suzanne. "What'll we do if we can't find it?"

He held her close, in spite of the heat. "I honestly don't know."

* * *

They were driving through a low open woodland area toward dryer territory now, the uneven ground covered in waves of prickly spinifex and saltbrush. Stands of a type of gum tree Ollie identified as eucalyptus bloodwood were thick amid patches of kangaroo grass.

"Campsite's not far off now," he said jovially, the river crossing long forgotten. "Soon as we get the tents set up, I'll get a fire going and we'll be feasting like kings, thanks to me mum. Reach back there and grab me a can, would you, luv?" he said over his shoulder to Suzanne. She opened the cooler and handed a beer to Ned, who popped the top and gave it to Ollie.

"You want one, too?" she asked.

Ned shook his head. He smiled to let her know everything was cool, but in truth he was feeling dicey. The skin on his arms and chest was stinging miserably, and it was impossible not to notice that the scale pattern had darkened. His vision went blurry and then cleared up a couple of times, and he was shivering slightly, not enough that anyone else would notice, but he could feel the tremors running along his synapses, vibrating in fast-forward.

They were climbing slightly now, leaving the grassy woodlands behind. Eventually they drove out from under the trees onto a broad savannah of waist-high grasses dotted with conical termite mounds, some nearly as tall as the Rover. It was then that Ned recognized in the spectacular vista overhead those eye-popping colors he'd painted in the surreal skies of his visions. A panorama of dark magentas and oranges and ultramarines filled his field of view from high overhead down to the horizon. He stared at it with a lump in his throat, understanding now that those outrageous skies he thought he'd made up were real.

"Found it!" Ollie announced, aiming the Rover at a copse of trees off to the left, their darker green promising a water source. It was a windswept canopy of myrtles, some up to thirty feet high with trunks two or three feet in diameter. An ancient sprawling fig with smooth light brown bark and round speckled fruit hanging in thick tags marked the entrance to the campsite.

Ollie maneuvered between gnarled trees so close together Ned was certain the door handles would catch on their knotty trunks. After a bit of twisting and turning along a barely visible path, they pulled out into a clearing big enough for the Rover and several good-sized tents. Ollie hopped out and stretched tall with a loud "Aaahh!"

Ned climbed down from the passenger seat and helped Suzanne unload their camping gear. With Ollie's help, the tents were soon pitched, and he'd found the charcoal remains of a long-dead campfire. They all helped in gathering wood and brush, and Ollie had a fire blazing just as the sun was going down.

"Look," he said, pointing toward the south. Flocks of bats were rising in spiraling drifts from the treetops, heading off to find food. The distant whumping of their wings came back over the glade.

"They're huge," Suzanne said, her head craned up to watch them flying in rough formation and then darting away on separate trajectories. "I've never seen bats that size."

"Those are flying foxes. Fruit bats to you," said Ollie. "They're harmless to the likes of us. If you're awake around sunup, you can catch 'em comin' back. There's a nice little creek just beyond this rise that we can take a dip in, but I'd advise waiting until morning. Don't want to step on something unpleasant in the dark."

Ned flopped down on the ground beside the fire, tired to the bone. He lay on his back for a moment, and then propped himself up on one elbow, looking for Suzanne. She was unpacking their food and spreading Mrs. Barnes's leftovers out on a plastic tablecloth. Ned had no appetite, but a great thirst invaded his throat.

"I'll just brew us up some tea in the billy, and we'll be all set," said Ollie. He plonked what looked to Ned like an old bucket with a bent handle and blackened base down on the coals and filled it with water. Once the water was boiling, he opened a bag of loose black tea, reached in and grabbed a good handful, and tossed it into the bucket. Then he brought out another pouch and selected a sizeable gum leaf, which he threw into the brew. Finally, he lifted the bucket, swilled the leaves around, and put it back on the fire. Then he set out three tin cups on a flat rock near the fire and poured what Ned hoped was sugar into each one.

As soon as the tea leaves had settled to the bottom, he took the bucket off the fire and with amazing finesse poured the clear dark tea into each cup. He set the billy back on the coals and gave both Ned and Suzanne each a cup. Taking the last one for himself, he unfolded a campstool, sat down near the fire, and took a loud slurp.

Ned sipped at the sweet aromatic liquid and felt better. It had a calming effect that settled his stomach and relaxed his muscles. He felt as if he'd been riding the last dozen or so kilometers with clenched teeth and fists.

"It's really good," Suzanne said, holding her cup in both hands.

Ned stared into the fire, letting his eyes go out of focus. He was suddenly so tired he would have fallen over onto his face if he hadn't been holding a cup of tea.

In the distance, a thin, high wailing howl filled the night air and subsided. Ned and Suzanne both jerked alert, but Ollie just grinned with his white teeth.

"Dingoes," he said. "They don't bark, y'know. But they sure do sing."

"Is that true," asked Suzanne, "they really don't bark? I thought they were canines."

Ned looked at the black wall of gum trees ringing them in. "Should we be on guard?"

Ollie slurped his tea with satisfaction. "No worries, mate. One or two might tiptoe into camp while we're asleep, but as long as we don't leave any food out for them to steal, they shouldn't bother us."

"What else do you know about dingoes, Ollie?" Ned felt somewhat revived from the tea, and thought he might actually be able to eat something. He sat up and reached for one of the cheese sandwiches Mrs. Barnes had packed.

"Depends on what yer asking … d'you mean their anatomy or their mythology?"

"The myths, I think."

"In that case, you'll be happy to know the sites along those river bluffs I'm gonna take you to are chock-a-block with 'em. Lots of dingo dreaming went on here, by which you might assume some of the long-gone Aboriginals who used these places were Dingo clans, right? Want me to tell you a Dingo Dreaming story?"

"Very much," said Ned. Suzanne moved close to him and lay down with her head on his thigh. He touched her hair, a river of flame in the firelight, and felt comforted.

Ollie lit a cigarette, inhaled, blew a ring of smoke, and commenced his tale. "Back in the Dreamtime, there was an old woman who had a vicious pack of dingoes. She commanded them to surround and kill blackfellas of many clans, so's she could drag them back to her camp and eat them. She was a cannibal, y'understand?" He laughed, relishing the tale. "Eventually, the wise men and women of the clans found out what was happening and they killed the old woman and all her dingoes. When they did that, a little gray-brown bird flew up out of her heart. Ever after, whenever that little bird shows up and cries its sad call, rain ain't far behind. All the dingoes who killed and mauled the blackfellas were turned into poisonous snakes, who still bite people to this day. Little dingo-snakes, heh heh."

"Well, I can't say that makes me feel any safer about going to sleep," said Suzanne.

"Ah, but it ain't the dingoes the blackfellas fear at night, nosirree."

"What do they fear?" Ned asked.

"Quinkans, of course."

"What?" Ned sat up, his brain wide awake. There was a distant murmur inside his head.

"That, mate, is where yer sorcery pictures come into play. Quinkans are evil spirits who like to eat people, just like our old dingo lady, and like her, they lure people into their trap by tricking 'em."

"How?" Susanne asked. Ned avoided her eyes.

"Mimicry, basically. They call to the child who strays away from the campfire, imitating the parent's voice and then grabbing him. They don't like the daylight, or even firelight, and you might encounter them mostly in dark corners of caves or outside at night. They mostly go after children, but they'll eat an adult if they don't find anything better on offer."

"What do they look like?"

Ollie yawned and swirled the tea in the billy. "Now, that's hard to say, 'coz they can take any shape they like to try to lure their victims. The Aboriginal blokes from Wujal Wujal, who took me to the sites I'm gonna take you to, showed me their pictures and told me what they were. They were right spooked by 'em, too. Couldn't wait to get out from under those particular overhangs, and then sat up all night yarnin' and telling stories to keep the Quinkans from snatching them up when they fell asleep."

Ned was sitting stock still although every nerve in his body was quivering. After so many years, he was finally getting the backstory on his childhood stalker.

"What were the shapes ... the ones you saw on the walls?"

"Tall, skinny, stick figures with funny little round heads and blobs on either side like ears, although some are squatty and round, like the ugliest frogs you ever saw, with white eyes or outlines around the body. Most of those paintings are very old, maybe thousands of years, and pretty faded. The paint's red ochre. Even the Aboriginals of today recognize them for what they are: Quinkans—evil spirits of the shadowland."

Ned's head was pounding, and he was finding it hard to breathe. He realized Suzanne was looking at him, her eyes wide.

"Neddy?" she whispered.

Ned doubled over and held his head, his tea cup falling to the ground. The din of voices was like the sound he'd once heard when he'd put a football-sized conch shell to his ear: surf roaring, but with the added difference of an occasional articulated voice. Sounds around him magnified, almost beyond enduring; the crackling of centipedes crawling in the grass and flying foxes stroking the air with leathery wings tore at his eardrums. His arms were on fire.

"Gnnnh," he moaned, rocking slightly. He could feel Suzanne's arms around him and her soft hands on his face while he fought the pull of that other world where the Rai held their ghostly vigil in the still gray lagoon. He heard Ollie's voice on the periphery of his consciousness, but it was inconsequential. His only thought was to cling with all his energy to his bright flame, his Suzanne, whose will to save him was at least as strong as that of those who wished him dead or worse.

Suddenly, an acrid odor of ammonium carbonate filled his nostrils, and the tumult in his mind receded. His blurred vision clearing, he wiped tears and sweat from his face and sat up.

Ollie held a broken capsule under his nose. "Smellin' salts," he said, giving another wave of the unpleasant stuff. "Kept it in my first-aid kit for a couple of years and never had a use for it, until now. Still seems potent enough."

"Neddy, what's happening? How do you feel?" Suzanne held his hand against her chest, and he could feel her thudding heart.

"It's better, I'll be all right in a minute." She held her cup of tea out to him, and he took a few sips, breathing deeply of its slightly medicinal aroma.

They sat silently, the only light coming from the fire smoldering beneath the ring of coals around the billy.

"Well, now," Ollie said, removing the bucket and stoking the fire till it roared awake, tossing orange sparks above their heads. "Why don't you just give me the duck's guts and explain why you and this lovely lady are *really* out here in the back blocks looking for dingoes and Quinkans? I'm bettin' it ain't to draw their portraits."

Chapter 28

December 1969

Ned and Suzanne looked at each other. Ollie chewed the stem of a eucalyptus leaf, waiting. Finally, he spat the stem out.

"The thing is mates, I like to know where I stand when it's a job I'm hired to do. I don't think you've been quite honest with me. In fact, Neddy, I'm thinking you're a right bullshit artist."

Ned studied the toes of his boots. "I'm sorry, man, really. You're right; we haven't told you the straight story."

"Well, let's have it, then. Fire away." Ollie strained the rest of the billy tea into his cup.

Ned bowed his head. This was it, the moment of truth where all his pretenses fell away. "I'm not what I seem," he said, staring at the ground. "I'm not what you'd call a normal person."

Ollie exploded into loud choking laughter, nearly falling backward off his campstool and spilling his cup. "Spare me days, mate!" he yelped. "I *know* you're not normal; I'd have to be barkin' mad to believe that! D'ya think I'm blind? I've been watching those so-called tats o' yers, going darker, and yer eyes do funny things. Yeah, I do notice things like that though you think I'm not payin' attention. And the way you wigged out just now … fuck yeah, you're not normal. My question is, what the bloody hell are you?"

Suzanne put a protective hand on Ned's arm. "Ollie—"

Ned shook his head. "He's gotten us this far. We owe him the truth." He looked at Ollie and took a breath. "I'll lay it out as plain as I can. My father was …" Ned hesitated, searching for the quickest way to describe his understanding of Lacy Rider, "a seer, you might say a shaman, and my mother pretended to be. She had her own skills, but true 'seeing' wasn't one of them. She used me for that. What she did was serpent conjuring." Ollie's eyes widened, but Ned kept going. "She used my blood as the fixing agent in her curse potions. By the time I was twelve, I had little scars all up and down both forearms. But the year I turned sixteen, something happened that changed them to this." He held out his arms, the dark green-gold scale patterns pulsing in the firelight.

Ollie sucked in his breath. "That's a real dog's breakfast, innit?"

"If you mean fucked up, yeah, it is. You don't know the half of it!" Ned could feel the heat rising in his face.

"Neddy, you don't have to—"

Ned brushed Suzanne's hand away. "No, he wants to know." He mopped his face with the tail of his T-shirt. "The bloody truth, as you would put it, is that I've been stalked most of my life by a creature that I now believe to be a goddamned Quinkan, and the reason I'm here in the frigging Outback is to try to get rid of it!"

"Jesusmary," said Ollie, his eyes round. "Don't shout shit like that out loud. Nobody says things like that at night in the bush unless you got a mutherfukin' campfire the size of Sputnik."

"Then you believe me?"

"I'm not saying I do or I don't. I'm saying you don't muck around with the local legends when you're in the bush at night."

"I thought you were the one who said there was nothing to worry about when those dingoes were howling," said Suzanne.

"Flesh and blood dingoes are one thing, but bloody Quinkans! You're not just havin' a go at me for fun, are ya, mate?" Ollie retrieved his stick and poked the flickering coals awake.

Ned slumped over. "I wish to hell I was." Suzanne buried her face against his chest. He could feel her sweat, or tears, dampening his shirt. "There's something else you ought to know. I have a totem, a guardian of some kind, that tries to keep the Quinkan away from me. It's an animal totem that shows up in my dreams and trance states."

"What kind of animal?" Ollie asked, poking the fire and cutting his eyes up at Ned.

"A snake."

"What kind of snake?"

"A taipan."

Ollie put down the poker and stared across the fire at Ned. "Fer fuck's sake, is there anything else you want to blow m'doors off with? Huh?"

"That's about it."

Ollie shook his head. "I can't believe this. Taipans and Quinkans. So all that shit about art books and illustrations and publishers was a snow job."

"I'm afraid so."

Ollie finished his tea in a single gulp. "Well, let me ask you this: d'you have any flaming idea what you're really looking for out here?"

"Suzie, hand me the pack, will you?" Suzanne eyed them both silently and reached for Ned's backpack. Ned opened the zippered side pocket and pulled out the one drawing he hadn't shown to Ollie. Now he handed it over. "Do you know what that is?"

"Sure, that's a sacred clan object. *Tjuringa*, in the lingo. Don't tell me you stole it and got a mob of angry blackfellas after you."

"Not exactly, but close."

"How close?"

"I didn't steal it myself, but I think one of my ancestors did. Whatever happened way back then is what caused the Quinkan to come after my father and now me. The taipan showed me a vision where this stone was made by some dingo-god. An Aboriginal taboo got broken somehow, but I don't understand that part of it. She keeps telling me I got to return this thing, but I don't know where it is or who to give it back to even if I could find it."

"She?"

"Taipan Ancestor. Sometime she looks like a dark-skinned woman with bronze-gold hair that streams out from her head in these long spirals." Ned gestured vaguely.

Ollie laughed. "I wouldn't mind havin' a gander at yer visions, mate."

Ned shivered. "You wouldn't want to meet her in snake form."

Ollie stood up and went to the brush pile he'd collected up earlier. He fed the fire until it was blazing up as high as a meter stick, with bright streamers swirling upward. "Okay, I'm getting' a picture here. You've been seeing this Quinkan in your dreams or visions or whatever, but didn't know what to call it. A Dreamtime Ancestor sends you on a quest after a Dingo Clan *tjuringa*. Maybe this taboo involves a curse, which is why you're so keen to find sorcery figures, which you're hopin' will lead you to a ceremonial site where you can do … something. "

Ollie looked at Suzanne. "I'm assuming none of this is news to you?"

"I believe Ned, and I want more than anything to help him get free from this thing you call a Quinkan. I believe it exists, because I've seen those same transformations in him you've seen, only worse. I want to help him make it all stop."

"Maybe lay off the dope?" said Ollie.

Ned glared at him and said nothing.

"Sorry mate, cheap shot." Ollie smiled with half his mouth. "So. You said a ways back down the road you were sure this is the right place. How do you know that?"

Ned shrugged. "I just feel it." He didn't have the words, or the energy, to try to explain to Ollie what it was like to have your head invaded against your will and your body pulled by forces you couldn't control.

Ollie stared at Ned, unblinking as a desert goanna. Ned wondered what he was thinking. Was he going to ditch them and be gone when they woke up, or would he decide to stick it out and help them? Either way, Ned had no intention of turning back.

"Neddy," said Ollie, poking at the fire, "you got any Aboriginal blood in yeh?"

"What? No, how could I? My parents were both born in Florida, in the USA."

"Hm. Just asking, 'coz what I'm hearing sure sounds like bloody 'clever man' work to me."

"Is that the same as a senior man?" Ned asked, remembering the old man at the Foundation in Sydney.

"Righto. What you blokes might call a witch-doctor, or maybe a shaman. When Aboriginal men learn mysteries beyond the regular coming-of-age initiations, they're called 'clever' or 'senior' men of knowledge. Then they can do things like diagnose what's wrong with sick people or go walkabout in the spirit world where they have supernatural guides, ghostly critters my bushie pal calls 'Rai,' and these spirit guides take them places where ordinary people can't go. The Senior man interacts with other spirits, good and bad, to help out their clans."

"I don't know how that could apply to me, except for maybe the spirit world part," said Ned, seeing the dark waters of the twilight billabong in his mind, with the storklike boatman in the canoe offering him a ride to the land of the dead.

He didn't want to remember any of that or the horrid burned man-thing in the hut of grass who'd cursed and shouted at him as he'd turned away, heading down the gray bank to the still waters of the lagoon in search of the shining cord that would lead him back to his body. Ned felt weary to the marrow, and at this moment wanted nothing more than to chill out on the floor of his Miami apartment with a joint and Jimi Hendrix on the turntable.

The distant flap of flying foxes and the mournful howl of dingoes beyond the campsite were as surreal to him as any of those visions. If it weren't for Suzanne's firm clasp on his arm, he might have thought this place just another hallucination.

But she was solidly here, as was this person called Ollie Barnes, as was the crackling fire he tended. The sound of distant thunder and the scent of rain on the night air seemed real enough. Ned tried to pull his scattered thoughts together.

"My father called it 'seeing far.' I never questioned how we did it, or where that ability came from. It was just something the two of us could do, a fact of life I grew up with."

Ollie shook his head. "Well, too bad we don't have some of my Wujal Wujal mates here. I'm thinking they'd be more use to you than me right about now. For a Yank, you've just spun me the damndest Dreamtime yarn I've heard in years. But here's the deal. I'm a man of my word, and you paid me to help you find this place of yours, so by jingoes, I'll make a stab at it."

"Thank you," said Suzanne, "you don't know how much this means to both of us."

"Oh, I have some idea," he said, grinning. "You're a lucky bloke, Neddy Waterston, if that's your real name."

"I know that. I'd probably be dead by now except for her," he said, clasping Suzanne's hand tightly.

"Then I suggest you two crawl into yer sleeping bag and rest up. The site we're heading for tomorrow is half a day's trek into the scrub, and I don't fancy carrying either of you on me back."

* * *

The laughing call of a kookaburra ricocheted across the clearing. Early morning sunlight spilled down into the campsite from a sky painted in pale blues, pinks, and yellows. The day promised to be fine following a series of late-night downpours that rolled across the area after Ned and Suzanne had collapsed, exhausted and drenched in sweat, onto their sleeping bags. Igloo-shaped, the tent offered a mosquito-screened window and zippered doorway, which they'd been forced to close during the rain. Overall, it had been a hot, damp, and disturbing night with neither of them sleeping for any extended period.

They'd made a quick breakfast of pan-fried bacon and damper, a pasty bread made of flour, water, and salt that Ollie prepared while they packed up their tent. Finishing breakfast off with coffee and mango slices Mrs. Barnes packed for them, they were ready to head into the bush. Ollie locked and secured the Land Rover, and made one last check of the three packs they intended to carry with them. As Ned understood it, the plan was to trek down to the most accessible rock art galleries that Ollie knew about, explore the area further by following Ned's instinct, camp near the river that night, and then head back to the campsite if they didn't find anything.

Ned watched, mystified, as Ollie gathered up three rough-cut quartz crystals from the campfire's edge. One was a shard half a hand long, milky around the base but clear at the point, and the other two were more rounded, golf-ball sized with clear faceted outcrops embedded in a coarse rock matrix. He didn't remember seeing them when he'd gone to bed last night.

Ollie put the elongated one in the breast pocket of his bush shirt and buttoned the flap, then he held out his palm with the other two.

"Take these and keep 'em on ya," Ollie instructed. Ned took a one, rolling it in his palm. Suzanne took the other and tucked into the pocket of her shorts.

"What's this for?" she asked.

"Quinkan protection," Ollie said, adjusting his backpack straps over his shoulders. "Lore from my Aboriginal pals. Those aren't just any old crystals. They got Senior-man business in 'em, made for the express purpose of warding off the nasties. If a Quinkan slips up to the camp, the crystal activates so the firelight shines in their eyes and chases 'em away, or something like that. My bushie friends never go to sleep in the Outback without putting 'em around the campfire, and neither do I."

Ned looked at Suzanne and saw what he thought was an expression of mixed bemusement and relief. Clearly, Ollie had decided to become an ally. The fact that he seemed to take the possibility of Quinkans at face value was the one thing that gave Ned any hope at all of succeeding in this hopeless task. The whole thing was madness, but now that Ollie knew, more or less, what they were searching for, Ned reckoned his chances at slightly better than even.

"Two things to watch out for," Ollie said, standing at the edge of the trees. "Keep yer eyes peeled for green ant colonies in the trees and bushes, and watch for snakes in the grass. Stay close to me and shout out if you need help. There are a couple of springs we can drink from once we get closer to the river, but it's a four-hour hike, so don't drink up your water supply all at once. Ready, mates?"

Ned took a deep breath. He was jittery, knowing in the back of his mind that somewhere ahead waited terrible things. But he hoped at the same time that whatever he discovered would bring this whole miserable business to an end. Ollie set off into the trees, following a faint footpath.

"You next," Ned said, motioning to Suzanne. She nodded and hoisted her backpack a little higher onto her shoulders, then followed Ollie. Ned took one last look at the campsite with its guardian Land Rover and turned to catch up with the other two. He was used to walking everywhere he needed to go, and was actually looking forward to the trek itself, as long as the weather stayed clear. It was warming up rapidly as the sun climbed higher, with an accompanying humidity that was enough to sap your strength long before your actual muscles were too tired to walk. Ned pulled his hair into a ponytail and stuffed in up under the bush hat that Ollie's mother had insisted he take along. A slight breeze evaporated the sweat on his neck and face, so he wasn't too uncomfortable, except for the unrelenting tiny black flies that bedeviled men and animals alike everywhere in the Outback. All you could do was swat at them.

Ollie made good time for the first couple of hours, which Ned kept track of with Grant's watch, but by noon they were all slowing and stumbling over their feet on the increasingly rocky, tumbled scarp. House-sized chunks of weathered sandstone, half hidden among groves of eucalyptus, jutted toward the sky, wind-blasted temples for goannas and rock wallabies. At last, Ollie headed toward one surrounded by thin-leaved stringybarks and a single sentinel palm standing tall on its bare gray-brown trunk.

The pinkish-red sandstone block was as high as a two-story building and nearly as wide, with fissures splitting its face into many small crevices and a few large enough for several people to stand up in. The shade inside the largest split was blessed relief from the baking noontime sun. Ned took his hat off and fanned his face, swatting flies. Suzanne flopped down on the sandy floor of the shelter, heedless of a couple of fat centipedes crawling in tandem near her foot.

"Look," said Ollie. He pointed over his head.

Ned caught his breath. A panorama of beasts and birds painted in ochres of red and yellow, some with white outlines, crossed the ceiling of the gallery as if on parade: kangaroos or wallabies, crocodiles, dingoes, scrub turkeys, fish, flying foxes, and more. The dingoes were of particular interest because they were remarkably similar to the one he'd drawn in the *tjuringa* sketch.

Suzanne pulled her camera out of her backpack. "I don't know if this will come out," she said, "since it's so dark up under here, but here goes." She aimed up at the rock ceiling and clicked the shutter.

"You might want to save yer film," Ollie said. "This is only the first gallery on the way to the bluffs and the river. Lots more where these came from."

"Any Quinkans?" Ned was craning his head back to see the entire scope of the paintings.

Ollie gave him a look. "If you mean paintings, I'd have to say no, but I'll show you a place pretty soon that's chock-a-block with 'em. We'll hang out a bit here whilst the heat of the day passes, then we'll see what we can find."

"Cursed flies!" exclaimed Suzanne, swatting at her face.

"Yah, Aboriginals use a paste of animal fat to keep 'em off," laughed Ollie.

"What I wouldn't give for a cold shower," said Ned, thinking that he'd never been so hot and sticky and miserable in his whole life, even though he'd grown up in the Florida swamps with no air conditioning.

"That's on the way, too," said Ollie. "Nice little spring and waterfall when we get to the bluff. Cool you off right smart."

They lapsed into silence, listening to the black flies buzz, when Ned realized that Ollie was watching him closely.

"What's on your mind, man?" He stretched himself out on the ground beside Suzanne.

"Just wondering if you 'feel' anything," Ollie said.

"No, I don't. But I'm a little spaced out, just being this close to places where Aboriginals once lived. I sense their presence, in a dim way, like breath on the back of my neck."

"How's your arms?"

Ned held them out. "Faded a bit."

Ollie took a look. "I dunno how you live with that. I'd be fed up to the back teeth long before I got to be your age." He stood and stretched. "Ready to move out?"

They shouldered their packs once more and moved out of the shade into the early afternoon haze and heat. Although white-hot sunlight blazed down on them, far to the west the sky was darkening with a massive buildup of purple thunderheads.

Ollie led them on an uphill track through gray-white box eucalyptus and spindly melaleuca, past an occasional termite mound, and through waist-high grass where Ned narrowly avoided plowing through a massive green-ant nest. He brushed the outer fringes of the yard-long colony with his knee where it was pasted with silken larval glue across a thicket of vines. A single ant clung to his thigh, pincers biting for all it was worth, but he was several feet down the trail before the rest came boiling out to see what had disturbed their tiny civilization.

"Goddamn, that hurts like shit!" Ned swatted the ant away and rubbed the swelling red spot where it had dug in, imagining what it would feel like to have your entire torso covered in such bites. Ned shivered in spite of the heat, realizing that, in a way, he already knew. His arms and chest weren't bothering him at the moment, but when the scale designs were pulsing, it could be close to unbearable.

They were off the track now, and Ollie stopped occasionally to check his pocket compass. At the top of a sharp stony ridge, he came to a sudden halt. "Have a go at that," he said, grinning.

Ned and Suzanne scrambled up the rocky scree and stepped onto a narrow plateau with a vista that was literally hundreds of miles worth of sloping scarps and rolling hills covered in an ocean of gum trees. The edge of the bluff dropped off steeply to form a narrow gorge with sparkling water far below. Ned felt dizzy looking at it; he estimated the drop at many hundreds of feet down. Riverine red gums filled in much of the area around the base of the cliff, their smooth, pale trunks thrusting nearly a hundred feet high along the sandstone wall. From that far away, their blue-gray foliage appeared dusted with tiny white stars in a wet-season flush of blossoms.

Ned held his breath. It wasn't the exact plateau in his paintings, but it was damned close. He had the sudden urge to leap over the edge to the bright ribbon of water below. Gulping, he stepped away from the precipice.

"Good god, Ollie, are we going down there?" Suzanne asked, hanging tightly to the trunk of a bloodwood rooted into the sandstone at the top of the ridge.

"Dunno, the route's up to his nibs here." He nodded toward Ned. "There's a huge shelter just below us that you can't see from here 'coz it's cut back underneath this lookout. You can access it from an ancient rockfall my Aboriginal mates call the giant's staircase. Want to give it a go?"

Ned nodded, still shaken from the brief couple of seconds where he'd imagined himself diving over the edge of the cliff.

Ollie turned away from the plateau and backtracked for a couple of yards, and then took a side trail that paralleled the rim. Then it angled down into a cut in the rocks, and Ned could see that indeed a steep ridge of boulders and sandstone slabs allowed them to carefully work their way down to another broader shelf some fifty feet below.

A flock of rainbow lorikeets swept up the gorge, calling and trilling, their shrill voices filling the canyon. The rocky terrain sprouted tufts of saltbush and other tough grasses, and an attractive flowering shrub Ollie called a goanna bush clung to the steep incline in a showy display of small lavender-pink flower sprays drooping like fern fronds.

At last they found themselves on level ground, with the scarp falling sharply away to their left and on their right a cave entrance tall enough to drive a double-decker bus through. Somewhere nearby, the sound of trickling water made continual background music.

"Y'see?" said Ollie. "Have a gander at these beauts."

Ned followed him inside the cave where it was blessedly cool. At first it was too dark to see much, but as his eyes adjusted, an incredible array of figures surrounded them on nearly every rock surface. He recognized the usual conglomeration of birds, fish, and reptiles, including a vast undulating yellow snake that stretched completely across one long back wall. But then he spotted the dark red ocher figures fronting the entrance to a smaller cave and his blood froze. He guessed what they were.

"Here's yer Quinkans," Ollie said cheerfully. "These fellas are just the advance guard, so to speak. Lots more through there." He indicated the entrance to the inner cave, which was still high enough for a man to walk through without stooping. "Take me torch and have yerself a look," he said, pulling his flashlight from his pack and offering it to Ned.

But Ned was rooted to the spot, staring up into the sightless white eyes of the nearest Quinkan. It loomed over them, larger than life, with arms outstretched and the seven digits of each hand splayed wide. Flaps like floppy dog ears sprouted from both sides of its head, and a long penis hung down between its thin legs. A host of similar, smaller figures were clustered around it.

Wordlessly, he took Ollie's flashlight and stepped through the entrance of the smaller chamber. Steadying his shaking hands, he played the light over the walls. More dark red Quinkans in varying sizes and shapes leapt up the walls and over the ceiling, flanked by numerous shapes of crocs, emus, and snakes. An inverted male figure with what looked like a barbed spear protruding from its head dominated a panel off to his left.

On the ceiling, directly over his head, an enormous spotted dingo rode the back of a wide-bodied snake painted in white and red crosshatch designs. Ned stared, open-mouthed. He jerked and nearly dropped the flashlight as the hissing voice of his tormentor announced itself in his head.

"Welcome, Neddy," it rasped across his brain cells. Ned felt himself slipping into a trance state, his fingers losing their grip on the flashlight and his knees collapsing under him. The death adder rose up in his fading vision, balancing vertically on its banded stocky body, its flat arrow-shaped head displaying impossibly long fangs phosphorescent in the dim light. Ned hit the floor, and a moment later a loud clap of thunder popped near his ear. Suzanne shrieked.

Chapter 29

December 1969

"Shit, mate, that was close!"

Ned opened his eyes and saw Ollie standing over him. Just a few feet away lay the body of a death adder, its head blown off by the pistol in Ollie's right hand.

Suzanne ran to Ned and threw her arms around him, holding on so tightly he had to pry her hands loose. "It's alright, baby, it didn't strike. See, I'm okay, you can let go." He took another long look at Ollie. "I didn't know you could shoot like that."

"That's what you're payin' me the big bucks for, matey, to save yer skin from the likes o' them." He kicked at the limp serpentine body and retrieved his flashlight. Shining its wide beam over all the recesses of the cave, Ollie appeared satisfied that no more surprises hid in the darkened corners. "All clear," he announced.

Ned got to his feet, brushing dirt from his shorts and legs.

"God, Neddy, if that thing had …" Suzanne let the sentence hang, her eyes wide with fear.

"Shh. It didn't, and I'm fine. This is the Outback. Those things are going to happen. We just can't afford to be careless."

"I know," she said, breathless. "But I would die if something happened to you."

Ned bit his lip. "Then I'll have to be even more careful." He smiled and kissed the top of her head, hoping to mask his own fears.

Ollie cleared his throat. "Perhaps you two'd like a cool swim after all this excitement?"

They followed him back out to the main cave entrance and up a tumble of limestone boulders to another terrace. At eye level, a stream of clear water emerged from a cleft in the rocks and splashed down into an elongated shallow pool, then spilled over the side and plunged freefall to the river below.

Ollie took off his boots and socks, emptied the pockets of his shirt and shorts, and waded into the pool fully clothed. He sat down in the cool water and cupped it in his hands, thoroughly dousing his face and hair. "C'mon in, the water's fine," he said, leaning back against a rock ledge.

Ned and Suzanne followed suit, and soon all three of them were sitting in the limestone basin. Ned lifted his face so that the spray coming out of the rock wall fell over his head and shoulders. It was ice cold and pure heaven to his sweat-soaked body. He sat in the water long after the other two had climbed out and set about making lunch from their provisions. He'd felt fevered when the Quinkan had invaded his mind back in the smaller cave, but now he was clear-headed and fully resolved to go forward and defeat this thing. And not just for himself. If he and Suzanne ever had children, he wanted to make sure their lives would be free of its shadow.

"Hey man," he called, standing up and feeling the cold water run down his legs like ice melting in the heat. "Why were some of those figures painted upside down?"

"Those are yer sorcery images. Aboriginal legends say that if a man is buried head down, when it comes time for the spirit to exit his nose and fly off to heaven, it can't get out, so instead, he'll be trapped between worlds as a ghost."

"And a spear aimed at the head?"

Ollie brushed flies away from his face. "Could be a curse. When a doctor-man points a bone at somebody, even in a painting, it usually means bad business. Sometimes you'll find sorcery pictures like that hidden way back in the darkest corners where nobody'll see 'em, prolly to keep the curse a secret."

Ned wrung water from his hair and went to join the others; he was hungry, but his mind was elsewhere. That bit in Ollie's yarn about getting trapped between worlds had struck a chord, and he couldn't stop thinking about it.

They ate a brief lunch of fruit, cheese, and tinned corned beef, and drank their fill of the cold spring water, refilling their canteens and water bottles for the trek down into the gorge. Ned walked out to the edge of the terrace and looked across the chasm to the other side. The reddish sandstone cliff was eroded into horizontal striations and elongated chunks like a Titan-sized brick wall peppered with tufts of green that he realized were the tops of trees and vine thickets. He spotted at least three narrow waterfalls tumbling down the flanks of the cliff into the gorge. The flat top of the bluff was covered in a green gum forest as far as he could see. Directly in front of him, the sky was bright blue with clumps of bluish-gray stratus clouds mirroring the formations of the land. Far away to the west, the sky took on a magenta tinge, and the clouds were darker underneath, pregnant with more rain.

"We got dozens of caves and shelters like this one all along the cliffs on both sides of the gorge," Ollie was saying. "I've explored a few, but I thought we might go further down toward the river and look for an overnight campsite."

Ned sat down, closed his eyes, and tried to calm his breathing, waiting to see if he could slip into his "seeing far" state. At once, he felt the Taipan Ancestor enter the top of his head and slide down his spine, wrapping her cool golden body around his shoulders and chest. Trembling, he framed the question in his mind: *Where's the site I'm looking for?* Immediately the answer came, whispered in his mind like the flick of a forked tongue in his ear: *Below.*

He opened his eyes, and the sensation faded, to be replaced by a sudden urge to jump up and run. The Ancestor was gone, but Ned knew Ollie was right; they should go down into the gorge. He was feeling the magnet's pull again, so intensely now that he would have dropped everything and flung himself over the cliff in order to get there as fast as possible if his rational brain had not held the impulse in check.

He stood up. "It's down there," he said. "I'm certain."

"Down we go, then," Ollie said, hoisting his backpack. He walked out onto the giant's staircase again. "I'll go first and find the best way down. Just follow in my footsteps, and take yer time. Plenty of dingoes and roos have gone up and down these rocks, so we can, too."

Ned felt lightheaded, stepping downward, following Ollie and Suzanne, but he kept his difficulties to himself. The sooner they got to the bottom the better, and he wasn't about to stop them so he could sit down and wait for the feeling to subside. Looking at his arms, he received a momentary shock as he realized the markings were gone. Not one scale pattern anywhere. He rubbed his palms vigorously over his forearms, but nothing appeared. He was suddenly, inexplicably, unmarked. Confounded, Ned stumbled after the others, his only clear objective now being to reach his destination somewhere at the bottom and face his worst nightmares.

* * *

The sun was low on the horizon by the time they stood on a ledge just above the waterline. The river was high in its rocky bed, and there was no sandy bank on which to camp. But from this vantage point, reddish light from the setting sun hit the rock wall above them at an angle, revealing a sizeable shelter not far from where they stood. A cluster of paperbark trees obscured the entrance, and further down, red gums stood with their feet drowned in the river. A small waterfall beside the shelter's entrance made a shining trail of silver down the ruddy cliff.

Ollie led them along the sandstone slabs and boulders, picking his way carefully and poking the clumps of shrubs and grass for snakes with a walking stick he'd fashioned from a fallen tree branch. At last they were all safely standing just outside the overhang of the shelter. Even in the fading light, they could see clusters of red spatter-painted hand stencils on both sides of the sloping entrance and finely executed paintings on the rock walls within. Beside the entrance, the weathered image of a large dingo was incised on a boulder that was vaguely dog-shaped, with rounded body, small head, and ear-like protrusions. Inside, more images of dingoes adorned the walls of the cave.

"Dingo Dreaming," Ollie stated. "Dingo clan people used this site."

Thunder boomed in the distance, promising more rain pouring onto the land and into the rivers and streams before the night was over. The shelter seemed high enough above the river, and after he'd checked the inside of the cave for "nasties," Ollie pronounced it a suitable campsite.

Ned dropped his backpack on the stony floor of the cave and sank to his knees, bathed in sweat. Voices filled his head, cresting and ebbing away, like the drumming sound of rain moving up the canyon. His vision blurring, he stared at the rock wall, trying to make out the tall reddish figures in conical headdresses topped with what appeared to be tassels or feathers. They did not seem to be done in the same style as those they'd seen in the large cave near the top of the bluff.

"Are these Quinkans?" he asked.

"Older," said Ollie, looking them over. "That mob," he said, indicating the largest of the humanoid figures, "those are Ancestral beings, but they don't look like any Quinkan figures I've ever seen. My guess would be that this is a ceremonial site, not a habitation shelter."

Suzanne stood beside him, looking at the parade of figures. "How can you tell?"

"Well, first off, there's that engraved rock by the entrance. Carvings like that are old, I'm talkin' thousands of years. And there's no occupational stuff, like campfire ashes, stone tools or shards, animal bones, or bark and wood sleeping platforms that I've seen in other caves. And look," he said, walking away from the entrance. "There's a dished area further back, see? For dancing, or some kind of rituals, I'd reckon. And here we have a stone slab long enough for somebody to lie on, or be held down on. My guess is that we have an initiation site, where boys would get circumcised and a tooth knocked out or senior men would be inducted into shamanic mysteries of some kind."

"Fascinating," said Suzanne. Her voice sounded hollow and distant to Ned, as if she were speaking through a tunnel. Other voices were calling him, pulling him. Ned staggered to his feet.

"It's here," he gasped. "The place is here."

"What? Are you sure?" Suzanne took his hand, but he was having difficulty distinguishing the warmth of her flesh from the fevered state of his own body.

"Not in this room, this gallery, but further back and down. There's a chamber connected to this room somewhere." He was beginning to see the outline in his head of the interconnected cave system and of the place where it exited through a split in the rock at the base of the cliff, except that now, during the Wet, that particular point of entry and the distinctive rock formation that marked it were under water. He would have loved to be able to go down to the riverbed and compare it to his drawings, but that wasn't possible.

Ollie stood in the cave entrance, looking out at the canyon. "It's getting dark. We ought to be making a fire."

Ned stumbled and nearly fell. "I don't think I can help you," he said, holding onto Suzanne for support.

"No worries, I'll go back to those trees we passed and collect some fodder." He was looking at Ned with a frown. "You look right knackered. Just sit and I'll be back in an eye blink." He strapped his long bush knife to his belt and went out of the cave.

Ned gripped Suzanne by the shoulders. His heart was thudding in his chest to the point of breathlessness. "I can't wait for him."

"Neddy, what do you mean?"

"Got to go now."

Suzanne grabbed his arms and then sucked in her breath. She was looking at his forearms.

"I know," he said, breathing hard. "They're gone. Please let go of me, Suzanne. There's a way into the cavern below, I can see it, but I don't want you to follow."

"Ned, please wait till Ollie comes back, and we'll all go together." She was gripping his arms with her thin, birdlike fingers.

Ned shook his head; he heard the Rai calling in their whispery voices. He went to his backpack and took out the drawing of the *tjuringa* and stuffed it in his pocket. It was then he remembered the quartz chunk Ollie had given him and that he'd kept in his shorts pocket; it was hot against his thigh. He pulled out his own flashlight and inspected the back of the cave, looking for an opening that would lead to the sacred site he knew was somewhere below.

Thunder rolled across the top of the bluffs and echoed inside the canyon.

"Ned, I'm begging you, please wait."

He was desperate now and pushed her hands away. "Here it is," he said, looking up. The flashlight beam rested on a small opening in the rough rock wall where the ceiling sloped down just above his head. He found footholds and handholds in the rock, and before Suzanne could stop him, he'd scrambled up to the opening and crawled inside. He could hear Suzanne's distraught voice behind him, but her words no longer registered. The only words he could hear were in the high keening song of the Rai, and a harsher voice that cackled and hissed in a rasping counterpoint.

Ned found himself wedged into a very narrow tunnel that barely accommodated his man's frame with its heavy boots. In his mind flashed the image of thin, dark-skinned people about the size of Suzanne moving on their bellies toward the chamber below. He pushed with his toes and worked his way over the rough surface of the tunnel, turning his shoulders left and then right, working his way down the sloping passage until it widened abruptly, and he fell headlong into the chamber below as the small ledge at the end of the tunnel crumbled and gave way.

Ned landed painfully, face-first, on a tumble of rocks and lay dazed for a moment. Sitting up, he tasted blood. Touching his mouth, he discovered that his upper lip was split. Touching it warily with his tongue, he also realized that one of his front teeth was broken off.

"Shit," he whispered to himself. His voice sounded thick and deadened in the still air of the chamber. He sneezed and wiped snot, dust, and blood on the front of his T-shirt. The air made him choke, and it smelled like a rat's nest or a snake's den. Gripping the flashlight, he looked around. The room was narrow and high, with many paintings on the slanting walls. Dingo images were prominent, but also ibis, flying foxes, barramundi and other fish, crocodiles, turtles, numerous snakes from only a few inches long to monumental serpents that stretched across an entire wall. Also prominent were Ancestor figures with large round heads and wavy lines emanating from them like rays of the sun. Ned was so astonished, he almost forgot the pain in his mouth.

Somewhere behind him, a long way off it seemed, someone was calling his name. But his focus was drawn toward the highest wall, where a number of sorcery figures in yellow and dark red, some twice as high as his head, cast their menace over the chamber. Trembling violently on his knees, Ned swung the flashlight upward, revealing their postures of aggression and death. Their colors were so vibrant, even in the minimal light of the flashlight, he felt an overwhelming urge to reach up and touch them.

With bloody, shaking hands, he pushed himself to his feet and stood, swaying.

"I'm here," he said aloud. "Show me what to do." His words fell like dry leaves in the dead air.

Turning around, he saw behind him dozens of shallow shelves chipped into the rock wall, each holding a bark coffin with its ends tied in grass twine. Some of the shelves also held implements such as boomerangs, stone axes, and small dilly-bags made of reeds or grass. It began to dawn on Ned that what he was looking at was a mortuary chamber, an Aboriginal burial cave. So Ollie had been right. Even with Ned's limited knowledge of Aboriginal customs, he knew this would be one of the most forbidden places you could stumble upon.

On a shelf nearest him, the light from his flashlight caught a perfectly chiseled quartz spear point resting on top of a bark coffin. Remembering, he put his hand in his pocket and drew out the quartz ball. It shone gold and white in the flashlight's beam. At the same moment, he heard a shuffling of heavy feet behind him, and claws scraping on the rocks.

Ned wheeled to find himself face to face with a dingo of monstrous proportion, its eyes red in the torchlight and its yellow fangs bared. A curling tongue slid over its front teeth.

"Helloh, Neddy," it growled. "You've come to see me at lahhst."

"Who ... what are you?" he gasped.

"Blimey," the creature coughed, "I've lived with you all your life, and you don't know me?"

Ned was shaking from his bloody face to the soles of his feet. "Is ... this your true form?"

"One of them," it huffed. "Many Dingo Clan humahhns have served me well." It licked its lips with a horrid smack. "When I appeared to them like this, they called me their god, their Ancestor. I found their young boys sent here for initiation most toothsome."

"The death adder, was that you ..." Ned was too shaken to think straight.

The Quinkan make a nerve-shredding attempt at laughter. "I used thahht form especially for you because your Snake Clahhn great-grandmother tried to interfere with me, but as you see, she's deserted you now, no more protection marks. She had business elsewhere."

Ned glanced at his arms, confirming what he already knew. The skin pattern had been a protective screen against shamanic magic, which probably explained how he'd managed to stay alive all these years, but now it was gone.

"I was making a nice living here, until your arrogant half-breed fool of a half-wit grandfather invaded this place with his delusions of grandeur. He thought he could hahhrness the powers of creation. A truly wicked, evil man," it snarled.

"You would know about evil. You killed my father." Ned barely got the words out.

The Quinkan growled deep in its throat. "He killed himself. I didn't have to touch him. He was useless, couldn't do the job I needed from him, but I have some faith in you, Neddy-boy."

Ned closed his fist around the quartz ball, drawing unexpected courage and comfort from it. Maybe what Ollie had said about it was true, that it really did have some senior man's Quinkan protection magic in it. At this point, he was ready to believe anything.

"Yer face is a right dog's breakfahhst," the devil-dog observed, adopting Ollie's voice and cocking its head. It took a step toward him.

"What did you want from my father, or from me?" Ned shone the flashlight directly into its eyes, and it took a step back. "I intend to do everything in my power to get rid of you, not help you."

"But that's the same thing, innit?" The devil-dingo grinned, showing its teeth. "This is the place where the mistake was done. As Black Hahhrrow's next of kin, it's your job to undo it. That's why you're still alive, wretch of a humahhn, to undo the magic! Otherwise, I would have just eaten you long ago."

"But how? I don't know how!" Ned backed away from the creature's stench, his stomach churning.

"Use the Dingo Clan *tjuringa*, fer fuck's sake!" it yelped. "That's why you're here, to fix the mess your stupid ahhncestor made. So whip it out already and cut the cord that keeps me tied to your sorry bloodline." It gnarred and chewed at its hide in a disgusting manner.

"Then show me where it is, this *tjuringa* thing, and I'll try."

"But that's the bloody point," it howled at him. "Hahhrrow spellbound it nobody knows where, sealed with his own blood, hid it away. You're his blood kin, you met him in the billabong. You didn't ask him where it was?"

Ned no longer felt the floor under his feet. "I-I didn't know ..."

"Whahht kind of pitiful shahhmann are you? With yer bloody face and another man's magic there in yer hand? You're so stupid, you didn't even bring the *tjuringa* with you!" It lifted its leg and pissed on a ledge, filling an empty oval-shaped depression in a rock ledge with its urine. "How did you think you could undo Black Harrow's sorcery without the clan *tjuringa* he stole?"

"But, I thought the thing was here, that I was supposed to find it and take it to some clan elders. I thought ..." Ned said helplessly. It was clear he had misinterpreted the visions, that he had staked everything on the hope that once he found the cave where it all began, he would be shown what to do.

"Curse Black Hahhrrowrowrow and all his brood," growled the Quinkan, snapping toward Ned. "Figure out how to do the job proper or I swear I'll eat you anyway!"

A scream cut through the chamber, and Ned saw Suzanne's head and shoulders emerge from the tunnel entrance. Her face was a mask of terror as she took in the scene.

The Quinkan turned toward her, and a red light blazed in its eyes. It stood up on its hind legs, balancing unsteadily for a moment, then turned toward Suzanne. Its guttural half-human voice froze Ned's blood. "Shahhll I eat this one, then? I'm soooo hungry!"

"NO!" Ned shouted and threw himself at the Quinkan, sending them both toppling into the black shadows of the cave. Ned kicked and punched for all he was worth as the Quinkan clamped its jaws around his thigh, shredding his flesh to the bone. A quick look at the tunnel showed him that Suzanne had retreated from the entrance.

"I'll KILL you!" Ned yelled, his mind a red blur. "If I have any guardians at all, I summon them NOW!"

The Quinkan shook Ned by the leg and flung him across the cave. He could feel bones breaking, but he was beyond caring about his own body. His only focus now was to do as much damage to the hated creature as he could manage. He could barely see it coming toward him through the flashlight's distant beam where it had landed against the painted sorcery wall. But then, a shimmering light that was not battery produced filled the narrow cave. Shining ovoid figures began to emerge from the rock walls, and Ned felt the icy touch of the Rai at his back. Snarling, the Quinkan stopped in its tracks.

We are the Rai. We teach, we guide. The shaman's path is our purpose. Their words sang in Ned's mind like cataracts and shrieking winds. Simultaneously, the tallest of the Rai plunged its amoeba-like appendages into Ned's body, ripping out his heart and lungs and viscera. It took the quartz stone from his hand and thrust it inside his body cavity, sealing the wound. Ned fell to the floor of the cavern, rolling and jerking as if in the throes of a grand mal seizure.

When he sat up, a bright light leaked from the sealed slit in his torso. Getting to his feet, he looked into the red eyes of the Quinkan but felt no fear, only a terrible burning sorrow. His body was numb and held no sensations of pain, and he marveled at the luminosity of his hands as he held them out. To his left, the Rai were faint ripples of light against the chamber wall.

"With my imperfect knowledge, I cannot unbind you," he said in a monotone to the Quinkan, as it circled him warily, "but I can restrain you until another comes who will learn fully what to do." Ned stumbled toward the tallest sorcery figure on the wall, his hands outstretched to it, just as the devil-dingo launched itself.

Both fell heavily against the painted wall, and Ned heard Suzanne's anguished screams mingled with the strangled howls of the Quinkan.

It was the last sound he heard as a mortal man.

Chapter 30

September 8, Thursday—Present Day

Alice sat on her deck swing in shorts and a Hardison Museum T-Rex T-shirt, savoring her next-to-last day of medical leave from the office. Barefoot, her right ankle and foot still wrapped in bandages, she sipped her coffee and contemplated the future.

The day, September 8, was her birthday, but that significance paled in comparison to recent events. She pushed the swing with her good foot, sipped at the cup, and took stock of things. This was the first day since Hal's death and the destruction of Dunescape that she had not taken the antidepressant prescribed by her doctor. Her head was clear, and she no longer felt guilty for being alive.

This was also Margaret's first week back at school and the first week of Nik's fall semester teaching gig at the university, his last before graduation at the end of the year.

She drained her cup. Twelve days since Hal's death, and she'd been thinking, sitting here on this placid late-summer morning, about a lot of things, some pleasant, and some not. On the pleasant side, Nik and Margaret were taking her to dinner that evening (she'd asked for no useless gifts). She was also relieved to be cleared of suspicion regarding Hal's sudden death and the destruction of the house. The autopsy confirmed natural causes (a heart attack), and the house fire had been ruled an accident caused by an oil lamp getting knocked over and igniting combustible materials in the upstairs area. She'd received a copy of Hal's will from his lawyer, and they'd agreed to meet soon. There was a lot of legal business to take care of, but the man assured her when it was all said and done there would be a tidy inheritance.

She thought about Nik. He'd been supportive beyond all expectations, asking few questions and taking up the slack in daily tasks, which included picking Margaret up from school during Alice's recuperation. Margaret had returned to school with enthusiasm, eager to stay in touch with several friends she'd met at science camp. Now that she was fourteen, she'd begun to change, in a good way. For some reason, she seemed less bratty and more reasonable, which Alice hoped wasn't just a phase. Margaret had spent a day crying and mourning for Carlisle, but now she seemed over it. About Hal, she'd said nothing.

Alice had wanted to come clean, tell her everything that had really happened in the attic, but she couldn't bring herself to talk about coming face to face with the Quinkan again, after all this time. In truth, she had been afraid that the mere mention of it might cause the thing to materialize again. But that, too, was changing.

She closed her eyes and pushed the swing, slowing her breathing. Finally, Alice allowed herself to think about Gull Harbor, to see the house in smoking ruins, to see Carlisle cradled in her arms, to see Hal's body stretched out on his deck chair. She tried regarding all these images dispassionately, as from a distance, seeing each one as a past event from which she was moving away, although a piece of her continued to mourn those two souls, man and dog, in their shared violent death. The greatest milestone in her recovery, the one thing not shared with her therapist, was her willingness to accept the Quinkan for what it was, to analyze it and know that she would survive, not on its terms, but on her own. If anything, she was more determined than ever.

"Hey, fella," she said, rubbing Dawg's belly with her foot. He lay sprawled underneath the swing, panting. He licked her toes and pounded the weathered boards of the deck with his tail. A few days ago that simple doggy response would have brought on the tears, but not today. Her mind was focused.

She got up and limped inside, heading with resolve to the small bedroom study. These days most of the available space was covered in books, trays of slides, and research materials related to Nik's dissertation-in-process. Alice moved around the piles of books and bent down to retrieve Milton Crouch's folder from the bookcase where she'd shelved it, unable to deal with its contents since the events in Gull Harbor.

Carrying the folder back to the living room, she flopped down on the couch and propped her injured ankle up on a pillow. Then she reread all the documents and made some notes. According to Milton, Patterson Undertakers, who'd handled the charred remains of the late Rev. Harrow, had gone out of business nearly fifty years ago. But now, thanks to Milton's bloodhound inquisitiveness, she had a lead on the Tanners, who'd made the funeral arrangements. Milton had discovered a Brumlie Tanner listed among the county's turn-of-the-century property tax rolls, and as this was the only appearance of that last name within the time frame, he'd felt sure it was the family in question.

The original location of the Tanner property, a twelve-acre farmstead, Milton further told her, was described as being about six miles southwest of Magnolia. He'd taken the liberty of trying to find it and had driven down the dusty dirt road shown on the county surveyor's map for that particular plat. But to his extreme disappointment, the stretch along the road where he expected to see fence posts and farmhouse foundations was instead a fairly new housing development carved out of open pastureland with a few surviving patriarch oaks dotted among the winding paved roads and cul-de-sacs.

But there was one other tantalizing piece of information. In 1915, the property had been sold for nonpayment of taxes, and the buyer had been forced to file for a quitclaim deed since the land was considered abandoned and no relatives of the missing Tanner family could be found. It had changed owners several times since then. Alice sighed. That pretty much ended her chances of finding a remnant of the Tanners, but it still made her wonder who these people could have been who'd taken it on themselves to bury the fiend. She could think of him in no other terms.

Alice tried to imagine the scenario. As far as she knew, no relatives were ever mentioned in connection with Harrow, who seemed to have descended on Magnolia out of nowhere—a loner with gold in his pocket and a burning mission in his soul. There was no indication, either from the article describing his demise or from his later obituary, that he had been survived by any wife or next of kin. It was likely, then, that the Tanners were members of the congregation wealthy enough to pay for the funeral expenses. If they were church members, Alice supposed there was some record of them, especially as donors or financial supporters. There was only one person she knew who might have that information.

She found the number in the phone book and dialed.

"Could I please speak to the Reverend Cecil Rider?"

The church receptionist sounded surprised. "I'm sorry, he's retired now. But I'm sure the new pastor would be glad to take your call."

"Oh. No, my business is personal. Could you tell me how to contact Reverend Rider?"

Alice frowned as the receptionist explained that he was not in good health due to his advanced age and that he now lived with his married daughter. Grabbing a pen, Alice scribbled the daughter's phone number and address.

"Thanks very much, and have a great day," she said, her heart thudding. She was going to have to go search out Cecil and his dark secrets. If his heart was bad, the last thing she wanted to do was spring surprises on him, but he was her last viable source. She picked up the phone again and dialed his daughter's number.

Chapter 31

September 8, Thursday—Present Day

Ironwood Drive, where Pearl Rider-Vincent lived, was in an older subdivision just off the main road past the Massalina County high school. It was fairly easy to find, and Alice pulled into the narrow concrete driveway of the modest brick house just after two o'clock. A boy's bicycle leaned against one of the tall pines that fronted the house, and a herd of half-grown cats scuttled for cover under a boxwood hedge as she got out of the car. She limped across the neatly mowed lawn to the front steps and pushed the doorbell.

A slender black woman in her late forties opened the door and considered Alice with a curious expression in her dark eyes. She wore faded jeans and a man's work shirt with the sleeves rolled up. "Are you the Miz Waterston that called?"

"Yes, thanks. I really hate to impose on you like this, but it's rather important. I promise I won't take much of your father's time," she lied, knowing that she intended to stay as long as it took. "I know he's not well."

"I guess it's all right, then," said Pearl, stepping away from the door and motioning Alice inside. "Daddy's in the TV room watching his soaps."

Alice followed her through the tiny living room to a den where Cecil Rider sat in an upholstered rocker in front of a large wood-encased television set. Although the room's concrete block walls were painted a cheerful daisy yellow and its floor wore a thick carpet of tan wool, there was no mistaking it as an enclosed carport.

"Daddy, that lady who called is here to see you." Pearl motioned for Alice to go in. "I'll be in the kitchen if you need anything," she said, glancing at Alice over her shoulder.

Cecil Rider looked away from the TV and up at Alice.

"We meet again," he said softly.

Alice sat down beside him in a wooden rocker, and laid Milton's folder across her knees.

"I'm really sorry to—"

"Stop, please. You didn't come here to apologize, you came looking for answers. It remains to be seen whether I can give you what you want." He muted the television program and turned his full attention toward Alice.

Cecil Rider seemed shrunken, smaller than she remembered from that freezing January afternoon when she'd shown him Harrow's notebook. Today, his slender, veined hands lay clasped in his lap, his boney knees visible through his thin trousers and his feet hidden in a pair of slippers. His hair had been grizzled when they'd first met, but now it was mostly white. Only his eyes were as bright and aware as Alice remembered.

"Well, then. I won't waste any more of your time than I have to," she said. Opening the folder, she pulled out the article from 1900 and read him the sentence that mentioned the Tanner family. "Do you know who they were?"

Cecil shook his head. "No, I truly have no idea. Some members of his congregation, I would assume."

"Wouldn't there be a roster from the early days listing the members of his church?"

"If there was, I've never seen it. My father Antoine may have known, or maybe there never were any such records. Why do you care who these people were?"

"I thought their descendants might still be living in the area, and I had hoped they might tell me something about … him." Alice couldn't bring herself to say the human name of the creature who'd masqueraded in the clothes of a minister of God.

"What could you possibly want to know that I haven't already told you? The most important thing is that a great evil was removed from this world by the power of our Lord."

Alice studied her shoes. She was not going to give up this time; she was certain Cecil Rider must know more than he was willing to say about the history of the church he'd led for nearly sixty years. She wondered how old he'd been when he'd taken over from his father. If in his thirties, which seemed reasonable, he must now be over ninety. A sense of desperation set in.

"I want to know where he came from," she said. She paused and took a deep breath. "I want to know what kind of curse he may have brought with him. I especially want to know about the thing that followed him around in the shape of a dog. Most of all, I want to know how it can be banished. Have you ever performed an exorcism, Reverend Rider?"

Cecil raised a thin brown hand and touched the corner of his eye. "Yes."

Alice sucked in her breath. "When? Where?"

"Do you have any idea how we, the good people of St. Christopher's United, were able to build such a fine brick church to replace the old wooden one?"

Alice shook her head.

"With stolen money," he said, and here his eyes shone liquid. "It was my father Antoine, a mere boy at the time, who found the remains of Pastor Harrow in the bell tower. My father took something from that room he should not have, a strongbox that contained a lot of money. He kept it for years, and finally, as pastor of the reunited flock, decided to use the money for a holy purpose, to build a new church as a gift to God and to the congregation. They were scattered, you know, after our Lord struck Harrow dead, and only after some years did they try to regroup and rebuild the church they'd lost."

"That's admirable," said Alice.

"It seemed so," Cecil murmured more to himself than his unwelcome guest. "But after work on the new church began, he started to think he was being haunted by Harrow's ghost for taking the strongbox. At that time, I was living in Birmingham, preaching and newly married. I had just convinced Estell, my wife, that we needed to move back here to look after my father, but he died suddenly before I returned."

Alice flinched. She knew, from Milton's photocopied article, how Antoine had died. She thought of Hal, frightened to death in his own home.

"After my father's death," said Cecil, "the congregation invited me to take up the pastorship in his place. It was then I decided to exorcise the old church of its evil past and bless the new one to our Lord's use, and I also saw to putting up a godly marker stone over the grave of Pastor Harrow, so the Holy Spirit would keep an eye on him. I loved my father deeply, and his loss was a great blow to me. Do you know how it feels, to suddenly lose the father you cherished, Miss Waterston?" Cecil Rider sat with bowed head, lost in his memories.

Alice shifted in her chair, embarrassed and guilty. "I can relate," she said. "I never knew my father. He died before I was born, but I've been able to learn a little bit about him recently." Opening her purse, she pulled out the passport and handed it to Cecil. "This is his photo."

Cecil took the open passport and felt around on the table beside his chair for his wire-rimmed glasses. Putting them on, he looked at the photo for several minutes without speaking, his hands trembling. Then he looked at Alice, leaning forward in his rocker. He continued to stare silently, the passport gripped in his hands.

"Is something wrong?" Alice squirmed uncomfortably.

Cecil looked back to the image of Ned and Suzanne. "I know this person," he said finally.

Now it was Alice's turn to stare open-mouthed. "But how? I mean, that's not possible."

"I always felt, you know, when you first came to the church to see me, doing your so-called research, that there was something secret about you, and something oddly familiar. I guess I saw Ned in you without knowing it. He came to me as a charity case, an orphaned white boy recovering from a near-fatal rattler bite. He ran away while we were tending him, and I didn't see him again for nearly twelve years. When he reappeared on my doorstep, he was a grown man who looked like this." Cecil looked at the passport photo once more and handed it back to Alice.

Alice's mind was reeling. "You're telling me he was from around here?"

"Yes. When he returned, as I said, he told me he'd come in search of his father. He'd recognized the man in a family photograph he'd seen in my house twelve years earlier, you see? I drove him back to his childhood home on the edge of the National Forest myself, except that it had burned down; he told me it was just a ruin, but he wanted to go there anyway."

"Where was this place? Could you find it again?"

"I doubt it. That was forty years ago, and obviously I don't travel these days."

Alice was thinking it wouldn't take much for her head to explode. "Why would Ned's father be in a photo of your family?"

"Because my grandmother raised him—Ned's father, that is— alongside Antoine as one of her own. I lived in the same house with him until he ran off and got married. I can show him to you." He turned slightly in his chair and called. "Pearl? Can you come here for a minute?"

Pearl came from the kitchen immediately. "What is it?"

"Don't look so worried," he smiled up at her, "I just need you to fetch me something. Would you bring me that photo of your great-grandmother that's on my dresser?"

Alice caught the look of confusion on Pearl's face as she disappeared into the back of the house. Alice rubbed her forehead, feeling headachy and drained.

"Let me get this straight. If I understand what you just said, that means my own grandfather was adopted by your grandmother. In some weird way that I can't work out, does that mean you and I are related?"

For the first time in the entire course of their conversation, Cecil smiled at her with the warmth she remembered from their very first meeting. "Yes, Miss Waterston, I believe it does."

Pearl returned at that moment with a framed photograph. Cecil took it from her and regarded the image with a wistful smile.

"That was a happy moment," he said. "Here, this is Ned's father, your grandfather. His name was Lazarus, but we called him Lacy." He pointed to a young man with liquid dark eyes and a bow-shaped mouth, seated on the front steps of a house beside a family who was clearly not of his same coloring.

"My father told me, when I was older," Cecil continued, "that Lacy's relatives had lived on a small farm or acreage of some kind near Magnolia. That was the most frustrating thing of all for Ned when he came back: knowing the place was somewhere in the county, but having no way to locate it or find out who had owned it. As far as I know, my grandmother went to her grave without telling a soul who Lacy's parents had been, if she even knew."

"A small farm?" Alice repeated. Something was pinging in her brain that threatened to undermine her reason.

"W-when was this taken?" Alice asked, barely able to think.

"I'm afraid I don't remember."

"The date's on the back, Daddy," Pearl said, looking at Alice with an expression that she probably reserved for homeless people and aliens.

Alice turned the photo over. "Yula and her boys," she read. It was dated 1934. Looking at the picture again, Alice touched the young man's face with her fingertips and shook her head. "This is my grandfather?" It seemed impossible.

"Pearl, would you mind giving us a private minute or two?" Cecil asked.

His daughter nodded, and headed toward the kitchen. "Call if you need me," she said, looking back.

"If Ned is indeed your father," said Cecil quickly, after Pearl had gone. "there's something I need to tell you. Money wasn't the only thing my father acquired when he stole the strongbox. That hellish book you once brought to me was in the bottom of the box, under all the money."

"So that's how you got it. I wondered," Alice said.

"While your father was with us that second time, he found the book and claimed the heathen scrawls in it moved when he touched them … he said they took him away to some alien world. He was beside himself with me for keeping the book after Antoine's death. He said I should have destroyed it. I know now that he was right. Please tell me it's gone, that you burned it as I once begged you to do."

Alice stood up. She'd reached a decision that had been taking shape in the back of her mind, and now it was time to get out of there. "Reverend Rider, I have to go, but I can't thank you enough for being so candid with me."

She started to leave, but Cecil reached out and caught her by the hand. He held it for a moment, looking up at her. "Ned's daughter," he mused. "And that beautiful lady in the passport picture was his wife?"

"Suzanne," said Alice.

"Take care of yourself," he said, and let go of her hand. He touched the photograph of Yula Rider and her boys lying in his lap.

"Thank you," she said, her thoughts in freefall. "I won't bother you again."

Chapter 32

September 8, Thursday—Present Day

Pulling into her parking bay under the house, Alice was relieved to see Nik's slot empty. The interview with Cecil had taken less than an hour, but she'd been afraid Nik and Margaret would beat her home, which would prevent her from carrying out her plan. She climbed the stairs, her swollen ankle complaining at every step, and went into the house. In her bedroom, she dug Harrow's notebook out of its hiding place. All these months she'd kept it hidden in a shoebox in the top of her closet under blankets and old pillows. She wondered now if having it in her bedroom, so close to her all this time, accounted for her insomnia and disturbing dreams.

Going to the kitchen, she collected a box of long wooden matches and a tin of lighter fluid, which she tossed in the shoebox beside the notebook. Then she took an armload of newspapers from the top of the pile stacked on the breakfast bar. Tucking the shoebox and the newsprint under her arm, she headed slowly down the stairs to the laundry room. Dawg followed her, his tail in gear. She gave his ears a scratch.

"I don't know if you ought to come along," she said. "Maybe I should shut you in here." Dawg wagged, and sat down on the patio, just outside the laundry room door.

Alice pulled a beach towel out of the dryer and draped it over her arm. Then she gimped painfully across the yard toward the woods behind the house. She found the trail that led to the pond and checked the time: nearly 3:00. This had better be over and done by the time Nik and Margaret got home.

Alice navigated her way down the trail, stepping carefully over tangles of cat-brier and poison ivy as Dawg ran ahead of her. It took about twenty minutes to reach a natural clearing just east of the pond. A red-shouldered hawk took flight from a nearby laurel oak as she walked out from under the trees, its sharp *KEER keer keer* adding to the sense of desolation. Looking around, she found an open spot and cleared away all the brush and leaves, making a pile of small branches and twigs that could feed a decent-sized fire once she got it going.

Checking her watch again, she crumpled the newspaper pages into balls and worked them into the small pile of twigs and brush where she intended to build the fire. Once everything was ready, she spread the beach towel over the ground and sat down on it. Gritting her teeth against the pain throbbing up her leg, she settled the shoebox in her lap. Dawg immediately claimed a corner of the towel and flopped down, his rump pushed against her thigh. Alice patted his backside and then opened the box.

She took out the notebook, intending to look through it carefully one more time, and then consign it to the flames for good and all. When she'd first discovered the folder containing the notebook on a dust-covered shelf in the county library, she'd used its contents to fill out details in her somewhat fictionalized history of the old church and its founder. And when she'd burned the manuscript of her book in a blind panic, hoping to rid herself of Harrow and his hideous companion, she hadn't thought of the notebook. But now, here it was—an artifact the man had actually held in his own hands. With trembling fingers, she turned it over, remembering the story she'd written about him and how it seemed to have come not from her own imagination, but told as if she were a silent observer to real events. Alice shivered. This plain, water-stained notebook was so much more than it appeared.

From a curator's perspective, the book was an excellent specimen of a late nineteenth-century folio, its covers bound in calfskin. Harrow had used the first thirty pages to document church business, and she read through them carefully this time, looking for names and dates of events. A paragraph on the second page alluded to gold brought with him in both nugget and dust form from gold-mining towns in Queensland. On the facing page was a tally of weights and amounts, and subtractions from the total in terms of U.S. dollars.

She wondered why she hadn't paid attention to this entry before, because here in Harrow's very own handwriting was the evidence that he'd come from Australia. And not only that, it was a clue as to what he'd been doing before immigrating to America. If he hadn't been actually down in the mines himself, he'd somehow been involved in the gold rush that afflicted the area in the 1800s. Perhaps he was connected to the Aboriginals who resisted the gold-mining invasion of their territory and were later eliminated from the land. Alice wished she knew more of the history of that time and place and resolved to research it as soon as she could.

She turned pages slowly, reading the entries. She'd seen all this before in researching her book, but now her perspective was vastly different. More stuff about worship services and lists of candidates for his so-called Body of the Church and Sisters of the Blood, groups she'd described in her aborted book as initiates who enforced Harrow's will over the congregation. Alice shuddered to see some names with checks beside them and others with lines drawn through them; did it mean that those who didn't pass his test of initiation were somehow eliminated? In the first year, more than half the initiate's names were crossed out. On another page, she found what looked like a floor plan of the original church, with cornerstones and the front steps clearly marked. She stared at it for a full minute, unable to pull her eyes away from the image. There was something there ... but finally she forced herself to turn the page.

On page thirty, which contained his final entries in the book (with the exception of the dozen pages in the back that Alice was saving for last), she saw what she'd been looking for. The top of the page was dated January 1900, and under the heading *Initiates* was a list of fifteen names, alphabetized by surname. Alice scanned the list and suddenly stopped. The eleventh name was circled.

"Holy shit!" Alice gasped aloud, and Dawg looked up, panting. Alice blinked. The circled name was *Tanner, Elise.*

She'd found her link. But more disturbing was the person's first name. Elise was the name she'd given to a character in her short-lived attempt to turn the old church's history into a work of fiction. It was a little hard to recall that scene now because she hadn't allowed herself to think about the manuscript in almost a year, but the gist of it was still in her brain. In her story, Harrow had assaulted a young woman chosen from his initiates. Reluctantly, Alice allowed herself to remember the paragraph in which Harrow had taken a knife and marked the girl's cheek with a serpent sigil. Shockingly, she'd felt the actual pain on her own face as she'd written the words down. It was that particular experience that had convinced her the story she thought she was inventing was something else entirely. It was Margaret who suggested she'd been channeling a history instead of inventing one.

Alice sat very still, thinking. Her mind was connecting the dots of something untenable, something so horrible to contemplate it made her sick to her stomach. What if that scene she'd written had been more or less true (according to the notebook entry, a real person named Elise Tanner had been one of Harrow's inner circle). What if Harrow had fathered a child with her?

That child would be a member of the missing Tanner family, who, as Milton had surmised, lived on a small farm near Magnolia. They'd buried Harrow, but had his offspring survived? Alice's mind spiraled into overdrive as it inched closer to the connection she was trying her damndest not to see. She suppressed the urge to whip out her cell phone and call Cecil Rider on the spot to ask him if he knew the birth date of the man adopted by his grandmother, the man he claimed was her grandfather, but she didn't really need to call him. The connection was already made. Lacy Rider, or Tanner, was Harrow's son.

Drenched in sweat, she turned to the back of the notebook. She had skimmed these pages cursorily in the past, but now she studied each one. If what Cecil had told her were true, this was her gateway to the spirit world where her father had gone. With damp fingers, she turned the pages, gripping them by the edges to avoid touching the images. She saw handprints, animal tracks, a doglike creature with fangs bared that took up an entire page, several man-shaped figures turned on their heads with spears or sharp arrow-like implements beside them, and finally, snakes.

One of them was drawn across a two-page spread, its blunt tail placed in the bottom corner of the left-hand page and its thick body drawn in wavy stripes diagonally toward the opposite corner where its oblong head and rounded eye rested in the righthand corner. Alice fumbled, losing her grip on the book, and then realized her fingers were turning numb. Frightened, she looked at Dawg beside her. He seemed to think everything was normal and yawned at her, his tail thumping a few times.

Alice turned back at the book, but found it hard to focus. The serpent's outline had gone blurry. Lines appeared doubled, then tripled, and then slowly began to wrap around themselves, forming a strand of twisted dots and stripes. Without thinking, she brushed her fingertips across the image. Instantly, her world went dark.

A warm night breeze breathed over her face and whispered in her ears. Some distance away, soft voices spoke to each other in a liquid language full of open vowels couched between rippling *r*s and *l*s. Alice rubbed her eyes and saw firelight. The sky overhead was full of stars so bright and piercing they seemed close enough to touch. Hard rock was under her hand, and a lone dingo howled in the distance.

Seated around a campfire in the mouth of a large rock shelter were two Aboriginal men, two women who could have been their wives but might have been some other relation, several children, and an old woman. An ancient man with frizzy white hair sat slightly apart from the others, his chin resting on his chest as he reclined against the cave wall, apparently asleep. They spoke softly among themselves, laughing occasionally and communicating as much with their hands as with words, while the children dozed beside or in the laps of their parents. It was a domestic scene of such tranquility that Alice longed to be one of those sleeping, protected children.

Abruptly, the ancient man sprang up with a spryness that belied his age. He looked directly at Alice and began walking toward her. The others seemed oblivious, never even looking in his direction. He grinned widely, revealing a missing front tooth. In his nose was a flat bone about the size and shape of a popsicle stick. He was totally naked, and his torso was covered in decorative scars that looped and spiraled around his chest and stomach.

She knew at once that he was a powerful senior man, a clever man or seer who could travel the spirit world while his corporeal body rested in the safety of his family grouping. Indeed, when she looked back at the shelter, she saw his body resting in its trance state against the rock wall. His spirit body walked right up to Alice and touched her on the forehead.

"We bin go now," he said and walked past her, heading down a path through rocks and scrub vegetation. Higher up, Alice could hear the tumbling splash of a waterfall. She turned and followed him, stumbling along the path in the darkness, hurrying to catch up. Off to her left, dingo songs filled the night.

"They bin sing you up, say you come soon," he said, walking faster.

"S-sing what?" Her voice sounded far away.

"You'll see."

They rounded a boulder higher than Alice's head and the solid ground under her feet came to an abrupt end. She looked over the edge into a sea of stars and distant galaxies. A small island of land seemed to float in empty space several yards away, like a raft moored by an invisible rope to the mainland. On it, a circular plot of ground was ringed in stones the shape of ostrich eggs.

In the center stood a tall Aboriginal woman with glistening mahogany skin and bronze-gold hair framing her head in a fine, curling halo of radiance. Beside her, an enormous white dingo sat on its haunches, its ears pricked forward on alert. Tiny red flames burned in its bright eyes as it watched the approaching strangers without blinking. On the woman's other side, a shining, coiled taipan with greenish-golden scales lay in great looping coils. It raised its head and tasted the air in their direction.

As they drew near, the woman held out her hand and rainbow light spilled through her fingers like mist. A chorus of howls filled the air, and Alice realized that at least a dozen normal-sized dingoes inhabited the shadows behind the three, just outside the rim of the circle.

"They bin waiting," said the Senior man. "You mob," he said to the three inside the circle. "I brought you this one, she bin come like you told me." To Alice he said, "Go on there now," nodding toward the circle. "Big Dingo Dreaming waiting on you. You'll see."

"Wait, don't leave me—" But he was already walking away on his skinny bent legs.

Her heart thudding, she turned back to the ceremonial circle. The rainbow light spilling from the woman's hand had formed itself into a semi-transparent bridge that just touched the cliff's edge at Alice's feet. Her pulse racing, Alice knelt down, reached out, and found the ribbon of light solid to the touch. Holding her breath, she stood up and stepped forward. The bridge was firm under her feet, though she could see stars through it. She took a breath and walked quickly toward the circle, trying not to look down.

The Senior Law woman watched Alice with large luminous eyes and beckoned her forward with outstretched hands. Terrified, Alice forced her feet across the circle until they stood face to face. The Dingo

Ancestor got off its haunches, and the Taipan Ancestor uncoiled its long body, raising itself up taller than the shaman beside it.

"Who are you?" Alice asked, shivering down to her molecules.

The woman smiled, and waves of rainbow light engulfed her as if flowing from every pore of her body. "*Great-great-grandmother.*" Her voice was ephemeral, like a sigh through the gum trees.

She took Alice by the hands, and the circle disappeared. They stood on a narrow plateau under a setting sun that painted the sky in purple and gold. Far below, Alice could hear water rushing. Stepping to the cliff's edge, she looked down at the storm-swollen river, its flowing current spattered with diamonds from the sunlight slanting into the canyon.

The scene rippled, and with a shock, she stood in a man's body, lean, sinewy, of medium height with longish sandy brown hair whipping in the wind that blew up over the lip of the cliff. He wore khaki walking shorts and a thin T-shirt that clung to his body. He peered over the edge. "It's down there somewhere," he said, his words flying away on the wind.

The Senior Law woman waited, the Dingo and Taipan Ancestors holding silent vigil behind her. Reading the man's thoughts, Alice panicked as she realized what he was about to do. "Noooo!" she screamed in her mind. There was a moment's hesitation, and then to her relief, he turned and stepped away from the edge.

Alice blinked, and realized she still stood in the circle, her hands in those of the Snake Clan's shaman, the Senior Law woman, her great-great-grandmother.

You come far to see the truth. Alice felt rather than heard the words brush through her mind. *Big Boss Wandjina say we make you see.* The woman held Alice's hands out, palm up. To her horror, the Taipan Ancestor pierced her hand with sudden fangs. Before she could even think to scream, the Dingo Ancestor bit down on her wrist. All went black and freezing cold for a second or two, then suffocating warmth enveloped her body and dust filled her mouth.

Alice found herself inside a cavern lit by a single flashlight. The air was stale and musty, and she wore the man's body again. He held the flashlight over his head, illuminating a painted figure at least ten feet high. She recognized it as a sorcery figure depicting a death curse placed on someone, and beside it towered the dark red stick figure of a Quinkan. A series of red hand stencils ran in a horizontal line underneath its feet.

Alice coughed in the fetid air and tasted blood. She touched her hand to her mouth and felt pain, then saw blood on her fingers, only they weren't her fingers. They belonged to the man's body.

Faintly, she heard a woman screaming. Coursing the direction of the sound, she saw a disheveled young woman's head and shoulders emerging from an opening high up on the rock wall. The woman looked familiar ... Suzanne! Then Alice knew whose body she inhabited. She'd been mentally chasing him for more than thirty years and now, not only had she found him, she *was* him. At least, she was inside his mind and body, experiencing what he was seeing and feeling.

She reeled from the waves of horror that coursed through him and then saw why. The Quinkan, wearing the guise of Gaiya the Devil-Dingo whom Alice knew from Dreamtime legend, was balanced on its hind legs not five feet away. Disoriented, she couldn't understand what was going on, but before she could make sense of the scene, Ned tackled the monster and fell heavily to the ground. Alice's mind was a blur of pain, fear, and rage as she fought in Ned's body with the Quinkan. She screamed soundlessly as his leg was ripped apart by its teeth and his body tossed into the air.

At that moment, Ned was gripped by a blinding flash of pain so intense it nearly unseated Alice from his body. She experienced with him the terror and ecstasy of the ritual evisceration, death, and rebirth that an Aboriginal Clever man undergoes when he becomes a seer. Alice felt first-hand the total panic and confusion in Ned's mind the moment it happened and the subsequent power flowing into him from his conjoinment with the Rai. They formed a curtain of pale light, rippling against the cave wall.

His mind, which moments ago had been a maelstrom of grief and rage, had now become as still as the waters of a lagoon. Alice felt the impact as his body hit the wall, pummeled by the devil-dingo's massive bulk, yet Ned's mind remained focused. He immediately reached overhead and fitted one palm over the largest hand stencil, and with his other hand he grasped the Quinkan by the heavy scruff of its neck. At once, the power of the Rai streamed through him into the painted images, fusing his body with the ancient sandstone. Alice screamed inside her own head as Ned's limbs turned to stone.

Looking out through his dazed eyes, she saw that more accurately Ned's flesh and blood, and that of the Quinkan, were being absorbed into the rock itself. Within seconds it was over, and where they had once struggled against the wall, Alice could see only a scuffle of dirt on the cavern floor. The Rai were nowhere to be seen, and the cavern was pitch black except for the pool of light where the flashlight had fallen. It took her a moment to understand what had happened to Ned, and then the terrible truth dawned on her: she was looking out of the rocks at the interior of the chamber. She could hear Suzanne sobbing and moaning in complete hysteria somewhere in the darkness. The Quinkan's guttural mutterings were muffled but unmistakable, and Alice could sense its quivering malice close beside her.

"Damn your entire bloodline," it gibbered from inside the rock matrix, but the essence that had been Ned was now firmly anchored in the molecules and atoms of the alluvial sandstone, and it cared nothing for empty challenges and curses. It held the Quinkan's raw hunger in a vise that would not be loosened until the Dingo Clan *tjuringa* was restored to its rightful place on the shelf beside a quartz spear point. She also felt, through Ned's remaining synapses, another distant tug, and saw for one brief flash a burned and blackened face, distorted in rage but easily identifiable to her.

Alice's horrified consciousness struggled to free itself from the fading shreds of thought and feeling that had once been Ned, desperate to escape before she too was irreversibly absorbed into the rock. *Father!* she screamed. There was a moment's suspension, as if all the protons and electrons of every atom holding the wall solid had lost their charge.

The Alice who was bound up in her father's small eddy-pool of the space-time continuum winked out of existence and gradually, inevitably, the twenty-first-century Alice, whose birthday was September 8, took hold of her consciousness, reassembled herself, and opened her eyes.

It was several minutes before she could move her fingers and toes and process fully where she was. The sensation of Dawg licking her hand finally brought her around, and she hugged his neck, breathing his doggy smell. Drained, she sat unmoving, the monstrous book of her ancestor still open in her lap as tears fell on Dawg's fur in silent lament for Ned, whom she'd found and lost in the blink of a cosmic eye.

Unsteady, Alice crawled to the pile of dry leaves and newspaper. Opening the box of matches, she set the paper on fire and nursed the blaze until it burned high enough to heat her face. Then she reached for the notebook. She tore the book apart and fed it to the flames page by page until it was completely gone. She then tossed the shoebox in as well.

Alice shivered, her skin freezing, and leaned as close to the flames as she dared. The sun was setting by the time she smothered the fire with dirt and kicked the remaining ashes around to make sure no coals remained. Then she knelt down and hugged Dawg around his shaggy neck.

"Thanks for sticking with me," she croaked, her throat scratchy and dry.

Wiping her eyes, she stood, gathered up the beach towel, and then stopped. There was no pain in her foot. She knelt down and unwrapped the bandages, holding her breath. What had been a ragged red and purple wound was now faint and disappearing. She touched the spot with trembling fingers and found the skin oddly cool instead of fevered. *Are you really gone, then?* she wondered. Tucking the beach towel under her arm, Alice headed toward the trail, walking swiftly along the path at first and then breaking into a run as she saw the outline of the house through the trees. Dawg galloped ahead of her, announcing their return in joyful yelps as he spotted Nik and Margaret leaning over the deck railing.

"Mom," Margaret called, ""Where've you been? Why are you running?"

"We were about to go look for you," said Nik, coming down the stairs to meet her.

Alice dropped the beach towel and flung her arms around him.

"*Hej*, what's this for?" he said, hugging her back.

Alice let go of him and collapsed onto the steps, holding her head in her hands. She'd gone in search of the truth, but the breadth of it was more than she could process.

Nik sat down beside her. "What's wrong? You seemed all right this morning."

Tears blurred her vision, but Alice blinked them back. She was done crying. "I went down to the pond, and burned Harrow's notebook. It's gone now."

Margaret slid down beside her.

"Before I burned it, I used it."

"Oh shit," Margaret yelped. "Kinigar warned me."

"I'll explain, if you promise to just listen and not judge."

Nik's eyes tightened around the corners, but he nodded.

"Tell," breathed Margaret.

Alice held out her hands. "My fingers got numb while I was holding the book. I wondered if Ned had felt the same, and in the next breath I was out of my body. I saw … and felt what happened to Ned in Australia. He fought the Quinkan in an underground cavern. They were both … I don't know how to describe it … transformed by some Aboriginal sorcery that was down there, painted on the wall. I was in his body, so I experienced his death."

"Mom." Margaret's eyes were black pools.

Alice plowed on. "Ned did something that may explain why the Quinkan won't go away. He didn't know how to undo what had been done by Harrow, who was his grandfather, so he took the Quinkan inside the rock wall with him, to trap it there forever, I guess. But I see now that it bound the thing even more tightly to his bloodline. So when Harrow materialized in this world again, the Quinkan came with him. Ned almost got it right about breaking the binding spell—but not quite."

Alice took a deep breath and bowed her head. She wondered how long it would take Margaret to figure out the dark shaman who'd terrorized them both was her great-great-grandfather. She decided to shelve that little shocker for another day, when she had the strength. Right now, she'd gone as far as she could.

"I don't even care if you believe me or not," she said, "I know what I saw. While I'm at it, I may as well tell you what really happened in Gull Harbor. The Quinkan killed Hal. It was up in the attic when I got there."

She looked at Nik, but he was silent, his face neutral, which was to be expected. At least he didn't get up and walk away.

"I have a confession, too," said Margaret. "I saw the Quinkan at camp, but I didn't tell anybody. I thought it wouldn't be a good idea, but now I wish I had. And I channeled for the first time, too. Kini says it probably runs in the family, being psychic like that. It might go all the way back to your dad."

"Further," Alice said, the horror of the cave playing again in her mind.

She cut her eyes at Nik. "Your thoughts?"

Nik studied the backs of his hands. "I need to say up front that I can't make myself believe in Quinkans or Dreamtime magic. I just can't. But I'll listen. I don't want to be left out."

Alice leaned against him. "Fair enough. I know you're not a believer. I wouldn't be either if I hadn't seen these things myself. As long as you want to be with me, and Margaret, that's all I ask."

They sat on the steps, a silent trio, until Alice finally said, "What I really want is access to a bona fide Aboriginal shaman, one of those shriveled old senior men who lives in the Outback and knows everything about the Dreamtime and how it manifests in the here and now. Fat chance. They've all been wiped out by white man's culture."

"No, they haven't. I know somebody who knows one," said Margaret, her eyes bright. "I'll e-mail him tonight, if you want."

Alice looked from Margaret to Nik. "What are you talking about?"

Margaret blushed to the roots of her hair. "I told you. His name is Kinigar, and he's wicked cool. Somebody in his family, an uncle I think, is one of those senior dudes."

Alice stared at Margaret and for once in her life was entirely speechless. Whatever else Margaret had done at camp, she had grown up, and Alice had been so wrapped up in her own drama she'd failed to see it.

"Yes," she said, "I *would* like to meet your Kinigar. If he could find me an Aboriginal man or woman who's willing to share Dreamtime knowledge with a stranger, I'd be beyond grateful." She had so many questions that needed answers. She knew the cave where Ned died was a mortuary chamber, full of dark sorcery. From those brief moments in Ned's consciousness, she'd gleaned that a clan object, an oval stone, had been stolen from there. Ned had searched for it and never found it, but she was beginning to think she knew where it was. The image of the church floor plan with its four cornerstones was sharp in her mind. Did she have the courage to go there and dig?

"I know you'll love him," Margaret was saying. "Kini's just ... total *win*."

Alice pulled her thoughts away from caves and totems, and gave Margaret her full attention. "And just how much about all this did you tell this boy?"

Margaret's eyes were shining. "Everything."

"Did you know about this?" Alice turned to Nik.

Nik shook his head. "But my intuition tells me it's okay."

Alice leaned against him. "You don't have intuitions. That's my job." She relaxed a notch, daring to think he might be right.

Margaret got up and faced them. "Well, now that's settled, can we go eat?" Alice startled. In the failing light Margaret's eyes were wide and black. "I'm sooooo hungry."

www.ingramcontent.com/pod-product-compliance
Lightning Source LLC
Chambersburg PA
CBHW030120180626
46812CB00002B/500